THE DAUGHTERS OF THE PRINCE

It is June 1938, and although war clouds are on the horizon, the sun shines down on six young people in the garden of the splendid Villa Magari, just outside Florence. A rich American, a talented pianist and an aspiring artist meet Lella, Roz and Fiamma, the beautiful daughters of Prince Giorgio Caeseri and the Principessa. Love begins to blossom in that perfect setting, but the outbreak of war in Europe, and 'The Blue Nude'—young Hamilton Johns' controversial painting of Fiamma—both serve to put an end to their romance. In the turmoil of war Ham and Fiamma are thrown together at the battle of Cassino—only to lose each other once again . . .

PUBLISHER'S NOTE

When Noel Barber died, on 10 July 1988, he had been working on *The Daughters of the Prince* for the better part of a year. He had written just over half of the book, and left a synopsis and notes. Since, as with his earlier novels, he had been working closely on the ideas and the research for the book with Alan Wykes, the publishers decided—with the concurrence of Mrs Noel Barber and of Vivienne Schuster, Noel Barber's literary agent—that the novel should if possible be completed. They accordingly asked Alan Wykes to take over the writing of the book and bring it to its planned conclusion.

CONTENTS

FOR
TANAMERA and PATRICK
My grandchildren
With love

For winter's rains and ruins are over,
    And all the season of snows and sins;
The days dividing lover and lover,
    The light that loses, the night that wins;
And time remembered is grief forgotten
And frosts are slain and flowers begotten,
And in green underwood and cover
    Blossom by blossom the spring begins.

—Algernon Charles Swinburne
(from *Atalanta in Calydon*)

PROLOGUE

SETTIGNANO, 1945

PROLOGUE

Ah! I used to think in the years between, those were the glorious sunlit, pre-war days of dreams: each of us—Steve, the American playboy, Kurt the German musician, and myself, Hamilton Johns, the English painter (of sorts)—all hopelessly in love with three beautiful Italian sisters. They lived in a large rambling villa on the hillside at Settignano below Fiesole on the edge of Florence, shielded from the road behind a drive of cypress tress, and looking down from the large untidy garden on to the silver thread of the Arno with the tower of Giotto soaring to the skies, and Brunelleschi's orange-coloured Duomo like a great ball in the background.

There we all lived our brief happiest moments in the breeze of the day, in the heat of the night, almost from the time in June 1938 when I first came to live in Florence and study art. I found myself sharing a house in which my painting professor had arranged for me to lodge with Kurt and Steve, and it was on the opposite side of the country road, lined for miles with golden broom in June, where the three beautiful sisters lived with their father, the Italian Prince Giorgio Caeseri and his English-born wife, Donna Margarita.

Now, in 1945, everything seemed to have changed—yet nothing really had. The narrow, crowded Florence streets, the Porcellino market, with its famous emblem of a boar, snout rubbed golden by those seeking good luck, was still filled with leather and basket work and other bargains. Procacci, the sandwich bar, still sold its delicious tiny bread rolls covered with white truffle paste in the Via Tornabuoni, a street not only filled with palaces, but also the elegant 'Bond Street' of Florence. Not far away Doney's still sold its dark brown boxes of chocolate, complete with a small spoon in case you preferred to scrape the chocolate off without soiling your fingers. Nearby, in the Piazza della Signoria, Frascati's served the best (and strongest) bitter Campari and soda as you leaned back admiring the magnificent reproduction statue of David, with the Palazzo Vecchio behind; while across the Ponte Vecchio crocodiles of tourists queued to see the masterpieces in the Pitti Palace.

True, a few new irritants now jostled the tranquillity of Florence, the most noisy being the Vespa—'wasp'—darting along narrow streets, and weaving between the tired horses that usually waited for tourists in the Piazza della Signoria.

But it was when I drove up in a borrowed Jeep to Settignano, where we had lived, where the town met the countryside, that the changes crowded in upon me. Nearer to Florence than Fiesole, nothing could spoil the view from the house of the beautiful sisters, in Settignano, but where, oh where, had *our* little house gone? It had been just opposite, but bulldozers—the modern world's great flatteners— had obliterated the building where I lived when I first loved Fiamma; the house where Steve had once vowed solemnly, 'I'll never leave this place'.

In front of the newly polished modern block of flats, still stood the girls' house, with its avenue of cypress trees. I could see the faded ochre of the building at the end of the short drive, but as I peered through the wrought iron gates on their heavy stone pillars, I could see only what looked like the empty grave of all our hopes and aspirations for eternal love. The Prince and Principessa— Principessa my foot! she was a Yorkshire woman named Margaret Monson who had married for the title—had long since left. The three girls had gone, the bright light of peace and love had given way to the flames of war and hate; and now they in turn had been followed by post-war lassitude, the cold grey skies of defeat, leaving no bright sunlight of love.

The house whose gates I now peered through was called the Villa Magari. The Prince explained its name the first time we three young men had been invited there.

'When I first set eyes on it, I fell in love with it,' he said, and the Prince not only knew English well but was very much an anglophile. 'I said to myself, "Magari! If only I could buy it!" Well, "magari" is one of those untranslatable Italian words, meaning roughly "Ah! If only . . . !" and I *did* acquire the property and so, in gratitude, I suppose'—the Prince beamed benignly—'I called it the Villa Magari.' He pronounced it 'mag*a*ri', with the accent on the second 'a'.

How much had happened since that week in June 1938! Love and passion had soon engulfed all six of us, secret thrusting love-makings until the bugles of defiance blew from Germany, and their shallow echoes sounded from an ever more truculent Mussolini, already branded as a warmonger in Abyssinia but not—so far—in Europe.

Our love affairs took on a sharper edge, all coming to an abrupt close in August 1939 when my beloved Fiamma announced that she was expecting a baby and the Principessa, in a fury, deliberately separated us from love, happiness, and each other.

Then the world outside erupted too. Steve went to America, Kurt to Germany, and I went home to Britain.

*   *   *

Above the side of the gate of the Villa Magari hung the same old-fashioned bell. I pulled the rusty chain and an old man hobbled out. I recognised his wizened face immediately.

'Enrico!' I cried. After all, it was less than six years since our last sorrowful goodbyes and there is little change in the face of an old man who has been grizzled by years of Tuscan sun.

'Who's that?' It was different when he first squinted at me. He peered almost crossly through short-sighted rheumy eyes, though he looked the same at sixty-five when he had first seen me as a boy of twenty-one, who had become a captain during the war.

'Goodness me!' he cried, finally, undoing the bolt. 'If it isn't Signor Johns. Welcome back, sir!' He gave an almost ceremonial blow. 'But,' he added, pointing to my stick, 'you are ill in the leg?'

'No, no,' I protested, 'and not in the leg anyway. A small thing, but I have to take care. Don't worry about it.'

He looked relieved. 'That is good—that you are back with us again.'

'Back!' I echoed the word ironically. 'Back to what?' I asked, adding bitterly, 'I don't suppose you know that Signorina Fiamma and I are married—married and parted.' I added explosively, 'Parted by what the big shots call "the exigencies of war".' His mouth fell open. 'Have you any idea what that means, Enrico?'

For a moment he looked nonplussed, fingering his cap nervously. 'No, sir, I haven't. But I heard that the Signorina had married—a nobleman, I heard. But it may be only servants' gossip. I—'

'You heard that too?' My voice was heavy with irony too subtle for Enrico to understand. Fiamma! The flame! A flame that had ignited another life before ... 'We had a baby,' I said brusquely. 'No doubt you didn't know there was a little boy. But there was. And I, his father, have no idea where his mother is.' I paused, letting the enormity of it sink in. The old man turned away not wanting to embarrass me.

'Come into the garden, sir.' Enrico tried to change the subject. 'The owner of Villa Magari lives in Milan and doesn't visit us very often. I'm kept on here as a sort of caretaker and they're away now. Remember there?' He pointed to one corner where from time to time the dogs of the house had died and were buried in a plot which became the canine cemetery. The old wooden crosses still stood, half buried in grass.

'And here,' he announced with pride, 'the first wild strawberries. They're just ready to be picked. Come on, sir, try a few. You always used to.'

I laughed. Gobbling fruit from the large sloping garden overlooking the distant bluish haze of Florence on a hot day had always been our favourite sport. Strictly forbidden of course, just like the love-making, but all of it such ecstasy.

'But most of all, *il ribes*!' I cried. We used to pick up the stalks of redcurrant, loaded with the tiny fat red berries, then pull them off the stalks with our

7

teeth. It had all been so beautiful, but now the grounds looked no more than a desolate wilderness. I remembered the vineyard and orchard as they used to be—burdened with grapes and pears and plums; peaches and nectarines that to my untrained eye with its love of brilliant colour were blobs in the first tin paintbox I had ever owned, with its tiny squares of Rowney's watercolours like postage stamps.

Now the trees were unpruned and bore more dead wood than fruit. Round the boles, streaky mats of unharvested ambrosia lay rotting in the shade, with buzzing wasps feeding on tender flesh. The grass was uncut, the nettles and dock leaves grew unchecked with butterflies hovering and darting over them. In the vegetable garden the sprouts had turned into long knobbed sticks and bindweed strangled the mauve-flowered stems of the chives. Overgrown ramblers had returned to their natural state as dog roses.

Whoever owned the villa now did not seem to care. Even the house itself had a shabby look. Paint peeled from the woodwork on the sunny side. Dandelions sprouted from cracks where the plaster had been chipped, through neglect. A wall was streaked where rain had run from a broken gutter. No doubt Enrico did what he could to maintain order, but it was impossible. A head gardener and two assistants had once mowed the lawns and sown and hoed. Handymen and house-boys had repaired and painted. In the house itself brass, copper, glass had been kept shining by trim housemaids commanded by a formidable housekeeper in black bombazine with a bunch of keys tinkling at her waist and an English butler called Fawkes.

Enrico burst into my thoughts.

'Any news of Signor Steve?' Instinctively Enrico used our Christian names as in the past when he, more than anyone else, had connived, had often been the secret link in making arrangements to meet the girls.

'Steve? Oh yes, happiness and tragedy mixed. He's in the US Air Force, in Rome, and Signorina Lella is there with him. But'—my expression must have implied a world of meaning, for Enrico shook his head sadly as if he too was no stranger to misfortune.

'And Kurt? A German, I know,' he spat, 'but I liked him.'

I could not find it in my heart to tell him what had happened to Kurt. I hesitated. 'He was at Cassino—' I let my words trail away leaving the thought in mid-air.

'It must have been terrible there.'

'It was. I was there too.'

I wanted to obliterate the painful memories. Kurt who was such a talented musician that Bernard Berenson, the renowned art critic and also a gifted violinist, often invited him to play at the *soirées musicales* Berenson regularly gave. Such a gentle German at heart, Kurt, so well mannered.

Abruptly, I said to Enrico, 'I must be off. I'm an out-patient at the hospital for the time being, but I'm staying at the Hotel Lungarno in the Borgo San Jacopo, right opposite the Ponte Vecchio. I'll come back and see you another day if I may.'

'There'll always be a few strawberries,' he chuckled as I started to drive down the hill to the hotel where I downed a bitter Campari and soda, this time spiced with a dash of vodka, and sat there,

9

facing the river, almost touching the Ponte Vecchio. I thought of Fiamma, of how I had wondered if she had died, and whether I should ever find her again.

Then I thought back to the Villa Magari and the first time the Prince and Principessa had invited the three of us to meet their three beautiful daughters, and the Principessa, with her sense of English humour, had nicknamed us 'Three Men in a Boat'—a reference which puzzled Kurt and Steve but which, of course, I understood. Jerome K. Jerome's book had always made me laugh.

PART ONE

FLORENCE, 1938–1939

CHAPTER ONE

I had only been living for a few weeks in the house which Steve, Kurt and I shared in the early summer of 1938 when we received from the Principessa the invitation to 'Supper in the garden' at Villa Magari. We had already heard about the sisters, even caught glimpses of them on the way to local shops or in Florence itself. The beautiful tranquil landscape around Settignano and Fiesole was lined with stops for the electric trolley-buses and often one of the girls would be waiting for a bus to arrive.

We could tell from the surreptitious glances they gave us that they knew all about the three young men in their twenties. But none of us had ever met, though once, when Berenson had sent me to study the Titians in the Sala di Venere in the Pitti Palace I passed one of the girls in the nearby Boboli Gardens. She gave me a faint smile of recognition and I smiled back, but we did not speak.

I think we were eventually invited because the Principessa—or Donna Margarita as she was usually called—was a bit of a snob who had never met the famous Bernard Berenson and must have been surprised when she heard that I was working with him twice a week under a fellowship learning the history of Renaissance Art; while Kurt was such a gifted amateur pianist that sometimes he played in the intimate concerts which Berenson gave in his fabulous villa, *I Tatti*, invitations being extremely rare and sought after.

When we were preparing for the evening at the Villa Magari, the three of us had a long discussion

13

on what to wear. Steve, being an American, insisted, 'Hell! The guy *is* a prince. We've got to wear a tuxedo.'

'Not me,' I retorted. 'Apart from anything else, I haven't got one here. I left it at home. And the invitation is quite clear—"Supper in the garden". Even if I *had* a black tie I wouldn't wear it on a summer's evening in the garden.'

'Ham is right,' said Kurt who, at twenty-three, was the oldest of us and at times answered with all the positive thinking of a German Nazi. 'To overdress is to insult,' he declared emphatically.

We liked Kurt, but sometimes he pontificated as though the answers had been provided by Hitler, or at least that he knew Hitler would approve of them. He was right now, of course. One of the odd things about Kurt, which I did not realise until much later, when the war was over was that he nearly always was right.

So in the end we dressed in lightweight flannel trousers, wore ties, carried our jackets, and pulled the bell chain—rusty even then—and Enrico opened the gates, and with a polite 'Buona sera' pointed the way to the house at the end of the short drive. I remember being impressed by the orderly rows of dark cypress trees, like a bodyguard of soldiers standing stiffly to attention, as though being inspected.

The Prince was waiting at the open front door and shook hands with us in turn. He spoke very good English and introduced himself merely, 'I am Giorgio Caeseri, and you?'—to each of us in turn.

'Kurt von Schill.' Kurt almost clicked heels as he shook hands.

'Ah!' said the Prince, with slight irony. 'The

14

other half of our Axis! And you?' He turned to Steve, a year younger than Kurt.

'Steve Price from San Francisco, sir.'

He shook hands and I said, 'Hamilton Johns, sir,' adding hastily, 'but I didn't choose the name and I'm usually called Ham.'

'Very sensible of you,' said the Prince gravely. 'Your given name is quite a handful.'

'After my grandfather,' I added.

'The sins of the father—and grandfathers—' he smiled—'can sometimes be quite a bore.'

The Prince was a handsome man in his fifties, tall, very thin in his light grey slacks and white silk shirt, with a coronet and monogram on his left-hand pocket and a thick mane of iron-grey hair above a narrow face and striking grey eyes. It gave him an almost uncanny sense of 'greyness'—the trousers, the hair, the eyes, all grey. But there was a twinkle in his eyes in those days. The element of greyness in his life was still to come.

'Come and meet my wife and daughters,' he said as he ushered us in. The house was long and low, amid a blaze of oleander and other flowers as we climbed half a dozen steps to reach the balcony outside the main door—a balcony 'guarded' by a pair of large terracotta dogs, long and sleek and looking down on visitors rather disdainfully. The outside balcony was deep and spacious and littered with basketwork chairs and cushions.

'We call this the Tea Room,' explained the Prince, 'because in sunny weather it's the shadiest place to have tea.'

The rest of the house was just as exciting and just as unusual. Through double doors at the back of the Tea Room was the dining-room, which

15

contained a refectory table for the elders next to a circular table for the girls—and us when invited. And since the house was built on a slope French windows from the dining-room led straight out on to the gardens behind.

Because the grounds—and the house—sloped, massive stone columns of different heights had been built to support the living space above—a big sitting-room, a study, the music-room, nurseries now used for all manners of things, and, as we were to discover, seven or eight bedrooms and three old-fashioned bathrooms, all linked by corridors covered with old photographs in dark-coloured frames on walls which in memory always seem to have been of faded wine-coloured patterned silk.

Near the French windows stood a tall, straight-backed woman, in her fifties, I suppose. I already knew that she must be English, a north-country girl whose father had made a fortune and had—to be brutal—used some of his money to buy herself an Italian title. Her first remark was, 'Ah, Mr Johns. So you are Mr Berenson's closest friend!'

I did not like to disillusion her, so murmured, 'He is very helpful to me. A brilliant teacher.' And then in came Kurt whose manners were perfect, and greeted her with a polite kiss on the hand which already contained a few brown graveyard spots. 'Ah! The gallantry of a good upbringing. Your manners are typical of the English upper classes.'

'I am German, Donna Margarita.' Kurt knew the short way to address a princess.

'Ah well, never mind, you *should* have been English!'

'I hope that's a compliment and not a threat. I

16

like being a German ally of the wonderful Italians,' smiled Kurt, whose English was impeccable.

Slightly nonplussed, the Principessa turned to shake hands with Steve and asked, 'You must be Mr Price, the American?'

'Sure am, Ma'am.' Steve pumped her hand vigorously. 'It's great to meet up with you, Prince and Principessa.'

'Ah yes, very interesting.' The Principessa looked helplessly to her husband for help but found none.

'Call me Steve!'

'Thank you Mr—Steve. The girls are in the pool. My husband suggests that you all have a dip before we eat. Fawkes, the butler, will show you the way. You'll find swimming trunks in the changing house. Just introduce yourselves.'

We walked along a beautifully decorated garden path, almost fifty yards long, all in decorated stonework. The gardens were a delight, especially in the hot summer, for Prince Caeseri had built a long tessellated walk lined on one side with rambler roses and urns and pots of flowers and, on the other side, an orchard and vegetable garden—lettuces, broad beans, peas, together with every kind of fruit you could think of—and, at the end of the walk, he had created what he proudly called 'the Indian Pool'. It had been built in oriental fashion by damming up the small river Mensola where the gardens changed into vineyards, olive trees and checkered plots of herbs. Near the entrance to the Indian pool, which he had also lined with coloured tessellated patterns, the water of the river flowing in could be stored when it was low, or let out when there was a danger of flooding. It might not have been as hygienic as modern pools but it was good

17

enough for the family—and us too. 'Indian Pavilion' changing rooms with rococo decorations completed the idyllic picture.

The girls were swimming as we reached the Indian Pavilion. Inside, I took off my clothes, put on a pair of borrowed trunks, dived in and introduced myself to the girls in a welter of laughter and splashes. They were delightful and exhilarating and, as we introduced ourselves, we discovered that each had a nickname. Raefella was the oldest at twenty-two but was called Lella. Rosanna—always Roz—was twenty, whilst the youngest Fiammetta, but always called Fiamma, the flame, was eighteen. Spluttering and splashing and laughing we cried out, 'I'm Steve!' 'I'm Kurt' and 'I'm Ham!' It was such a liberated, happy-go-lucky introduction that nobody bothered with surnames at that first meeting. We had certainly dived in at the deep end, only to rise to the surface and fall in love.

We larked about for twenty minutes or so and then the butler Fawkes in one of those old-fashioned waistcoats with black sleeves and horizontal yellow stripes across his chest—looking just like a wasp—announced to Lella, presumably because she was the eldest, 'Signorina Raefella, supper will be served in thirty minutes.'

It was the signal to jump out of the water, and make for the two adjoining dressing-rooms. The pavilion was liberally supplied with towels. We showered—I wanted to as I could not see any signs of filtering in the reservoir-cum-pool—borrowed Steve's comb and tried to slick down my unruly blond hair which was always getting into my eyes.

'Trying to look pretty?' teased Kurt. 'Which one are you after?'

18

Quite naturally, with no hesitation, no affectation, I answered simply, 'Fiamma.'

'Ah well! Don't get burned in the flame.'

'I guess it would be a kinda nice death,' drawled Steve. 'I'll take Lella, the other blonde.'

Kurt laughed, 'So that leaves only Roz, the dark-haired one, for me. *Das ist gut!* She suits me.'

'Odd, one of the three being dark,' Steve said, shrugging off the observation.

We hurried, knotting our ties and—how strange it seems now, looking back—our laughing first suggestions in the Indian Pavilion turned out to be a perfectly judged arrangement.

When we reached the large outside balcony facing the garden—not the Tea Room near the entrance to the house, but at the back of the house—one half contained the supper table, big enough to seat a dozen people, and the other half a selection of more basketwork chairs and sofas, with us sitting on the edge, the girls decorously sitting opposite all dressed in summer frocks, asking for what looked like lemon squashes, and presumably non-alcoholic, until the Prince said laughingly, 'All right, girls. It's a beautiful evening. Would you like a bitter Campari and soda?'

A chorus of assent greeted the invitation while we were offered more substantial alcohol. 'A gindiano?' asked the Prince, deliberately and for our benefit using the current Italian slang for a gin and Indian tonic water.

'Or if you like Campari,' the Prince looked round, 'perhaps you will do what I do—add a little gin to it. Tones the bitterness down a bit.'

'I'll try that, sir,' said Steve eagerly, while, seeing Kurt hesitate, Fawkes suggested, 'Perhaps an
19

Italian beer, Signor?'

'Perfect!' beamed Kurt. 'I'm afraid most of us Germans like a cold beer on a warm evening.'

The silence that embraced us as we sipped our drinks was one of those silences which seem to presage events, cast uncertain shadows into the mind. It was not my gindiano, I think, that was responsible for the secret emotions I felt.

★   ★   ★

Half-way through that first evening, another man quite suddenly appeared after we all finished splashing in the pool. I saw Fawkes approach in his stately way, as a dark man—he looked about thirty—entered. He wore the uniform of a *capitano* in the Italian army. He was muscular but not tall, and so like the Prince that he *had* to be his son Vanni, whose name we had already heard, but in conversations which seemed suddenly to change direction or dry up, as if he were some sort of black sheep who had disgraced the family. It was all a bit mysterious.

Even more odd, he was only introduced as 'This is Vanni!' Did he, as the son of a Prince, not merit some sort of title?

He nodded, in a rather surly fashion, and I did not much take to him—perhaps because I hardly got to know him, I saw so little of him. He was, I learned, the Principessa's stepson, presumably by an earlier marriage of the Prince.

He said, 'I've just popped in for a day!' and dashed off to the Indian pool. But it was only later that I heard from the girls that he shared his father's passion for beautiful women, and it did not

20

take much intuition to guess that he preferred the bedroom to the battlefield.

The only time he unburdened himself just a little was when he asked me to pass the salad and said rather condescendingly, 'So you're an artist! The army's marvellous if you don't have to fight a war. I always had romantic dreams about war, but I began to dislike it when I was first in the army in Abyssinia and ordered to arrange for poison to be poured into the water wells to kill off the poor bloody natives who hadn't done anyone any harm. As you British would say, it's hitting below the belt.' Then he added with a twisted grin, 'As you British would also say, all's fair in love and war, but give me love any day.'

With that he finished his supper, cried ''Scuse me! Must dash off. Got a date!'

Watching him almost run to the front door, Roz whispered, 'When he's on leave, Vanni's got a couple of girls—or a dozen for all I know—in a flat in Florence.' She trilled with laughter. 'He really just comes here for a swim now and again, and if he's hungry, for a meal. He's not really one of the family.'

I did not give the matter much thought, though it *was* odd, the way in which, when Vanni's name was mentioned, distractions seemed to occur—or had been made. But we learned nothing more about the mysterious brother, and perhaps because of the idyllic circumstances in the brilliant summer of 1938, we were not curious enough to press the matter. After all, what was really so odd about having a brother serving in the army?

★   ★   ★

Fiamma sat next to me at supper and I found her charming. She spoke excellent English, as did her sisters, though with an occasionally delicious wrong use of words that made me burst into laughter but did not seem to embarrass her at all. She laughed a lot, and I loved her tall, willowy figure with her father's steady grey eyes, her head topped with an almost whitish mop of blonde hair.

'As far as colour is concerned,' said the Principessa, 'you two are a perfect match. Tell me, Mr Johns—'

'I wish you'd call me Ham,' I interrupted.

'Very well, then, Ham it shall be. Such an *odd* name, though. Sounds like a sandwich. I believe'—she spoke almost too eagerly—'that you know Mr Berenson quite well?'

'Both Kurt and I know him,' I nodded. 'I have my own art teacher, but Mr Berenson gives me a lecture twice a week on how to appreciate Rennaissance art. He says no one can be a good artist until he has mastered art history. I went to Oxford. Berenson had established two fellowships—one at Harvard, one at Oxford—and I won the Oxford fellowship. I am very honoured. He is the greatest art historian in the world.'

'And Kurt?'

'Mr Berenson is a highly accomplished amateur musician, a violinist, so when he has his small concerts, Kurt often plays the piano. He's a very good pianist.'

'I would love to meet Mr Berenson and attend one of his musical evenings,' said the Principessa wistfully. 'Is it hard to get tickets?'

'By invitation only,' I replied, knowing that it

22

was virtually impossible to acquire the tickets, which were strictly limited to his friends and, turning to Fiamma, asked, 'Do you *like* classical music?'

She hesitated.

'Of course she doesn't,' laughed the Prince who had been listening to the conversation. 'She only likes Fascist sing-songs.'

'Oh, Papa!' She coloured, a rose pink.

'You even used to wear the young Fascist girls' uniform,' said the Prince.

'I had to,' she protested. 'If you're not a member of the Party, whatever you may think—you can't get in anywhere—'

'Oh, I know. The Fascists have cleaned up Italy and done some good, particularly in clamping down on the Mafia, but I can't stand them. Especially that awful Mussolini. What a braggart and bully—everything that's contemptible in comparison with an Italian gentleman.'

As we all dipped hungrily into a second helping of spicy *vitello tonnato* Kurt ventured, 'But, sir, we've signed an accord with Italy.'

'Worthless!' snorted the Prince. 'Il Duce should stick to building roads and cleaning up stretches of marshland and Mafia crime, and leave international politics to his betters. Abyssinia! Disgraceful! Made my blood boil, treating countries the same way that Hitler'—he spluttered—'would do. Look what Mussolini is—an overweight little newspaper reporter with ideas above his station.'

I listened to the outburst in silence. Obviously the Prince did not like the Fascists!

'But Prince,' Kurt persisted, 'Abyssinia was quite a big idea for what you call a little man!'

23

'Not that I approve,' interrupted Steve, 'of edging round territories with threatening gestures.'

'I hope so,' muttered the Prince. 'You are quite right. And with all respect to you, young man,' this to Kurt, 'I don't approve of the way Hitler overran Austria and is—as your friend describes it—threatening Czechoslovakia.'

After a pause the Prince said, 'For the one thing only will I give Mussolini credit, as even the devil must have his due. He crushed the Mafia, not by strong-arm tactics but by education and keeping people out of mischief with widespread programmes of employment. So I tip my hat to Mussolini for that. But that's all. The man's nothing but a thug.'

Steve looked puzzled. 'I find it kinda surprising that he didn't team up with them. Weren't the Mafia thugs in a big way?'

'Like our Sturmabteilung, who started as the Brownshirts,' Kurt remarked.

'Not quite,' the Prince replied. 'Those are ... what do you call them? "Storm troops"—a bodyguard of bully-boys. The Mafia had their bully-boys all right, but their methods were usually more subtle. Blackmail mainly. The rich and socially vulnerable always paid up to be "protected" by ever-increasing payments.' He paused, peering into his glass.

'Gee, that'd be like USA in the Volstead Act,' Steve put in.

'What is that?' Kurt enquired curiously. 'The Volstead Act?'

'Prohibition. When the country was forced dry by some zany law that's got Congressman Volstead's name on it. Y'know? No liquor. By law. So what the country got was bootlegging and

24

gangsters. One led to the other, sure as God made little apples.'

Kurt shrugged, mystified. I think it was the term 'bootlegging' that baffled him.

The Principessa got up, and went to supervise the tricky business of preparing the zabaglione.

The Prince, smiling in reminiscence, went on. 'I was vulnerable myself, being of a disapproved-of social order. But I paid up. It was all done very discreetly. The Mayor himself was "godfather" of the cell that operated this side of the Arno. Oh, he was very polite—coming here as if on a social call instead of summoning me to his office. But to a Prince he displayed what he thought were princely manners. There was a photograph which had been "found" (as he called it) and which he returned with his compliments, saying with a smirk that he was sure I would like to have it. No question of money, of course, but it was a picture of ... a somewhat compromising situation. It gave me no qualms, yet the public consequences could have been embarrassing for the Caeseri family. I knew perfectly well that a negative of the picture existed and that this was his way of offering it to me—particularly as a dignified appeal for a contribution to the founding of a new hospital had preceded it. A non-existent foundation, I may add. I made a contribution and the negative arrived, anonymously and mysteriously. And Mafia funds were enriched by half a million lira.'

'Yeah,' Steve nodded. 'That figures. "Protection money" we call it in the States. If you didn't subscribe to your gangster protectors you got your kids beaten up or your premises damaged in an automobile "accident". It was scary the number of cars that found themselves driven off the roads into shopfronts when the patrolman was sneaking a quick coffee for which he'd got a hundred-dollar bill on the side.'

Kurt shook his head in seeming disapproval. 'I think the Brownshirts and the storm troopers were incorruptible in that way. They were bidden to burn down synagogues and shops owned by the Jews. I don't think you could buy them off. They were dedicated to eliminating the Jews.'

'And you, Kurt—?' the Prince let his question hang in the air.

'I am not dedicated to anything. I was a member of the Hitler Youth because my parents would have gone to prison if they'd forbidden me to join. I am just'—his brow furrowed—'a German.'

The Prince's expression changed. 'We are seeing this "dedication" to the elimination of the Jews here too. And the Fascist thugs are no less vicious than the Mafia—but with less purpose, for they do not need money to support their violent activities. They are government funded.' He gave a hollow laugh. 'Still, I tip my hat to the Duce for that one good act.'

'Yeah, you're well rid of guys like that,' Steve agreed.

I was curious about the origins of this sinister society and would have liked to ask more. But at that moment the Principessa returned.

'That's enough of politics, Giorgio,' she cried. Then she turned to me, 'Perhaps, Ham, if you were to ask Fiamma as a friend of yours to one of Mr Berenson's concerts, he might invite her, and I could go as her chaperone.'

'Really, my dear,' the Prince replied almost

26

tartly. 'You're just trying to get Mr Johns to wangle an invitation to a concert that will merely bore you.'

'That's not true, Giorgio,' she protested. 'It's just that—Mr Berenson has such a remarkable house—fifty acres of grounds—'

'We have twenty. That's quite enough,' laughed the Prince.

'Maybe I could help,' suggested Steve. 'I get around quite a lot. I talk fluent Italian, and sometimes there's a few tickets secretly on sale from people who don't want to go. It'll cost you something though.'

During this exchange I had been thinking hard—about how I could manage to see Fiamma again—and again, and again, just the two of us. And suddenly I knew how to do it.

'I've got a wonderful idea,' I burst out. 'If—your daughter, Fiamma—will help me—'

'She doesn't know Mr Berenson,' said the Principessa sharply.

'Let Mr—let Ham have his say,' said the Prince tolerantly.

'Well, sir,' I addressed him, 'Mr Berenson wants me to paint my first portrait, and my art teacher, Signor Umberto, agrees. I would love to. But to Mr Berenson it's an exercise to prove that I've learned the theories behind Renaissance art. So he wants to choose the model for me to paint—or if I find a suitable one, he would want to approve. It's all part of my studies, you understand.'

'And you mean Fiamma?' asked the Principessa.

'Well, yes, Donna Margarita. And if Fiamma loves music—then I'm sure that as my model she would be invited to the next concert.'

'Clever Mr Johns,' cried the Principessa. 'That's

27

why the English always win their wars.'

And that was the way my romance with Fiamma started, for I did all of my actual painting (apart from learning theory and history) in Umberto's studio when he was not using it. And it meant that I would have to spend hours with her—alone, at his studio on the top floor of a thin building in the shadow of the Torre de Marsali, near the Via Barbadori, a stone's throw from the Ponte Vecchio.

CHAPTER TWO

Umberto was almost a caricature of a stock actor playing an artist, even to a beret and beard. He was on the fat side, had a round face and a permanent smile. He wore dirty trousers, old and covered with smudges of paint. He painted savage (and sometimes unsaleable) scenes of Florence, often before dawn because he was fascinated by lights shining in the dark. He had been born and brought up in the same tiny Florence studio-flat, and was an orphan, but never seemed concerned about it. I doubt if he or anyone had ever renewed a pot or a pan, a sheet or a suit, since his mother died.

In short, he was one of the sights of the city, trundling along with his portable easel, holding a wet canvas in front of him. And essentially he was a very kind man. He gave lessons because he needed petty cash—and he needed the cash because he rarely *sold* any paintings. He always swapped them. He had a regular clientele among shopkeepers and other similar people who believed that one day his paintings would be famous. With them he would exchange a new painting for groceries, the rates, a couple of sacks of wood or coal in winter, and especially he bought tubes of paint and canvases from Sangallo's, the largest dealers in painting materials, just off the Via Martelli. He always paid with paintings.

But above everything else, Umberto could teach. He had an uncanny flair for singling out the only way you *should* paint according to his feeling for a pupil. A few strokes of my brush, the way I put paint on the canvas, and he could pick out the one method of painting at which he was convinced I would do best.

I remember one budding oil painter whom Umberto doomed to a life of painting watercolours, beautifully, while to me, after futile experiments to discover the metier which suited me best and what I *enjoyed* doing best—for that is the secret of painting, enjoyment—he suggested that I was happiest and most professional using a palette knife rather than a paint brush, filling canvases with vast slabs of bright colours, then using the edge of the knife to some parts, even scraping off sections I did not like, in others leaving a thick impasto which at times stood out in ridges from the canvas.

The result was exciting, but I did not have the faintest idea if I could employ the palette knife technique on a portrait.

'Only if you don't try to paint a likeness,' growled Umberto. 'You have no experience of this. If you want to attempt a portrait—if Berenson says you must'—he scratched his long white beard—'paint one. But as a *painting*, not a photograph. Don't expect it to look anything like the sitter. You're not painting a portrait for money or to please a sitter. It's a *painting*. The end is what you are after, not the beginning.' He said this with a stern grimace that had the character of a warning.

★ ★ ★

No doubt delighted that I might be able to arrange for an invitation to be sent to her, the Principessa readily agreed to 'lend' me Fiamma as a sitter for her portrait; but before I took Fiamma to start work I told Umberto more of my plans.

'Splendid,' he cried. 'It's time you enlarged your scope. I only hope she'll be able to stand the strain. It's no joke you know, employing an amateur model. It's hard work—for them.'

He ran two paint-stained fingers through his beard. 'You must remember that, though you are the *maestro*, your sitter is a human being like you and everybody else. And there is a great difference between the experienced sitter and the one casually plucked from a crowd because of a smile . . . a sadness . . . a look of lust . . . some . . .' He took his fingers from his beard and pushed his beret back on his forehead, pondering. 'I don't know what you call it in English. *Espressione*, we say here.'

'Expression,' I smiled.

'So. There is this expression, this reason that you pluck the sitter from the crowd, like your Fiamma, because she is beautiful in the body or the smile of the teeth or the way the head is sculptured to the shoulders. But she is not like the hired model, who is blasé about her attractions and sees them only as little handfuls of liras and has learned patience and stillness and detachment from her own body'—he touched his forehead with a finger—'so that in her

30

head she can write letters or think of arguments with her landlady while to you, with your palette, she is no more than the unmoving medium between you and your canvas. She has learnt this over many years, and at the bidding of different painters she will hold an arm aloft or stretch a leg and become immobile for as long as she knows it's necessary.'

'For hours?' I asked naively.

Umberto chuckled. 'You know as little of the body as you do of painting, my young friend.' Seeing my glum look he added hastily, 'No, no, do not be discouraged. You have the painter's ... *visione?*'

'Vision,' I smiled again.

'Good. This is happy, this likeness of our languages.' He leaned forward. 'You have the vision, the inside, of the artist, but you know little yet of the way. For there are perspirations to this business of the painter as well as inspirations.' The fingers combed the beard again. 'As you know from what I have told you, in matters of brushes and pigments and the way to half-close your eyes sometimes to get the view you want. So I tell you now about the poor girl who sits there on the dais, so self-conscious as she must be and not at all concentrating on sitting still because she is your lover—'

He held up his hand to stop me as I was about to protest—a protest that was half wishful thinking.

'—in her mind if not *yet* in bed.' He smiled mischievously. 'I am old. I know about these things. I have had many women. But there she is and you want her to sit still and she is restless. So remember, please, that she is not the professional and will need much rest. Even for the professional,

31

the hireling, it is troublesome to remain for more than twenty minutes if the pose is not one of—of—*relaxment*. Even to be peaceful and in a pose of meditation is not a happy thing for the body; for the muscles need not to be taut and we shift them to ease them, even in sleep. It is unnatural to stand rigid like soldiers. So I tell you to remember: be patient with your Fiamma, for she knows nothing of the difficulties of being a model and will also be half curious about what you are painting and half fidgety. It will be disturbing for you because *you* can concentrate for much longer periods. But you must restrain your impatience and remember that any discomfort she feels will be reflected in her face and will therefore give you not the portrait you want. But'—he wagged his finger solemnly—'again I say to repeat myself, "Do not try to get a likeness. A camera is for likenesses. A painting is for *espressione*." Now you understand?'

I understood only too well. There was an area of conflict here between my teacher of history and my teacher of technique. It was not the only area of conflict into which we were destined to wander.

*   *   *

Two days later I brought Fiamma to Umberto's studio. He took a long look at her.

'She is magnificent,' he agreed with me. 'Beautiful white teeth and I can see the lovely young breasts peeping through her thin dress. What colour are your eyes? Grey. Hair good, but I have to ask you a question,' he spoke casually. 'You have been to bed with this man?'

'Certainly not!' cried Fiamma.

32

'More fool you. He's a handsome young devil.' His laugh robbed the original question of any offence. 'But you probably will do—if you follow my advice.' He laughed again and she did not protest.

He turned to me. 'Ham, you will never be able to paint a pretty chocolate-box face. Thank God for that. So far, since we started using the knife, you have been painting strong, vibrant exciting buildings, roads, even a field of cabbages with houses in the background—remember that one? Striking, but always with a kind of architecture. Yes, even a field of cabbages can be painted that way. Now, this girl.' He held out his hand to Fiamma. 'Her body is vibrant, and like a beautiful piece of architecture—sculpture, if you like—those legs, breasts, thighs, hips, belly—perfectly constructed—imagine!'

I could! I was getting sexual stirrings, secretly undressing her, so that I blurted out, 'You mean a nude?'

Almost ignoring Fiamma, who was beginning to look embarrassed, he said to me, 'Of course! What else? The face doesn't matter.'

'I couldn't—'

'Mama would never let me,' Fiamma broke in.

'Paint her like the flame she is.' Umberto ignored Fiamma's interruption, regarding her only as a convenient object to be painted. 'You can paint her here—while I'm out giving lessons. She's got a beautiful body. Don't strive for *any* likeness, though. The *essence* of beauty is what you must strive for.'

I could not help thinking how right he was, and how exciting it would be. The sex was something

33

else—and very, very present, as the bulge in my trousers grew larger and more urgent, especially when Umberto said, almost without thinking, 'Let's have a look at you, my dear. Make absolutely sure you're right for the subject.'

'You mean—undress?' For a moment I thought Fiamma was going to run for it.

'Of course. And don't feel embarrassed like a baby. I can hire a dozen nude girl models, like that.' He snapped his fingers.

'I've never—'

'Just smell the paint in this room—and remember that we are artists, not sex maniacs.'

'All of me?' she asked faintly.

'All of you,' roared Umberto. 'Keep your pants on if you wish. I'm interested in your body, not your pussy.' He used the Florentine slang word *passera*, meaning sparrow. 'Now, come on.'

By sheer force of personality—and his inner sense of kindness combined with the knowledge that he was not being lecherous—Fiamma started slowly to undress. Was it delicacy that prompted her at first to turn her back to me? As she started to undo the buttons on her silk dress she suddenly said, 'In this hot weather'—hesitating—'it's so very hot and I've got no underclothes on at all.'

'Who cares,' cried Umberto, and then, with a multi-coloured silk dress like a halo, she slid it down, the halo round her feet, and stood upright and still and turned round, pert breasts pointing upwards, a flat belly, and under it the echo of her thick blonde hair, a darker shade, but as thick as on her head, and I groaned inwardly at the sight until Umberto brought me back to earth.

'Perfect, my dear.' And to me, 'You should paint

34

her first in off-white, with touches of blue and a faint touch of green shading to accentuate the parts you feel *should* be accentuated. And a plain background. It could be a sensation. You start a week on Monday. I'm going off to Siena in two weeks. Here's a key. Remember, the face doesn't matter. Leave the head off if you like! There are plenty of headless statues in Florence.' To Fiamma, 'Yes, yes dear. Pop your clothes on. We'll see what you've done wrong when I return.'

'Thank you. *You* don't mind?' I said to Fiamma.

'I suppose not. It's, well, exciting.'

'It's always exciting showing off a beautiful body,' said Umberto.

'I suppose it is,' Fiamma agreed slowly. 'I don't know why, but you're right—I will enjoy it—for you—' She gave me a shy smile.

Almost in a trance of frustrated desire, I managed to mutter, 'Mr Berenson won't be so delighted. *He* wants me to try my hand at a portrait.'

'That guru of yours, the sacred Berenson. He's the nearest thing to a charlatan,' jeered Umberto.

'You can't say that,' I almost shouted. 'BB is a genius. He knows more about art than you'll ever know.' I felt suddenly angry.

'Genius! He's a fake. Okay, he might be useful teaching you the appreciation of historical art as an expert in his field, but don't let him try to turn you into a failed Michelangelo.'

*　　*　　*

After we left Umberto's, I suggested we had an espresso at Doney's and, sitting in a corner seat, I said rather awkwardly, 'I'm sorry about

35

that—Umberto making you take off your clothes. I was as astonished as you were.'

She lowered her eyes. For the first time I noticed how long and dark her lashes were. With a toss of her head she shook her thick blonde hair back into place.

'I *was* surprised and a bit shattered for a moment, and then, well, I realised it was a sort of compliment.' She gave me a dazzling smile, showing her white teeth, and asked, almost shyly—no, that's not fair—almost *teasingly*, 'You don't mind?'

Before I could even begin to think about cutting out my tongue, I blurted out, 'I loved it. You're so beautiful. But not only that. It did make me feel—well, I don't know what the polite word is, but you know—so excited I thought I was going to blow up. I can't wait to paint you.'

'Paint and look?' She gave a laugh, almost a suppressed chuckle.

'Look and paint,' I corrected her seriously.

'And we'll be alone during these sessions?'

'I'm afraid so. For two weeks! And it's not going to be easy,' I added less gravely. 'It's the first time I've done anything like this alone. In classes, yes, but I'm not used to standing and looking at a beautiful woman *alone*. I don't know whether I'll be able to take it. And then there's—your mother. The Principessa might not like the idea of a young man painting you without any clothes on.'

'Don't tell her.' She fiddled with her napkin.

'You mean that?'

'I do. I was fascinated by the problems Signor Umberto was discussing. I want to see what happens—what you make of it. But Mama wouldn't understand. On the other hand, so long as she meets Mr Berenson ...' she added with a touch of irony.

'You're a very tempting young lady,' I smiled. 'And forthright.'

'You're a very tempting young man,' she replied. 'No, let's carry on, say nothing, pretend the portrait is a failure—and see what happens.'

'I know what I'd like to happen.' My voice was husky.

'Let's change the subject,' she said. 'You're trying to make me feel like you say *you* feel. What about Mama's invitation to the next concert?'

'Let's go. I told Mr Berenson that I'd chosen a model, which is why he asked us for lunch, today.' I paid for the coffee. 'Now let's go and meet him.'

As we made our way to *I Tatti* I explained how, as an historian, Berenson had advised me that I should try my hand at painting a portrait as part of what he called 'the process of making a painted appreciation of the value of art'.

'I don't understand,' she admitted.

'Neither do I!' We both laughed and I held her hand as we walked out into the street, and we squeezed our hands in a gentle but definite way. The very modest touch sent a surge of tenderness through me, tenderness more than desire. What a girl! I thought. And to let Umberto order her to take off her clothes and she did so without a murmur! And in front of a healthy sexy man like me!

'Not you,' she read my thoughts and reproved me with a smile. 'In front of Signor Umberto. You just happened to be there.'

She laughed as we jumped on the No. 9

trolley-bus at the Piazza San Marco, which deposited us at the Ponte Mensola over that small river. From there we took a ten-minute walk along a country lane on the slopes of Settignano, to one of the entrances to *I Tatti*, where a narrow path bordered by cypresses led us to the entrance of the villa. The scents and sounds of summer filled the air. Above the stream dragonflies hovered, their wings gaudy with sunshine.

'Prepare to meet a genius,' I laughed.

'But what I don't really understand,' she confessed as we passed through the ornate front gates, 'is—*why* he's so famous—and so rich.'

I tried to explain. 'Basically I suppose, it's because he's the greatest expert in the world on Renaissance paintings, and he's of enormous help to big international dealers like, say, Duveen. He can spot fakes. He gets paid a percentage of any transaction. Always. Even before the turn of the century he was making 15,000 dollars a year in commissions and sales. He has the *real* knowledge, you see, more than anyone else, and it is important when you're dealing in fortunes to spend a little extra and make sure.'

'But even that . . .' she faltered.

'He explained once during a lecture that he only had to look at the hands to see if a Botticelli was genuine—because Botticelli always painted hands with square nails. That and the paint itself—and age—he has invented what he calls "tactile values"—I'll explain it sometime—he needs to touch to make certain. Did you know that Titian always painted the ball of a thumb in the same way? Berenson knows an awful lot. I've been helping him with some Florentine drawings, and I've learned so

38

much from him.'

'But still? All the money for I Tatti?'

'He bought the lot—the villa, two cottages and a chapel *and* fifty acres for about six thousand pounds in English money. Sixty million lire in yours. Ridiculous! He's also got another little place in Poggibonsi where he retreats to when he wants a change or things become a bit too hectic here. And as for the money—well, he has one other attribute. He's Jewish. I'm not against them. And I worship Berenson. But he's very smart as well as clever. He's quite capable of selling a painting twice.'

'Not to two people at once?'

'No, no. But he'll recommend an old master to a client, take a percentage, then later advise the client to sell it and replace it with a better painting. So he gets commissions on resales *and* new purchases.'

The gardens of *I Tatti* were magnificent. Berenson had transformed fourteen of the fifty acres into formal Italian-style gardens, the beautifully manicured squares of lawn criss-crossed with gravel patches as immaculate as a newly cleaned carpet, with not a blade of grass out of place, not a flower in disarray.

'It's so ... so *elegant*,' gasped Fiamma as we approached the front door. The rather plain and unpretentious Tuscan villa was topped by a pretentious clock tower which years before had been erected by Berenson's wife as a surprise when he returned from a trip to America.

'That's more impressive than elegant.' Fiamma sounded as though she had to say something polite but was doubtful as she looked up.

'He hated it!' I said cheerfully. 'When he first saw it he wanted to pull the whole thing down, but

39

structurally it was too difficult. They'd have had to take the roof off. So it's still there.'

The entrance corridor behind the front portico was short and a table covered with hats stood by the front door. The walls were lined with old master pictures that looked as though they had been arranged to stay in the same position for ever.

Lunch was always arranged in the same way. It was preceded by the vaguest of cocktails in a large rather rococo room where half a dozen celebrities had already gathered. Mrs Berenson—Mary—an art expert and author in her own right, introduced Fiamma to the others Count this and the Marchese that; and while we waited for BB, as he was known world-wide from the initialled certificate with which he authenticated pictures, we were offered minute glasses of vermouth flavoured with a little lemon.

Finally Berenson arrived—but only when he had been told that all the guests were present. It was as though stage-managed for effect. Perhaps it was? The semi-circle of admirers and acquaintances, including Fiamma, nervously awaited the first sight of the small, immaculate, white-bearded man with, as usual, a carnation in his buttonhole.

Afterwards, Fiamma described him to her mother and me, 'He's like a small ivory statue of a saint.'

He *did* have a saintly look about him. Speaking in Italian mostly on Fiamma's first visit, he made the rounds of the guests, kissing the girls' hands, lingering for a moment longer than he needed to savour the fragrance of beauty of Fiamma before sitting down in his 'own' deep leather armchair and motioning Fiamma to sit on his right. I, as usual, sat on a stool inside the large fireplace, ready if need be to refill any glasses of vermouth while Berenson told one of his interminable, oft-repeated, allegedly funny stories and we laughed dutifully. In between he started making one of his regular anti-Fascist outbursts.

'You should meet my father,' Fiamma smiled. 'He hates the Fascists, can't stand Mussolini. He's always getting into trouble.'

'One of us!' Berenson raised his eyes to Fiamma who remarked later on his beautiful grey eyes. 'I must ask him to come around.'

After a lunch dominated by talk from Berenson, he led the way to a large structure—the only word I can think of—which he called his *limonaia*, a sort of glass barn filled with lemon and pomegranate trees, a kind of *orangerie*, until three o'clock when he always went for his siesta, followed by his afternoon walk.

During lunch he never mentioned the reason for Fiamma's visit, but once installed in the limonaia he turned to me and said, 'So this is the young lady who's to be your model? Very beautiful, I must say. You sit here.'

'If you approve.' I knew he would.

'I do,' he replied in his gentle, almost silky voice, the sound almost like a caress.

He paused, looking at Fiamma. 'I suggest a head and shoulders.' I was startled—especially after Umberto's decision, but said nothing. 'You agree? Good. Now, when do you start? Two weeks? Good.'

I wondered what Fiamma was thinking. I was always careful when talking to BB not to overstep the limits of familiarity. I had warned Fiamma to avoid discussing abstract art—to him a subject for

41

contempt. It was not always easy, for I also had to deal with Umberto, who was much less rigid in his approach to representational art.

'It is for pleasure—art,' Umberto had insisted. 'So if it pleases the artist to convey pleasure by shocking the beholder—well, why not?'

Tentatively Fiamma put this view to BB without mentioning any names (Chagall and Picasso whould have been like red to a bull). BB paused reflectively before explaining what he called 'the flouting of rules'.

'In all arts and sciences there must be rules; otherwise chaos,' he explained to Fiamma. 'Take perspective: the Greeks followed the rules in the fifth century BC, and the Renaissance painters developed them because they so often had to depict interiors. To ignore them gives you nothing but an outline, a profile, as on a coin. But this is perfectly all right for those who make coins, which *are* flat and have no third dimension other than their thickness. But an artist may *want* to give that impression.'

He paused and contemplated the cypresses. 'So he may break the rules as long as he knows them first. In music too, the same. It is good to be defiant if you know what you're being defiant about. Beethoven knew perfectly well that consecutive fifths flout the rules of harmony, but he used them joyfully.'

He raised his stick to point at the cypresses. 'The charlatans would have us believe that those trees are pink or blue or yellow—not because they want to make a statement about the importance of colour but because they want to draw attention to themselves and to what they think of as their

42

cleverness. Conceit: a manifestation of conceit: that is all it is.'

I kept quiet. I knew he was getting at me because he had recently seen me closely examining a print of Dufy's *Harvest*, with its startling red horse in the middle of the team of three drawing the threshing machine. I wanted to say, but if it brings forth an emotional response in the beholder, does it matter? I did not, though. It amused me to think that both my professors used the word 'charlatan' in different ways. And I had got it into my mind that my portrait of Fiamma was going to be called 'Blue Nude'—for the simple reason that blue was the intense colour in which my inner eye conceived it. A conception, I thought wryly, that would hardly please BB.

'Well,' said BB to Fiamma. 'I hope I haven't bored you. You are too beautiful *ever* to be bored.'

He tended at times to speak in clipped phrases. To me he said, 'I would like to see your preliminary sketches if you don't mind, while I swallowed, trying to see my way around the problem I now faced. 'Not important at this stage.' With a shrug of his shoulders he turned to Fiamma. 'But you are a very attractive young lady, and I'm anxious to see how this young man here interprets your face.' And after taking some tea, he apologised, 'Now, I have to have a little sleep. But, you must come again,' declared Berenson, preparing to leave. 'I have met Prince Caeseri at a large dinner, but not his wife. Yes, perfect for a portrait. You agree, Ham?'

Hesitating to tell him that I had already seen much more than head and shoulders—and hoped to see it all again—I merely said, 'I haven't really thought about the details,' and knowing that it

43

would please him, added, 'I just wanted you to approve the choice first before I go to Umberto.'

Turning to me he suggested—and this was a *very* rare honour—'Why don't you take the prince's daughter to have a look at our library, and my study if you like. I'll see you before you go.'

We made a very quick tour. What impressed Fiamma most was that details of all the old masters were carefully explained, each room containing a folder with a transparent cover giving details in Italian and English of each picture on the walls, while in the centre of the library was a really magnificent, huge fifteenth-century table. We just peeped into his study, where one painting made all the others seem ten times less beautiful: it was a Madonna by Domenico Veneziato.

'We'd better go, he'll want to say goodbye.'

Back in the limonaia, where Berenson was standing, looking at his watch, he saw us arrive.

'I just wanted to say goodbye.'

'Very considerate of you,' he murmured. 'You'll be back to study for your Renaissance thesis on Monday, Ham?'

'Of course, Mr Berenson. And—'

'Well?'

'The Principessa, Fiamma's mother, she's very keen on music. And she's a friend of Kurt's. She'd love to hear you all play.'

'Would you like to come too?' he asked Fiamma.

'It would be an honour, Mr Berenson.'

'Then you must come—both, of course.' He was obviously more interested in Fiamma. 'I'll send a double invitation to your mother tomorrow.'

It was as easy as that.

And to both of us, he said, 'Now you've seen my

44

library, the next time I must show you all over the house.

We both thanked him, but my mind was not on his house! I was much more concerned about finding a way to please both of my art masters! One wanted a nude, the other a head and shoulders. And I could guess which one the Principessa would choose! But I had seen Fiamma in the nude, she had agreed to pose for me naked, and there was no way I was going to stop her doing that!

CHAPTER THREE

Kurt von Schill was studying to be a pianist, and the next musical evening at I Tatti promised to challenge him with one of the most difficult evenings he had so far faced. He *was* promising, but this was a tricky piece, even though Berenson, in his silky voice, very beautifully dressed, with the inevitable carnation in his button hole, had announced, 'I'd like you to have a go at Mendelssohn's B-minor quartet. Youthful music, but I think you're up to it, being youthful yourself. I won't be able to play the violin. Don't feel up to it at the age of seventy, but I'll be there to listen to you.'

Kurt had practised hard on the upright piano which was part of the furniture of our house—in fact, it was the main reason why Kurt, who was the first of us to take up residence, had agreed to rent the place.

'But now,' he said, 'that you tell me the Principessa is coming, I shall have to do really well to impress her.'

'You always play well,' I assured him without any real conviction to back up what I said, 'so—why especially for the Principessa?'

'Well, Roz. Rosanna's quite a girl. And it's important I keep on the right side of the old lady.'

'She's not that old,' I protested. 'Smitten with the girl?'

'Are you—with Fiamma?'

'Well, I *am* going to paint Fiamma.' Then, pausing for dramatic effect, I added casually, 'In the nude!' And when Kurt gave a low whistle, I added even more airily, 'Yes, it's all been arranged. She undressed so that I could make sure I thought she would be suitable.'

'Lucky bugger!'

'I don't see why. All *you* have to do is seduce Roz with your music. If music be the food of love, play on—but you wouldn't know that being a German. Shakespeare.'

With a laugh he threw a newspaper at me, deliberately missing. 'You ignoramus! Hitler wrote it.'

No one was ever very serious for long at our 'villa'—villa for want of a better word. It was close to the road, had a tiny patch of garden behind, just a plot of ill-kept grass, three bedrooms, a sitting-room with the piano, and a dining-room table which I often used for sketching; and—this was heaven—we had an old beamed Tuscan kitchen, with a large table in the middle, a stove, and a fridge. An elderly woman called Maria cooked lunch for us and left us a cold meal for the evenings. If we were not in for the evening, she would heat it for the following lunch; or, if we did not like the look of it, we took the food out in a paper bag and threw it away.

'Do you think you'll go to bed with Roz?' I asked, not only out of curiosity, for though Roz was great fun in some ways, she had hidden depths of reserve.

'I know what you mean,' agreed Kurt, reading my thoughts. 'Sometimes she looks as though she's got the whole world on top of her, weighing her down. But she's twenty, and she can't remain a virgin forever. I'm prepared to wait'—with a grin—'for a week or two.'

Steve bustled in.

'What gives?' He walked over to the drinks shelf behind the kitchen table and poured out a stiff gindiano.

'Ham tells me he persuaded Fiamma to strip—all for the cause of art! An old dodge,' cried Kurt.

'Jeez!' Steve took a long gulp of his gin, while Kurt mischievously played *Plaisir d'Amour* on the piano. 'How much you charging for visits, Ham?'

'Vulgar shits,' I said without rancour. 'This *is* art for art's sake. And a good painter never notices the body in detail—or the sort of thing that's making you squirm in your pants. You disgust me!'

'Balls,' cried Kurt.

'Crap!' cried Steve.

I explained how Fiamma and I had wangled a ticket for the Principessa to visit Berenson.

'The Principessa? I know. She's as delighted as hell. The invitation's already arrived,' said Steve.

'She told you? Already? When did you meet?' I asked.

'Every day.' Steve was almost smirking.

'How? Tell us!' I begged him.

47

'Nothing to tell. I know you two guys are both hard workers, but me—waal, I'm just a gentleman of leisure!'—'leesure', he pronounced it—'and you may remember the Principessa *did* mention casually that we should feel free to use the pool. Well, with an invitation like that, we Americans don't waste time. I took her at her word. I walked up the morning after that first evening, arrived with a large box of Doney's chocolate, and my swimsuit, and asked the old girl if I could go swimming, adding "with Lella, if she happens to be around". Well, she did happen to be around, so I told her to make sure it "happened" every day.'

'What cheek!'

'It worked,' said Steve cheerfully. 'That girl Lella ain't going nowhere if I'm around the Villa Magari. And her Mom thinks I'm great. Love me, love my daughter. That little girl Lella is something, I can tell you. I'm already crazy about her. And when I tell her about the way you made her sister strip—it should be kid's stuff to make her swim in the altogether.'

'No, no, you mustn't tell, for Chrissake,' I cried. 'Her mother doesn't know. Even Mr Berenson doesn't know. They think it's going to be a head and shoulders. Berenson's idea.'

I explained in some detail the double problem I faced—that I might even have to paint *two* portraits, one to please Berenson and the Principessa, the other to please Umberto—and myself.

'You sure have a problem,' Steve said. 'Nothing you can do about it, though.'

He was wrong.

I did, however, do one thing. Since we had some time to spare before the painting sessions started, I decided to join the morning sessions at the Indian pool, especially when Steve and Kurt mentioned casually they were going to Florence the following morning—Steve to take Lella to meet a friend, Kurt for one of his master-class music lessons. I said nothing, just decided to turn up the next day—and every day when I was free.

Quite apart from the girls, it was heaven. We were royally treated, with Fawkes or a maid carrying trays of lemonade, ice and alcoholic drinks along the long walk with its left-hand side a riot of rambler roses. The water was cool, the surroundings perfect.

'Here's something that might please you as an Englishman,' said Roz, the dark-haired member of the family.

'Father spent three years at Oxford, you know'—I did not but let the remark pass—'and he fell in love with one summer fruit which we don't often see in Italy though it does grow in some parts. But ours was planted specially by Papa. Do you like "uvaspina"?' She used the Italian word.

'Haven't the faintest idea what "uvaspina" means,' I laughed.

'Come on, I'll show you. It's a bush. Father planted four. They're behind here.' Dripping with water and leaving our wet footprints on the rim as we both climbed out of the pool, she led the way to a corner of the garden beyond. 'Look! There!'

'Oh!' I cried. 'Gooseberries! I love them. What did you call them?'

49

'Uvaspina,' she laughed, almost a deep throaty chuckle.

'Never heard of the word. What's it mean?'

'Prickly grapes.'

'Can I have one?'

'As many as you like. Papa's grown out of them, I think. He never usually eats more than a couple of uvaspina pies with cream a year. So you can eat and eat until you have tummy ache.' Then, without any warning, she asked, 'Do you like me?'

'Well, of course!' What an odd question! 'All three of you are superb. But why do you pick on me? I thought Kurt had his eye on you. All this daily swimming.' I picked a couple more gooseberries, topped and tailed them, and with an attempt at a laugh in advance I said, 'Take care of Kurt. You know what happens behind gooseberry bushes?'

'I've already taken care of Kurt.' She gave a secret smile. 'What does happen behind gooseberry bushes?'

'Babies!' I laughed.

'Oh *that*,' she shrugged her shoulders as if the possibility had not occurred to her. 'You like Fiamma, don't you?'

'Well, she *is* attractive.' I looked towards the pool not longingly, hopefully, just to avert what might become an embarrassing situation.

'But don't you think I'm attractive too?' she asked. 'After all, my other sisters are both dizzy blondes like my father used to be before he turned grey. I'm very dark. I've always been told that it attracts men because they wonder—well, *you* know!' she teased suggestively.

'Why one girl has dark hair?' I asked, knowing

50

perfectly well what she meant.

'Well, I *am* the black sheep of the family.' This time I did not understand. 'Didn't you know?' she asked with assumed innocence. 'The Prince is not my father. I'm the result of one of Mama's slip-ups.'

I didn't know what to say! I gulped miserably and finally managed to utter something like, 'Oh God, I am sorry'. She ignored my look of embarrassment.

'Don't worry. I love life,' she replied cheerfully. 'And as for Mama—why, Papa's had his own *garçonnière* in Florence since he married Mama for her money. And he still has.'

'You can't be *sure*.' I had a mental picture of this tall, suave, good-looking and perfect specimen of apparent rectitude.

'I *am* sure.' She seemed to be enjoying my discomfort, for she added, 'because I've been to the place. After all, he's not my father.' That was a curiously suggestive remark, but she didn't enlighten me any further, so I asked hastily, 'And your Mama—she's not upset?'

'*Upset*?! She's adorable, she's loving, we all worship her, but she's tough. She insisted once on taking us children to see England—the north where she was born, where it never stops raining, and when we returned to Italy we christened her "The Princess of the Yorkshire Dales".'

I could not help laughing, but I was still thinking, this daughter is illegitimate!

'Mama plays around quite a bit—or did, I suppose. I don't know what she's up to now. You, though,' with a knowing wink at me, 'I *do* know she can become very fond of young men.' She laughed

51

again. 'I don't mind. Officially I'm the daughter of a prince—well, I *am*. And I'm just like Mama. I also enjoy playing around a bit. And I find *you* attractive. I love your thick blond hair—and your freckles. But'—what a sexual tease she was, and I was staggered at her next remark which was almost whispered—'I bet I've got more hair down there than you have! Want a peep?'

I began to become aroused and, looking down, she saw the tight bundle in my close-fitting swimming trunks and, laughing, pointed, 'I told you. One day—who knows. Anyway, watch Mama. She's always ready for a handsome young man. My! You have grown!' This with another glance at my trunks. 'You'd better have a quick dip in the pool!'

Then as we ran towards the pool over the grass and shrubs that divided it from the garden she held hands as we jumped in with an almighty splash, gasping and exhilarated while I was thinking, 'My God! *Thrown* herself at me!' What a girl! I do believe she would have let me try and do it there and then, behind the gooseberry bushes.

And yet, when I emerged again from the depth of the pool to sit on the tessellated pink and grey decorated stone edge, I found myself next to Fiamma.

I thought, she is the exact opposite of Roz with her black hungry look, and her flagrant invitation which she had so skilfully implanted in me. But I longed much more for the girl next to me now—Fiamma with her long legs swinging idly, as different from Roz as chalk from cheese, figs from gooseberries, asparagus from artichokes. Fiamma seemed to hint at a stifled desire for love with sex, Roz an enticement to experience sex without love.

Still, an experience. I would not mind it, I thought a trifle guiltily, as I sat talking to Fiamma, mostly about our first meeting with Umberto, and her forthcoming modelling session.

And then she asked, and was it with a touch of envy or sarcasm? 'I see Roz has been taking you for a walk.'

'She wanted to show me the gooseberry bushes.'

Laughing loudly she said, 'I've had my English lessons from Mama. We all know what happens under gooseberry bushes.'

'Well, I don't,' I said almost crossly.

'Sorry,' she apologised. 'But Roz—well, she's a bit of hot stuff. We all know that. And we know all about her as well. I expect she's told you. She tells everyone—loves to cause a stir. But we all love her. She's great fun. But at the same time she's ... sort of, well, I don't know quite how to put it, but there's a *secret* side to her, as if all the fun-loving side of her was a screen to hide something different, something she didn't want people to know about, which she keeps to herself.'

'She'd make a good spy,' I said jokingly.

Fiamma laughed. 'To me, she's just a sister. Completely.'

'Of course,' I agreed. 'And I know what you mean. She is fun. But you—you're more serious—I like you very much.' I hesitated, splashing my foot in the water of the pool.

'Even though I cheerfully got undressed so your artist friend could have a good look at me? And you too.'

'Yes, because of the way you did it.' I was thinking, Roz with her 'want a peep' had *invited* me. 'You just agreed in the course of work.'

'Don't be too sure,' she teased me, 'we all have a touch of Mama in our make-up.'

'Promise,' I asked huskily, touching her foot next to mine. 'Tell me, Fiamma, if you want to, about your mother and Roz, and her husband.'

'Papa? Oh dear. It's rather sad really, but it's a long time ago. And it's only what I've heard really—older friends told our younger friends—you know how stories get around. But it seems that Mama, who is very rich, not only married Papa for his title, but fell in love with the dashing young man he must have been when he'd been married to Vanni's mother, who died.'

'Nothing wrong with falling in love,' I smiled.

'Of course not. And illegitimacy's hardly a crime. Just the result of a spell of . . . well, in Mama's case, disillusionment.'

'With the Prince?'

'Well, yes. You see, she did hanker after a title but she really adored Papa and when, after Lella was born, he quite openly took a lover, it almost broke her heart. She thought it was confirmation that he'd wanted no more than her money—which wasn't true; but you know the old saying about being born in sunny climes leading to passionate times. It was just his Italian love of beauty, of'—she broke off—'what's the word I want?'

'Sensuality?'

'That's it. He adored her just as much as she adored him, but could never resist an occasional romp in the hay, as you English call it. Mama was too young to take it calmly, as a fact of life. Her English bulldog spirit was aroused. She adopted the "what's sauce for the goose is sauce for the gander" attitude and took a lover herself—a young Jewish

54

film director from America whose father was putting up money for a film that was being shot in Florence. They used Magari for some location shots and when they moved off Mama moved off with them, leaving a letter telling Papa that two could play at his game. It was all very dramatic, but it brought Papa to his senses. He realised that the difference in their temperaments had caused the rift and he was ... he was—'

'Contrite?'

'Well, yes. And after Roz was born there was forgiveness and understanding all round and Papa lavished just as much affection on her as he did on Lella. And to seal the renewed loving relationship between Papa and Mama—'

'Ah!' I interrupted. '*You* came along?'

'That's it. And we all lived happily ever after, like in the fairy stories.'

'But, your Papa, now—'

'Oh, you mean—nowadays?' She shrugged her shoulders. 'That comes with being married for twenty or thirty years I suppose.' The casual way she accepted a middle-aged man's infidelity as perfectly normal shocked me.

'But just because two people are married,' I began. 'Would you like to marry a man who loved you and then expect him to—behave like your Papa? would you *like* that?'

'Of course I wouldn't *like* it, but I've always assumed that all men do that after a certain time, and there's nothing you can do about it. It's a fact of life.'

'Well, if I married a beautiful girl like you ...'

'Ah!' she said wistfully. 'That might be different.'

At that moment there was a shout 'Hey! Buon giorno!' from the back balcony of the villa, and against the harsh light I could see the burly outline of Vanni, the step-brother.

'Just came for a swim,' he said after he had loped along the path to the pool. 'Staying the night at my flat, then back to Spain in a few days.'

'Stay for a meal,' said Fiamma. 'We never see you.'

'The best way to keep friends—never see them,' Vanni grinned. 'But I will—I'm bored.'

'You mean your latest girl's walked out on you?' asked Fiamma.

'Just that! Val al diavolo!'

She *could* go to the devil, I thought, but so what? Yet Vanni seemed to be in a better mood than on the first occasion we met. An age gap can consist of months or decades, it has little to do with the age of the people concerned, but in this case the two 'A's'—A for art, A for army—constituted a far more potent gap than the differences in our years. Yet after dinner Vanni did say to me, 'Must be fun being an artist, but I can't paint a bloody straight line. All they've taught me is to use a straight bayonet. Tell me, do you get around to many nudes?'

'Well, some,' I admitted.

'Give you a stand?'

'You Italians!' I laughed. 'Never!' I lied, thinking of the nude I was about to paint with such passion. 'At the moment I'm doing landscapes.'

'Ah! Pity. I'm off back to my military duties in a few days,' he added a little pompously, 'but next time, maybe?'

'Sure,' adding with a smile, 'I'll pick out a real winner for you.'

Summer was on the way out when next I saw Vanni, and that was in very different circumstances.

* * *

A few days later the Principessa herself arrived to watch us at the pool one morning; not to join in the swimming, though she had a good if slightly angular figure, but for drinks on the large terrace between the Indian pavilion and the pool itself. As usual, it was charmingly furnished with swinging hammock-type sofas, low tables and casual chairs impervious to water.

'Come and sit next to me, Ham.' She patted the adjacent cushion on her hammock. 'Now tell me, when are you starting your painting of Fiamma?'

'Monday next, two days after Mr Berenson's concert.'

'Of course—the concert!' Her face lit up with excitement. She was very good-looking, no lines or wrinkles, and I had noticed how she took great pains to keep out of any direct sun.

'Sun is fatal for your face,' she declared. 'If you don't want to end up looking like a bit of wrinkled old leather, keep out of the sun.'

I adored sunbathing, but thought it best not to comment because certainly her skin—arms and neck as well as her face—was without blemish, as smooth as silk. Not a wrinkle to be seen except small ones at the corners of her mouth. In fact, I thought, she was *very* good-looking; a small straight nose, a wide generous mouth that smiled easily, and auburn hair that looked as though it had never been tinted.

'You come from Yorkshire, don't you?' she asked. 'Where exactly?'

'Richmond.'

'Richmond Lodge?' I nodded. 'Oh! Of course, I should have guessed. Sir Henry Johns. I nearly married him! Your father?' I nodded again. 'I'd have been your mother!' She almost giggled. 'I spent several weekends at your father's house when I was Margaret Monson—Monson's Famous Yorkshire Jams.' She laughed. 'Ever taste them?'

'Many times.' I laughed too. 'Father was in love with them!'

'Perhaps he preferred the jam to me?'

'That's impossible,' I cried. 'Where do *you* come from?'

'Just outside Harrogate.' Watching Kurt and Roz splashing each other in the pool, she asked, almost idly, 'Someone mentioned that you went to Oxford?'

'I did. Oriel. But I left after a year.'

'Why? It seems such a waste.' She shook her head when Fawkes offered her a drink. I took a gin and Pellegrino limonata.

'I couldn't stand it,' I admitted. 'My father was in the Foreign Office, still is, and he wanted me to follow in his footsteps. But I was always messing about with pencils and crayons, and then brushes and paint, and my work at Oxford bored me unbelievably. So finally Father saw reason and managed to wangle me a place at the Slade School of Art. I studied there for two years.'

'And now?'

'On the strength that I had been to Oxford—Berenson had been there too—and that I

58

had studied at the Slade, I qualified for the Berenson Fellowship to study the history of Renaissance art. Mr Berenson believes that you have to study the greatest painters thoroughly, if you want some of that greatness to rub off on you—me.' I laughed. 'But of course Berenson always has—how dare I describe it?—a kind of ulterior motive. He hasn't the faintest notion of how to *teach* me, so believes that the easiest way to learn is really to make me an unpaid assistant. He's trying to catalogue his great tome of Florentine Sketches—he's done it once, wants to revise it—and, of course, helping him does help me to appreciate them.'

'I hope it does. But where does Signor Umberto come into this?'

'That's the technical side. *How* to paint. *What* to paint. He's a genius at that. My father pays for the lessons and gives me an allowance.'

'I see.' She hesitated as she watched the others sitting on the edge of the pool, then asked me bluntly, 'What made you choose Fiamma as a model?'

Also hesitating, I replied, 'I don't really know. I suppose that, well, as a model she appealed to me. I can't remember exactly how it happened.'

'I hope'—the smile robbed her next remark of any offence—'you didn't ask her because you found her too attractive to resist.'

I must have blushed for, with a laugh, she added, 'I don't mean that really. But artists *do* have quite a reputation for, well, mixing work with pleasure.'

'Not me, I promise you, Donna Margarita.'

'Of course. I trust you implicitly, Ham.' She almost trilled with laughter as she added, 'As a

59

Yorkshire girl who nearly married your father!'

I laughed too, feeling a trifle awkward, thinking of the picture of Fiamma I still carried in my mind. Would I ever forget it! The tall slinky naked body of Fiamma standing there, facing me directly.

'Perhaps,' suggested the Principessa, 'I could come and see you at work. It would be a fascinating insight.'

Panic-stricken at the prospect, I cried hurriedly, 'Umberto doesn't like me to have anyone watching when I'm painting. He says it's off-putting.'

'I understand,' she replied. But did she? Was she suspicious that perhaps I might take advantage of Fiamma? Rushing politely to my defence before there was any need, I blurted out, 'After all, Mr Berenson suggested that he would prefer me to paint a head and shoulders.'

'Did he?' Was there a touch of relief in her voice as she said, 'I didn't expect anything else, of course. But I wonder why Mr Berenson stipulated head *and* shoulders.' Was this because she wondered if I had invented the entire story? Well, in for a penny I thought, and said recklessly, 'We'll ask him at the concert. He always has what he calls historical reasons for everything he suggests. The other day he was even suggesting a visit to the monastery at Cassino to study some fifteenth-century frescos. He is always saying, "The very heart of art lies in the Renaissance".'

*   *   *

It would be wrong to dismiss the Principessa as a foreigner who had decided to live in Italy merely because she enjoyed her title. Her character was deeper than that and her desire to meet Berenson was based on more prosaic reasoning: 'I wanted to meet him before it was too late,' she had confessed to me. 'After all, we've been next-door neighbours for goodness knows how many years.'

I saw her point of view. Berenson was now, at the turn of 1938, over seventy years old, though as sprightly as a man of fifty, with an acute yet sensuous knowlege and appreciation of art which had in no way diminished with the years; but he was not immortal. One thing the Principessa did share with Berenson was a love of Florence and above that—literally—a love of Settignano, only five miles out of the city yet, as Berenson himself wrote in his diary after watching oxen dragging a plough near the vineyards, 'a feeling I experienced that I was looking at what had been going on here ever since civilisation began'.

Clearly the Principessa shared many of these feelings of past and present intermingled. After all, Michelangelo had spent his youth in Settignano; Gabriele D'Annunzio had enjoyed his tempestuous love affair with Eleonora Duse in the Villa Capponcina within sight of the Villa Magari. The past brushed you every day and it was impossible for the Principessa not to feel its delicate touch, especially as Settignano was the automatic choice for many rich Florentines—especially the patrons of art—who had built their finest houses, their most splendid gardens on the traditional patterns of parterres with a fountain in the circle at the crossing, and some with views of the blue and distant haze of Florence itself. The Principessa might not have known much of the history of the area when she took up residence, but she felt it deeply now. Odd,

61

I thought, that she had never met Berenson.

She did now. I took her and Fiamma to I Tatti, and we all listened to Kurt playing the piano with—to my musically untrained ears—what seemed great skill and feeling. Perhaps fifty people were perched on uncomfortable gilt chairs arranged in the music-room and after the quartet had ended, Berenson led the applause and asked Kurt to play a solo encore, which he did, announcing it as 'A Prelude in G minor by Rachmaninov'.

It was disturbing music. The opening was a sinister theme, faintly martial, like softly repeated drumbeats growing in a tremendous crescendo to a tumultuous downward rush of octaves fading to a yearning song-like tune, then more of the thunderous martial theme until finally tenderness returned and the drums of war faded into the distance.

It *was* disturbing, but love did finally triumph over war. I determined to ask Kurt to play it for me again, at home.

Immediately the music ended, the silence gave way to clapping, then chatter as the guests filed into the spacious limonaia for coffee or wine with biscuits and small sandwiches.

We installed ourselves in one corner and Berenson hardly hesitated before approaching us, as dapper as usual in a dark grey suit with a grey silk tie partly hidden by his neatly trimmed short silky white beard.

His eyes twinkled at the sight of Fiamma but of course he extended his hand first to the Principessa.

'It's terrible that we haven't met for all these years,' he confessed in his gentle voice almost as silky as his beard. 'And now that we *have* met, I can see what I've been missing!'

The Principessa made a polite 'thank you' and I could see that she was delighted at the compliment.

'And only a beautiful woman,' Berenson continued, 'could give birth to such a beautiful young girl as the one Ham has chosen for a model—your daughter. Ah!' he sighed. 'Her head and shoulders will make a perfect Renaissance picture.'

That was what I had wanted to hear! I had thought that I might perhaps have to engineer the questions to make him tell Fiamma's mother in some roundabout way what he expected me to paint, but no! Confirmation had come from the master himself that he had decided on a head and shoulders. That would surely satisfy the mother she did not have to worry about me as a painter.

'We start work on Monday,' I said to them all, 'and I'm dying to start painting.'

'How long will it take?' asked the Principessa.

'He must not rush it,' Berenson advised. 'Rushing a painting is a big mistake. Remember that Raphael took three months to finish his portrait of Giuliana de Medici. And don't worry, Donna Margarita, I shall keep an eye on my star pupil.'

I blushed. It was very kind of him, but I was hardly his 'star'. I was the only one! And a kind of apprentice helping to sort out what Berenson called his 'lists' of his Florentine drawings. On the other hand Berenson was convinced that you could not succeed at one without the other.

He might be right, I thought as we walked back to the Villa Magari, but I was only interested in one thing—to paint, and not her face.

The Principessa walked into the house ahead of

us, and as I said a clumsy goodbye to Fiamma—clumsy because I had a sudden desire to kiss her—I said, 'See you on Monday.' Adding with a laugh, 'And you still don't mind if I don't bother with the head and shoulders?'

'No, I don't,' she smiled and whispered, 'Au revoir', as she ran up the balcony steps and into the house.

CHAPTER FOUR

On the Monday morning when I was due to begin work on the portrait, I thought I had better make an early start—before Fiamma arrived—to tidy up Umberto's living quarters in the Borgo San Jacopo, pretending to myself that Umberto might have left the studio in a mess.

That was not the reason though, the *real* reason. When I jumped on to the No. 9 trolley-bus at the Ponte Mensola I knew that, in my heart, I was trying to cloak signs of nervousness at the prospect of our meeting.

After all, I was wondering as I walked across the Ponte Vecchio, how do you start work with a pretty young amateur nude model? All kinds of possible future phrases passed through my mind. I would perhaps suggest, 'Please put your clothes on the peg there'. Or, 'You'll find the bathroom at the top of the stairs'. Or maybe, 'You're sure you won't be too cold?' Even though it was summer!

The early life class at the Slade School was one thing: a group of artists all working industriously hardly gave you a moment to think of the model

64

herself. But with a girl you found attractive! Alone in someone else's flat for hours on end! No wonder, I thought, as I unlocked the outside front door and made for the rickety lift to the fourth floor, that I approached the first encounter with more than a little trepidation.

Curiously the apprehension began to subside the moment I entered Umberto's studio. It was due to a strange factor: the overwhelming smell of artist's paint in the studio immediately made it clear in my brain that I had entered a place of work and nothing more.

The furniture, or rather the lack of it, increased the feeling. In the centre of the large room was a six-foot-square platform with a chair on it. The platform was of light wood and could easily be moved to make the best use of the light. There was a large north skylight. So you could easily arrange a pose in the proper place. It was very practical. There was a rather shabby sofa at the far end—clean but old—to be used mainly by the model to rest when she became tired. Near that were a couple of equally shabby armchairs and another table.

There was no carpet—just wooden floor covered with blobs and splashes of paint. Against one wall were stacked paintings, some unfinished, standing in their dozens. Mostly unframed, others half-completed, waiting for inspiration. Against the opposite wall were scores, no hundreds, of gouaches and watercolours, painted on paper of standard size, many depicting dramatic street scenes at dusk or dawn, witness to Umberto's favourite hours for painting. Some were very good. At the back of the room was an old-fashioned china stove for the winter cold. A large mirror on the wall above it caught reflections of the lamps hanging from the ceiling.

Umberto had left his big easel near the model's wooden square, and I would use it. I had my own painting materials, my overalls—after all, I was learning how to paint in his studio unless I was painting in the street—and Umberto had also left our portable easels, each with its own three-legged folding stool and its canvas seat. I had bought myself a liberal stock of thin charcoal sticks for preliminary sketches on canvas. All the paraphernalia was part of the art of learning and thus encouraged me to regard the new venture as just another painting to be done.

The rest of the furniture increased the feeling. In what was little more than a partitioned cupboard hidden behind a large four-sectioned screen which Umberto had made and painted, there was a tiny kitchen, not big enough for real cooking, but with a sink and a plug for making coffee, of a sort. Behind the 'kitchenette' a spiral staircase led up to Umberto's untidy bedroom and a bathroom.

I went upstairs to examine it—and immediately the sight of the bed made me forget the smell of paint below! I beat a hasty retreat and waited for Fiamma to arrive. She had promised to arrive at eleven o'clock.

Looking around the room, I suddenly had an exciting idea. In a split second the shabbiness of Umberto's studio ignited a spark. I would not just paint a nude reclining on a chair against a plain contrived background. I would go further. I would paint the entire studio, filled with its rubbishy junk, with Fiamma unclothed, sitting in the middle. How much more exciting to paint an entire scene, dominated by Fiamma, rather than just an 'exercise' in trying to deal with only the human body. I would have the chance to experiment, to paint the background with the same sort of vigour that I had seen in paintings by the post-Impressionists.

'It suits my style,' I muttered to myself, only to laugh at my own temerity. *My* style! I had *no* style. Not yet!

Something else teased my reason, a casual remark once offered by Umberto. 'Don't be afraid to copy other paintings—but only copy the best,' he had said, pointing out that Monet had spent hours copying the wonderful *Olympia* by Manet; to improve his painting, yes, though eventually one painter's work would be worth as much as the other.

I would depict the room and, near the centre, my blue nude. Some long-ago advice by Gauguin flashed through my mind. In effect it was, 'You must liberate painting from the shackles of probability. And never worry if you want to paint a yellow tree—paint it yellow.' I would do just that—in every detail, in wild colours. I would paint a masterpiece of my own interpretation of Umberto's studio—and Fiamma. Whatever Berenson might think.

*   *   *

The clock in the old tower opposite the Hotel Lungarno had hardly finished discreetly chiming the hour when the front door bell rang and I shouted 'Hullo'. A disembodied voice from four

67

storeys below cried, 'It's me.'

I pressed the button to release the outside door of the flats, and shouted, 'The lift's at the end of the corridor. Fourth floor.'

'I remember.' A moment or so later I heard the sinister rumbling of the lift, which never sounded strong enough to groan protestingly up four flights on its perilous journey. But a few moments later I opened the front door of the studio and a ravishing, happy-looking Fiamma, her loose hair like a halo of gold dust, pulled back the trellis door of the lift and breathlessly cried, 'Hope I'm not late? I ran all the way along the Borgo San Jacopo.'

'Dead on time, come in,' I smiled. She really *was* stunning. 'You shouldn't have rushed,' I added laughingly, 'you remember what Berenson told us. Never rush a portrait. So you don't have to rush and be out of breath tomorrow.'

'I'll be on time again tomorrow,' she promised. 'I like being punctual and not out of breath. Especially when we've got a job to do!'

She was wearing a silky sort of dress, white with a small red pattern, and a red cardigan slung over her shoulder. She looked for a place to put it.

'Sorry,' I said. 'Here. I'll take it.' I hung it on one arm of an ancient-looking hat-and-coat stand with a top like a curling wooden flower and a circle around the middle of the tall 'stem' for sticks and umbrellas. I was so excited about my new plans, that instinctively I thought, what a wonderful oddity the old-fashioned stand will look in my painting.

'It's all a bit primitive,' I apologised. 'The bathroom's up those circular stairs behind the screen. You can just see the top half.' I pointed

68

them out. 'But would you like a coffee first? I'd love one. Didn't have any breakfast today.'

'All right, I'll make it.'

'Behind the screen.'

There was a mischievous look of complicity in her eyes, a hint of hiding-places and secret assignations, as if she were anticipating some pleasurable experience. Or was I deceiving myself?

★   ★   ★

We sipped our coffee, sitting on the sofa. She put her cup on an occasional tea table next to it, and wondering when to begin, we looked at each other in an embarrassed way for less than a minute—then simultaneously burst into laughter.

'I'm sorry,' I spluttered, swallowing hot coffee. 'It's all too silly.'

'It is,' I agreed. 'I spent months at the Slade looking at girls with no clothes on—and yet now—'

'Perhaps you should get some of your artist friends to join you and turn it into an art class.'

'Don't joke, Fiamma,' I begged her. 'You know how I feel about you'—ending lamely—'it's nothing to do with painting a nude model. I know that. But if you—er—want to keep some of your clothes on, well, I'll have to make some preliminary sketches, with you just sitting naturally on a chair. You don't have to—well—take all your clothes off yet. I want to do preliminary sketches of your face, arms, legs and so forth. Work which I will use later when I've perfected the sketches.' I did not know quite what to say next. 'I'll do these on a large sketch pad, then go on to charcoal when I start on the big figure.'

'Look,' she laughed and finally said, 'I haven't

69

the faintest idea what you're really talking about. But if you want to make preliminary sketches of, say, a thigh, or my shoulders, you can't do it with my clothes on. I'm sure you're right, but I'll sit on this chair if that's what you want. And ready for anything!'

Almost with one movement, and before I could say or do anything, she seemed to slide out of her dress, though still keeping on her panties, which she had not worn the time before. Her breasts were bare, perfect, not too large, the nipples, I noticed, pert and upturned with no brown circles around them, only pink.

'This right?' She sat down.

'Perfect. I've got the big canvas over there.' I pointed it out. 'I've already done the ground. I've washed it down with white starch to isolate the canvas from the paint. It prevents the paint being absorbed into the canvas and prevents cracking if the canvas has to be rolled.'

'But that isn't white.' She was forgetting she had no clothes on, and becoming more interested in the technicalities. 'It's more bluish.'

'I've already put on a thin coat of paint, a tint of the blue I plan to use in the painting. We call this the primer. It's to give even more help against absorption. It is all ready, but first we'll do some of the studies for different parts of the body.'

Laughing, I added, 'I might even show some of the studies to BB or your mother—not today but when I go there. In the meantime'—picking up a large sketch pad—'I think I *will* start by also doing some full-length studies as well—only preliminary sketches to be thrown away later—with you just sitting naturally on the chair.' I did not know quite

70

what I was saying, I jumbled up the words, partly to make her feel more at ease by talking so-called technicalities.

It was quite astonishing how that first laugh had lit the spark of effort on my part, had brushed away the stupid shibboleths, so that I caught myself thinking as I sketched, 'There's nothing like hard work to take your mind off sex!'

It was not hard work. Later, after she had gone, I would draft out the picture of the entire room, but my first task was to sketch the outline for a full-length sitting portrait, and I had to accentuate the curves in exactly the right places to give the sensuous effect I wanted. Yet at the same time I had to make sure that I took heed of the muscle structure I had painted so painfully so many times at the Slade, if I wanted the overall picture to be good enough to show to friends. Plus, I had to create my own illusion of her beauty and my desire while still guarding the underlying structural truth behind her body.

In the intense struggle to capture some of the flowing lines and subtle curves I became so engrossed in my work that I hardly noticed the model. I was totally preoccupied with the difficulties I was trying to surmount.

Finally, timidly, Fiamma pleaded, 'Can I just have a rest? I'm getting stiff.'

'Oh, I'm sorry.' In a split second the concentration vanished, to be replaced by the image of a desirable young naked girl. 'Here, put this on.' I handed her a towelling bath robe. Normally girls rested after each half an hour, but because I had let Fiamma choose her own natural pose she had not felt any strain.

71

'I didn't realise ...' I started. 'We've been hard at it for over an hour. I'd no idea.'

'Can I look?'

'Not yet, please. It's all so rough. Just relax. Let's stop for this morning. Let's go and have something to eat. I'm starving.' It was easier to talk to her when she had fastened the belt of her robe. 'Shall we go to Celestino's just round the corner?'

'Wonderful. I love the place.' It was famous for its fresh peas, hand-picked in front of you and cooked in virgin oil and sugar.

'You can dress behind that screen,' I suggested as I took off my painting overalls and washed my hands in the kitchenette. I had not used any paint, but there was the dirt of the place itself, and of the charcoal.

*　　*　　*

We ate at the corner table at Celestino's—hot peas to start with in a way never cooked better anywhere in the world—then skipped the main course and finished up with a large plate of fresh raspberries.

'No uvaspina for you today?' she teased.

'Not today. I'm sharing your tastes,' I laughed back. 'Seriously though, Fiamma, it's early days but I'm delighted with my ideas and how well we're getting on. It's not difficult—you're so beautiful.'

'You shouldn't say that.'

'I do. You are. I think you're the most exciting girl in the world.'

'But you still only see me through a painter's eyes?' Was she being ironic?'

'Only when I'm painting. Now, here in this restaurant, you're just—' I hesitated—'a one

72

hundred per cent desirable female.'

'Do we work after lunch—the painter, I mean.' She was still teasing, maybe as a kind of defence.

I shook my head. 'Tomorrow morning at ten. But you go home after lunch. I'll stay behind and try and tidy up some of the loose elbow joints I've been working on. Little bits that need improving.' I laughed. 'Not the face. The limbs, legs, arms, shoulders. I can rub off the rough corners better when I'm on my own. Then tomorrow...'

'I'll be on time,' she promised, and I kissed her gently when she said goodbye at the door of the restaurant. And she kissed me back.

★   ★   ★

For five days I drew or painted, and she posed, in peace—or nearly in peace. No more than the occasional faint tremors of anticipation through close contact rippled inside me, but I tried rigidly to hold myself in physical check. What I did not realise at first was that I was not the only one to feel frustration. She too, I slowly realised, was starting to feel as I did.

She began to fidget more. She demanded more rest periods as I started using the palette knife. Lunch time started earlier and earlier as we started to fight within ourselves, but never with words.

Men of my age too often forget that in those dim late days of the 1930s, fighting repressed desires was not a predominantly male preserve. Women may not have shown it so openly—they could not show it in the most obvious way a man can—but they were (and still are) as desirous of sex as much if not more than most men.

And, finally, it was Fiamma who cracked first. We had finished our first week of work. I had now sketched and started painting the whole scene. I had often worked far into the nights on the 'household' section of the picture, which was beginning to glow with excitement. I had started with my version of the floor—a dirty blue, streaked with the brown lines of the floorboards—using a pointed palette knife. I painted the *entire* floor. I would overpaint the furniture later. I had already painted the rough outline of Fiamma's body.

On Saturday and Sunday we swam in the Indian pool with the others, and were invited for Sunday lunch, having fun, plenty of drink, and a 'summer' lunch including a seafood salad, followed by a wonderful 'sandwich' of layer upon layer of Parma ham and fresh, squashed figs.

On the Monday morning, back in the studio, it happened.

*   *   *

Suddenly, without warning, when I thought we had conquered the first stirrings of sexual desire, and I had lost myself in my work, she burst into tears. I was so immersed in my attempt subtly to change the white outline of her body into flesh tones tinged with a blue outline, that I hardly noticed the figure posing on the small platform.

I was intrigued, not only by the use of other colours on a big room, but by the echoes of colours near her body, which gave a warm reflection on to the white. Of course it was not quite as Umberto had suggested, for our 'inner eyes' saw things differently, but he had taught me a great deal about

74

the influence of using one strong colour near another. To put it simply, I had learned that if you painted, say, a thick white square on a blue background, it would give the white a different shade.

Fascinating, I was thinking. Then I suddenly realised that Fiamma was grabbing her towelling gown.

'Darling!' I had never used the word before. 'Fiamma, darling, don't cry,' I begged her, rushing over to the chaise-longue on which she had sunk, sobbing. 'What's the matter? Have I done something wrong?'

She shook her head and through the tears managed to say miserably, 'No, it's my fault. I'm sorry. I'll go on in a few minutes.'

'No, no!' With a turpentine-soaked rag I managed to scrape the smudges of paint from my hands, took off my overalls—I never wore a smock, just an old paint-daubed jacket and trousers—and sat beside her.

Instinctively, it seemed, she dropped her head against my chest, and the soft strands of her hair, so thick, so fragrant, propinquity making it smell stronger even than the smell of paint, as she lay there, the crying stopped, not even sniffles, she just slumped there at peace.

Her towel robe had no buttons of course, just a belt and she had put it over her body, but she had not fastened the belt. One breast—which I had seen so often when working—had slipped out and, still wordless, she cuddled towards me and I gave her our first kiss of comfort. As I did so, I caught out of the corner of my eye the beautiful breast and below where, because of movement, part of the robe lower

75

down which had fallen open, leaving the partial view—even more exciting than seeing all—the flat tummy, half of the thick patch of the hair in her groin, then one slim thigh and down the calf of the leg, even down to the ankle.

We were locked in an innocent kiss, lips hardly open, and I could not have choked out even one word of sympathy or love at that moment.

I wanted her so badly—yet I had no wish to 'make' her in the vulgar way some men love, chalking up another sexual victory; for strangely, there was nothing *really* sexual about this moment. I remember wondering, what had taken its place? I wanted her of course, now, in the nearest thing to a bed. Of course I did. I would not have been human otherwise. But I did not want any impersonal victory. And above all, I did not want to hurt her.

Could it be love that I felt—the absence of guilt where a feeling of guilt should have been present? A feeling of 'you shouldn't' when all I felt was 'you must!' I know we all describe 'love' in a lover's sort of way, even sign letters 'with love' when all we really mean is 'yours sincerely' at most.

But all I could realise was that this *was* love. How ridiculous! At the age of twenty-one, immature except for a few fumbling caresses followed by spurts of excited manhood, a feeling born of curiosity rather than love.

And yet now, to a girl barely eighteen, without any forethought, no demands, no need of acceptance on her part as she clung to me, still kissing, I found myself feverishly kicking off my loafer shoes, struggling to tear off the bottom of one trouser leg, kicking it off—to hell with the other!—no waiting to take off the second leg.

Then, feeling the delicious sense of freedom as leg touched leg, the special kind of freedom as something so long imprisoned in the hate of clothes, sprang into real life, she knew it too and, still wordless, twisted on her side. She put her hand down, held me there, gasped with the delight of discovery and then she spoke, in a voice swimming with love and desire, 'How beautiful.'

I moved slightly, giving her room, feeling the beat of her heart, no, much more than a beat, a pounding. She turned on her back and I moved on top of her, stroking her, feeling the heat, the wetness, while she gently guided me whispering, 'Please, I'm ready. You can tell, can't you?'

I stroked her thighs. Yes, I could.

'Now,' I whispered as I felt her tremble with anticipation. 'Now. The first moment of our true love.'

CHAPTER FIVE

She lay in my arms for a long time, speechless but not sleeping—that I knew because occasionally she touched me with a kind of gentle stroke, on the face, on the chest, or she would tighten the grip of her fingers as we enfolded each other.

How long we lay there, uncomfortable on the small sofa, I do not know. Finally, it was something as mundane as cramps that made me whisper, as my muscles knotted with pain, 'Darling, I *must* move.'

'Oh! Don't,' she begged. 'I'm so happy. Don't move, just love me, Ham.'

'I do love you.' I edged over, almost falling to the

77

ground, and then stood up, pulling on the missing leg of my trousers. Only then did I balance on the side of the sofa, and rub the hurting calf of my leg. Suddenly, almost shyly, she strugged into the sleeve of her towelling robe, then firmly tied the belt.

As I looked at her, wonderingly, she turned to face me, and holding my cheeks in her hands, kissed me tenderly on the lips, not inside but just on them, as though sealing something, a promise of eternal love perhaps, if there is such a thing.

Then she looked at me and, holding one of my hands, asked simply, 'Why? Why did we? It was so beautiful.'

'It was like being transported to heaven,' I said.

'Or hell? We sinned.'

'Love isn't sin, Fiamma. We made love, but we didn't do anything really, good or sinful. It was done for us. I didn't set out to try and persuade you. And you didn't—what's the phrase?—set out to get me. In the way that Roz might. It *happened*. Did I—did I make you—well happy?'

'You know you did.' Shyly she added, 'I didn't know it would be like that. I didn't know anything except that I couldn't wait any longer—even before you came to the sofa. But I could *never* let you if I hadn't known that we love each other. You *do* love me, don't you?'

'Of course. With all my heart. I fell in love with you at the Indian pool. The first time.'

'So did I. From the beginning.'

'You didn't prefer Steve,' I teased her. 'Or Kurt?'

'Never. It was only you. As though I'd been waiting all my life to meet you. A very strange feeling. It sent shivers down my spine.' She spoke quite gravely. 'But Ham, what now?' Her anxiety was as innocent as a child's.

'Now?' Slightly startled, it passed through my mind like a flash that perhaps she expected me to start making love again—and I would have been happy after the half hour of what Steve always referred to as 'recharging my batteries'. But I realised immediately that she was referring to something deeper.

'My darling girl.' I took both her hands in mine and looked at her full in the face. 'We've started. There's no turning back. We go on just as we started,' I said.

'And do this again?'

I could not help laughing, for she asked the question so innocently, and I realised that it must have been her Catholic education that had made her frightened at the prospect of repeating such a moment of forbidden bliss.

'Of course!' I cried. 'It was heaven, it was wonderful! Of course we're going to repeat it, over and over again, for all our lives.' Then, trying to explain, with all the wisdom of a man of twenty-one talking to a girl of eighteen, I said, 'Listen, Fiamma. It's done. You may say we shouldn't have. But if we've made love once, we can do it again. Nothing really changes the sin once we've committed it. Now, it's repetition of the same act—and remember, we're one person now. So that when we make love, it's *our* secret. We never tell anyone.'

Almost helplessly, but still knowing the facts of life, she asked, 'And us together, when we're, well, a bit older. Shall we just remember?'

Again I looked at her then I took her hands in

79

mine again, squeezed her, kissed her, and then a moment later I held her out in front of me, undid the belt of her robe so that the front fell open, and looked at her and said a little unsteadily, 'When you're an old lady and I'm a famous painter and our four children are grown up, think back to this day when we're sitting by the fire in London.'

'You mean?'

'Of course,' I said recklessly. 'Anything can happen, I know, but I want to marry you. Do you think I'm the sort of man who goes around seducing women while pretending to be a painter?'

'Oh darling! Mr and Mrs Johns.' She laughed outright. 'Doesn't it sound wonderful.'

'Eventually Sir Hamilton and Lady Johns. But not yet,' I added hastily. 'I have to work first. I have to start to make my reputation. But as for now—let's say we're secretly engaged. And as for work—well, now I have a divine urge to paint—you. I've always been told one thing about life—that as a creator, a painter, an author, a musician, you do better if you've just made love—because love-making gives you an urge to work. Actually, it's true. Doing what we just did releases something—something that before was bottled up.'

'Till the urge comes again? Like—now?'

I nodded. I could talk no more. I had probably talked a lot of nonsense, but I had wanted to try and show her the beauty of love-making, I wanted to try and wash away any thoughts of sin, and dwell on the beauty of what had happened, the difference between real love as against the sordid hole-in-the-corner kind of sex for the sake of sex.

80

For the whole of the following week, with Umberto still in Siena, we gloried in splendid isolation and love. I painted. She sat. We stopped to make love. Then, reborn each time—as far as my painting was concerned—I started again with renewed vigour on 'The Blue Nude', a title which, in my imagination, was slowly acquiring capital letters.

I had started to fill in the savage colours of the studio—the old-fashioned circular heater with its pipe through the ceiling, all in blue; the ancient hatstand in dark green, the electric lamps spluttering light on the ceiling. The sofa, tables, all were vaguely blue, though I had painted the wooden platform a dirty brown, with the chair on it in yellow, and the white and blue figure of Fiamma draped on it—in what to me looked like a sensuous and yet comfortable pose.

At the beginning I had taken sketches home at night to work on—to the ribald laughter of Kurt and Steve—but that phase had passed now. I was working in deadly earnest, spurred on by the love-making as it increased the intensity of my effort.

I painted the figure at first in off-white, edging the outline in deep blue so that, except to me, I could hardly see where the blue background ended as it fused from one colour to another. *I* could see it of course. But then, for me, I could see the picture all the time—even before I painted it. I knew what I wanted to do. *Not* the figure based on Umberto's suggestion; but then that was before I included the background of the entire room. Fiamma's face would never consist, as Umberto had suggested, of flat planes, 'a kind of architecture' he had thought. Nor would it become merely what BB warned me against—'a chocolate box painting'.

There was nothing chocolate-boxy in portraits by men as different as Toulouse-Lautrec or Van Gogh; they were living people, but stamped with the authority of the artists who not only knew how to handle paint, but how to penetrate into the soul of the sitter, so that no two great painters could produce similar portraits, even though they were painting the same model, yet you could recognise something in each one.

I wanted to find the inner love that had changed the face of Fiamma in the short time since I had first met her. But that I could not deliberately paint; it had to come from within, applied by a palette and brushes, used as though by magic with hands that did only what the brain dictated.

We no longer stopped work for a big lunch. We ate a couple of sandwiches or a baguette and half a bottle of wine followed by what Fiamma, stroking my face whispered, 'our siesta'. And then I would start to paint again, using for the most part the palette knife, though from time to time I changed to brushes, striving for a strange mixture of truth and imagination—a likeness that would be recognisable, but one which might disturb, cause anger, perplexity or whatever.

But I had to do it.

*   *   *

We were approaching the end of the second week but I was not too worried, for though the painting was by no means finished, I had reached a turning-point and produced much more than the outline which was all I had expected to achieve in two weeks. Much of the detail—the furniture, for example—had been almost finished and the nude in the middle of the picture did astonishingly bear quite a resemblance to Fiamma. Altogether I was delighted (and not a little proud of myself) at the result. I would soon have to use the studio, often without Fiamma being there, touching up, re-painting, sometimes with Umberto in the studio. When he was away—and I knew of Umberto's arrangements—Fiamma would come to the studio.

One thing worried me. How should we be able to continue painting from day to day without arousing parental suspicions? The Principessa knew I only had the use of the studio for a fortnight.

Almost at the end of the fortnight Fiamma arrived one day crying out, 'Keep September free!'

'September? Why? It's only July,' I laughed, thinking as I looked at her and kissed her gently that one of the joys of loving Fiamma was that she seemed to spend all her days laughing.

'Well, I like September!' She smiled with a secret look.

'Come on—what are you up to?'

'Nothing—except that I'll be free all September.'

'Free? Stop talking in riddles,' crying as a mock warning, 'or I won't let you undress.'

'Sorry, Ham, my darling. Listen. I'm serious. We're closing the Villa Magari for the whole of September for repair work.'

'For a *month*! Repairs? The place looks perfect to me.'

'It *is* perfect. At least *we* all think so. But it's some silly new law that old Fatty—Mussolini—calls *la gran pulizia annuale.*'

'What the hell is that?'

'It's a plan of Il Duce's to increase employment. He's passed a law that all estates over a certain size have to be inspected annually by a civil servant who decides what repairs and renovations need to be carried out, and then—'

'But can they *force* you?' I asked.

'In Italy they can even force you to drink half a pint of castor oil if you don't do as they say.' There was no laughter in her voice. 'But the *pulizia*—I suppose it's a kind of tax on the rich, but Father has been able to fix the time of the repairs for September so that he and Mama can go touring in Britain.'

'And you?'

'We'll be more or less on our own, the three of us. Papa's brother has a small villa behind the pineta at Forte dei Marmi. It's a summer place, and Uncle Federico rarely uses it. The plan is for us girls to go there. Maybe you could come? After all, even artists need a holiday and a month in September—the mosquitoes'll have gone, the beach is huge, the sea will be beautiful, Lucca is next door—a heavenly place—and towards the end of the month we may even be able to find some thin wafers of tartuffi bianchi—white truffles served on melted Fontina cheese. Terribly expensive.'

'Sounds revolting.'

'It's heaven! You wait. And if you and Steve or Kurt just *happen* to be in the area, well—' she shrugged her shoulders with assumed innocence— 'there's not much we could do about it, is there? We won't even need to *tell* Mama or Papa.'

'But that's wonderful,' I cried. 'I know Kurt is

84

going to see his family in Germany sometime in September, though Steve hasn't told me his plans.' And then, with a sudden switch in tone I said with pretended severity, 'What about work? Isn't it time you got undressed?'

*   *   *

Although Europe was boiling up to the crisis that was to be falsely resolved by the Munich 'agreement', that last week was gloriously happy even more than we thought it might have been, partly because both of us were so excited about 'The Blue Nude'. I knew in my heart that it promised well. And though there was no way I could ever show the painting to BB or to the Caeseri family, I *was* looking forward to displaying it to Umberto. I knew his teaching, his advice, his almost cold-hearted appraisal instinctively, though, and knew it would please him.

'On the other hand,' I laughed to Fiamma, 'I wouldn't dare show it to BB—or to your mama.'

'Better not,' she laughed back. 'It's too precious. We don't want to risk having it thrown across the room.'

This was a reference to the fact that in an impulsive moment I had told Fiamma I wanted to give it to her—'when you find a place to hang it. But you mustn't sell it. We'll hang it in our bedroom if we get married.'

'If?'

'Sorry, when,' I corrected myself. 'But with all this talk of Fascism, mutterings of war and Hitler annexing countries for what he calls "Lebensraum", I wonder sometimes what's going

85

to happen to all of us.'

'Don't be so depressing,' she protested.

'Sorry. Let's stop work for today and stroll through the streets instead, and find a frame for the sketch I'm going to give to your mama.'

For though we could never show 'The Blue Nude' to BB or to the Caeseris, I had produced several study sketches and one that was a fairly good likeness, though very 'orthodox'. So we bought an old frame in the long corridor-cum-junk shop that had over the years grown in the long arcade in the Uffizi and it looked good enough to present to the Principessa, for which she thanked me, though not too enthusiastically.

I had the feeling that, although she patronised the arts in a fashion, she had once said to me that painting was not really a painting unless it had paint on it. As for BB, I gave him one to see and merely mentioned that I had thrown the other sketches of Fiamma away, they were so bad.

All BB commented was, 'Don't worry. Takes time to learn to paint.'

I could have left 'The Blue Nude' in Umberto's studio, I suppose, but we decided that it deserved a better fate.

'Take it home,' Fiamma insisted. 'After Umberto's seen it. Hang it on the wall in your house, then I can sneak in sometimes and admire it.'

So we did that. And when we took it up to the house, who should be there, drinking beer, sitting back in our small square of garden lawn, but Steve and Lella.

'Hy'a,' cried Steve. 'Wanna cold beer?'

I did not need a second glance to see where *they*

had been just before we arrived—the too jovial look, Steve's unbuttoned shirt, a slight fluster on the part of Lella who was breathing more heavily than usual. They had been upstairs in the bedroom and had, by sheer chance, come down into the garden just before we unexpectedly arrived. Still, it was none of our business. Indeed we were doing the same ourselves as often as we could. So all I said was, 'I'd love a beer. To celebrate finishing my portrait of Fiamma. Come and look at it. It's in the living-room.'

Lella jumped up, crying, 'I must see this!' She almost ran into the sitting-room, where the portrait was propped up on the piano. It was a big painting—after all, there was a lot in it—nearly three feet long and a good two feet in height—a blaze of colour, the blue highlighted by the faint yellow circles of overhead lamps shining out of their thin opalescent circular lamp globes. I do not know what prompted me to pretend it was dark, but when I lit the lights, so to speak, it had transformed the entire scene.

When we reached the piano and the painting blazed at the four of us, I could hear Lella's sharp intake of breath. She actually gasped. For a moment she said not a word, then she cried, 'It's superb! It's unbelievable! Oh Ham, you're a genius!'

'Holy mackerel.' Steve's voice was equally enthusiastic. 'How the hell did you get this likeness. You ain't painted Fiamma's face—you've painted her soul. Boy, Lella's right. You're a bloody genius. That should go right into the Museum of Modern Art.'

Delighted—even with a touch of embarrassment

—I laughed, 'Glad you like it. I only wish I dared to show it to Berenson.'

'You're not going to?' Steve looked up in amazement. 'For Chrissake, this guy Berenson has *got* to see it.'

'Nor to Mama, I suppose.' Lella looked at Fiamma, whose face was shining with happiness.

'I don't think so.' She shook her head. 'I'm heartbroken because I'm so proud of it. But it's so—don't you find it sexy?—she'd have a fit. And,' with a rueful laugh, 'she'd probably never let me see Ham again.'

'What I can't understand,' Steve was examining the portrait more closely, 'is that it looks just like Fiamma—it's a wonderful likeness—but there's no real detail on the face. It's *suggested*. How the hell did you do it?'

I hesitated, then explained. 'I made several sketches, showed one to BB, then when I got the right one—the one I gave to the Principessa—I began painting the actual canvas, and started to eliminate as many of the features I had sketched as I dared. I only hope I knew when to stop!'

'It's amazing—the suggestion in the face,' said Fiamma. 'I think it's really beautiful.' Turning to me, holding out to take my hand, 'Beautiful in Ham's wild, untamed way.'

'I can tell you, lady,' Steve's American twang cut in, 'that *that* shows right through. It just reeks of satisfied sex.'

'Heh!' I protested. 'Hold on!'

'Hold on,' Steve mimicked my voice. 'We know what you like to hold on to!'

'You're a fine one to talk,' I retorted, not angrily, but determined to let him know I knew what he and

88

Lella had just been up to. 'You two look as though you've just come out of bed.'

'Ham!' cried Fiamma, shocked.

'You're darned right,' agreed Steve cheerfully, 'and goddam wonderful it was too. Not true, honey?'

Lella gave her joyful smile. Then turning to Fiamma, who now seemed amused at the way the conversation was developing, asked, 'And you? We have no secrets—we girls, do we?'

Fiamma waited for what seemed a long time and finally said, with an assumed nonchalance, 'Anything to further the cause of art. Sorry. Shouldn't have said that.'

I said nothing. I knew that the sisters talked among themselves—about everything, about sex, of that I was sure.

'No need to apologise,' cried Steve. 'No use living unless you're determined to enjoy it. I am. Soon be time to open a bottle, and I don't mean beer. There's a couple of bottles of Spumanti in the fridge, let's celebrate!'

The front door closed with a bang. In came Kurt, back from a music tutorial. Standing against the wall from the top of the piano, the painting shone like a sparkling blue jewel.

'Gott im Himmel!' cried Kurt, almost as though spitting out an oath. 'It is a treasure, this piece of painting.' His voice was almost guttural. 'You are the best, my friend. One day—and soon, I hope—you will become a master. What does our Jewish friend think of it?'

'Jewish?' I suddenly felt angry.

'You know, Berenson.'

'He's not a Jew—not specially. He's a citizen of

89

the world, and one of the finest art historians in the world.'

'Sorry,' apologised Kurt with a slightly sardonic smile. 'In Germany we get into the habit of classifying—'

'That's the trouble with the Germans. You classify but you never think.'

'Not Germans,' interrupted Steve. 'Nazis.'

'Okay, okay!' Kurt held up his hands as though to defend himself, but for a moment I had a vision of him dressed in an aggressive black uniform, arm outstretched in a stiff Nazi salute. Instinctively I shivered and Steve noticed.

'Someone walk over your grave?' he asked.

'Something like that,' I tried a smile, 'but I managed to sidestep.'

CHAPTER SIX

We were in the Tea Room when the messenger arrived. We had been swimming and the girls had gone upstairs to change when I heard the roar of a powerful motor-cycle suddenly stop as the engine was turned off. Enrico spoke to someone and then opened the gates. I was standing, waiting for tea, so saw the man dismount, wave imperiously, then walk through the gates—an effete-looking man wearing a pale blue uniform and impenetrable dark glasses.

With a supercilious lift of his eyebrows, the Prince murmured, 'Looks like someone from the Foreign Office but you can never tell these days. Everyone seems to wear a uniform—from street

90

cleaners to cabinet ministers. It's difficult to tell if he's from the railway or Mussolini's praetorian guard.'

Fawkes waited for the messenger just outside the front door, and though I had never seen the English butler put out before, he was obviously ruffled now.

'This ... person'—the note of contempt was subtly subdued—'insisted on seeing you, though I assured him, sir, that I had been entrusted with many more important things than telegrams.'

The messenger almost minced into the room, superciliously flourishing a sealed envelope embossed with a crest. In a pseudo-pompous voice he said, 'My orders were to give this personally into your hand, sir. I am the personal courier of the Count Galeazzo Ciano.'

'Ah, Ciano, how interesting,' mused the Prince taking a stiletto from the top of a cabinet and slitting open the envelope.

'It is usual,' he said to me, as though explaining a point of etiquette, 'in noble circles, for even an ambassador, never mind an ordinary courier, to wait to be invited into the presence of a prince.' The man turned pink.

'However,' continued the Prince, 'let us in the circumstances dispense with protocol. Thank you, Fawkes, for your observation regarding telegrams.' He looked down at the crested letter he had drawn from the envelope. 'But this, I think, is rather more than a telegram.'

It was, in fact, a letter written in the most precise italic hand announcing that His Excellency Count Ciano, Secretary of State for Foreign Affairs in the Government of King Victor Emmanuel III, was, by the order of Il Duce, touring Tuscany as Il Duce's personal envoy and would expect to be received at the Villa Magari on 9 September. He would stay a week touring the area, and together with attendants ('guardia del corpo') would be delighted to avail himself of the Prince's hospitality.

The Prince looked up with a quizzical smile. 'A royal command, I take it?'

'Of course,' the man replied, almost offensively. Turning as if to go, he said, 'I have delivered the message, sir.'

'You have indeed. And if you will wait a few moments I will write a reply to it.'

'No reply is necessary.'

'I hardly think it courteous to leave His Excellency in the dark regarding my absence on the date he mentions.'

'Absence? *Absence*? But—'

The Prince crossed to a small bureau. 'I shall explain that in September I and my family are turned out of house and home for *la gran pulizia annuale* as laid down by Il Duce himself. I cannot change the time.' It was true, Mussolini's plans for increasing employment had been decided by the officials.

'I shall be enjoying the hospitality of friends in England during *la gran pulizia*.' He folded and sealed the note he had written, and handed it with a smile to the messenger.

'So as you see, a reply *is* necessary.'

I shuddered as I watched the man's mouth twist into a sort of snarl and could imagine the hatred in his eyes behind the black glasses.

*   *   *

We stayed on, as we were so often invited to, for a scratch supper in the open air, all of us together eating prosciutto with fresh figs, followed by large bowls of fresh fruit from the garden, washed down with the Prince's own home-grown white wine, light but fruity. Then we played the portable gramophone and danced on the Tea Room veranda so that the noise would not disturb our host and hostess.

The girls had a good selection of records—old sentimental favourites like 'Good Night Sweetheart', 'Ramona', and one that was a huge success in Italy, 'It's a Sin to Tell a Lie'.

Towards eleven o'clock the Prince popped his head through the door leading to the veranda and called, 'Goodnight, everyone. Your mother and I are going to bed.' He smiled cheerfully. This was the time-honoured way of saying he thought we had stayed long enough, and he added to me, 'I'm going to have lunch with your friend Mr Berenson tomorrow.'

'You are?' I must have looked surprised.

'I've met him before, you know,' he smiled. 'He just wants some advice about the appeal for a subscription to Fiesole's ancient *Teatro Romano*.'

'Oh good, sir. I'm working at I Tatti tomorrow, so I'll see you.'

'Hope so. Goodnight.'

As the three of us walked between the cypresses to the gate and across the road to our house, I was thinking, what a hell of a good chap the Prince is. No side, no snobbery, no suggestive remarks such as, 'Now don't get into mischief, you three'. The way we were deceiving him gave me occasional qualms of conscience.

93

'But he wasn't so tolerant with that bloody pimp of a messenger!' I said.

'He sure roasted that guy,' Steve chuckled.

As we crossed the road, Enrico locking the heavy iron gates behind us, Kurt almost spat out the words, 'That man deserved to be shot!'

'Gee,' protested Steve, 'the guy wasn't *that* impolite.'

'Not for being impolite,' explained Kurt, 'but because he hadn't learned the protocol—about waiting to be announced before being received by a prince.'

'Shooting's a bit rough for that.'

'In Germany we *learn* the right things to do, the correct way to behave when addressing our superiors. And in Germany, we don't forget, *ever*!'

*   *   *

I had not realised that the Prince had lunched several times with BB, probably because the dates had never coincided with the times I was 'on duty' at I Tatti when I always joined any lunch party, though (thinking back) the reason I did not know was because it was not my business. Yet (looking back) I should have realised the clues which the Prince occasionally dropped, such as the time when he said something like, 'What a joy with such an intellectual—especially one who is so charming'. And I also realised that the Principessa had now been to several of BB's concerts. It seemed as though they all got on well together. There was no question of Berenson 'title hunting'—he knew more famous people than did the crowned heads of Europe. No, but it might have been that Fiamma

94

was always invited with her mother to concerts, and that Berenson enjoyed her company. And probably he enjoyed lunching virtually alone *en famille* with the Prince who was witty and knowledgeable.

That was certainly the impression I received when I lunched at I Tatti the following day: just BB and the Prince, with me as helper, his wife Mary, and Nicky Mariano, his resident mistress, too old to be 'active' so that the two ladies lived happily in an amicable ménage à trois.

This always allowed BB to forget for a short while his overwhelming fascination for art. If a guest like the Prince did not appreciate the deeper aspects of art history to the same degree as BB, it gave him an intellectual holiday—though the Prince did enjoy artistic surroundings and often went to church at the fifteenth-century parish church, the Assunta, and afterwards would work up an appetite by strolling through the magnificent gardens of the Villa Gamberaia, not far away. 'Four hundred years old and still exquisite,' he said to Berenson.

'As beautiful as any painting,' BB agreed.

'It's strange how much more beautiful *things* are than human beings.' The Prince went on to describe the distasteful visit by the messenger from the Foreign Office. 'I can't stand that man Ciano, and I'm damned if I'll give him hospitality, even if I'm not present. He's a posturing playboy—it's a joke to make him Italy's Foreign Secretary just because he's Mussolini's son-in-law.' The papers had been full of the appointment and had made much of the fact that when Mussolini had proclaimed the annexation of Abyssinia the playboy Count had 'done his share'.

'By which was meant,' the Prince said, 'that he

95

had led a squadron of bombing planes which had indiscriminately dropped bombs and poison gas. And that hardly amounts to bravery,' he added with heavy cynicism, 'when you consider that the Abyssinians had no air force to resist with. And anyway, he was only appointed Foreign Minister in June this year.'

'Even so,' BB replied, his frail hands clasped over the ivory handle of his stick, 'I have heard of kindnesses shown by Ciano towards Jews who have found themselves at the mercy of *Fascisti.*'

His eyes misted with reminiscence of such acts—and reminiscence of another kind: 'I have long left Lithuania, my homeland. But I remember in my childhood that there were two factions of the Jewish people. My family's, which tended to think of scholarship as life's greatest secular target, in which they were encouraged by the Rabbis; and the Hasidim, who were all against scholasticism. They were all for fasting, dancing, and ecstatic prayer, and the others looked down their noses at this rejection of the Mosaic law. The Hasidim were banned, as if they had done something disgraceful. But eventually it was seen that there was good in them and that they were only following a different route to the same goal. They were assimilated, faults and all.'

'One cannot assimilate blatant evil,' the Prince said.

BB leaned forward, a wry smile in his eyes. 'Perhaps not. I will say only this: you know the requirement is that one of those dreadful garish pictures of Il Duce be displayed in every home. I have one, of course; but I have a grim sense of humour too, and it hangs between two of my

96

choicest Renaissance portraits. Thus I can comply with the law and please myself with the incongruity of it at the same time, though paradoxically it is also horror and torture to display such dross among the gold.'

The Prince laughed. 'So now you tell me that evil has been assimilated among the good. For myself, I have hung mine in the servants' lavatory and there it will remain.'

*   *   *

A few weeks later, Steve approached me one morning when I was at home and Kurt had left for his musical studies. I was working on some sketches laid out on the kitchen table, the back door open to a sunlit patch of lawn.

'Wanna coffee?' We had an electric machine that made a kind of amateur espresso.

'If you make it,' I grinned.

'Can do.' Steve busied himself with the water and the coffee, and when the tiny cups had been poured, turned to me and asked, 'You going to stay with the girls, come September?'

'You know about that?' I had thought that so far—it was already late August—Fiamma had made only a casual suggestion to me. I did not know about the others.

'Of course I do. You must come with us.'

'In theory I'd love to,' I said cautiously. 'Why do you ask?'

'Waal, I'll tell you,' Stevel drawled and sipped his strong bitter coffee. 'God, this tastes like shit. What wouldn't I give for a good Fifth Avenue delicatessen cup of coffee.'

'What stops you going there?'

'I like this goddam place—and besides the truth is, Ham, I was left one hell of a lot of dough by my father. My share of the family loot. But in New York I've got relatives on my tail every hour of the day, trying to persuade me to work. Hell, I don't want to work ever, for God's sake.'

Hell and God in one sentence seemed a bit much, but I let it pass.

'So you're rich!' I laughed.

'Not stinking rich,' he laughed back, 'just more than comfortable.'

'Makes me envious. I can't see you've got any problems. Yet you seem to have.'

'Not really, but this place Florence—it's what I've always imagined heaven to be like when I die. Sometimes I have the goddamndest dreams. Imagined I was dead the other night and ran into my father in the Via Tornabuoni. Palaces, paintings, the most beautiful countryside I've ever known. It's a land of eternal peace and beauty.'

'Quite lyrical, for an American.'

'Aw shit, stop kidding, Ham. I'm trying to explain something that's difficult to put into words.'

'You did it beautifully,' I soothed him. 'I feel just like you do.' I could not help adding slyly, 'Does the delicious Lella make you feel more in heaven?'

'You bet she does. Heaven on earth. Two things for the price of one.'

'I like that, nice way of putting it. But since you're obviously in love with the place, am I presumptuous in asking if you love her enough to want to marry her?'

Steve hesitated, put down the empty coffee cup and admitted, 'That's kinda different—love and

98

marriage. You know, my parents before they died seemed to spend all their lives fighting. Sometimes my pa couldn't bear my ma, but she never helped out. Came out with a sharp, "Don't be so goddam rude". And once I heard her threaten, "I don't know why I stay with that sonofabitch". Poor old pa just suffered in silence. Well, Ham, if that's how married life ends up, I ain't that sure it'll fit in with my notion of paradise, a heavenly Florence. Live for today is my motto. And fuck while you've got the balls to do it.'

'Sums up what seems like a comfortable existence!'

'How's about you, Ham?' asked Steve. 'Got sumpin' strong going for Fiamma? She sure is a honey.'

'Yes I have.' I smiled at his descriptions. 'Very strong. Enough to believe that *we'll* get married one day.'

'Wow!' Steve pumped my hand over and over again. 'Gonna name the date? Think the Principessa'll have you?'

'She'd better! She nearly married my father, apparently. As for naming the date.' I shook my head. 'I've got to make my way in the world as a painter.'

'That's okay.' Steve waved his hand airily. 'I'll employ you!'

'Like Rubens was the paid court painter of Philip IV of Spain and Lely to Charles II of England,' I smiled.

'Yeah. And talking of working for me'—he grinned, almost with a kind of affection, and added, half joking, half serious—'I'd like you to undertake a painting commission for me, payable of course.'

'Anything to oblige.' I thought at first he was joking.

'Sure you mean that?'

'Why? What?' I felt a trace of uneasiness.

'A nude. In your special style—the room filled with junk. I thought that background of yours was great.'

'Well, I'll try. I'd have to find a model.'

'I've got one. Lella.'

'What?'

'That's the girl.' He laughed at my look of blank astonishment.

'But I *couldn't*.'

'Why the heck not?'

'Well'—thinking hard—'Fiamma. She'd be horrified.'

'Why? What the hell's wrong with art?'

'I know, Steve. But I couldn't. She and I—'

'Chickening out, eh?'

'No. Don't talk balls. But two nudes in the same family,' I protested, 'and both good-lookers.'

'But in different colours,' said Steve slyly.

'I can't do it,' I muttered. 'I'd like to, but I'd never do anything that would upset Fiamma.'

'Ask her if she'd mind?' Steve looked at me.

'No, of course not. You only just made the suggestion.'

'Well, you ask her then.'

'She'd never agree. And I'm not sure I could stand the strain of looking for days at another member of the family in the nude.'

'Now it's balls to you, Ham,' retorted Steve. 'All you've got to do is to have it off with Fiamma just before Lella poses for you, and that'll keep you quiet before the morning session. If you paint her when we go to the seaside—we've got two beds so you pop into your room with Fiamma first. Come on, buddy. Be a man!'

I could not, though the challenge of painting Lella, who was beautiful but in a way different from Fiamma, was tempting. To a painter, the two girls had a natural family resemblance; but their beneath-the-skin *characters* were different. Lella, I was sure, could be ruthless if she wanted to be, while Fiamma had kept more of her childhood innocence. As for Roz, I felt that her challenging sexuality was little more than a mask for the 'secret self' she'd wanted to hide. But Fiamma was the love of *my* life—whereas the love in Lella's life lay in her single-minded pursuit of Steve. It had become all too obvious.

Indeed I wondered whether it was Lella who had persuaded Steve to ask for me to paint her—vying with Roz for kicks, more than for art. Maybe she too wanted to see if I could withstand her charms! I knew that the final decision would rest with Fiamma. But halfway through my discussion with Steve, who should walk in but Lella herself.

'Hullo both.' She blew a kiss at Steve. 'I'm not interrupting anything, I hope?' She spoke in the tone of voice that made it clear she knew perfectly well what we were talking about and *wanted* to interfere.

'Oh that!' she said after a few words with Steve. 'You've been talking about my nude. Come on, Ham, don't be so stuffy.'

'I don't think it's stuffy.' I tried to lighten the conversation. 'I think it's wrong of me to be—er—led into temptation when I'm such a close friend of Steve's.' With a laugh I added, 'I may not

101

be able to resist you.'

'Aw, let the poor guy relax,' said Steve. 'I'll find someone else. But, hell, it's a shame. I've got the dough—plenty of it, and I love your style. I was going to offer you five thousand bucks. That's about a thousand pounds in English money.'

A thousand pounds! I gulped. What I could do with that kind of money! I'd never earned a penny yet from painting, and here was a crazy rich American prepared to offer me a king's ransom just to paint his girlfriend in the nude. And I was a would-be professional, supposed to be unmoved by nudity. A thousand pounds! And yet I baulked at doing something I knew I could do well—just because it was Fiamma's sister and there might be consequences. Yet how could I turn down a sum which in the Italy of the 1930s would keep me for years?

'I'd love to,' I admitted. 'But I think I should ask Fiamma. I'm seeing her this afternoon. Can you wait for my answer until this evening, Steve?'

★   ★   ★

When Fiamma and I met for a walk along the banks of the Mensola, Fiamma, to my astonishment, blithely told me, 'Oh! I know *all* about the picture of Lella. Grab it! For the money Steve's offering.' But she did add, 'I know she's the eldest but in some ways she's the most innocent and is trying to get some of Roz's sophistication to rub off on her.' There spoke Fiamma's innocence!

'You must be crazy even to think I would have anything to do with it.'

'You haven't seen her stripped. She's got the

102

world's biggest patch over her pussy, and some man—she's never told me who it was, maybe it was herself—shaved her and cut it into the shape of a heart.'

I must admit I twitched in my trousers. 'Sounds interesting.' I tried to be casual. 'But I don't think I should.'

'Come on. Aren't you a *professional* painter?' she taunted me. 'The money's a fortune.'

I *had* been thinking a lot about that thousand pounds. 'Do you think Steve feels I'm hard up?' I asked Fiamma. 'And it's a sort of charity effort.'

As we sat down on the grassy bank with the sound of the Mensola tinkling below she said cheerfully, 'Charity begins at home. *Your* home. Of course you must take the commission.'

I was still hesitant—not because I was *really* afraid of watching Lella pose in the nude, but because some instinct was warning me that it might land me in trouble.

'But you *can't* afford to turn down an offer from a real patron. And that's what he is.'

'I'd like to think it over.'

'Well, I'll tell you what you do. Wait until we go to Forte dei Marmi in September. We'll be absolutely alone. If you agree then, the villa there will be the perfect place to paint Lella. And you'll have a whole month free.'

'That's fair,' I admitted.

CHAPTER SEVEN

Lella and Fiamma planned to leave for Forte dei Marmi on 1 September, after seeing the Prince and his wife on board the train at Florence for Milan, where they would catch the international express to London.

Roz, the third girl, had decided suddenly to accept an invitation from Kurt's parents to spend her holidays with them. I was not surprised at her change of plan, as in my own mind I had begun to call her 'the double-sided one', recalling Fiamma's saying she had a hidden side to her obviously sexy, fun-loving nature.

According to the photographs which Kurt showed us, the Von Schills lived in some style near Lübeck, north of Hamburg; but they also kept a house on the Danish island of Bornholm in the Baltic Sea, where they spent their summer holidays.

This was where Roz was going, following a very prim and formal invitation from Kurt's mother: 'Kurt has told me all about you, and you would be very welcome ...'—that sort of thing. Roz never hesitated.

'Anything for a change,' she cried.

'And the Danish food! It's even better than German,' Kurt cried.

'Don't tell Hitler!' teased Steve.

The holiday in Bornholm was the main reason, of course, but there was another: Kurt was really beginning to make his mark as a young musician and was hoping to win a German music scholarship to continue his studies in Florence. The chance had come his way after he showed a rare musical talent at his first public concert with the pupils of the Florence Academy of Music, of which Toscanini was the president until earlier that year he left for America to escape the Fascists.

The music critic of a Milan newspaper wrote that 'Herr von Schill has intellectual depth and a formidable technique. His solo was well chosen, for the F-minor Ballade, one of the greatest works of Chopin's maturity, poses a great problem to any pianist, let alone a young one. It has two tremendous climaxes divided by *pianissimo* falling chords, and the difficulty lies in making the second climax effectively greater than the first. No pianist has really solved what is, after all, approaching the insuperable. But this young player has got as near a resolution as any mature virtuoso I have heard. His may well become a name to conjure with.'

Kurt had sent a clipping to Lübeck and the authorities had replied with a form to be filled in, after which Kurt had agreed to play for his scholarship. Why not take Roz, he thought, and so it was arranged. But we could hardly discuss with the Principessa our own holiday plans, though I had lied cheerfully when she asked once if I would go to Yorkshire during the summer.

'Hope so,' I had replied, 'but it depends on whether my father will be at home.'

Unsuspecting, she apparently never gave the matter another thought; and in the last week of August Roz caught the train to Milan; thence, with Kurt in Germany and Denmark. Fiamma and Lella went by train to Pisa, and on to Forte dei Marmi by taxi. Three days later Steve and I packed our bags, my canvases and paints, and at Pisa the girls met us and took us on by bus to Forte dei Marmi.

It was a cheerful enough seaside town, with the word 'resort' stamped all over it—selling buckets and spades and beach balls, shoe shops with windows bulging with espadrilles in every colour of the rainbow, dress shops filled with the latest bathing costumes, each year more 'daring' than previous ones. On the right-hand side as we drove in, gaps between the line of shops opened up glimpses of a huge stretch of sand, with restaurants near the edge of the sea; and on the left-hand side of the road were pine trees among which nestled the villas.

'Come on, we get off at the next stop,' cried Lella, while Fiamma smiled inwardly, hugged me and whispered, 'For this month at least—two happily married couples!'

'Here we are.' Lella led the way up a slight incline along a sandy path strewn with pine cones, the fragrance of the trees and flowers lingering in the air. The path opened up on to a pretty flower-edged lawn and a small square house washed in pale pink. Very pretty, very unpretentious.

'Just somewhere to stay,' whispered Fiamma, 'but the sea's only a hundred yards away, through the woods and across the road. You can go to the beach in your costumes!'

'And the guests will only be occupying two of the rooms?' asked Steve cheerfully.

It was the first time I had realised that, as Fiamma had said, we would be 'married'. In our brief love affair all manner of exciting prospects had so far eluded me—waking up together, after a night's blissful sleep in each other's arms, sharing a bath, cooking, washing up . . . a *complete* love for a few weeks. Cooking breakfast together—it might only be croissants and coffee, but still it would be *our* breakfast. And lazy love-making—sometimes 'inspired' by reading each other some of the tales in the *Decameron*, of which there was a well-worn copy in our bedroom. How wonderful!

My second sensation was very different—and nothing to do with love. The dwelling was a quite ordinary house; pleasant but—what was the word I was looking for?—unadventurous. Like the functional sort of ski lodge the Swiss rent you. And there was no way I could see, in the practical kitchen, the neat bedrooms, the small living-room, of making a background as exciting as the bric-à-brac at Umberto's which gave such life to my 'Blue Nude'.

That was what Steve wanted—not a carbon copy of 'The Blue Nude', of course, but something with a background as bizarre—something I also badly wanted, irrespective of the figure: something so startling that it would make the viewer gasp in surprise. I had stumbled on this technique by accident because of Umberto's crazy studio. There was no way, though, that I could achieve a similar excitement by exaggerating the details of this holiday villa.

'It's going to be a problem,' I admitted as Steve and I lay on the long wide stretch of sand after we had settled in and taken half an hour to unpack and (as Steve whispered to me) 'christen the bed'.

'You see,' I tried to explain, hoping it did not sound self-important, 'I think I hit a small jackpot with Fiamma's portrait because the studio triggered off a crazy idea. But I just can't do it here. Trees? A rather ordinary villa like this house? Exaggeration?

I don't see how. I can't just paint the beach green and the sea red and the trees blue, can I? The trouble is—'

'But can't you *imagine* something?'

I shook my head miserably. 'I wish to God I could. But so far I just can't. I might elaborate, like I did before. But I had something to paint *there*—the studio, the hatstand, the ceramic stove. Okay. I accentuated the blue, but it was like putting an accent on a word that had already been written.'

The girls came rushing up to us, grabbing towels to rub themselves down.

'Lazy!' cried Fiamma. 'Lovely water—and you laze away...'

'The journey tired me out,' I said.

'The journey plus—' retorted Lella cheekily. 'Can't say I blame you. Takes more out of a man, I suppose.' Then, 'When do we start work on the painting?'

As I hesitated, searching for a valid excuse, Steve retorted, almost crossly, 'The genius doesn't like the background.'

'What's wrong with it, darling?' asked Fiamma.

Shrugging my shoulders I tried to explain. 'It doesn't—well, inspire me. Steve wants something dramatic like "The Blue Nude". There's nothing dramatic about sea and sand or the villa. Nobody's fault. We just picked the wrong place.'

'Can't you imagine it?'

I repeated what I had already told Steve. 'If you want, I'll paint you in the garden—a normal nude, I suppose you'd call it—that is, if you would like me to. But Steve wants something more exotic.'

'Yeah, I guess I see his point,' Steve admitted. 'It

108

ain't his fault that he's come here. The object of the exercise is pleasure, not painting. But that "Blue Nude"—he sighed—'it's a beaut! We'll think of something later. Meanwhile, we'll settle for a standard portrait. Otherwise it's just bed and breakfast from the local shops.'

'Before I strip to pose?' laughed Lella.

'Why?' Steve echoed the laugh. 'Give the natives a bit of fun.'

'*That's it*!' I almost screamed, so loudly that two or three groups of sunbathers turned to stare. Something had suddenly clicked in my mind, as if a screen had been spotlit. '*Of course*!' I yelled. 'I'm blind.'

'Gone off your rocker?' asked Steve.

'Darling—what is it?' Fiamma gave me an almost anxious look of concern.

'The painting! *There's* the background! In that tiny, ultra pretty-pretty street of shops stocking all the accessories needed for an innocent holiday for the wife and kids and there, right in the middle of the pavement—'

'A pavement?' asked Steve.

'Sidewalk to you. And there on the pavement is Lella in the nude, standing full frontal, maybe pointing out towards the pineta on the other side of the street. It'd be sensational!'

'You mean, pose in front of the shops?' Even Steve stood up in astonishment.

'Certainly not while I was outside being painted,' cried Lella. 'Even you wouldn't dare to paint me naked in the main street of Forte dei Marmi.'

'Don't interrupt!' I cried, forming a semi-circle with my hands spread out in front of me, to emphasise my plans, 'And this won't be blue. It'll

109

be golden! This is summer at the seaside—yellow paint splashed everywhere, a yellowy sky, even an echo of yellow in the sea. Emphasise the dullness, the *conventionality* of some of the shop fronts, but that's all. Names, appearances, nothing changed, only maybe exaggerated. And you, Lella—outlined in yellow, almost in a vivid gold, and in the centre against the shops, your golden body in stark contrast, and—'

'We know all about the middle bit,' interrupted Steve with an excited grin, 'at least I know that you've imagined it. But I can assure you it'll make one helluva startling contrast. But, Ham—will you dare? How the hell can you get away with it?'

'You wanted something exciting,' I said. 'Scared?'

'Hell, no. But a nude in the street...'

'Oh no, come off it. I'll do what I did with Fiamma—make detailed sketches—this time in the street. I'll sketch the street scene—the shops, and displays. In the villa, I'll sketch the nude figure of Lella, and then transfer the sketches to a large canvas and start painting.'

'So nobody'll see Lella in the nude?'

'Not unless they peep through the pine woods,' I said cheerfully.

'It's pure genius, Ham!' Steve had jumped to his feet by now, and said, 'It'll cause one hell of a stir if this secret ever gets out.'

'It's for your eyes only,' I warned him. 'And for mine—just for a short while, until the day I hold my first exhibition.'

'In Sydney, Australia.'

'Sydney? Why Sydney?'

110

'Farthest place away I can think of. Come on, Ham. Race you to the sea for a dip.'

*   *   *

The 'nude bit', as Steve described the times when Lella was sitting for me, did not, surprisingly, affect me at all. Her mane of hair was so thick, so heavy, I was prepared for a surprise and it was true that the very first time she slid off her panties, the sight of her huge thatch of pubic hair, cut into the shape of a heart, was enough to make me forget painting for a few moments. But as I was looking at it, Steve bustled in, kissed Lella on the lips with perhaps more casual familiarity than passion as he affectionately but gently slapped her bottom, and cried to me, 'Kinda cute hairdo, don't you think?'

Instinctively looking at her long, thick, shining hair cut in a straight line a third of the way down her back, I murmured, 'Beautiful, beautiful.'

'Not here, dope, *there*. The heart!'

'Oh, I see. Yes, perfect.' I fumbled for words.

'Here, dear.' Carrying a cup of coffee, Fiamma spoke in the soothing voice of a well-mannered woman, quite out of tune with her age of eighteen, as much as to say, 'There, there, dear. Don't let anything worry you.'

I almost laughed, everything was so happy-go-lucky. I had thought I might be embarrassed at this naked beauty—but numbers make for a kind of dampening of emotions. It even reminded me how once at Oxford I had, for a 'dare', attended a nudist dance. The prospect of walking naked into a room filled with pretty naked girls had terrified me. I might show my feelings! I could not disguise them like a woman could. But to

111

my surprise no visible signs shamed me. So many naked men and women made me act normally. It was like that now. We were all friends together with hardly a lecherous thought between us.

*   *   *

The painting posed no real problems either, largely because I did not feel any great sense of urgency so that I was much more relaxed. It went very well. To start with, I spent three or four days sketching the little shopping street, trying to put into shape the smells of the sea and salt, of the pines and the countryside. I know you cannot really paint a smell! But you have to try and evoke these things so that you can, for instance, smell a picture of bacon and eggs cooking when you paint them. The tiny unspoiled village and the villa life of Forte dei Marmi had a curious innocence as though it had just been discovered, and I wanted to catch that too. The best way, I thought, would be to copy it exactly. I did so accurately, setting up my easel on the opposite side of the street and, when I finished the rough drawing, I drew the outline of the block of shops, the trees, the people I had sketched, on another piece of paper, but only the outline.

On this outline I then spent two days roughly sketching my final nude studies of Lella against the sketches of the street background. I painted her as though I had stood on the opposite side of the street, where I *had* stood when sketching the shops. This allowed me to put Lella into perspective, making her the large nude in the foreground, with the shops in the background, with glimpses of sand and sea.

112

'It's going to be a bit tiring,' I warned Lella when I was sketching her. 'I can't just have you standing there doing nothing. But if you're waving, as though waving to Steve, it'll look very realistic, though I think you'll have to suffer. Holding up an arm can be very tiring.'

Once I had the figure right I began to transfer it to my outline of the street shops, then a complete outline in charcoal on canvas, of the nude itself, standing legs apart full frontal, arm waving and that huge dark blonde heart dominating the centre.

★   ★   ★

With the Munich 'agreement' having calmed down the European turmoil, we had been in the Forte dei Marmi for nearly four blissfully happy 'married' weeks, and the portrait was developing in an exciting way, all yellow hot summer, smelling sea and sun and sand, grapes and figs. The four of us had finished our pre-lunch swim of the broad, nearly deserted beach, the water cooling but the sun boiling—and, as the others crossed the road to make for the villa, I hung back, still in my swimming trunks, to get a packet of cigarettes and half a dozen bottles of Drago beer to put in the fridge.

'I'll just pop into Dino's.' I moved in the direction of the local general store where Dino handed over the beer and cigarettes with a 'Buon giorno, Signor Johns, ha finito il quadro?'

I had not yet completed the centrepiece—the nude—but he did not know what that was going to be like! 'Si, grazie,' I smiled.

The others had disappeared into the pine woods

shielding the villas when I caught sight of a curious figure, loping across the road then disappearing into the trees. He was ungainly, dishevelled, and not at all the sort of man who would normally grace the dully elegant and rather snobbish Forte dei Marmi. As he approached closer I thought he looked as though he needed a bath, a shave, a haircut. In short, he was a down-and-out tramp and, I have no idea why, but suddenly I had a thought of Flanagan and Allen singing *Underneath the Arches*.

He drew nearer and I felt a sudden spurt of consternation, almost apprehension.

'Johns!'

I spun round at the soft voice, the odd name, surname transposed with Christian, rarely heard in Italy.

'How the hell—'

'I must shelter in the woods before anyone sees me.'

He spoke with a gasp of despair. 'For Chrissake, don't you recognise me?'

I looked closer through the bearded stubble, and dark face and glint in the eyes. Curiosity superseding fear.

'Vanni!' I almost shouted aghast. 'I thought you were in the army.'

'I should be!' Vanni said bitterly as he ran towards the trees. 'But I seem to have lost my way—on purpose.'

It did not take much imagination to realise what had happened.

'On the run?'

He nodded. 'I jumped ship, reached Naples, made for this villa, but can't remember where the bloody place is.' He was breathless.

114

I pointed out the villa ahead.

'I haven't been there for years. It's all built up now—changed. God I need a drink.'

I burst through the door shouting, 'Vanni's here!'

'Who?'

With a less cordial, 'Hiya!' from Steve, I shouted a warning, 'Prepare for a shock, he's in a bit of a mess.'

Once through the kitchen door and next to the front entrance Lella gave a scream. Tears sprang into the eyes of the tenderer, the more demonstrative Fiamma. Steve, for a moment, just gaped, mouth dropping open. Then the four of us burst into simultaneous, uncontrolled demands, questions, until above the din and confusion, Vanni roared, 'A drink, for God's sake, a drink!'

Only when he had taken a mighty swig of grappa straight from the bottle did he start to relax, and then Fiamma begged him, 'Vanni darling, we want to help you—'

'I know,' he grunted, 'but I'm so bloody hungry—'

'Just tell us what happened while I start to boil some water for a plate of pasta.'

'All right.' He heaved a big sigh, as though even explaining was something of an effort, but that he felt it was his duty to tell us in return for a meal. At least that was what passed through my mind.

His story was simple. Vanni was disillusioned, a man whose enthusiasm for Fascism had been drained. He was also, as we guessed, on the run, pleading for help, no longer, it seemed, the enthusiast for what Mussolini had proclaimed as 'the glory of a Fascist Empire'. And he had fought hard and long.

'Yes,' Vanni continued as he lit a cigarillo and took another sip of grappa. 'It wasn't always the triumphant advance that the propagandists had put out, even then, when we were supposed to be chewing up Abyssinia. Those Abyssinians may have been without aeroplanes and had very few modern weapons, but they certainly weren't without courage. And when it came to spraying mustard gas from the air—which with no Air Force they had no means of resisting—our faith in Fascist supremacy began to rot. The action was hushed up or denied by the propaganda people,' he added, 'but soldiers on leave told their families that the streets of Addis Ababa were full of blind people. We of'—he paused and smiled cynically—'We of rather less than ardent sympathy with Il Duce were revolted.'

Vanni drummed his fingers on the table and turned his head with a startled movement as someone let loose a shot at some pigeon. It was the instinctive fear of a man being pursued.

He continued: 'I got sent to Spain when the Duce agreed with Hitler to supply men and arms to General Franco to fight the Republicans. And in Catalonia there were similar brutal attacks—not mustard gas, but merciless bombing of villages that had absolutely no defences. One of those finally sickened me. One day, there had been an attack—one of the few successful ones—by the villagers. They'd sprayed us with bullets from ancient Lewis guns. For a few moments our chaps fell like ninepins until we routed the defenders. I suppose I'd been shocked by the explosions of the shells so close to me. I was more or less in a daze. I wandered about among fallen bodies, some of them doubled up with pain, others lying grotesquely with

116

limbs distorted and blood sticking around ghastly wounds. Then I saw an even more sickening sight. Some of our own men were looting the bodies of their dead Italian comrades—watches, pens, money, anything they could find, even the wedding rings off their fingers. I couldn't believe it. And, dazed as I was, I simply walked away down the hill and kept walking, not believing that war could also mean this. And I never went back. I've been living rough and on my wits for weeks. So officially I am a deserter.'

He smiled his twisted smile. 'With a price on my head. With a court-martial to face and six shots to be fired into my body for cowardice in the face of the enemy if I am found guilty.'

'You'd better get out of here right away,' said the practical Lella, 'but first some pasta. The water's boiling, I'll put the spaghetti on.'

'Not a second more than six minutes,' shouted Vanni without thinking of the mess he was in.

But he never did eat that spaghetti. Almost at the moment Lella left the kitchen, a heavy boot landed one savage kick on the bottom panel of the flimsy front door. It cracked, then split open like matchwood, the door, or what was left of it, flew open, and in the space left, brutally outlined against the background of hot sun, stood the burly figures of two men, both carrying guns.

CHAPTER EIGHT

I recognised them immediately from their almost deliberately shoddy clothes. They were members of the Guardia Segreta, the Secret Police. Originally Mussolini's private guard they were now the equivalent of the dreaded German Gestapo. Their job was not to arrest—the uniformed polizia did that. The Guardia Segreta checked and traced criminals or Jews whom they would persecute, bully—and break their spirit. They were notorious throughout Italy for their almost fanatical love of brutality.

Their idea of enjoying themselves was to track down some helpless victim and then, before anything else, kick him hard in the testicles. Which is precisely what they did now.

With lightning speed, and as Fiamma shrieked, the smaller of the two men moved to her left along the wall against which we stood, brandishing a pistol, firing one round, smashing a window, and leering, 'See what happens if you misbehave?'

As he threatened, the big man seemed to leap across the small room, charging into Vanni before he could take any evasive action and, with Lella in the kitchen, we stood stock still for just the split second as the big man headed to slap Vanni hard twice across the face, then, in one movement it seemed, grab his jacket, pull the shoulders round the back, effectively trapping his arms and—all again in one horrifying movement—jerked his knee with all the strength of a big brute into Vanni's crotch. Vanni groaned and slumped. As he did so, the man—so obviously adept at just this trick—hit his jaw with an uppercut with the might and precision of a professional boxer.

Fiamma gave a cry and moved towards him.

'Get back!' roared the smaller guard.

The big man saw me move and also shouted, 'Get

118

back. Who are you?'

But it was Lella who acted first. Spotting the man with the pistol through the half-open door, pretending not to see him, but having heard the smash on the door, she came screaming through from the kitchen as though enquiring what was happening, but carrying the large saucepan of boiling water and spaghetti sticking out. She managed to spill it all in front of the legs of the two men. She shouted a frantic 'Sorry!' and, as she did so, they managed to fall into the lake of hot water and greasy spaghetti in front of them. They slumped, but then both slipped on to the floor. Already Vanni was out like a light. A couple of shots pierced the silence.

Steve seemed so terrified that, accidentally on purpose, he lurched against the table so that it blocked the back door.

'Shut up, everyone,' shouted the big man. 'Silence! Or you'll be sorry. Now'—after silence—'who the hell are you?' He pointed his pistol at me. 'Come on, quick!'

'I'm English.'

'Papers. You English, you will be next!' As he flicked through the passport, which I always carried, he jeered, 'Remember! Nice, Corsica, Tunis—and Britain next on the list.' [*I was to hear this phrase more than once. It apparently referred to fanatical feelings of resentment harboured by Fascist Italy for past losses of territory. Nice had been ceded to France as the price of French help in the nineteenth-century Italian war of liberation; anti-Italian sentiment in Corsica had aroused the fury of the Fascists who attempted to start a movement for the restoration of the island to Italy; and the special*

119

privileges accorded to the Italians in Tunisia had been revoked by France and caused more smouldering resentment among Fascists.]

Turning to Steve, he barked, 'And who are you?'

'American.'

'Oh, you won't be next. The Americans never fight'—he added sneeringly—'until they know the other side is nearly beaten and they're in no danger of losing.'

'What about Caporetto?' screamed a furious Steve. The Fascist thug made to hit him but thought better of it, warning him threateningly to hold his tongue. The two men now wanted to know everything about the two girls, jeering to the boys from time to time. 'I suppose the three of you are all having it off with whichever happens to be handy! Degenerate shits, no wonder Italy won so easily in Abyssinia. Makes France just a target-practice joke.'

As they made to go, the big man said, 'This area will be under surveillance until further notice and don't worry about your brother El Capitan. The polizia will pick him up soon—and he won't give us the slip.'

'Now listen here,' shouted the big man again. 'No bloody nonsense, understand? Especially from a Limey and a Yank. And you two glorified tarts—leave that bloody man alone or you'll be in trouble.'

'I'm going to wash his wounds,' shouted Lella defiantly. 'Are you going to stop me?'

'I won't be here,' the big man chuckled. 'Our job is to find people, and if they deserve it, beat 'em up a little. So be warned. Don't do anything. Just wait for the police. You may think it strange that we

120

don't take this villa shit away with us. We followed him on foot. And even if he recovers and bolts, we'll find him again. This is the speciality of the Guardia Segreta. We always find our men. And when we've taught them a thing or two, we hand them over to the polizia. Or the army police. So'—with an evil smile and an exaggerated gesture of courtesy—'I will be bidding you au revoir, ladies and gentleman.' He almost bowed, before adding, 'Or should I say whores and foreign shits?' With that he banged the door behind him.

'Calm down.' I put an arm round Fiamma, who was crying, while Steve was trying to help Vanni, who was now sitting up and trying to get to his feet.

'Oh, what'll happen to poor Vanni? They'll kill him,' cried Lella.

'Knowing him,' Steve shouted over his shoulder to her, 'he'll manage somehow. Anyone who can travel all the way from Spain to Naples without being caught must have learned a few tricks. He'll be okay.'

'Oh, but the poor boy—'

'He's not a boy,' retorted Steve, 'he's a grown man who should have known better than to bolt like he did. And he's tough enough.'

Astonishingly, it was not long before Vanni *was* standing up and making sense.

'That kick in the balls,' he began. 'And my jaw.' He felt it tenderly. He sipped a grappa, almost choking as the fiery liquid slipped past a sore point. 'Can I take the rest of the bottle with me?' he asked. 'And if you've got a loaf of bread or some pâté or something portable?'

'You can't go,' I cried. 'You'll never make it before the police get you.'

'Care to bet on it?' he croaked.

'No, I wouldn't,' said a more cheerful Steve. 'You'll make it. Here's to you, Vanni!'

A funny thing, I thought, all of us raising our glasses to toast an army deserter. And an officer. No, I thought again, not so funny really. He was not a bad fellow, Vanni, and I could only feel sorry for him.

'Where are you going to make for?' I asked.

'Ah! That'd be telling.' Vanni gave another twisted grin. 'Once I've got a square meal inside me,' he patted the bottle in one pocket and the bread, 'I'll be as right as rain. But time is of the essence.'

Blowing a kiss, and without another word, he hobbled out before any of us could stop him.

* * *

And that, I thought and hoped as we started to clear up and board up the broken door, was the end of our problems in Forte dei Marmi. Now, for the last few days, we would have to put Vanni out of our minds, and peacefully dawdle away our time in an otherwise flawless unmarried honeymoon, passing the days and nights in a sublime mixture of love and painting.

No such luck. A few days later just before lunch, the phone rang in the living-room, startling us so much that Steve nearly spilled his gindiano.

'Must be the police,' said Lella.

Not one single time had the phone rung and disturbed us. We had no friends in the area. We needed no servants, we mostly ate out, and the only daily chore the girls did was throw back the sheets

122

and the one blanket.

Now the bell was stuttering impatiently, as though demanding an answer—and the first word Lella uttered when she picked up the phone was answer enough.

'Papa!' she screamed, adding, 'you're in Pisa!'

I realised later that she had deliberately shouted—to warn us.

'Oh no!' she said. 'How awful! Yes, Fiamma is here. We'll both take the bus to see you in Pisa. Where shall we meet?'

Silence as the Prince talked.

'Oh! You're coming here. Wonderful.' But less enthusiastic. 'Yes, here's Fiamma, longing to have a word with you.'

'Papa darling,' cried Fiamma while Lella beckoned us out of earshot.

'He's coming here in an hour,' she cried, almost panic-stricken. Urgently, briefly she explained: 'Papa received a telegram from Enrico, telling him that Fascist thugs had smashed up part of Villa Magari and gardens. Nothing that can't be mended, but Papa must oversee it. So Papa took an Imperial Airways flight from Croydon to Rome—there's a twice weekly flight. Then the train to Pisa. Now he's about to set off for—here!' The last words almost a wail. 'What shall we tell him? What can we say? When he sees you two he'll—'

'Bye-bye, Papa. See you in an hour.' Fiamma put the old-fashioned phone back on its hook and looked at us blankly. 'What shall we do? What *can* we do?'

'Do a bunk!' Steve never hesitated. 'If we want to preserve the status quo—if we want to maintain a beautiful friendship—let's get out of here pronto.'

123

And then to me he said, 'Come on, big boy, and don't forget to take the painting with you.'

'You've got to go, darling,' Fiamma agreed, but almost in tears.

'I know.' I looked around the modest but heavenly 'home'. 'Robbed of a week of heaven. How could he!'

'Darling—think of poor Papa. Goodness knows what's happened to Magari.'

'We'd better step on it, Ham,' urged Steve. 'Otherwise we'll meet him on the steps here. Better take a cab to Pisa station, then make straight for home.'

The painting, 'The Yellow Nude' as I was going to call it, posed something of a problem. Parts of it were still wet. But I knew from experience what to do. I had a spare canvas on its stretcher, and this I laid on the painting but separated from it with halves of wine bottle corks, one in each corner, through which I drove thin panel pins to hold the two stretchers together. To be on the safe side, I secured them with cord tied in each direction like a parcel.

As Steve remarked afterwards, our journey to Florence—or anyway the early part of it—would have done credit to an old Mack Sennett film. Carrying the unwieldy canvases—which did nothing to make us less conspicuous!—we made for the cab rank, which was but a few yards from the bus stop at which the Prince might at any moment arrive. As bad luck would have it, on this occasion there were no cabs standing there, so we had to retreat into a little ice-cream parlour from which we could watch, and fill in the time until a cab returned to base by eating butterscotch flavoured ice-cream—a pleasure we would have appreciated much more if we had not been shaking with anxiety.

We were halfway through our second dish when finally a cab did arrive and, to the horror of the proprietor, we dashed out leaving it unfinished. But, as the taxi stopped, who should jump out but the Prince! There was nothing for it but to dart back into the ice-cream parlour and screen our faces by holding the canvases high.

Mercifully, the Prince almost ran up the sandy path towards the villa and the moment we were out of his sight, we dashed into the taxi, then to the station. We had to wait over an hour for the train to Florence—terrified that the Prince might phone Villa Magari and be told by Enrico that he had not seen us for a month. There was nothing we could do about that, however; and the rest of the journey was uneventful, and we finally caught the No. 9 trolley-bus to Settignano.

*   *   *

'I guess I know what we ought to do,' suggested Steve. 'Dump our stuff in our house, then cross the street to Villa Magari before the Prince arrives, and look as though we're helping Enrico to get the place in order.'

No sooner suggested than done. We had little to unpack, so we left it, and I blew a kiss to the painting of Fiamma, still standing on the piano, then rushed to the villa and pulled the entry bell at the front gates of the Magari.

'Oh! Signor!' Enrico dashed out to unlock the heavy gates. 'The catastrophe!' He was wringing his

125

hands, almost in tears. 'Oh, the swine! Our beautiful house and garden. And all for spite.'

'Tell us what happened, in your own time,' I said gently, trying to calm him down. 'Already, I hear, the Prince is on his way.'

'You know?' he exclaimed. And, then, as some sort of comprehension dawned, yet thinking slowly, he wagged a finger and muttered, 'Ah yes, maybe I see . . .'

'See?' I asked with mock innocence.

'The Prince. He telephoned me and say he will telephone his daughters. Perhaps,' with a slightly cunning look, 'perhaps you overhear, eh?'

'I overheard nothing,' I said severely. 'Now, promise me, understand—that you know nothing. Nothing! And that includes backstairs gossip. Right?' I said briskly. 'Understood?'

He nodded, hardly bothering to conceal a conspiratorial smile.

'Now, let's go and look at the damage,' I said, while Steve swore under his breath, 'Quizzy old bastard'.

'Grazie, Enrico.' I patted his back. 'Much appreciated, and perhaps one day I'll be able to help you.'

Enrico's hands trembled as he told us of the damage.

'Villano,' he kept mumbling while he tried to get the order of things into his narrative. 'Ah! Villano!'

'And what did the villain do?' I asked patiently. I understood the need for the ceremonial telling of the tale, the importance to Enrico of explaining; that he had been defeated by brute force and that the dignity of his appointment as guardian of Magari had been wrenched from him.

126

'Not one,' he exclaimed. 'Not one villano. Two!'

He pointed to wallpaper that had been scored and stripped as if with age; at tiles wrenched from their surrounds; at ceilings with gaping holes in the plaster; at light fixtures torn from the walls; at a bathroom with no taps; and to a door stripped of its handles and hinges.

'You see the personal property—the piano, the pictures, the furniture—all left alone,' I said to a horrified Steve. 'Only the house itself, the fabric, has been ripped up. It is easier to claim that the estate needs repair work. What bloody thugs!'

In the grounds it was the same thing. Tiles chipped on the beautiful rose-lined walk to the pool. Plants and shrubs torn up in the gardens. Tressels pulled down. Paths damaged. Coat hooks wrenched out of the walls in the changing rooms by the Indian pool. Fencing uprooted, all the result of 'slipshod work' deliberately made to look like this to show negligence on the part of the owner. And much, much more.

We did lend a helping hand in clearing up some of the more obvious mess, and were working hard replanting stakes that had been torn down in the garden by the time the Prince arrived in a taxi with the girls.

He waved his hand to us in the garden. The two girls waved to us decorously, and then I saw the Prince beckon to Enrico who shuffled inside the house, returning with a paper. I saw the Prince scrutinise it, then tap it, obviously pointing to a signature.

Only then did he stroll towards us, tap the paper—the form officially authorising the work to be done—and in a fury almost shout, 'I knew it.

127

The bastards. Look at the signature! Luciano Neri. The Mayor's number two, and if my intelligence is correct the same upstart who brought that message from Ciano. This is the work of the Mafia.'

'Are you sure, sir?' asked Steve.

'Of course I'm sure,' replied the Prince, irritably. 'But I'm sorry, you two,' with his charming smile. 'I forgot my manners! It was very kind—more than kind—giving up your time to help Enrico. Trust the Italians to over-egg the pudding. Makes you feel ashamed to *be* an Italian.'

'We didn't really do anything,' I protested, afraid he might believe we had been working for days. But he knew we had not for, with an ironic smile, almost taunting us, he turned to Steve and said, 'Oh by the way, Steve, these are your espadrilles, I think. You left them behind.'

*   *   *

For a few days we did not dare visit the Villa Magari, though we felt we should have been volunteering to help repair the damage. The Prince had discovered all—and for the moment I did not want to run any risks. And though the Prince had let us off with a caution, and the Principessa had not yet returned to Italy, what had the Prince said to the girls? Had he exacted any promises? Had he issued any threats? And now that he had discovered *our* guilty secret, had either of the girls told the Prince about Vanni? There was no way of knowing.

We might have remained puzzled and separated—had not the Prince invited himself to BB's for lunch a few days later. It was my day for duty at I Tatti so of course I went for lunch too,

128

together with our guests.

As the Prince and I walked down to I Tatti to join Berenson, I tried as best I could to apologise for the incident of Steve's espadrilles. It was not easy.

'I was very upset indeed—and angry at first,' admitted the Prince, 'and whatever my feelings, I can't abide stupidity! But, well, forget it.'

He paused as we almost reached the entrance to BB's house, before adding, 'I thought you'd both do what you did, but I'm of a forgiving nature.' And after another slight pause, almost for effect, he added, 'I believe it was Oscar Wilde who said that all advice is dangerous but good advice is fatal. Even so, fathers are *meant* to give advice and as I can't in my heart blame you, I will just say this: Don't let my wife find out—or I doubt if you'll ever be invited again.'

After thinking, he said, 'I suppose my *real* anger and annoyance is directed at Neri.'

With that he walked into the house with an almost languid sign of dismissal.

'Well, I'll be buggered,' gasped Steve later, when I told him. 'What a man! Caught red-handed—and forgiven.'

'Not forgiven,' I was still shaking, 'so much as warned. He's the worldly type—doing it himself all the time, so there's damn all he can say about it. But I must say, he's a gentleman all right.'

'Yes,' I added, 'and we must express our gratitude by offering to help with the clearing up at Magari.'

★   ★   ★

'I really invited myself because I'm lonely,' the Prince laughed to BB when he had been offered the usual minuscule glass of vermouth. 'My wife won't be back for another fortnight.' And with a smile to me, 'You and Steve seem to have deserted us. Come over, both you boys, whenever you like, there won't be much swimming weather left and I believe both girls are in.'

'I'd love to,' I replied eagerly and dashed over to the villa as soon as lunch was over and I had finished helping BB to hand round coffee in the limonaia.

It was a sunny day, but there was no swimming—the pool water was too cold. When I reached the back balcony overlooking the garden, Fiamma was swinging on a sofa dangling from thin chains attached to an iron frame.

'What happened?' I cried. 'I've been dying to see you, but I didn't dare come. Where's Lella?'

'Gone to Florence.'

'Your father has been very decent.'

'Darling Ham.' Almost falling as she jumped off the swinging sofa, she flung her arms around me and all but squeezed the life out of me as she showered me with kises.

'Hey!' Breathlessly I tried to disentangle her arms. 'I'm the one who is supposed to do that! I won't have any neck left.'

'Sorry,' she laughed—a laugh of pure happiness—well, happiness perhaps mingled with a touch of relief. 'I was so frightened at first—and Papa gave us such a lecture! For a moment I wondered—I had all sorts of fears—that he'd never let us see each other again, never let you into our house. But then he began to calm down a bit and

130

then—then he looked at me, stroked my face and said something very sweet. "All I want is for you to be happy."'

'And you are?' I laughed with the sheer joy and excitement of it all.

'Utterly! Now I want nothing more out of life.'

'We think alike,' I said gravely. 'There's only one thing more I need.'

Fiamma knew exactly what I meant. 'But where?'

'In the garden behind the uvaspina bushes. It's such a lovely day. It won't take long. Shall we?' I asked.

She nodded.

'Come on, then,' I said hoarsely. We ran along the tessellated path. For no reason a phrase from a D. H. Lawrence book came to mind—one so evocative that I had never forgotten it in the two years since I had first read it: 'I took her, short, sharp, and finished like an animal'.

'It'll have to be that,' I gasped, heart beating double fast with physical and mental excitement.

She ran ahead, carrying a blanket, to look for a warm patch of sun facing the vineyards, such a beautiful, innocent creature with long legs below a simple white linen dress, held round the waist by a thin gold leather belt, and on her feet, matching gold-coloured sandals.

In the sun behind a few trees she lay down on the blanket almost moaning, and crying, 'Quick, quick! I can't wait.'

As I lowered my trousers, she held up the white dress, almost with a flourish. Nothing underneath.

'I've been waiting so long.' She was touching herself above the join in her legs, and her knees, bent and supple, were already moving as she arched her back gently up and down.

With my trousers half-way down, I could feel the beauty of everything as I slid between the heat of her thighs, but then she made one ecstatic arch and cried with a gasp, 'Sorry—it's all over. I couldn't wait.'

Then she seemed to flop as though almost fainting and I came too, only before I could enter her, over her legs, just with the tenseness of trying to help and get inside her, to love her, but she had come first and, knowing that at any moment we might hear a gardener's footsteps, I rolled over.

Almost gravely, sitting up she slid a finger along the inside of her wet thigh and then with a secret smile pushed the finger inside her.

'You,' she said simply. 'The next best thing.'

         ★   ★   ★

A beer was needed.

'All that exertion,' laughed Fiamma, teasing.

'All that effort at control ...' I replied.

'I know! Always the woman's fault.' And then, as we strolled back along the stone-patterned walk, the last of the rambler roses still clinging stubbornly to the carefully placed wires running along the red-brick wall, she hugged me and said, 'I love you so dreadfully that sometimes I'm afraid.'

'Afraid of me? Am I such a big, bad bully?'

'You're my idea of heaven.'

Once back on the balcony, flopping on the swinging double-chair, Fiamma brought me a cool Drago, with its label of a fire-spitting dragon, and I took a long drink.

'God! That's good.' I smacked my lips and

offered her a sip. 'By the way, is there any news of Vanni?'

She shook her head. 'You saw what happened.'

'But did he say where he was going?'

Swaying gently on the swing-cum-hammock, Fiamma took another sip of my beer and shook her head.

'No,' she said. 'He didn't want to get Papa involved, but I am afraid—'

'That Vanni will be found?' I asked.

'Not that so much—but if he is a *deserter* then eventually Papa is bound to get involved. The Military Police will come round and, well, Fascists making enquiries don't bother much about sparing people's feelings.'

'I wonder if'—I was almost thinking aloud—'it would be fairer to tell the Prince—to warn him. It's going to be a terrible shock if . . .'

'If,' she echoed. 'There's always an if! Let's wait and see.'

I said no more. After all it was none of my business; but at that moment, somewhat to my surprise, Steve walked in.

'I didn't think you'd dare come,' I cried.

'I was just going into our house when I heard Enrico at the lodge shout out, "Mister Ham is at the Magari with Signorina Fiamma." I couldn't believe it.'

'He's quite a guy.'

'He likes you both,' said Fiamma demurely.

'And he knows there's fuck-all he can do about it,' chortled the more down-to-earth Steve. 'He does the same thing himself so he's decided that if you can't fight 'em you'd better join 'em.'

'You shouldn't talk like that about my papa,'

133

Fiamma reproached him.

'Sorry. But that reminds me, Ham, what about my painting—I don't seem to have noticed any activity with the nudes lately. Getting bored sitting there painting pussy?'

'I'm getting on,' I replied tolerantly. 'We're on the last lap. We finished all the background. On Tuesday I have the use of Umberto's studio, so if Lella's free, I'll more or less wrap up the last touches.'

'Oh boy!' cried Steve. 'Then I'm gonna hang it right in front of my bed as a substitute for the horny nights I have to spend alone.'

*   *   *

When the Prince went to lunch with BB his main reason had been to offer practical suggestions to Berenson about a forthcoming visit to the famous monastery in Cassino, about eighty miles south-east of Rome—in fact, midway between Rome and Naples, beautiful but high in the mountains. BB, who was an indefatigable traveller, wanted to study the Renaissance frescos in the abbey, and though I knew that he could easily have arranged the trip without the help of the Prince, I also knew that BB enjoyed looking things over in advance. He had once said to me, 'Shared anticipation is the best part of an excursion.'

What made the trip more exciting was the fact that Kurt and I were to accompany BB. 'I like having people around me,' he confessed to the Prince. 'And an artist and a musician—what better friends can I have?'

I *was* excited—I did not have that much money,

and BB was paying for everything. And there was another thing: any change from the routine of I Tatti was welcome. After all, despite his pretensions of modesty, I knew that in fact Berenson was vainglorious, could be a bore, told his stories over and over again, and that he was a tough taskmaster especially in the beautiful rectangular and classical sixteenth-century villa, with its library of 50,000 volumes, all in this treasure house hidden from the roads by alleyways of cypresses and ilex and banks of flowers and formal gardens.

A heaven—but you could have too much of a good thing. A break in the mountains would be closer to heaven. And there was one thing more: as Kurt said, 'Cassino's the kind of place that neither of us will probably ever see again. So let's have a look this once.'

'Well, I'm glad you're going soon,' said the Prince. 'The war situation is still looking pretty grim. It's that that makes me so angry when the Mafia wastes energy in attacking other Italians instead of preparing to fight foreigners.'

It was not until this lunch, ostensibly to arrange suggestions for the trip to Cassino, that I realised that, though the Prince still appeared to accept life with all its drawbacks, his almost debonair take-it-or-leave-it attitude masked his real, deep hatred of Luciano Neri, the Mafia director on the mayor's staff.

'After all,' he said to us that lunchtime at BB's, 'it looks as though Europe *is* moving inexorably into war. Despite Munich. Germany's bent on it. Why *should* Italy waste time trying to smash up people's houses out of spite when we may soon be fighting?'

'You don't think it was Ciano's doing?'

Caeseri shook his head. 'No. Ciano knows which side his bread's buttered. "Do as Papa tells you"—and Il Duce *does* disapprove of the Mafia. But he hasn't got around to clearing up Florence yet. Probably because Neri has some hold over him.'

'Do you really think, Prince,' asked Mary Berenson, 'that we're heading for war?'

'Most assuredly I do.' Gravely he looked in the direction of Mrs Berenson.

'But I just *can't* believe it.'

'Maybe not in Italy, not yet,' he was thinking aloud. 'But look at it this way. Spain is going Fascist. The German fleet pounded Almeria in Spain. Spanish cities like Guernica, Santander, Gijon, Oviedo are all in Fascist hands, with the help of the German Air Force.'

'But couldn't you just regard that as Hitler using Spain as a training ground?' asked BB.

'For what?' asked the Prince, answering the question himself. 'It can only be for war.'

'But not Italy?' asked BB.

'I'm not so sure. No—yes, I *am* sure. Italy can't be left out, especially since she's part of the German-Japanese anti-Comintern which is referred to as the Axis. It's war, I tell you. Especially as England is,' he coughed apologetically to me and smiled, 'shall we say not very strong and doesn't *want* to realise that Hitler is telling lies every time he promises a thousand years of peace. Mr Chamberlain is pitiful—his very presence, appearance, his whole *attitude* is an invitation to Hitler to increase his aggression. And Italy? Nice, Corsica, Tunis—the old resentments still burn,' he said mockingly. 'Il Duce is not going to stand up and let Hitler take all the rich pickings in Europe. France will fall like a ripe plum, I'm afraid—there's no *will* to fight in that country—and Mussolini will be unable to resist asking Hitler if he can have the Côte d'Azur! A perfect alternative playground!' he laughed, but bitterly.

Berenson gave a sigh and stroked his neat white beard. 'It all makes your problems at Magari sound very unimportant,' he smiled.

'Indeed,' cried the Prince. 'But one of the only good things Il Duce has done is to curb the activities of the Mafia, only he hasn't got around to Tuscany yet.'

'Why not?' I asked. 'And what *is* the Mafia exactly? I mugged up a bit on Italian history before I came out here, but I seemed to draw a blank whenever I followed up that line.'

'Yes, you would,' the Prince replied, 'because it's really Sicilian history that will supply some of the answers—but not many of them; not even the meaning of the word itself, which is Sicilian, not Italian. Not surprising, really, since it's a secret society. But like all secret societies its activities got embroidered by the gossips and nowadays you can't see the wood for the trees—which pleases the Mafiosi immensely, I'm sure.'

'Concealing their real tricks, no doubt,' BB put in with a touch of asperity.

'Exactly. Because on the surface they support whatever government is in power. They take good care that nothing of a rebellious nature can ever be pinned on them, though their creed is "Gridare vendetta"'—with a nod towards me the Prince added, 'or as you might say, "Cry aloud for vengeance".'

137

'But vengeance for what?' I asked puzzled.

He paused as if collecting his thoughts. 'That would take more time than we have to explain. But basically it was because in 1860 the Sicilians were conscripted and they called it being enslaved by Italy. The conscripts were mostly brigands anyway, robbers'—another nod to me—'"highwaymen" you might call them. And they sank further into the criminal underworld to avoid being dragged into the army. Not that they'd have been any good anyway, brigands having no loyalty except to themselves. But their resentment was active. They assassinated the politicians they thought were responsible for their so-called slavery and, when they got caught and brought to justice, their fellow brigands banded even tighter together and plotted for even greater vengeance.'

'They should have known something of the persecution of the Jews,' BB said wryly. 'It would have taught them tolerance.'

The Prince mused on that for a minute. 'Maybe. But what they actually did was to organise themselves into cells like in a honeycomb, which they called "families", with each family bossed by a "godfather" who in turn served a more powerful boss in the bigger cities. Whatever the form of Italy's government it was riddled with the tentacles of the Mafia, whose "families" always held the reins of real power through its own wealthy patrons. The unwilling rich were forced by extortion to join—in fact I became a victim myself, but that's another story—and one I think I've told you. At the bottom of it all was a sort of violent and distorted loyalty to each other and the vendetta motif; and those who betrayed it never lived to tell the tale.' He gave his shoulders a mock shudder. 'Disturbing, very—especially when these things invade one's own premises. And the reason there's still Mafia activity in Tuscany is because Mussolini doesn't know.' And suddenly, after thinking in silence for a few moments, looking into the distance across the vineyards beyond the limonaia the Prince slapped his thigh and cried, 'Yes, by God, I'm going to. I will!'

'Will what?' asked Mary Berenson.

'Go and see Mussolini. Just very politely tell him what the Mafia's doing in Florence.'

'You can't just walk in to see Mussolini,' I said, almost laughing.

'I can, and I will. I met him once before, but better than that, I'm an hereditary member of His Majesty Victor Emmanuel's court—the equivalent of your British Privy Council—and I have access to him and his requests, if it's all properly handled. I'll ask His Majesty to arrange for Mussolini to grant me an audience.'

'But does Mussolini ever take any notice of the King?' asked BB.

'Oh yes, they're in frequent communication,' the Prince said. 'I don't say,' he laughed, 'that if the King asks Mussolini to change all the uniforms to bright blue or green, he'd do it, but for innocuous requests, he listens. And he's certainly very interested in suppressing the Mafia. Yes, I'll write to His Majesty this afternoon.'

And he did.

A couple of days later, a formal letter to His Majesty was on its way to Rome.

A hint of mischief in his eye, the Prince said, 'It wouldn't be fitting for a nobleman of the Caeseri to
139

address the monarch of the ancient House of Savoy with a typewriter, so I've had a letter handwritten on parchment paper in the formal flowery phrases of Court protocol.'

He showed me the letter which Victor Emmanuel received:

Sire:

In presenting my humble duty I crave your Majesty's favour on behalf of Signor Benito Mussolini, and beg of you to do me the honour of arranging for me to have a private audience of Il Duce to discuss with him a matter requiring some delicacy, in which the presence of clerks and other minor officials would inhibit its presentation. When I say that the subject is that organisation for so long an intolerable burden on Italian society, the Mafia, your Majesty's concern will no doubt seem to be warranted.

I hold myself in readiness to obey your Majesty's summons at any time appropriate.

I am, Sire, ever obedient to your Majesty's commands.

Giorgio, P

There was no reply for months, but that was only to be expected. It all depended on Mussolini, and though he ruled the efficiency of the government with speed when ordering wrongdoers to drink castor oil, or despatching poison to the water wells of Abyssinia, he was inclined to be more dilatory in matters concerning the King. But after all, Mussolini had met the Prince years previously and maybe that counted in Il Duce's decision. The letter did not come from the King, but from one of

Mussolini's acolytes, telling the Prince that Il Duce would grant him an audience in the late afternoon during the last week in May—just as the international tension between Britain and Germany was again intensifying.

'Not exactly the best time,' observed the Prince wryly to me; 'but still, with luck I will be able to get my own back on that bastard, Neri.'

'You'll be careful not to get into trouble.' The Principessa had by then returned from England.

'I will be careful.'

'And do tell me what it's like—the Quirinale Palace, I mean,' I asked him on the eve of his trip.

'I promise,' the Prince laughed, and he kept his word—telling us in fascinating detail what happened.

CHAPTER NINE

The Prince had visited the Quirinale several times for official functions before Mussolini came to power, but he was astounded at the changes since Mussolini had installed himself in what was obviously one of the largest rooms in the house. The King still lived in the Quirinale, of course, but Mussolini had a large 'suite' and while the Prince was waiting—out of respect he had arrived early—a pretty young secretary showed him round one or two of the different rooms in which from time to time Mussolini 'received' or held conferences.

The most astonishing was a small annexe in which children could be left while interviews were conducted, for Mussolini liked to give the impression that he was a man of the people. After all, he had five children of his own. The room had toys and a rocking horse in it and though no one ever seemed to use the room, it built up the impression that Mussolini was very much the family man.

Finally, the Prince was ushered into the reception room itself—referred to behind the Duce's back as the 'gabinetto', the lavatory. The Prince took in the huge rectangular space with Mussolini's outsize desk on a podium at the short end. Behind it was a vast window framed in a tasselled pelmet and curtains of 'imperial' purple. He had heard that, depending on whether or not Mussolini wished to be seen by his guest, he had arranged spotlights controlled by buttons under his desk. These he would switch on or off so that Mussolini would appear in silhouette against the brightness of the window, or so that his face would be illuminated, as though by photographer's lights, to emphasise the strength of his aggressive jaw.

On a table alongside the desk stood photographs of his wife Rachele, his three sons, Vittorio, Bruno and Romano, and his daughters Edda and Anna Maria. A portrait in oils of Clara Petacci, his mistress, on one wall was flanked by badly proportioned portraits of two revolutionaries, Garibaldi and Mazzini. Other opulently framed pictures that hung on the panelled walls included Marshal Radetsky and Napoleon III. Where the panels were visible, the Prince could just see that they were decorated with elaborate scroll work in gold leaf. The same pattern of scroll work was repeated in the purple-and-gold carpet—said to have been designed by Salvador Dali.

All this he saw after passing two permanently posted guards, who took turns to come from the army, navy, air force or, as on this occasion, from the Vatican's Swiss guards.

'I must say,' the Prince continued when he met us, 'that Il Duce was very angry when I told him what had happened to the Villa Magari and that the Mafia had been responsible. He almost went purple with rage—the colour of the carpet!—and summoned some official—he didn't even bother to introduce the man—and almost flayed him for not attending to what he called his "anti-Mafia" duties. "I want a full report on the situation in Florence by tomorrow!" he thundered. "And fire this man Neri from his job as Deputy Mayor. Also by *tomorrow*." And in front of the official, he said, "I'm glad, Prince, that you wrote to His Majesty and that he reported the matter to me. You, Prince Caeseri," with a look at the cowering official, "are the sort of public spirited man we need to come forward and help to keep Fascist Italy the great country it is."'

The Prince paused and added, with his usual wry smile, 'Frankly it was not my intention to boost the ego of Mussolini, or to help make Fascism great. But you have to hand it to the man. He's a master of propaganda.'

With that (as the Prince continued his account of events) an astonishing thing happened. Mussolini looked at his ostentatious wrist-watch and then gave the Prince what he could only describe as a metaphorical dig in the ribs and said, 'Prince, what are you doing this evening?'

'A quiet dinner at the Jockey Club, Duce, and then the first train home to Florence in the morning.'

143

'You're a man of the world,' said Mussolini with the next best thing to a conspiratorial leer. 'I've heard a great deal about you—well, we'll leave it at that!' The Prince coughed apologetically, probably grateful that the Principessa was not listening to his story. And then Mussolini said that he would like the Prince to meet Clara Petacci. She, of course, was Mussolini's mistress.

'So,' Mussolini slapped a thigh, 'when we are off duty we live simply. Come round for supper. Not dinner—just a plate of spaghetti and a few glasses of vino. I would like to know you better. We need help from your stratum of society. What better way than over a meal? Which hotel are you staying in?'

'The Excelsior.' The Prince hesitated, for, although the project was fascinating, he was not sure even so that he wanted to get involved. Mussolini jumped immediately to the wrong conclusion.

'Of course! I should have known.' He almost clapped his hand to his forehead. 'You have a girl at the Excelsior. Is she presentable? Bring her along if you wish.'

'No, no,' the Prince cried. 'I'm alone.'

'Ah! Well, perhaps it's better if we want to talk.' Mussolini would not take 'No' for an answer and, after a brief telephone call, he beckoned the Prince to follow him and strode, as though on parade, across the long purple carpet, jaw jutting out, to the door which opened miraculously as he approached. Still 'on parade' he reached the front door and, the flunkeys bowing and scraping and hastening to open his Fiat limousine, engine already purring, they made their way across side streets in a small motorcade, so that it was difficult to follow the route they had taken, and finally drew up, almost with a flourish, at the house which the young lady from Cremona shared with her lord and master—indeed the lord and master of all the empire of Italy—for the time being.

'This is Miss Petacci's house.' Mussolini opened the modest front door with his own latchkey, and, turning to his bodyguard and driver, shouted the equivalent of 'That's all, boys, you can go now. Come and pick up His Highness the Prince at ten o'clock and call for me at seven o'clock tomorrow morning.'

The car roared away, with a squealing of tyres as it twisted round a sharp corner, and Mussolini strode ahead into the hall, calling, 'Clara! I've brought a guest for supper' and when the lady of the house called, 'I'll be ready in five minutes,' Mussolini turned to the Prince and waved him towards a door, saying, 'There's the living-room. You'll find a table of drinks inside. I'll be a couple of minutes changing into something more comfortable.'

The Prince had hardly started sipping a glass of vermouth when Clara Petacci entered, smiled, shook hands, and made some inconsequential remark along the lines of, 'I'm delighted to meet any friend of Il Duce's', adding with a look at his glass, 'There's some ice here. Don't you want some ice?'

As the Prince told us later, he was impressed with her manners and charm. She seemed genuinely concerned that he was drinking slightly warm vermouth. 'Please,' she took the glass from his hand, 'we shall have some wine later.' The Prince found her tall and dark and very attractive, and remembered a phrase Oswald Mosley had written about her. She had 'a full figure'. He had also heard that Mussolini—who had only met her earlier that year—refused to be photographed with her unless she was sitting down or on a low step of any staircase because she was taller than he was.

When she asked the Prince again whether he was sure he did not want any ice, she said quite unaffectedly, 'Benito really prefers wine. But,' with a laugh, 'quite a lot of it with his pasta.' The Prince had heard that Mussolini could quite easily drink a bottle of wine with a meal. Yet he never appeared to be drunk—perhaps because he had put on a lot of weight and so it took a long time for any alcohol to seep into his brain. And also, the Prince was thinking, as Miss Petacci offered him some olives, Mussolini's father had kept a pub, and Il Duce had met his future wife when she was serving his father as a barmaid in 1910.

The Prince heard Mussolini's footsteps clattering down from the bedroom and he entered the modest living-room, in which there was a dining-room through an arch. The Prince hardly recognised him at first. Mussolini was wearing slacks and an open-necked shirt—though he almost always preferred breeches to trousers so he could show off the calves of his shapely legs, of which he was very proud. He was a fanatic about uniforms and had two valets to look after them, but they only came after he had left his flat during the day. And of course there was something else that puzzled the Prince until he realised what it was.

'I don't think I had ever seen him, either in a crowd or in a photo, without his hat on,' he told us. 'He was completely bald. But being extremely vain,

146

he always covered his head and this came as quite a shock, I can tell you. But otherwise Mussolini couldn't have been more agreeable. He even offered to sign copies of a novel called *The Cardinal's Mistress* which he had published in 1928.'

Apart from that, Mussolini, as the Prince continued with his story, was talking of ways in which the Prince might be able to help the Fascist cause. The Prince—and his title—could be useful, said Mussolini, to further the cause of Fascism, especially among the people who worked on the land and were often short of money.

The Prince, of course, did not relish this—he was ardently anti-Fascist. Although, as he insisted, he was too much of a gentleman to argue against Fascism with his host, Mussolini in any event was so busy wolfing food and drink in the grossest possible way that he would hardly have had time to argue back.

'It was appalling,' confessed the Prince. 'Mussolini looked as though he hadn't eaten for a month, and all good, solid, peasant food. We started with a dish of tinned tuna fish and white beans, and when I politely refused, Mussolini grabbed the full dish of beans and tuna fish and a spoon and fork and not only ate from the bowl, but finished the lot. The same with the spaghetti—and I must say that it was beautifully prepared. He *wolfed* it down, like a pig. The girl didn't seem to notice, but I must say the whole evening threw quite a new light on the modern leader of Italy.'

And there the evening's 'entertainment', as the Prince described it, might have ended but suddenly, with the meal barely finished, the front door bell stuttered as Mussolini was opening a second bottle of red wine and he grunted, 'You answer it, Clara. Don't let any journalists in!' adding to the Prince with a laugh, 'I don't like journalists quite as much as I did when I was one myself!'

The Prince was laughing when there was a noise of other laughter in the hallway, and then in walked a pretty girl who embraced Mussolini and cried, 'Papa! We were on our way home and thought we'd pop in and see you and Clara.'

Mussolini introduced the girl. 'This is my daughter Edda Ciano, wife of our Foreign Minister.'

'Honoured to meet you.' Edda smiled as the Prince touched her hand with his lips, and an instant before Count Ciano himself came bustling into the room, shook hands and said very politely, 'Delighted to meet you, Prince Caeseri. I'm only sorry that you were away during my visit to Florence.'

Thinking it better to be polite, the Prince said, 'The loss was mine, sir, but,' with a smile, 'when Il Duce gives an order, who is there who dares to disobey!'

'What's that?' asked Mussolini.

'Nothing,' said Ciano, while Edda Ciano, also laughingly, said to the Prince, 'Father's bark is worse than his bite. But we all love him. And,' with a sigh added, 'and we do tend to come and see him here—with Mama it sometimes leads to scenes.'

The Prince laughed outright. All these people were so human that they forgot their rank and their pomposity! Ciano was not such a bad fellow after all! At that moment, in fact, Ciano beckoned to the Prince that he wanted to talk to him privately, and

148

when the Prince had followed him back into the dining-room annexe, he said, with some difficulty, 'I'm sorry, Prince, to learn the bad news about your son Vanni.'

The Prince remembered how he felt, as if his heart had missed a beat, a lead weight seemed to have hit him in the stomach, and a dull pain struck him across the chest. It must be that Vanni had been killed in action.

'My son?' He must have sounded stupefied.

'You didn't know?' Ciano looked startled.

'You mean—killed in action?'

'No, no. Not that. But Prince, I thought you knew. I hate to say this, but he's missing. Posted as a deserter.'

A great weight seemed to lift from the Prince, but at the same time—what a family disgrace! 'What happened?' he asked dully.

Ciano started to tell what he knew and was just talking about 'extenuating circumstances' when Mussolini came into the annexe.

'What extenuating circumstances?' he asked.

With an apologetic look at the Prince, Ciano repeated the story.

'But the extenuating circumstances?' Mussolini's voice was no longer light and cheerful, it had suddenly become almost a bark.

'Because of his connections, I had a report made on the Prince's son,' said Ciano. 'It seems that he might have suffered some sort of brain-storm or heat stroke or something. There was an ugly incident which upset him. We lost a few Italians in a skirmish, and Captain Vanni Caeseri saw some of our Italian troops looting anything they could from

149

the bodies of their dead comrades. It sickened him so much—'

'Impossible!' Mussolini almost screamed, banging his hand on the table. 'No Italian—'

'They did, sir,' Ciano insisted, while the Prince's heart started to beat more normally.

'Find the culprits, and have them shot!' shouted Mussolini. 'That's an order. And when you apprehend the Prince's son, arrange to have him freed immediately so that he can return to his regiment and no charges will be brought.'

The news had been shattering to the Prince—even though the stern decision by Mussolini that the matter should be forgotten helped to mitigate the original offence—that his own son had been branded as a deserter from the armed forces. However great the provocation, nothing could warrant such action on the field of battle.

The Prince spent a sleepless night, twisting and turning in the Excelsior's large and luxurious bed, and even on the train that took him back to Florence the following morning he was wondering what the outcome would be.

'Ah well,' he sighed as he finished the story, 'Vanni hasn't been found yet. We'll meet that problem when we get to it.'

CHAPTER TEN

When all was ready for the trip to Cassino, a town of about twenty thousand people with the abbey perched above, there was a sudden change of plan. BB fell ill with a particularly virulent form of influenza. At his age—he was now seventy-four—there was no question of his making the trip and I naturally assumed that it would be postponed.

Not at all. From his sick bed, and with a rheumy cough, he insisted that Kurt and I should make the trip ourselves.

'You know the latest series of articles on frescos I am writing,' he said. 'This flu won't stop me writing, but I *do* need some research on the texture of the fresco surfaces.' He paused. 'I have been studying Giotto's technique and the heritage he passed on to the true Renaissance painters. I think it's a fair assumption that the route by which the inheritance came was via Giotto's pupils and followers—numerous and often anonymous, but known as Giotteschi. Some of them have demonstrated their abilities in remarkably well-preserved frescos in the monastery at Cassino. I say "I think" because there is little documentary evidence, but the influence is ...' He broke off, shutting the book with a snap. 'Well, see for yourself. Try and detect which have been painted in true fresco style—known as "buon" frescos, and which were added later, "secco". I have my own opinions, which I am anxious to confirm. Would you check that for me, Ham? It'll make a change from your normal work.'

I was delighted at the prospect, indeed had been looking forward to it.

'Then arrange it with your friend—Kurt, that pleasant young musician.' He looked up sharply. 'Of whom, I may add, I have great hopes. He played the "Appassionata" at one of my soirées when you were—er—studying with Signor Umberto, and his performance, though naturally

151

youthful, had a certain brooding quality I think Beethoven would have approved. Perhaps he too could enjoy a little relaxation with you.'

Fiamma and I had been lovers for so long now—deeper in love every day—that we had reached the stage where we could afford to be parted for a few days. She quite understood—after all, it was Berenson who had asked me to help.

'But be back in a few days, promise?' She kissed me. 'Otherwise I'll come looking for you!'

'I adore you, my Fiamma, and every day away from you is a day lost. Never fear, I'll be back.'

I also had to tell Umberto that I was leaving and with a snide smile he laid a finger alongside his nose, and spoke in conspiratorial tones. 'You will find the frescos most "interesting" shall we say, will we not? Yes?'

'I expect so.' I was mildly confused.

'Indeed, yes. For they are sensual to a degree quite surprising until you recall that God does not deny even the celibate their vicarious pleasures. Well, you will see. Frescos are the ancient equivalent of today's—what is it you call them that are in the newpapers but with no words, for children sometimes, but also for their papas and mamas?'

I suddenly tumbled to what he was getting at. 'Oh, the strip cartoon.'

'The strip cartoon: that is it.' He resettled his beret. 'The story in pictures. With no words.'

'Well, sometimes they have words written in balloons that are linked to the speakers' mouths.'

He winked. 'At Cassino you will find that the pictures need no words. They tell earthy tales. You know Boccaccio?'

'Oh, yes,' I said smugly. 'Fiamma and I have read much of the *Decameron* together.'

'Of course, of course. Favourite reading with young lovers.' Umberto was under no illusions as to the course of our affair; and I knew he approved.

But now as we—Kurt had joined us—sipped our cappuccino in the little café, his demeanour changed. 'I think of Berenson not only as a charlatan,' he said without rancour, 'but also as a man, a *Jewish* man, he is human like the rest of us—like I am—and I would not like him to go—to go'—he snapped his fingers irritably, trying to conjure the right word—'I have it! I would not like him to be *unwarned*.'

'Unwarned of what?'

He lowered his voice as he looked across the table at Kurt and me. 'In Germany more and more Jews are seeking shelter from the persecution and'—his voice fell to a whisper—'and soon it will happen here, for Il Duce is a great puppet of Hitler and we are seeing it take place, now that the new anti-Jewish laws have been passed in Italy, forbidding Jewish music and books, and even dressmakers and artists.'

'I don't think BB's a practising Jew.'

Umberto spread his hands. 'Of no matter the *quantity*; it is the quality of the Jewishness that they find out, and even if'—his fingers indicated a tiny amount—'Pouf! So small as not to notice, they still find out and persecute.'

'I think your friend is maybe a dangerous man,' said Kurt suddenly. His Nazi Youth years were revealing their teaching, though he was trying hard to remain polite.

'No, no.' Umberto shook his head sadly. 'I think

153

it is this Signor Hitler who is the dangerous man; and I think Signor Berenson should be advised to make his way to a safer place while there is still time.'

★ ★ ★

I did not repeat Umberto's warning to BB. After all, Umberto was a bit of a crank, and anyway, two days later, after a lazy day in the country with Fiamma, Kurt and I set off on the leisurely and uncomplicated journey. The train from Florence seemed to be invested with a somewhat pompous dignity of its own. Not being an express it made a great to-do about huffing and puffing at level crossings, as if determined to assert its authority over the impatient motorists who were reluctantly obeying the law and demanding that they give way to the 'ferrovia'. At Arezzo we passed through what seemed to be countless miles of dazzling wild flowers.

'Very beautiful,' murmured Kurt, peering from the window. I was so overcome by the brilliance of the scene on both sides of the railway that, in my mind's eye, I was reducing it to the dimensions of a canvas, trying to imagine how I would cope with translating it into terms of palette colours. How would Dufy have done it? Or Monet? I could hear Umberto being cross as he wagged his finger at me—'Do not follow other people's minds, boy. Your imagination is your own priceless gift. Use it.' All very well, but the impact of such a scene as that riot of colour aroused emotions that could scarcely be controlled. I gazed silently away from the window thinking that only in retrospect could I

154

arrange my own interpretation of such profusion.

In Rome we did not stay long, thinking, I suppose, that the mighty city had to be seen properly or not at all. A quick and unsatisfactory visit to the Colosseum—which, as Kurt said, needed a week on its own even to accept its immensity—and we were on our way south again, through countryside that was often of dazzling beauty, particularly where it stretched down to the distant Pontine Marshes.

'One of Mussolini's engineering triumphs,' Kurt reminded me, 'was to recover that land from the inundations of the sea.' But I was more concerned with such pastoral scenes as the winding course of the River Liri as we clattered our way towards our destination, this time in one of the new esprèsso trains that were another of the Duce's triumphs.

Umberto had warned me that the way up to the monastery was too difficult to be popular with tourists even though a funicular linked town and abbey; and indeed its great grey pile above the town dominated Monte Cassino with the forbidding air of a castle defending a realm—which indeed it had been since the sixth century when St Benedict founded it. But we hired a car, chugging up the stony road that zigzagged through arid scrubland dotted with patches of yellow gorse and moss-covered boulders.

'An invincible defence,' Kurt muttered as we bumped our way up.

'Oh, I don't know,' I said, 'a neatly aimed bomb would demolish even those walls.'

'I was thinking,' Kurt replied scornfully, 'of the terrain rather than of the building itself. Defenders

155

on a hill always have the advantage over the attackers.'

The monastery was impressive. Its massive walls and towers were bastions against even the biggest guns, I thought. But it was the frescos I sought; and the lay brother who had been appointed as guide smiled secretively as he conducted us to the seminary. As Umberto had said, many of them were extremely 'earthy', showing intertwined figures, rebuses that were undeniably phallic, and scenes of jollification that must have owed a great deal to fertility rites in a world even more ancient than that of St Benedict.

I spent three or four hours examining the texture of the surfaces and noting down details that I knew BB would want, such as the depth of the incising lines that had sketched out the designs when the plaster was still wet, and the tone values of the tempera effect used for the figures' robes. There was also a picture gallery, the catalogue raisonné of which, I noted, had been prepared by BB himself. But in contrast to the boldness of the frescoes the pictures were of a strictly religious nature. And I was deeply affected by the tranquillity of the church with its immense bronze doorway and mosaics overlaid with the patina imparted by centuries of monkish feet. And as we sat peacefully in the hard stalls, monks entered chanting plainsong, moving like eerie ghosts through the moted beams of sunlight patchily illuminating the paved way linking the Stations of the Cross.

Time seemed to stand still; but as we strode into the sunlight I felt an unaccountable shiver in my bones. I have no idea why. I shrugged it away, and when Kurt raised his eyebrows I walked quickly through the archway of the basilica and looked back from the deep shadows to see him standing there in the sunlight, his head in a golden nimbus. But the chill did not altogether leave me until we left the precincts of the monastery.

*   *   *

Back in Settignano I spent three hours composing what I hoped would be a lucid account, with many bracketed references to higher authority, of my 'findings' at Cassino, and though BB was not one to bestow praise lightly he must have been highly pleased for, in a matter of weeks, I saw my modest effort at writing Renaissance history printed word for word in London's *Review of the Arts*—under BB's name!

But he did show me the article and then explained, 'You gave me exactly what I wanted. So I didn't see the point of changing anything. And now a surprise: we have a distinguished visitor coming to see us for a few days. None other than Lord Duveen.'

Duveen! I tingled with excitement for I knew the name, of course, as BB had mentioned him more than once and there was also the fact that he and BB were supposed to have quarrelled. You could not ignore Duveen's name, his power, his ability as an art dealer and—how can I put it?—his rather secret association with Berenson which even gave rise to whispered suggestions that from time to time they connived at 'arranging' sales.

It had worked in a very simple way, so the rumours ran. BB had by now become so highly respected that any Renaissance painting that bore a certificate of authenticity by BB was virtually a

157

guarantee that it could not possibly be a fake. The words 'Certified by BB' were the international art world's equivalent of a British hallmark.

Duveen had started life as a salesman and had gravitated to the art world. A dapper man with a neat moustache, he could charm anyone into believing anything. More than that, this Englishman's biggest clients had included all the most famous American art collectors—multi-millionaires like Pierpont Morgan, Rockefeller, Frick and Bache were totally uninterested in the sordid matter of money. All they wanted was art. Genuine art.

So BB provided the guarantees. But, the critics whispered, supposing BB wasn't quite sure? A painting might *look* genuine, but if there was *any* doubt in the art world, it should be stated openly. Unless, that is, Duveen, talking in millions of dollars, was never as fastidious about a painting's authenticity. But, as part of my job at I Tatti I regularly had to check on financial details and had to keep certain records, and so I had to admit (to myself anyway) that there were discrepancies in the accounting that I could never understand, and not until many many years later did I learn that BB's certificates had earned him over thirty million dollars.

I found Duveen delightful, a little too suave, yes, and looking far from well, but still he oozed charm and when BB was called away from time to time Duveen asked me to show him the formal garden behind the limonaia, treating me as an equal fellow artist. Indeed, when I told him that I painted, he treated me as a man of superior talents, saying, 'You are to be envied, Mr Johns. The world

158

consists of men who do and those who wish they could.'

Pausing to light a cigar, he asked, 'What does BB think of your paintings?'

I hesitated before replying, 'He hasn't seen them, sir. You know how he feels about the Renaissance period, and you know too, sir, that he doesn't approve of modern art.'

'I do know.' Duveen pulled on his cigar before chuckling, 'I myself am very partial to Picasso and Derain and Vlaminck, but I never discuss them in front of BB. It only makes him irritable. I must see your paintings one day.'

And he did. I am not sure how it happened, but I suppose it was because Duveen seemed to be such a nice man—and so kind that he allowed people to talk to him. That, perhaps, was the secret of his charm. That and the inner knowledge that you must *never* pass up the chance of making a possible future contact. Had I invented a new car, he would hardly have given me a second thought, but art! To him it was a magnet so that when he was leaving and BB, who still had a touch of flu and was looking frail, suggested that I take 'His Lordship' to his car on the main road, I gladly acceded and without thinking said, 'You never saw my paintings, Lord Duveen.'

'No more I did. Is your studio far?'

'No, sir!' I pointed to our tiny house opposite the Villa Magari.

'Let's go. It'll only take a few minutes.'

We walked up the road, lined with wild flowers and huge banks of wild roses in the thorn bushes, and to me scented with happiness and excitement. I

159

said apologetically, 'It's a very small place, I'm afraid.'

'Let us see, Mr Johns.'

I had finished four nudes by now, including the yellow one of Lella. First I showed him 'The Blue Nude', still standing on the piano (unless Kurt was practising).

Duveen took a long look at it, stood back behind the sofa to see it better, and then said softly, 'It shows magnificent promise, my boy. No, it *is* magnificent. Inspired!'

I almost blushed.

'It was inspired?'

I nodded.

'By a girl?'

I nodded again.

'I thought so. It has *great* merit, Mr Johns—may I call you Ham, like BB does?'

'Thank you, sir.' I found my voice quite husky.

'I could sell this easily tomorrow,' said Duveen decisively. 'Easily. Not for a fortune, but for enough. Where are the others?'

I do not want to give a blow-by-blow account of his visit. Suffice it to say that he seemed to be really impressed.

'Very exciting indeed,' he said. 'Now, Ham, I want to be your dealer in London. Work very hard now, and if these Germans allow us to live in peace, I want you to try to prepare for an exhibition. Work harder than you've ever done before. Produce twelve big nudes, all with the strange exotic backgrounds, and I will arrange a show for you. Yes, that's a promise. I'm very excited, Ham. Very.'

With that, he jumped into his car, the chauffeur revved up the engine, and he was gone.

Leaving me with a glowing sense of achievement.

'I've done it!' I cried to myself. 'I've bloody well done it!'

*   *   *

A few weeks later, sadly, Duveen was dead—July 1939. But before that I had sent colour photos of my nudes and had received ecstatic promises from one of his assistants, together with another letter from the gallery assuring me that they still expected to show my paintings when I had sufficient for an exhibition.

I showed the letter to Steve.

'Great!' he cried. 'I always knew you'd make it. And now *I've* got big news.'

It was the middle of 1939, with the 'victory' of the Munich crisis in 1938 almost forgotten—and the signs of imminent war had become more and more ominous. With the conquest of Abyssinia complete, Mussolini had looked inwards, so to speak. He had already signed a far-reaching act of legislation dealing with the oppression of the Jews.

Libya had long been a part of Italy. And just before 1938 turned into 1939 Italian deputies were again claiming, 'Nice, Tunis and Corsica!', the old chant. And the Italian Chamber of Deputies held its last session, to be replaced by the Chamber of Fascisti and corporations. A few days later the new Chamber denounced the 'bon voisinage' treaty Mussolini had concluded with France and Britain in 1938, thinking that friendly relations with them might conceal his intentions. All this looked grim, but the severest blow came when Mussolini launched a carefully prepared 'blitz' (before that

161

word had entered the European language) on neighbouring Albania, invading with such ferocity that he swallowed the country in a matter of days and King Victor Emmanuel III accepted the crown of Albania barely ten days later in April 1939, to be followed the following month with a ten-year alliance between Germany and Italy.

And it was this, the threat of a war that could engulf all Europe, which more than anything else made Steve Price cry out, 'I've got big news.' He asked the two of us to dinner at Celestino's—'My treat,' he said with a lordly air. 'Special reason!'

'What is it?' Kurt and I both cried at the same time. He had yelled to us from his room, and in a way I hardly heard what he was saying because there he had put up 'The Yellow Nude' on the wall directly in front of the bed and its golden glow, growing better and better each time I looked at it, almost stunned me.

'Still like it?' He followed my eyes as he came in from the bathroom.

'Yes, I do,' I admitted, adding with a grin, 'I wish I could afford to buy it!'

'Well, it's mine now,' Steve chuckled. 'Sorry pal, but that's the way the cookie crumbles. Come on, let's make for Celestino.'

We arrived in the Piazza Santa Felicità in a few minutes, a trolley-bus arrived at the bridge just as we did, and, once in Celestino's, Kurt, sounding almost impatient, asked, 'Well, what's all the big mystery?'

'Ah, yes, the mystery!' Steve spread out his arms as though about to make a speech. He loved dramatising speeches or events for effect. 'Gentlemen, I thought we ought to have a dinner

162

because of a special decision I've made.' He paused for effect and then announced, 'The truth is—I've decided to leave Italy.'

'You're joking!' I blurted out.

'Why?' asked Kurt.

'How? You're deserting us!'

'When?'

I must say the sudden announcement gave me a queer feeling of sickness in the pit of my stomach. Steve was the fun man of our party. How would I fare only with the more serious Kurt, and at a time of rising tension between Britain and Germany? Would this disprove the old saying that two's company, three's none? Before the flash of thought really had time to register, I cried, 'Give us a break! Tell us why you're leaving.'

Steve took a gulp of his Italian 'champagne' and I had a definite sense that he was not telling us the whole story. He was keeping something back.

'I'm afraid,' he said finally, 'afraid of the war that's going to come soon.'

'Come off it,' I snorted, slightly annoyed. 'You're an American. Did you forget that Roosevelt has always been telling us that in no circumstances will America be dragged in again to save Europe?'

'I'm not afraid for *myself*.' Steve gave a pseudo-innocent look at the ceiling, just as the waiter leaned over and murmured, 'Another bottle, sir?'

Steve nodded.

'Then for whom?' I asked. 'Stop talking in bloody riddles,' while Kurt actually started to scowl.

'Oh Christ! I forgot to tell you,' Steve grinned, 'I'm getting married!'

163

'You're *what*? You phoney! I distinctly remember you telling me that marriage ruined love!' I cried. In my excitement I half stood up, my knees knocking the table, upsetting two of the three glasses of wine, staining the tablecloth with bubbles.

'Don't worry, sir.' The waiter rushed up. 'Non si preoccupi.' Deftly he took the glasses, then the tablecloth, and spread out a new one.

'Lella?' I asked.

'Of course. A summer wedding—the last week in August.'

'Well, I'll be damned. And how long have you known? Why didn't you tell us? Has Lella told her sisters? Is she going to America?'

The questions poured out. Yes, the Principessa did know. She had approved. No, the girls would know by tonight. When we had sorted out some of the details of his replies, and started to eat our first course of mushrooms, Steve sobered up a bit—not that he was really *drunk*, only drunk with suppressed excitement—and said simply, 'You're right, Ham, I never wanted to get married, not then. But this bloody world is changing. And I don't see any way that Europe's two biggest shits—Hitler and Mussolini—won't become involved.' Kurt started scowling again. 'And if Italy gets into the war, what's going to happen to us? Okay, I ought to remain neutral, but we all know that there's no guarantee of neutrality anywhere, and I don't want to have to go and drop bombs on Lella. An enemy! Jeez, Kurt, you're getting Europe into the shit.'

'It's not *me*,' cried Kurt angrily.

'Well, your buddy,' replied Steve, good-

164

humouredly. 'So we talked it all over and decided to make Lella a beautiful, young American citizen.'

'Are we involved?'

'You sure are. You two guys are both going to be my ushers. Not that I'll have many guests.'

'Ushers?' I must have sounded surprised, for I asked, 'Is it going to be a formal affair?'

'Well, pretty formal. At the cathedral in Florence. But strictly family and close friends. Then a reception at the Grand Hotel, followed by an evening party at Magari. But Lella and I'll have gone by then. We're sailing that night from Genoa on the *Conte Verdi*.'

'Well, I'll be damned!' I cried.

'Never mind the damnation,' cried Steve cheerfully, 'what are you two guys going to give us as presents?'

CHAPTER ELEVEN

Steve and Lella were duly married in the last week of August and it was quite a wedding, though it turned out to be impossible to hold it in the Cathedral. Like St Paul's and Westminster Abbey in London it was reserved, so far as weddings were concerned, for the highest in the land. Papal dispenation was required. And though Georgio Caeseri was a Prince, Steve certainly was not and there would have been endless applications and rebuffs, with priests and higher church dignitaries intervening, before approval could be got from the Vatican—if at all. Certainly not in the time Steve and Lella had available. So it was arranged in the lovely fifteenth-century parish church of the Assunta. And if it was not exactly a cathedral the ceremony was just as grand. The Principessa had seen to that. But though the day was filled with the sun and joy of two people in love, it ended in tragedy and disaster for Fiamma and myself.

I was the best man. Steve not only insisted, but actually gave me the ring to keep several days before the wedding—he was afraid of losing the thin band of faceted platinum with 'Stephen/ Raefella 1939' engraved in tiny letters on the inside.

'Very smart,' I said. 'I'll *try* not to lose it.'

He looked suddenly frightened, but then realised that I was joking. 'I've had enough hassle fixing the music,' he said. 'That'd be the pits.'

'Not to worry,' I promised with a smile. 'What's the problem with the music?'

'It's the goddam ban on Jewish composers. Mendelssohn's *Wedding March* is out. So it's gotta be Wagner and the good old Bridal March from *Lohengrin*; that or something so obscure nobody knows it. I don't like it but I guess I had to settle for it. Lella's furious, so's the Prince. Says it's interfering with personal liberty. He sure is right.'

There were difficulties over Lella's dress too. Fiamma told me it had been designed by Schiaparelli but there had been trouble getting the oyster satin and Brussels lace for it—again because of Jewish suppliers. But someone had slipped a 'dono' to the right man in the offices of the Secret Police, and in the end everything went smoothly.

I kept out of the wedding preparations as far as possible, but BB took me once (before the ceremony) to the Cathedral of Santa Maria del Fiore where, at that time, we thought the wedding was to

166

be held, to show me the architectural merits and Renaissance features of the cathedral.

'A wedding is every day,' he said rather pompously, 'but Brunelleschi's dome is for ever. And where can you match the beauty of the campanile, the red, green, and white marble contrasting with the black in the baptistery? Or the treasures within—sculptures, mosaics, frescos, bronze doors which, as Michelangelo put it, are "worthy to serve as the gates of paradise"? And while you are young,' he added wistfully, 'you should climb those four hundred and sixty-four steps to the top of the cupola for the most wonderful view in the world.'

*   *   *

Steve's aunt had come over from New York for the wedding and was worried about the international situation. 'Just as well Steve and his bride are coming back,' she said to me. 'My husband says there's trouble ahead in Europe, that's for sure.'

Apprehensions, however, were all cast away on the day. The church resounded with the organ and voices of the choir. There had been a nuptial mass and Communion the previous day, and the sombre interior of the Assunta was still scented with incense and fragrant orange blossom. As I waited at the altar beside Steve—both of us in hired morning dress with grey stocks at our throats and grey spats over our polished shoes—I was unable to turn round and see Lella approach down the aisle on the Prince's arm, but when she arrived at Steve's side, I gasped, she was so dazzingly beautiful in her ivory dress with its heavy lace veil screening her face and her two sisters elegantly spreading the short train of her dress across the purple carpet.

The bishop and his assistant in their gorgeous vestments were illuminated by hundreds of candles in sconces and the sweet-scented smoke from the acolytes' censers rose into the nave to soften with haze the angles of the Gothic structure.

As a compliment to Fiamma and me, Steve had engaged one of the boy sopranos to sing a short aria from Respighi's *La Fiamma* and, as the organist and choir made joyful sounds with the anthem, passers-by and tourists and crowded into the church. Steve was really nervous. I could feel his fingers tremble as I handed him the ring, but he managed to slide it on Lella's finger while with her right hand she turned back the veil to reveal her sparkling eyes—sparkling with happiness of course, especially after the ceremony was over, and we made our way to the Grand Hotel for the reception, to be followed by the evening party at the Villa Magari after Steve and Lella had left for Genoa to catch the boat.

The speeches were short and to the point if not especially witty, and the champagne flowed, as Steve's aunt put it, 'Like there was no tomorrow'. White-gloved waiters offered silver salvers of Parma ham and other cocktail snacks, moving among the guests, while the Prince and Principessa, together with the bride and groom, remained receiving congratulations for a full hour before Lella went off with Fiamma and her mother to the Villa Magari to prepare for her honeymoon journey, while Steve and I were driven to our own house opposite to pack. The Prince, together with Roz and Kurt, stayed on at the Grand enjoying themselves.

As Fiamma was about to leave, she suddenly darted across to Steve and me and clutched my hand. Her eyes shone with tears.

'There's something about a wedding—' she began, then buried her face on my shoulder.

'There is indeed,' I said, trying not to let her sentiment affect me. 'A day to remember. See you this evening.'

*　　　*　　　*

In the car, Steve turned to me and said, 'I'm tuckered out, Ham. Absolutely shattered,' adding with a grin, 'This is definitely the last time I'll ever get married. The strain's too great!'

'It'd better be!' I laughed back.

'I know.'

We were standing alone—he had recovered now—and he said, 'We've got to catch the train from Florence to Genoa at seven o'clock and board the *Conte Verde* before midnight. Thanks for coming along to help finish my packing. We won't be seeing you for a long time after today. Anyway, need you for a special job!'

Steve always had a habit of leaving out the pronouns at the start of a sentence.

'Such as?'

'I'll show you. It's "The Yellow Nude". I'm taking that States-side. Got to be carefully packed.'

As we walked in the front door Steve said, 'Gonna miss you guys. But I gotta hunch you'll be on your way to the UK before long—to become a soldier.' He paused and added, 'And what's going to happen to you and Fiamma if there is a war?' A friendly finger poked at my chest. 'You'll have to marry the right girl, Ham—give her English nationality. Then you'll find out what a strain the whole business of getting married is.'

'I can face it,' I said, laughing. Then I went on, 'You may be right. Everything points to war. And if it's to be, well, I suppose I'd have to join up. I'm in the Territorial Army—a sort of reserve—anyway. I'm going to miss *you*, Steve,' I said. 'My first Patron. You're the one who gave me just the right amount of encouragement—financial and spiritual. Of course I was delighted with "The Blue Nude", but that was more personal.'

It was true. The passage of time—and the money in my pocket—had encouraged me to paint more nudes with professional models, and I had 'invented' my own way of producing bizarre background effects. It took time, but it was worth it. Sometimes, helped by Umberto, sometimes alone, I would search out unlikely but appealing spots and start to sketch them in detail. They had to offer something of the unusual, but when I found such a place I roughed out the background, then superimposed a nude model on the rough. Such a place was Le Mure, a wonderful garden restaurant near the town hall in Lucca which not only had attractive open-air tables, shaded by trees, always filled with grateful clients, but a large circular table of hors d'oeuvres, the table built round an enormous old tree. Round this, diners would circle picking out the tempting dishes they wanted to eat. I drew them. I painted one version roughly, for then later I drew in the model, a professional whom I could now afford with Steve's money. And the model was nude. I placed her choosing what to start the meal with, together with all the other diners

170

grouped round the tree. It was not exactly an original idea: Manet had used it in his 'Dejeuner sur l'herbe'; but my technique was completely different. And the effect was staggering. Others had to follow and they soon did.

'One day you'll be famous, and I'll have the first art bargain of my life—only, however much it will be worth one day, I'll never sell it. Not even if we're divorced!'

'Already?'

'Figure of speech. I guess we'll make a go of it. Hope so, anyway.'

Steve had already bought a roll of thick twine and corrugated paper in which he wanted me to help him to parcel 'The Yellow Nude'—quite a feat for, after all, the street scene was six feet long.

'Quite a picture,' sighed Steve. 'Now I've got to find a house with a room big enough to show it off.'

'I shall miss that,' I said with a laugh. 'Almost as much as you. We had a lot of fun in that small village. And now you're off across what they call the Big Pond. Oh dear! It's so sad. I don't suppose we'll ever meet again.'

'Don't be so bloody depressing!' said Steve. 'Of course we'll meet again. Probably in the most unlikely place.'

At that moment I heard voices at the garden door—we preferred to call it the garden door rather than the back door—and a pseudo-girlish voice trilled, 'Are you there? It's Lella and me.'

'Sounds like the Principessa!' Carrying on with his last-minute packing, Steve cried, 'Come on up,' adding teasingly, *Mother!!*'

We never gave it a second thought—why should we?—as I heard the sound of her footsteps as she

171

climbed the stairs and cried, 'I just thought I ought to see where Steve lives before he takes Lella away.'

'Right this way,' cried Steve. 'No secrets!' whispering to me, 'no longer, anyway.'

But there was one. I was just about to start putting the outsized sheets of paper on the floor and laying the canvas face up next to the bed when the Principessa saw it.

She screamed! That's the only word for it. She took one look at the uncanny naked likeness of Lella, flaunting her patch of hair in the shape of a heart.

'How vile!' she screamed. 'Who did this awful, terrible, filthy thing?' She made as though to stamp on it, as though to ruin it with her high heels.

'Donna Margarita!' I cried. 'Be careful, please!'

'Careful!' she railed. 'With this filth, with some so-called artist leering at my daughter, licking his lips as he paints this disgusting muck!'

'It isn't filthy, Mama,' cried Lella. 'It's beautiful!'

'It's disgusting,' shouted the Principessa. 'Wait till I find out who did it. I'll make sure he never paints another picture in Florence. I'll have him ...' she hesitated, breathless, searching for words. 'I'll have him kicked out of Florence.'

It seemed as though she railed and stormed unendingly, though I suppose it was only a matter of minutes before she stopped, looked at me almost with sudden loathing, and, as I listened in silence, spluttered, 'It wasn't—it couldn't have been—it wasn't *you*? You weren't the artist?'

My silence was far from golden. Silence was the clearest possible indication of guilt. Even a shake of the head would have been enough. An unspoken

172

lie. But I could not do it because, while she fumed with rage, I knew she was wrong. It was a fine picture.

She looked at me full in the face and said, '*You*, the son of a respected diplomat. I'm ashamed of you. I'm ashamed to know you, to have met you, a purveyor of filth.'

'Shut up, Mama!' cried Lella furiously. 'You're a fine one to talk—not even telling Roz who her father is!'

As Steve took Lella's arm and said, 'Hush, honey, that's enough,' the Principessa flushed scarlet and before anyone could do anything, she slapped Lella hard across the face.

'Come on!' shouted Steve. 'I've had enough of this. Let's get outa here. And to you, lady, Principessa or not, you ever do that again I'll kick you so hard up the arse you won't be able to crap for a week!'

And with a sneer he added, 'It just happens that this guy Ham has the makings of a great painter. You ask what Duveen, the art dealer said. And if you don't believe me, go take a look at his "Blue Nude" of Fiamma!'

The Principessa turned around, with a withering look at me, and shouted, 'So this isn't the first one, eh? I should have known. You used this as a trick to seduce my daughter. Where is this monstrosity?'

'Downstairs, on the piano!' I cried, defiantly. 'And I didn't seduce her. I want to marry her.'

'Over my dead body,' snorted the Principessa. 'Let me look at this new evidence of your filth.'

'It's going to go on exhibition,' shouted Steve, furious now as the Principessa clattered angrily down the stairs. 'With my picture, which I commissioned.' Whether the Principessa heard this or not, Steve added jeeringly. 'Might be fun if we exhibit first in Florence so that your family can see their daughters in toto.'

'Shut up,' I hissed. 'I'm already in the shit, why the hell did you have to tell the old girl about Fiamma?'

I heard the door bang below as the Principessa searched for 'The Blue Nude' and finally she must have seen it for I heard another scream of fury and a shout, 'Vile brute! Disgusting libertine!'

I clattered down, fearful in her rage she might try to hurl it from the piano and smash it, and sure enough she was about to smash the centre of the canvas across the top corner of a chair which would have torn it to shreds.

'Stop it!' I grabbed the canvas, and panting I shouted, 'You beast! I'm not going to let you smash it, my beautiful Fiamma! For Chrissake, calm down.' Trying to wrench the painting away from her, we almost fell.

'I'm going to marry her!'

'Marry her!' the Principessa gasped. 'Never, never, never. My daughter is never going to marry a pig like you!'

'You're a fool,' I cried, finally wrenching the painting unharmed from her grasp—not easy, considering its size. She had managed to scratch one corner, but that I could touch up.

'Now get out!' It was my turn to shout now. 'You're making a stupid row out of an attempt at pure art. The nude is the highest form of art. You're making a fool of yourself.'

She gave me a malevolent look—coming from a woman I had first thought of as thin, but who now

174

to my eyes seemed scrawny and nasty—and then she hissed, the only way to describe the low-pitched hate-filled words, 'You'll never, never marry my daughter. You're forbidden to enter the house. I'm going to take her away as soon as I can. You'll never see her again. Never!'

Somehow—reaction perhaps with high feelings and the reckless words we had used—the ultimate possibility had never entered my head: that this old harridan, who thought I was a filthy brute, was now threatening to break up our love for ever.

'That's impossible!' I shouted. 'You can't do that. I won't let you.'

'And how, pray, will you stop me?' Her shouting had given way to the icy scorn of a mother whose daughter had been wronged.

'We'll run away!' I threatened.

'With what?'

She waited for no answer, just gave me a last, withering look and said as she left, 'As far as Lella is concerned, what's done can't be undone. She's out of my life. They'll have gone. But you can't come back, you don't come to the party tonight. And Fiamma and Roz—I'm going to make sure they don't—' I did not hear her finish the sentence, for she banged the door and stalked out. Nor did she hear my furious last words, 'You're sure it's not too late, you old bag!'

★　　　★　　　★

The bride and groom would soon be on their way to Genoa, but Kurt and I had been invited on an official card to the post-wedding reception being given by the Prince and his wife at the Villa Magari.

The invitation had, it seemed, been rescinded. But I still could not believe that the outraged. Principessa really meant to separate Fiamma and myself. Apart from anything else, surely the Prince—who had behaved so understandingly over Steve's forgotten espadrilles—would sort things out. Especially when I told him that Lord Duveen had given me a virtual promise of an exhibition in London which his gallery had confirmed, and that I already had four pictures to start the collection, plus 'The Yellow Nude' which I would ask Steve to lend to the exhibition. I also had enough money to be able to get married now. Surely the wedding would blot out the Principessa's sense of anger!

First of all though, I must see Fiamma. But how? I did not dare to walk boldly to the Villa Magari and demand to come in. In fact I doubted if Enrico would let me in. Still, though I could not go to the evening reception, I had to try to go earlier. I had no idea where Kurt and Roz were.

They were probably resting after the wedding celebrations. The evening party was scheduled for nine o'clock. At seven o'clock, dressed in slacks and an open-necked shirt, I tentatively approached the locked gates and rang the bell.

My apprehensions were well founded. When Enrico shuffled out of the porter's lodge, he took one look at me, his face seemed to freeze with fear, even at the prospect of the Principessa's rage, and he cried, 'No, no, Signor. You cannot come in. It is forbidden by the Principessa.'

'I know, Enrico,' I pleaded, 'I understand. But your wife—she is here?'

'Lucietta—what do you want with her?' Suspicion mingled with genuine concern.

'She works in the house when there's a party like this.' I lowered my voice instinctively, though we were a long way from the house itself.

'And so?'

'Maybe she could get a message to Signorina Fiamma?'

'I don't know,' Enrico seemed doubtful, yet I knew he liked us and would help us if he could. 'One moment, I'll fetch my wife. She will speak to you. I do not want to know what she says in case the Principessa asks me.'

Lucietta was younger than her husband and a pleasant, well-built lady with grey hair done in a bun.

'Buona sera,' she started.

'Please. Lucietta,' I begged her. 'Help me if you can. I want to marry the Signorina but the Principessa won't let me in to see her. Can you get a message to her?'

Lucietta looked round fearfully, as though spies were hidden in the cypress trees or the shrubbery that edged the drive.

'It is not easy,' she faltered. 'My mistress—she has given Enrico very strict instructions not to let you or Mr Kurt in.'

'I know,' I was still whispering. 'But I *must* see Fiamma. There's nothing that says that she can't come to see *me*, is there?'

'I don't know, sir,' she hesitated. 'I suppose not.'

'Do this favour for me, Lucietta. I love the Signorina. Try and get her alone and ask her to come and see me for five minutes. You don't even need to ask Enrico to unlock the gates. We'll talk *through* the gates. I just want to talk to her and explain.'

She hesitated, hummed and hawed, the warm good-natured peasant woman vacillating between the emotions of a young boy in love and the duty to a stern patron of whom she was afraid. Finally love triumphed, the key to her agreement, I am sure, being the fact that the gates would not be unlocked—which was the limit of the orders the Principessa had issued.

'You're an angel, Lucietta,' I whispered, blowing her a kiss through the gates. 'Tell the Signorina Fiamma that I'll be at the gates in an hour—at eight o'clock, before the guests arrive.'

*   *   *

How long I had to wait! How long that miserable hour of anticipation stretched and yawned into what seemed like an infinity. Kurt had not returned. Almost as soon as I had come back from talking to Lucietta, Steve and Lella left by chauffeur-driven car for Florence on the first leg of their journey to catch the boat at Genoa. Of course there should have been a grand send-off from Magari, with all the traditional trimmings of rice, old shoes, confetti and rose petals. But as Steve said, 'It'd be phoney, Ham. We don't want to leave in an atmosphere of tension. Sooner just fade away.'

I shook his hand warmly and embraced Lella with genuine affection. 'Listen,' I said, 'there was an old music-hall comic my father used to talk about. He had a sort of pay-off line that went "Life ain't all you want, but it's all you 'ave, so 'ave it. Stick a feather in your 'at and be 'appy." Do that, both of you.'

'Darling Ham,' Lella said. Her eyes were misty.

They both got into the car.

'Keep fighting the old girl! Be seein' you, Buddy!' from Steve and a whisper from Lella. 'Don't worry about Mama. It'll all blow over,' and they were gone.

But would it all blow over? As I watched the honeymoon couple depart down the hill towards the city, I don't think I had ever felt so down, so low, so utterly dejected and dispirited. She was going to tear my beloved Fiamma away from me, separate us. She could not! But she would! I was thinking in a torment, as the minutes of the hour went ticking away with damnable slowness. If only I could see the Prince! Surely he would understand me, intervene. Meanwhile there was no way I could make contact with a living soul. That old Yorkshire bitch! I swore at her as I strode up and down the tiny living-room, put 'The Blue Nude' back on the piano from which the Principessa had wrenched it. I even wondered whether I should confess all to BB—after all, *he* could phone the Prince on my behalf. I was still simmering with pent-up rage and looking at the clock—not quite half an hour had gone—when the angry silence was shattered by the phone ringing.

It must be her! It *must* be. Hardly another soul knew our number. Almost tripping over the rug where it was frayed by the door leading to the hall—and with the only phone in our house—I reached the phone, stopped the stuttering bell and cried, 'Pronto! Johns here!'

A voice—no woman's voice this, but a man's voice—its usual resonance and strength diminished by distance, cried, 'Is that you, Ham?'

'Hello—who's that?'

'Your father. Goddammit, don't you recognise me?' Father was always irritated when speaking on the phone, though he spoke only rarely to me, but he shouted now, 'Ham, listen carefully. The balloon's going up. Can you hear me? Good. It'll be a week at the most. You *must* get the next train back to England.'

'What? I can only just—'

'You must, and you will. Listen, Ham, don't be a fool. Every day counts.'

'But Italy won't declare war,' I cried.

'Listen, Ham, Italy will declare war. Dammit man, I'm your father and I work on the inside. You *think*—I *know*. We'll be at war with Germany within a week. I know! I tell you. Now you get right back to England as fast as you can.'

'I can't. There's someone I must see.'

'A girl, no doubt?'

'Yes, Father, it is.'

'Well, forget her. She'll soon be an enemy alien in Italy. Now come on home—and now. It's too late tonight, but get the first available means of transport before you get yourself locked up and remember, for a year you were in the KOYLIs as a Reserve Territorial lieutenant. They'll be expecting you. So—it's not only necessary to come, it's your duty. And remember. I *know* what's going to happen, in my position.'

'But Chamberlain—'

'He's an ass. A waffler. He'll be out of a job within weeks or months. Sacked. He's hopeless. No time to talk any more. Get home right away.'

With that he hung up. No goodbyes, no discussions. Just 'orders'. True, I had trained with the Territorials until I went to the Slade, but surely

180

that did not bind me? He was a tough old bird, my father—and probably he was right. He certainly was in the know, in the Foreign Office. But war or no war—or rather *possible* war or no possible war—there was no way I was going to walk out on the most important love of my life, one that my future mother-in-law (if I was lucky) was doing her damnedest to wreck and ruin—and all because I had chosen Fiamma as a model for a painting which Duveen had described as 'brilliant'. How unfair!

Almost feverishly, I looked at my wrist-watch. Ten to eight. I must go to the gate. I must be in good time—in case. In case she could only sneak out a bit earlier than anticipated. It was such a warm balmy August evening—a perfect day for a wedding, I thought bitterly—that I did not even put on a jacket as I walked across the road to the gate, waiting in an agony of doubt.

Would she come? Had Lucietta been able to get a message to her? Perhaps the Principessa had locked her in her room to prevent what we were trying to do? No, surely not. But my doubts were intensified by Father's urgent phone call, virtually ordering me to get out of Italy as soon as I could. Was it true that we were on the edge of war? It was hard to believe, yet it was equally hard to disbelieve—for Father really did move in the highest councils of the land and even Steve's aunt from America believed it. All kinds of mad thoughts rushed through my brain—maybe we could at least run away—as far as France. Would that help? But if I *did* plan to escape, how the hell could I ever get Fiamma out of the prison in which her mother had incarcerated her?

No, it did, in theory anyway, look like a parting

of our ways, forced not only by her family, but by the fortunes—or misfortunes—of war between our countries. There was no way I could beat the savage force of circumstance. We would, I thought, have to wait: just wait until the war was over. But how long would that be? Who could tell? At least with the end of the war, a reconciliation between the Principessa and me could be much easier. Relief would supersede anger. Or else we would force a marriage. I don't know, but oh! How I loved Fiamma. Yet now both sides—even though one was far away in endangered England—both sides, both families, were in effect making it impossible for us to see each other, though for different reasons.

*   *   *

Ten minutes later—ten years later it seemed—a white fluttering dress appeared on the balcony and the young, lovely, forbidden apparition of Fiamma rushed down the drive, beautiful, oh so heavenly, with the light making her look so airy, framed in the forbidding looking cypress trees. With a gasp, she reached me as I pressed my face against the gates and cried, 'Beloved, oh darling heart, I'm so unhappy.'

We tried to kiss between the space of the intricate scroll work of the gates, but the iron was too thick. Even when we pouted our lips—until she put out her tongue and so did I and for a moment we had a kiss of a kind.

'I'm so unhappy,' she repeated the phrase, born of anguish, veiling unshed tears. I could get my arms through the holes in the iron and put them around her. 'I can't leave you,' she said.

'Listen, beloved,' I said urgently, conscious that at any moment she might be torn from me, 'we'll meet again—your mother—'

'You don't understand, darling,' she was almost wailing.

'The same thing's happened to me,' I cried. Briefly I told her what my father had said on the phone. 'Of course I can send him to hell, and if your mother lets me see you—dammit, I would, even if I do have to be interned later.'

'You mustn't, darling.'

'Maybe,' trying to force a smile, 'if I did, would you come to see me once a month?'

'Don't joke. Even *my* father says war's inevitable. But there's something'—there was a sudden twinge of anxiety in her voice—'Oh, darling,' she was starting to sob now, sounds that tore me in two.

'Don't, beloved,' I begged her. 'Please don't. Whatever happens we'll always love each other, even if we have to wait for a war to end. At our ages—we're young—do you think I couldn't wait? I will always wait.'

'You don't understand—'

'That your mother's taking you away? That my father has virtually *ordered* me to leave? I do understand, precious.' Aware that the minutes were ticking away, I was concerned only with trying to console her. If we could meet again so be it, I would fight to demand of the Prince the right to say a proper goodbye—and I felt in my bones that he would understand and agree. Especially if he knew that I was going to leave. But at that moment, with the guests due to arrive shortly, and the fear that Fiamma's absence might lead to more anger on her mother's part, all I could try and do was still her

183

fears, to promise that on the morrow—or the day after, of course I would wait another day—we would meet. But it did seem as though the war, if nothing else, would tear us apart.

'I know, beloved Ham,' she was crying softly, 'but Mother is taking us to Rome first thing in the morning. She says it's because war is imminent. But still—'

'It *is*, my darling Fiamma. And we are not the only couple in the world going to be separated by the war. Forget it!' I cried. 'We'll meet tomorrow—we'll make it up with your mother—somehow. And then we'll meet again when the war is over. And get married that very day. There, do you believe me?'

I still had my arms around her and of course I was facing the house. Out of the corner of one eye I caught a glimpse of Lucietta stumbling frantically across the drive towards us, beckoning, obviously trying to tell Fiamma to come back to the house. Her actions spelt trouble.

'Lucietta's calling you.' I unclasped my arm, and tried again in vain to kiss her properly.

'You don't understand—' she said again.

'You keep on saying that,' I laughed gently, 'don't worry, darling, I *do* understand. It may be sad, but we're going to get married as soon as the war is over. Nothing else matters. Now you must go. I'm going to try and see you tomorrow if I can get hold of the Prince.'

'But Ham, darling, beloved husband to be I hope, you don't—understand.'

'Understand?' I laughed again.

In a dull sort of voice she said, hands holding

184

mine tightly through the decorative gates, 'I've missed twice.'

'Missed? I don't follow. Missed what?'

And then, almost at the moment Lucietta reached her and cried, 'Signorina, the Principessa', Fiamma uttered the last words she said to me before the war came.

Half turning, she looked back at me, eyes brimming with tears and she cried with a sad smile, 'You don't know? It means, beloved, that I'm expecting your baby.'

★   ★   ★

My feelings can be imagined. They were half triumphant for the forthcoming birth of our child, half tragic for the separation already forced on us. For whatever happened, I would have to catch the train home the next day. My first years in Italy had come to their end.

But there was still what Kurt would have called, using the musical term, a coda. A dying fall, as it were, to a period that was a milestone in my life.

I returned to the house. It was silent. 'The Blue Nude' on the piano taunted me. I could not rest. I clattered about, pouring myself a grappa, lighting a cigarette, forgetting I had lit it and lighting another one. My hands were trembling as I poured another drink, but I knew that was not the answer and flung it in the sink. I thought of packing, but could not get down to it. Some time passed, I do not know how long, but it was still early, the brilliance of the summer day still lingered, as if reluctant to accept the dying fall of dusk. When at last I looked at my watch I saw that barely half an hour had passed, and it was not yet nine o'clock.

It would have been impossible to sleep, my mind was in such turmoil. In those days people did not think of tranquillising pills, if there were such things. What I needed was not the solitude of a silent house but the solitude of a noisy city.

Florence! I thought. When might I see it again?

Carrying my jacket looped to my finger over my shoulder I made for the bus stop. I paced restlessly, wishing the trolley-bus would come. Then I saw a figure approaching from the direction of Magari—hurrying as if, like me, anxious to escape.

'Roz!'

'Ham! Oh, Ham—I simply couldn't face it all after that horrid scene, so I left Kurt helping with the party . . . and escaped!' She shivered slightly. At the wedding, with the photographers' flashes going off and the champagne bubbling in the glasses, she had looked radiant in her rather special way. It is difficult to describe, for she was always the 'loner' among the three daughters of the Prince—or, in her case, of the Principessa. Unlike my darling Fiamma, who was like a bud unfolding in the warmth of love, and Lella who assumed something of a sophisticated dignity as the first-born, Roz always seemed to be holding something of herself back (except when she was inventing a mischievous sophistication of her own!). Now, though, as we waited for the No. 9 and she greeted me with a fluttering kiss on the cheek, there was an appealing look in her eyes, as if she sought comfort. The appeal was mutual, and there we were, both heading for Florence 'to get lost among the crowds', as she put it.

'Me too,' I said feelingly.

'Poor Ham! You must feel wretched. I can see

186

Mama's point of view in a way. She's really old-fashioned at heart though she sometimes pretends to be awfully modern and unconventional. But she should never have behaved like that.'

She can damn well be unconventional for real when she chooses, I thought maliciously, slinking off with some American film director when she wants to get her own back on the Prince; but it would have been unfair to speak my thoughts. I suspected that something more than the false gaiety of the party was troubling Roz.

'You feeling pretty low too?' I queried.

'Mm.' She nodded, her dark hair falling to conceal one cheek; but I could see the gleam of a tear. I sensed it would not be right to ask her straight out what was wrong. She would tell me in her own good time. I thought of telling her about Fiamma, but did not want to add to Roz's own worries, nor break Fiamma's confidence. So we were just good companions finding strength in each other's company. I gave her my hand as we alighted from the bus and we remained linked as we wandered the streets of Florence as if in a dream.

Of course the city was familiar to both of us—to Roz because she was born a walk away, to me because I had studied its buildings and pictures and sculptures, could have found my way blindfold to the Pazzi Chapel, the tomb of Leonardo Bruni, the library of San Marco, or sketched from memory the scene down the Arno, looking towards the Ponte Vecchio.

It was there we found ourselves, having walked hand in hand in silence through the bustling streets. The river was rosy in the glow of the setting sun, the bridge was haloed with a mist that smudged its

187

outline. The shops of goldsmiths and leatherworks stretched across its length like the shops on old London Bridge, and above them was the covered way linking two ducal palaces along which Grand Dukes used to wend their ways on secret errands—some of them as sinister as those of the Mafia and as mysterious as those of Roz.

'Look!' I pointed to the space that separated two shops in the middle of the bridge. 'The space makes a frame for the view the other side, like a picture within a picture.'

'It's almost like a look into the future.'

I said wryly, 'The present's got enough trouble for me.'

She managed a smile. 'Don't you know it's a sin to pity yourself? You couldn't have counted the penances I had to do at Fiesole convent school! Reverend Mother had her hands full with me, I can tell you!'

'And now Kurt has.'

I only meant it in a light-hearted way but I felt her shiver. So that was it. 'Doubts?' I asked.

She shook her head and again the curtain of hair fell forward. 'Oh no! Not *that*! We adore each other, we do, we do. It's just the thought of what they're doing to the Jewish people in Germany, and Kurt's—well, it's hard to explain, but he's *part* of it. And me—you know about me, my father, he was American—and Jewish.'

I nodded gravely. 'Of course. And you're frightened.'

She was suddenly angry. We stopped in our tracks. People passing looked at us, startled at her vehemence. 'Ham! You don't understand at all. It's not for me, it's for him, a Nazi ... I suppose. I

188

know what it's like in a Fascist country. You have to join a youth organisation—we did, Lella and Fiamma and I. If you don't you're marked, your family's marked. Kurt's told me all about it. I don't know about his parents. I met them at Bornholm, they're nice, his father's a sort of scientist. I wouldn't want to put them in any kind of danger, especially Kurt. And perhaps, in Germany, if the secret police, the Gestapo, knew about me it would be like a red rag to a bull.'

'Or a Blue Nude to a Principessa.'

It was a small joke, but she giggled, breaking the tension.

'Oh Ham, that lovely picture! What are you going to do with it if you have to ... go away?'

I shrugged. It scarcely seemed to matter any more.

'It must go somewhere safe, Ham. Out of Mama's reach. With Signor Umberto, perhaps?'

'Perhaps. Anyway, this threat of war—it'll all blow over.'

Such silly wishful-thinking!

We spent the rest of the evening almost as tourists, as if we had shaken off part of ourselves and were marvelling at the sights—the Dante Stone near the cathedral where the poet used to bring his stool and sit and meditate; Michelangelo's tomb; Orcagno's fresco 'The Triumph of Death' in Sante Croce; the wrought iron doors of the baptistery of the Campanile. The grim faces of 'The Blind and the Halt Soliciting the Attention of Death' in the fresco made Roz tremble, and when I thought of the Black Death stalking through the city so many centuries ago I shuddered too. The sacristan gave us a smile as he watched me put our contribution in the box and waved to us as we left Sante Croce.

'He thinks we're lovers,' I smiled.

Roz smiled too. I believe the thought amused her.

★   ★   ★

I waited up for Kurt that night. There would be too much to do in the morning for any but the most cursory of farewells—packing, deciding what to do with the painting, a hundred last-minute things. And I could not find it in my heart to leave him with a 'So long; see you sometime', as if we were casual acquaintances. Our friendship was keen and deep.

He was dejected, had gone through the motions of helping and being entertaining at the party—'But my heart was not in it, Ham. Nor Roz's. She found it painful and left.'

'I know.' I told him how Roz and I had teamed up, comforted each other, but nothing else.

'That was kind, Ham.' He sat down wearily, elbow on knee, chin in hand. There was a touch of stiffness in the changed tone of his voice as he said, 'I suppose this must be the parting of the ways for us.' It was German efficiency, as if cutting a cord.

I smiled faintly. 'Well, if you mean we're going to be on different sides if there's a war—yes. But that can't turn us into enemies, Kurt. Not *real* enemies.'

He looked at me directly, blue eyes frank. 'No. Of course you're right, Ham. Not *real* enemies. We never could be.'

And so we said our farewells.

'Auf Wiedersehen, Ham.'

'Arrivederci, Kurt.'

190

PART TWO

SECRET SERVICE, 1939–1940

CHAPTER TWELVE

I arrived back in England on that balmy Sunday in September when we declared war on Germany, distraught and unhappy. I remember, even now, the sunshine—someone playing tennis at the very moment when Chamberlain was uttering his fateful words committing Britain to war with Germany, and then the first sirens of the phoney war wailing into action.

Yet for me, the prospect of fighting—or whatever I planned to do—was nothing compared with the struggle to overcome the heartache of not being able to make any contact with Fiamma. I had tried to work out a dozen ways of doing so. I could not write. Censorship would be coming into force immediately, and though Italy was so far neutral, all out-going letters would be opened and read. How could I write and bare my innermost secrets to some ignorant moron who would probably only gloat over my words of love. And even if I did it would be intercepted.

As I sat in the rattling train from Dover to Victoria, I wondered for one moment if I might be able to phone Steve in America—two neutral countries who might be able to make contact. But then I realised he would not even have reached New York yet!

One thing I was determined upon. I wanted to stay in London while I decided on my future; obviously I would end up in the forces, but I was not sure in what branch.

You do not think very lucidly, if at all, when

your heart has been broken by a girl's vindictive mother; and when the pain is compounded by a feeling of guilt for the unexpected result of that forbidden love. A child on the way! My God, I sighed, yet not entirely a guilty sigh. A touch of curious pride was there too. I was not only a cad! I was about to become a father! But my sudden surge of excitement took a steep, swift, downwards plunge into misery—a father maybe, but a father without a legal wife; at least not until the bloody war was over.

As I looked out of the window at the passing scenery, fields where the crops had been harvested, a few leaves beginning to flutter in the wind, the fleeting glimpse of a station as our train passed through, I was reliving that last morning when I reached the gate of the Villa Magari at eight o'clock, only to find it empty, locked, and deserted, except for Enrico who, almost in tears, more dejected than I had ever seen him, said simply, 'They have gone. To Rome. The Principessa told me. They say it is the war. The Prince is driving. He also says it is the war coming.'

'But Florence would be safer than Rome.' I kicked a stone savagely. 'It's not that. Were both the girls in the car?'

'Si, si. The Prince he drives. He says this morning he will return in a few days but he leaves no address. Just says to guard the house till he is back. He doesn't smile. He is very stern. My heart is grieving for you, Signor Johns.'

And that was all. I even went to see Berenson, confessed all, but he was even more blankly astounded than I was. There was no option but for me to do as my father had suggested—go back to

England. I took a cab to the Borgo San Jacopo had left my precious 'Blue Nude' and the others with Umberto whose bitter comment was, 'Better not let the Germans see them if they come to Italy. They'll have them burnt as decadent trash.'

After that I set off with my modest luggage to catch the train, crossed France, then the Channel and when the train finally drew into Victoria, I was able to carry my suitcase after someone had directed me to the No.25 bus which took me to Hyde Park Corner, then a No.14 which went along the Fulham Road. Umberto had given me an address there.

'Do you remember meeting Mario Manenti?' he had asked when I went to say farewell to him. And I vaguely did—at one of Umberto's occasional wine and cheese parties—a big jovial man with a wide-brimmed hat and an attractive wife. Was she Russian? I could not remember.

Manenti was an artist but, more than that, a bit of an entrepreneur as well. He told me how he had built up what he called 'My Italian village' of over twenty studios in the Fulham Road, adding, 'And there'll always be one for you if you want one. Just ask the porter and use my password, "Firenze".'

I did. Manenti's group of studios (all with beds and baths) lay behind two grey, dull-looking houses between Stamford Bridge, Chelsea's football ground, and Walham Green Underground station, and the caretaker, a scraggy man with a built-in cigarette dangling from his lips, said when I came in and uttered the magic password, 'Mr Manenti is 'ere, sir. The last studio on the right.' He led me to it.

We recognised each other immediately.

'So you have come home—to fight, I suppose?'

I nodded.

'Well, I'm going—been advised to do so. But there is one studio to let—£3 per week furnished—a big living-room, a gallery along one side, a tiny bedroom, a tiny kitchen, and so on. Come and have a look at it.'

I took it on the spot, 'Studio H'. Surrounded by other studios, it overlooked a patch of lawn on which grew one large pear tree, now nearly leafless, and as I had plenty of money left out of Steve's payment for my painting, I had no hesitation in paying a month's rent in advance.

'If Italy and Britain'—he made an expressive Italian gesture—'I suppose you'll have to pay the rent to the custodian of enemy property. I don't know, I suppose they'll keep it for me, but whether we'll get anything I don't know.' With a sigh he added, 'And I don't *care*, I'm so depressed. I *love England*.'

'And I love Italy,' I laughed, but sadly.

Manenti could not have been more agreeable. As we walked into the garden with its pear tree, a woman and her daughter were just leaving an adjacent studio and he cried to me, 'Ah! Come è bella! May I introduce the lovely Ferida to your new neighbour. This is Mr Hamilton Johns, an artist, this is Ferida Forbes and her daughter Juanita,' and as we shook hands, my heart gave a wrench of sadness. The daughter—fifteen or sixteen, I suppose—was like a younger version of Fiamma: long and leggy, a beautiful face filled with laughter, who, with wide open eyes looked at me and asked, 'Are you really a painter?'

'I was,' I smiled back. 'But the war got in the way.'

I had the telephone number of my father's London flat at the bottom end of Curzon Street, and with all this war planning and panic I did not expect him to be up in Yorkshire for the weekend. I was right.

'Glad you got home, Ham.' He answered the phone himself in his usual, brisk way. 'Stirring times, eh, my boy?'

'Stirring and sad,' I muttered.

'Girl trouble? Forget it, man. You'll be in the KOYLIs soon. You've still got your Territorials uniform? They are waiting for you!'

When I reached the Curzon Street flat—what a long time since I had last seen it—my eyes lit on an old photo of Mother. She had died some years ago, but not before she had persuaded my father passionately to let me study art.

'Do you miss her a lot?' I asked, handling the photo in its silver frame.

'Less each year if the truth be told,' Father sighed. 'And I don't mean that in a nasty way. It's just that with the years memory tends to fade, perhaps because the load of work increases so much that I never have time to think—especially of the past.'

'Don't overdo it,' I said.

'I am,' Father admitted. 'I've never worked so hard in all my life. Never. Organising difficult projects should be the work of businessmen. I *am* a businessman at heart. A lot of politicians don't like businessmen. It's very tricky as you move up the political ladder. And it's going to get even worse.'

'But why you? Yes, I would like a Scotch, thank

197

you.' I saw him indicate the decanter, as though inviting me.

'It's simple. The government is filled with windbags. It needs a businessman to run a government department, and it's going to be even more necessary now we've got this damned war. That bloody man Hitler is no pushover. But Chamberlain certainly is.'

The one thing about my father, despite his occasional short temper, had always been a reasonable attitude to differences of opinion. If I wanted to do something different or unusual (like studying art) I was never afraid to tell him. Never. It was one of the foundations of a firm father-and-son relationship.

So when he asked me again about going to join the KOYLIs, I knew that as a part-time soldier who had left Yorkshire, I had no real obligation to go, other than to be with friends, and so I said, 'I'd rather not, Father.'

'Oh dear.' He sounded surprised but not upset. 'Why not?'

'Hard to explain.' I had picked up the habit from Steve of sometimes dropping my pronouns. 'I've been in Italy too long. I'm so much a part of it, I just couldn't face becoming—well, a Yorkshireman. I don't mean that as an insult.'

'I'm sure you don't. But there *is* a war on.'

'Do you think Italy will join in?'

'Eventually—absolutely.' He was emphatic. 'Bound to, if only to pick up a few spoils of war.'

As though changing the subject entirely he asked, 'Where are you staying?' Father was the sort of man who always assumed you would stay in a hotel if you were in London.

198

'I've taken a studio for a few months in the Fulham Road. Part of a kind of village built by an Italian.'

'For several months?'

'Well, even if I join up I'll have to have some base—where am I going to go when I'm on leave if I join the army?'

'If?' A slight note of asperity.

'Well, *when*,' I smiled. 'But I want to get into something where I'll be really useful—and which I might be able to enjoy.'

Drily my father said, 'Well, Ham, shooting people or dropping bombs on them is quite useful.'

'I mean in a different way.' I hesitated. I knew nothing about modern war. I had not read a single book on the subject. A few newspaper magazine articles but that was all. So it was difficult for me to explain that, since I was completely bilingual in Italian and if, as Father said, Italy would be at war with us, there *must* be some way in which I could put this specialised knowledge to good effect. And I did not mean just as an officer translating for possible Italian prisoners-of-war. Something more heroic than that. But what?

'Anything I can do to help?' asked Father. 'You seem worried.'

I tried to explain and he listened attentively.

'I think I know how you feel,' he said finally. 'You mean something along the lines of SIS?'

'Sorry—meaning what?' I had not the faintest idea what SIS stood for.

'Well, it's an offshoot of counter-intelligence,' my father explained, thinking as he spoke, then almost laughing as he added, 'You don't want to go back to Italy as a civilian spy, I take it?'

199

'Not much. Probably mean getting shot?'

'If you're caught. But let me think. There's no hurry about joining up. The most important thing I did was to get you home before they interned you. As to the future—I've been co-opted on to a committee planning ways in which we may be able to send secret help to Allied people overrun by the Germans.'

'I don't understand,' I confessed. 'You're not suggesting that the French will lose?'

'Of course not—though I do *not* have much faith in the Maginot Line. But think of the speed with which Mussolini took Albania. Or, if *we* go to war with Italy, the poor Abyssinians will become our allies, even if they're occupied. And with the Italians all over parts of North Africa, British East Africa will be threatened. What we're discussing at the moment is possible plans to have a force of fully trained men ready to help any subversive movement—anywhere. Rebels against oppressed governments. Men who won't recognise defeat if it comes. They would need help—caches of arms, leaders, experts at blowing up bridges and so on—generally disrupting life in conquered and occupied countries. After all, I don't imagine the Abyssinians are particularly fond of the Italians!'

'But all this is supposition, isn't it?'

'Of course. But I've been brought on to the committee because too many people think the whole thing is nonsense, whereas I believe that in war you've got to prepare for the unexpected—for *any* eventuality, even as you pray that such an eventuality will never happen. And by the way, you mentioned some girl in Italy?'

'I did.'

'Serious?' Father lit a cigarette and I wondered what to tell him, then suddenly I thought, what the hell, here I am old enough to prepare to fight for my country, I'm old enough to be able to tell the real truth of an agonising problem.

'Yes, I have got a girl. And she's expecting a baby.'

'Oh, my God!' groaned Father. 'I might have expected it.'

'And she's the daughter of an Italian Principessa who nearly married you!' I retorted.

'Don't talk nonsense.' Father was beginning to show signs of anger. 'I don't know any Italians outside the embassy.'

'Well,' I could not resist a smile, 'this is a Yorkshire girl. Came from Harrogate. Became the Principessa Caeseri. But I can't remember her maiden name. However, she's quite a woman. And why should you remember? It was a long, long time ago. But her father used to make jam.'

'Harrogate? Jam?' Father was thinking back, trying to fit a tiny fragment of the past into a whole picture of the present, the one missing piece of a jigsaw puzzle.

'No,' he said, then finally. 'Yes, I *do* remember! It was Monson, wasn't it? Monson certainly made jam. But if you've fallen in love with her daughter why didn't you marry the girl?'

'I'd like another drink,' I said. 'May I? It's a long story, ranging from art to love. And Father, you might be able to help if I tell you everything.'

I was thinking that Father might be able to use his influence to contact the British Embassy in Rome, and so I told him the whole story—including

201

my meeting with Duveen and his promise to sell my paintings.

And in the end, that is what happened—that and the fact that for the months of the war that never seemed to start, Italy remained happily neutral and Father's ominous fears seemed groundless.

At last, and after a lot of thought, and a few more whiskies for Father, he suggested, 'Maybe—for the time being anyway—it might be better for you to take a—well, a civilian job. I know we're recruiting a great many young fellows to pose as foreign businessmen and infiltrate into Europe. Dangerous work, y'know—more or less shot on sight if you're caught—that's if ever there is a war with such a thing as an occupied country. Well yes, Poland of course—but thank God you can't speak Polish.'

'But I *can* speak fluent Italian—' I was beginning to see the drift of his rather rambling discourse. 'Ah! If only I could go back to Italy.'

'You just left!' cried Father.

'You more or less ordered me to,' I retorted.

'Sorry, Ham.' He laughed awkwardly. 'So I did. But I'm just thinking aloud. I can't recall his name, but we have some chap in Rome working as a double agent and running a small bureau—oh yes, they're useful even in peacetime, believe me. I'll sound out the prospects and let you know. Meanwhile keep in touch.'

*　　*　　*

Apart from casual lunches and dinners with my father, I heard nothing of interest for some months—and still the war strangely never seemed to start. Everything was peaceful. The only reminder of the war was the rationing and the

202

blackout, the barrage balloons, more uniforms on the street, and a miserable shortage of whisky and cigarettes. I got a temporary job working in the Italian section of the BBC Overseas Service, basically consisting of making speedy translations of news items which arrived just before they had to go on air.

It was at times quite exciting—or would have been had there been any news worth reporting!

And then, late in March 1940, out of the blue, Father called.

'I'm speaking on a private line,' he said. 'Got to be careful. But go at eleven tomorrow to this building'—he gave the address of 54 Broadway in Westminster—'and ask for—the name is Pilbeam. He'll be waiting to see you. Now then, don't ask any questions. No, don't worry about the BBC—they've been told you won't be reporting for work tomorrow. Just go—and see. You may feel scared—but you might be excited.'

★   ★   ★

I arrived at the rendezvous five minutes early, tingling with excitement—and a touch of apprehension at the unknown future ahead of me, disguised for the moment behind the drab street scenes of Westminster. Father's instructions had seemed so vague, it looked like playing some kind of game—yet surely you did not play war games in wartime? And normally Father was not dramatic, rather the opposite in fact. But this smacked of a *Boys' Own Paper* serial. Secrecy. Code names. Unknown addresses. Mysterious instructions. What could it mean? And what did they propose to do with me? Already I was beginning to think that my temporary job at the BBC was not so bad after all!

Father had told me to make for the fourth floor when I reached 54 Broadway, with its sign proclaiming officially that it was the Passport Control Office.

'Don't be put off,' my father warned me. 'Other kinds of business are transacted there.'

Inside the rather scruffy waiting-room, people were waiting, and the three counter positions were filled with men and women applying for visas. But I spotted a door with an arrow pointing down a corridor. Roughly written in pencil beneath it was a sign: *Other Business*. Very cryptic, I thought; and that was not the last time I said that word to myself.

The corridor led to a kind of niche—hardly more than that—in which a big cheerful man with a handsome moustache sat at the desk. He raised a questioning eyebrow.

'I'm afraid if it's a visa you're after . . .'—a shrug of the heavy shoulders indicating that I would have to queue in the waiting-room like everybody else.

I shook my head impatiently. 'No. I don't want a visa. I have an appointment with—' I looked down at the name I had written on the card, '—with Mr Pilbeam.'

Immediately the man at the desk looked more interested. 'Ah! Actually *Miss* Pilbeam. Take the lift up to the fourth floor. She'll see you right. It'll be "C" you need to see.'

I must have looked mystified. Indeed I was.

'Don't worry, old boy. All will be revealed. Only'—he nodded in the direction of the passport office—'we've got to separate the sheep from the goats. Two sorts of business, eh?'

The big man smiled at me from his desk. I was later to learn that Morris (I never discovered whether it was a real name or a pseudonym; code names were as abundant as leaves on trees) topped the section of the SIS—Secret Intelligence Service—dealing with recruitment. A good many names that were to move from the shadows of secrecy into the limelight of fame: Graham Greene, Hugh Trevor-Roper, and Malcolm Muggeridge for instance, started their careers with SIS at his desk.

The lift clanked and creaked as if needing oil, and as it slowly passed each floor I glimpsed corridors that were even shabbier than the ground floor offices. At the fourth floor the cage groaned to a halt and I pulled back the lattice gates. Empty. I could see no sign of any Miss Pilbeam until she suddenly stood before me as if conjured up by a genie of the lamp—a rather formidable lady with greying hair plaited and coiled round her ears. Evidently she had heard the lift gates clang. She said in a low voice as if walls had ears, 'Mr Johns? Mr Hamilton Johns?'

'That's me,' I said, and she looked directly into my eyes as if searching for a sign of deception. Then she led me across a threadbare stretch of carpet and showed me a rickety chair standing outside a door above which a red electric bulb glowed fiercely.

'When the red light goes out and the green one comes on C will see you,' she said conspiratorially. I suppose I must have revealed my amusement for a look of reproach came into her eyes (they were blue, I noticed, and had a sparkle of merriment in them despite the reproachful look) and she said, as if to a wayward child, 'I would reserve any judgement that comes to your mind, Mr Johns, until you have conferred with C.' And with that she disappeared into what I supposed was her own office. Evidently C's secretary, I thought. It was one of the few accurate guesses I ever made about that extraordinary place, 54 Broadway.

When the green light came on I knocked hesitantly and responded to a cultured voice which said, 'Please enter.'

C was seated at a battered desk. I noticed it had a wedge of paper under one leg to keep it from wobbling. The few plain chairs might have come from a shabby kitchen. On a hatstand was perched a bowler hat. There were two green filing cabinets and on one wall a map of Europe with one corner curling. That was about all, except for the candlestick-type telephone on the desk and a wire basket containing files tied with red tape.

C himself might have been any city worker: dark, a rather shiny blue suit with a fountain pen in the top pocket of the waistcoat, white shirt, plain blue tie slightly frayed where it was knotted. He would have passed unnoticed in any crowd of commuters emerging from Victoria Station after a journey from the suburbs. [*I was later to discover that Stewart Menzies, C's real name, came from a wealthy aristocratic family. His mother was a Lady-in-Waiting to Queen Mary, he still held a commission as Colonel in the Scots Guards, and he had, in his present capacity as Chief of SIS, direct access to the King and the Prime Minister.*]

'You will be known as Painter,' he said tersely as he signalled me to take a chair. 'We don't use real names in the service, only initials or code names. I understand you're a painter by profession?'

206

'Well, I've hardly had a chance to estab—'

He waved my hesitation into thin air. 'Are you by chance also a philatelist?'

I could hardly avoid expressing my astonishment. 'Good Lord, no. I think I collected stamps when I was a schoolboy, but I certainly don't—'

Again a wave of dismissal. 'It's of little consequence. It might have helped a bit if you'd been able to use the jargon—"imperforate", "overprint", that sort of thing. But no matter. Your ignorance may even serve you better.'

I felt slightly irritable and could not resist saying, 'Look, sir, I'm afraid I haven't the slightest idea—'

'—what I'm talking about.' He completed the sentence for me—and he too seemed slightly irritable. 'Of course you haven't. Nor are you intended to. "Secret" means, if you recall, "covert", "concealed", "disguised", "confidential". This is a secret service, Painter. Need I say more? And it works both ways, you know. I know little more about you than you know what I'm aiming at. I know you're fluent in the Italian language and are not suspected by the Fascists and their kindred of being anything but a harmless artist.'

Standing up, as though to stretch, and still holding his pencil, he added, 'I also know you have a second-lieutenant's commission in the KOYLIs. I learned that from your father. I need to know no more at present.' Sitting down, he tapped with the pencil on the desk. 'You will discard your uniform for the time being and forget your rank. You have been seconded to me with War Office approval. And I intend to use you. That is clear?'

I frowned. 'Well, yes; clear enough in itself. But—'

He seemed amused. 'Your curiosity will serve you well, Painter. But for the moment, stifle it.' He wrote something on a scrap of paper. 'Memorise this address and destroy the paper. Then go there. You will find that it is a philatelic dealer who is well-known to other dealers and collectors. It's a small shop in a side street in the Parioli area of Rome, up near the Tiber. Say that your name is Painter and that you're enquiring about the Cape of Good Hope.'

'Rome!' I whispered to myself. 'Rome— Fiamma!'

C took an envelope from a drawer. 'Money and travel documents are here.' He held up a hand, anticipating my bewildered questions. 'That is all you need know, Painter.' He tapped again with the pencil on the desktop. 'I need hardly tell you that the less you know the less you are able to—er—reveal.' There was an implied hint there which I did not like one little bit.

And that was my induction into the SIS.

*　　*　　*

Bewildered almost beyond belief, I made my way to Joe Lyons' Corner House at the far end of Trafalgar Square, and ordered a pot of their excellent tea. A Nippy brought it quickly and then, pouring it at a lonely table in the corner of the large room, I just sat and puzzled over the past half-hour. C had uttered one additional note of warning, 'This packet containing your travel documents and so on—don't open it in a public place. Go home and examine the contents in private.'

But first I needed my non-ration tea. I *needed* it. I felt exhausted, drained, by my secret instructions. The packet of papers, still burning a hole in my pocket, still so secret I had no real idea of what they contained, apart from the cryptic—that word again!—reference to a meeting in Rome. Could I *really* be returning to Italy? It sounded too good to be true. A thousand and one questions plagued me.

I did not even bother to finish my second cup of tea, I was so anxious to open the packet. I would have taken a taxi home but I could not find one, so I queued until the next bus arrived, jumped on it and half an hour later I was back in Studio H, flopping into the one deep armchair that went with the studio flat. Excitedly I tore open the packet of papers.

There was a wad of money—French francs, Italian lire, a few English pounds. There was a passport. Neat, new, blue and shining gold, with the name John Painter, and there was my photo staring out on the third page—and attached to it, was a piece of paper with bold red letters on it, 'SIGN THIS IMMEDIATELY'. My occupation, I noticed, was 'Businessman', an all-embracing term that could cover anything, including the ever popular import-export dealer which I had believed was the standard trade of most people engaged in my line of work. There was a travel permit also bearing my photo, allowing me to leave the United Kingdom, a cross-Channel ticket, and railway tickets to take me across France and on to Italy. Destination: Rome.

In one way I was more excited at the prospect of returning to Italy—and to being reunited with Fiamma—than anything else, but another emotion niggled at my subconscious, disturbing the idyllic dream: a few words that C had uttered in a casual sort of way: 'Of course you must be extra careful because if anything goes wrong it would be very—er—uncomfortable for you, and we of course wouldn't be able to do anything to help you.'

It was not fear that battled with the exhilaration to search for Fiamma. It was more a burst of sudden loneliness, sitting there in Studio H, an uncomfortable awareness that all the warmth and friendship—to say nothing of love—I had experienced in Italy would have vanished when I returned, a different man. I was being thrown in at the deep end, and I would be utterly alone, save for some unknown stamp dealer! Otherwise, not a friend in the world. I would not even be myself.

Talk about a stranger in a strange land! I did not even have the faintest idea what I was to do, where I was to go—except to my rendezvous—and if as an amateur I bungled my assignment, well, *tant pis*, as they say in France. I imagined the worst: caught, tortured, finger-nails pulled out, cigarette burns, all inflicted by sadistic enemies like those in spy stories.

I fingered the passport again and again, not lovingly, but with the strange mixture of excitement and apprehension I had experienced before. But this mood passed, to be replaced with a new sense of excitement. This was adventure with a captial A, the sort of derring-do stuff of which dreams are made! And whatever else I did, even if I disobeyed instructions from my unknown boss, I would do everything in my power to find the girl of my heart.

I fortified a pretty poor lunch at a local restaurant on the Fulham Road with half a bottle of red wine, and that made me feel better, less tense, thinking less of what I did *not* know I would have to do, more of the girl I was determined to find. After lunch I went to a matinee showing of *Mr Deeds Goes to Town*, Frank Capra's comedy about a small-town hero who is not so simple as he seems. I found it quite amusing to identify with Gary Cooper's character.

The next day I lunched with Father at the Carlton Club in St James's and, after ordering two pink gins, he said briskly before uttering another word, 'Ham, I understand that you've been to see my friend. Before we do *anything* else, there's just one thing I must say: I don't want to hear any—repeat *any*—confidences. Your plans have nothing to do with me. Understood?'

'Understood,' I repeated meekly, and we had one of those dreary lunches in which all my pent-up excitements, doubts, thrills, remained pent-up and we hardly mentioned a war which, so far, seemed to consist only of false claims and rumours, as though each side was too afraid to fire the first shot.

CHAPTER THIRTEEN

Arriving in Rome at seven o'clock on a still quite wintry morning in April, after an agonising night tossing and turning on the train, was like being given a glass of champagne. Never has tiredness been tossed away so rapidly! Never mind my bleary eyes! One rub of my exhausted eyelids, one scratch at the stubble of beard, one jump from the dirty train steps on the the broad busy platform, and it was as though I had been transpirited to another world. I coined a phrase in my mind: 'Fiamma-world!'

I was back! Less than three hundred kilometres from Florence, my spiritual home. Somehow I would have to go there as soon as I had reported to my new masters.

Which reminded me: I had better go and start talking knowledgeably about philately. At least after breakfast. I had already discreetly tucked all my French and English money in different pockets, so now, my jacket pocket bulging with lire, I walked into the station buffet and ordered a cappuccino and was about to take a croissant when I spotted a dome-shaped *pannetone*, so I ordered a section of the currant-studded, light as air, semi-cake, dunked it into the coffee and ate breakfast.

I did not know where to stay, what to do. So I had first of all to meet my stamp-collecting contact. It took a bit of finding, but armed with a street map I finally reached a nondescript shop in a side street called ironically Via Amicale, flanked by an abandoned greengrocer's shop, the old vegetable crates visible through grimy windows, and a *tabaccheria*. In between was the philatelist, his name displayed in black letters on the glass panel of the door:

ANTONIO PRIVITERA
FILATELICO

He was almost gnome-like with a pink and smooth face like a child's; he had slightly bowed legs, tiny blue-veined hands in one of which he held

212

a jeweller's loupe, or magnifying-glass.

'Good morning.' His voice was aristocratic, it reminded me of Prince Caeseri's, and his well-tailored suit added to his bizarre appearance. But you could not make fun of his small size; he was much too dignified.

'My name is Painter,' I said, 'and I'm enquiring about the Cape of Good Hope.'

I felt stupid. How ridiculous they were, these Secret Service agents on whom presumably the safety of many lives depended. Behaving like schoolboys with code names and secret 'drops' for messages, and cloak-and-dagger activities lifted from the pages of *Sexton Blake*! How the enemy must be laughing up their sleeves! [*Klaus Fuchs, the spy who betrayed the secret of the atomic bomb to Russia, was once told to go the Lower East Side of New York carrying a tennis ball in his hand to meet a man wearing gloves and carrying a spare pair and a green book.*] I had not yet realised that the transparently simple is often the safest guise for the immensely complex.

'Really?' Antonio Privitera said. He might have been responding to some casual remark made at a cocktail party. I waited for the next step, marking time, as it were, by looking round the dimly-lit shop, with its one green-shaded lamp over the counter—a glass case filled with albums, magnifiers, packets of transparent envelopes, all reminding me of my youth.

One wall was stacked with shelves of solemnly titled books—one I noted was *On the Falsification of Postage Stamps*. There were displays of carded stamps, some mounted individually, others in bulging envelopes with transparent windows. Again

I was back to my schooldays when I would trot into the local 'corner shop' that sold everything from pins to potatoes and spend my pocket money on a packet of '500 of all countries'.

Finally he put the loupe on the counter and caressed his chin with his tiny hand. 'Your observation fits your name.' He laughed. 'The artist's vision, eh?' After a pause he added, 'The Cape of Good Hope, you said? Conspicuous by its shape, wouldn't you say?'

Bewildered, I tried to remember what the tip of southern Africa looked like. There was nothing remarkable about it. I suppose my bewilderment showed, for he laughed, then opened a heavy volume and showed me a picture of a triangular postage stamp.

'Oh,' I said, light dawning. 'You mean *triangular*, as compared with a square.'

He shrugged. 'Or oblong, or hexagonal.' He shut the book with a snap. 'And an excellent place to order a cup of cappuccino, I'm told.'

Really, I thought, this is lunatic—to go to South Africa for a cup of coffee. The man's barmy!

'You will go there,' he continued, 'with a copy of *Vita di Mussolini*, Volume One, under your left arm, the title displayed outwards. You will find a table for two—which at mid-morning should not be difficult—and await a companion, keeping the book tucked under your arm. You will find the place quite easily. It's quite close to the Palazzo Doria.'

I said sarcastically, 'I understood we were at the Cape of Good Hope.'

'My friend,' he replied, 'the ways of our—shall we say our "cameratismo"—are devious. It is never wise to let the ear know what the lip pronounces.

214

You take my meaning?'

Almost crossly I replied, 'No, I don't. It seems to me—'

He put a finger to his ear. 'The place is at the junction of three roads. It is called, naturally, "Trattoria Triangolo".'

I could not help laughing as I left the shop. All that melodrama to tell me the name of the rendezvous! But I could have saved my laughter. I had a great deal to learn.

★   ★   ★

I had been in the Trattoria Triangolo long enough to drink three cappuccinos before anything happened. The restaurant had only a few people in it and I was beginning to wonder whether I should order a meal when a big man (he looked to be in his sixties) hovered over me. He was brusque, rather untidy, with the sort of eyebrows that meet over the eyes, which some people say indicates bad temper.

'Painter!' he said with assumed joviality. 'Regrets for being late.' I saw that he was carrying a volume to match mine. 'Brought you vol two,' he boomed. 'Meaty—very! Required reading—huh?' He snapped his fingers. 'Waiter, bring me an espresso.' He grimaced at my cappuccino. 'Can't stand those things. Milksop stuff.'

If he is trying to draw attention to himself, I thought, he is doing well. I could not understand. He did not fit into the cloak-and -dagger introduction. But, as I said, I had much to learn. Including (I may mention now) the fact that my companion in the restaurant that morning was in fact C's Number Two in the service—a man with the given name of Claude, [*Colonel Claude Dansey, a Territorial Army officer who had served in the first world war and subsequently made a career of Intelligence.*] though I knew him only by his equally odd code name, Access.

The name, I discovered, was a play on the initials of his title. He was the ACSS—Assistant Chief of the Secret Service.

'You'll need a place to live,' he said. 'Here's the address.' I was provided with a rent-free room—or rather allocated one—and later that day discovered that it had been used by my predecessor before he had left for another destination. It was a large bed-sit over a café in the arty-crafty Via Margutta, central, not far from the fashionable Via Condotti, opposite the foot of the Spanish Steps. Later I discovered that the British Foreign Office, under suitable cover, actually owned the building, and rented my room to me for nothing. It was comfortable, the walls pale blue, and it contained all the things I needed—hanging cupboards, a small table for eating, a kitchenette, a divan bed. The only thing it lacked was a telephone.

'Your drop is the café on the ground floor,' explained Access. 'I will leave messages with Marco the barman—he also handles the espresso machine—or you'll leave messages with him and I'll arrange for them to be collected. Understood?' His attitude was, 'It'd better be!'

I had a number of meetings with Access after we established contact—usually in public places, parks or railway stations or cafés. He told me that there had been a disaster in November 1939 at Venlo.

'Where's that? I asked.

'On the German-Dutch border. Two officers of
216

the SIS, Major Stevens and Captain Best, [*Stevens and Best were kept in Gestapo jails until the end of the war.*] were kidnapped there,' explained Access. 'A German agent had promised to introduce them to an anti-Nazi German General. Best was carrying a list of British agents with him, and from this, other indiscretions, and from interrogation, the Germans were able to arrest many British agents in Europe. So you see,' he added drily, 'there's a need to replace them.'

'And I'm one of those to be thrown to the lions?'

He sneered. 'Wind up? If so I'll attend to the matter.' There was an implied threat in his tone.

'A joke,' I said. Another thing I had to learn was that one avoided making jokes with Access. He was too dedicated to action to appreciate subtleties.

'You're Oxford, aren't you?' he shot at me on one occasion.

'I was there briefly,' I told him. 'Why?'

'SIS is full of 'em,' he said. 'Lot of old women. Oxford and Cambridge dons. MAs, BAs, Professors. And queers at Cambridge.' He shrugged his large shoulders. 'Oh well; make the best of it.' His glance implied that he would turn me into a man yet, given the chance.

I cannot say I liked him. He always seemed to be threatening—an attitude of 'if you can't do it, we'll get someone else who can'. Slightly derisory, almost bullying, bossy, and at times a little vulgar. But apparently dedicated to his job.

I found out about his vulgarity when I decided to tell Access everything about Fiamma's disappearance. I wanted to try and find her, at least to tell her I wanted to marry her, and if I needed help, I had better be honest.

'Watch it,' he growled a warning, adding with a sneer, 'Remember—a standing prick knows no conscience.'

I coloured angrily and he saw it for he added, 'No offence meant. Just an old axiom. But in matters of the heart it's easy to betray a confidence. However, Painter, I'm beginning to trust you. Done a bit of checking.'

'I don't seem to have done anything worth checking yet.' I managed a wintry smile.

'Checking you out. You don't get drunk, you don't seem to be a nancy boy. What's the name of the girl's father?'

'Prince Giorgio Caeseri. He had dinner with Mussolini not all that long ago.'

'Did he now! That'd be interesting. I'll check *him* out, I promise you,' he assured me. 'And as for your romance—all right, you go to Florence on Thursday for a week and see what you can find. I'll give you details of your drop in Florence. Check daily. Let me know when you return.'

'Why on Thursday?' I asked.

'Why not?' he retorted.

★   ★   ★

Beautiful Florence seemed unchanged, even in April, at peace with the world, a thousand miles away from the conflict between Britain and Germany. Shortages, perhaps; petrol rationing was beginning to bite, but being Italy there was always a way to get round any problem. Florence—all Italy, for that matter—seemed filled with motorists whose non-existent mothers needed special petrol coupons to allow them to drive them daily to hospital.

But there was plenty of food and wine in this wonderfully abundant country, and with it plenty of laughter and music. After life in England in what was already nicknamed the phoney war—until the fighting began in Norway when the Germans invaded on 9 April—arriving in Florence, where all the world seemed to smile, was like arriving at the pearly gates of heaven.

I had already experienced this in Rome of course, but Florence—ah! Florence was different, unique. Florence to me was 'home', filled with friends amidst the bower of sweet-scented spring flowers, the heavy perfume of love and living, of art and talk of art that seemed to envelop all this exquisite garden.

I could not return to our old house of course, it would be rented to someone else by now, so my first thought was to stay a few days at the Lungarno Hotel, next door to Umberto's. I knew that Umberto would surely offer me a mattress, but I did not fancy sleeping on the floor. After all, I was actually saving a little money as I had free board and lodging in Rome on top of my officer's pay, so I could splurge a few on the very modest Lungarno.

At the last moment, though, I had cold feet. For I faced the first of the problems that bedevil all agents. They knew Ham Johns at the Lungarno! How then could I walk up to old friends at the reception desk and present a passport made out in the name of John Painter? It was unthinkable. No one in Florence knew of Mr Painter, and though people like Umberto or Berenson would never have reason to see my passport, in an hotel where I was already known it was a very different matter.

No, it would have to be Umberto's place, and the

219

rather grubby bed Fiamma and I had shared for so many brief encounters. I remembered that, though there was no spare bed, he did possess not only a spare mattress, but sheets and pillows.

I took the creaking lift up to the top of the building, each passing dark floor an agonising memory of the times Fiamma and I had taken this way to the stars—the sanctuary of Umberto's rough-and-ready studio. Rough, yes, but ready too, and so blissful that each memory tugged at me with an almost physical pain, as though my heart was hurting with every tiny memory or snippet of loving.

I pressed the bell. Umberto let out a gasp of disbelief when he opened the door and saw me. Then his round face dissolved into a smiling joy and he threw his arms around me, crying, 'It's like seeing a ghost! I never thought I'd *ever* see you again! It's wonderful. Let me look at you.' He held me out at arm's length as though to examine me, and went on babbling, 'Let me make you some coffee. Or you can make it if you like. No, better, a drink. Might still have a tiny sip of Scotch left—it's getting hard to find. But some—'

'No, nothing,' I pleaded. 'I just wanted to see you.'

'You're staying where?'

I hesitated.

'Here! Fine. Okay. Shut up! The artist returns. How did you get back?' He rushed into the kitchen spilling questions, and did find some bitter Campari and a bottle of soda, then produced a couple of none-too-clean glasses, and insisted on celebrating.

'It's not every day that a friend returns from the

dead!' he cried. Again asking, 'How did you get back? Why?'

Pretending innocence, I said, looking mildly surprised, 'What's all the fuss about? I just came! Italy isn't at war. Why shouldn't I come? The Germans don't seem to want to fight, there was nothing really for me to do, so I got permission to make a short visit. It meant crossing France, and she's a friendly ally. No problem.'

I had to be careful, though, for Access had warned me to admit nothing, to regard my return as the normal behaviour of an outraged lover who had been spurned, and above all, to be casual. Any undue curiosity by anyone should be shrugged off. My only slight fear—a risk I discarded immediately—was the faint possibility that someone travelling from Rome to Florence might stop me in the street when I was with friends and cry, 'Hullo, Signor Painter.'

But even if that happened, I thought, I would be able to laugh it off, as if it were someone complimenting an artist.

After Umberto had again insisted that I sleep at his place, and we were having a drink, he wrinkled his fat jovial face into a grimace and sighed, 'Sorry to hear about Fiamma. She was a great girl.'

'Sorry,' I cried, disbelieving. '*What* did you say?'

Before he could reply, I felt myself go ice-cold all over. Fear—of the unknown above all—gripped me like a vice, and almost shivering, I asked hoarsely, 'Sorry? What do you mean—*sorry*?'

As he realised I had not the faintest idea what he was talking about, his face creased with anxiety at his stupidity, and he muttered, 'Oh, my God! You didn't know? I'm so sorry.'

Grabbing him by the lapels of his velveteen

jacket, I shouted, 'Didn't know *what*, damn you?'

'Heh! Take it easy,' he shouted back. 'I assumed you'd know. She's married.'

'*Married*! Fiamma? Are you mad?'

'No—yes. To some Spanish marquis—or something. I know he's got a title. Saw it in the papers. And I also read last month in the papers that they'd had a baby. I thought—'

'Don't *ever* say that *they* had a baby.' I grabbed him again. 'It's *mine*. Don't ever say that. Mine. I know. Where is she?' I was wondering aloud. 'Where is she?' But also, 'How could she?'

Suddenly I could hardly control the tears, as the full force of the shock hit me. And then they burst out, my eyes smarting with salt, the tears dribbling down my cheeks, into my mouth as I cried, 'Oh Fiamma! My own Fiamma. How could you?'

I cried, looking round the studio of memories, the famous 'blue' studio which had grown into our own particular trysting place, nurtured by our love and my imagination—but now no longer the romantic setting for true love, instead, suddenly transformed into a slightly sordid scene—how could she! 'How could my own Fiamma do this to me?' I asked Umberto. 'Where is she? And my baby! Is it a boy or a girl? Can't you bloody well tell me *anything*, except lousy news?'

'I didn't know anything about this.' Umberto tried to soothe me, to calm me down. 'I haven't the faintest idea, but I'm sure that her father's here—his photo—'

'And that bloody wife of his?' I asked savagely. 'I'll kill her if I get my hands round her scrawny neck.'

'She's gone. There was a photo I saw. Remember

the Caeseris are a famous family in this region,' said Umberto. 'Anything they do is always in the local paper. In the photo the Prince was kissing his wife goodbye and the caption said she was leaving for an extended holiday at a flat she's taken in Switzerland—near Interlaken, in the Ticino, the Italian section of Switzerland.'

'Bloody good riddance,' I shouted. 'Hope she never comes back. And the Prince?' I was beginning to recover a little from the terrible shock. 'How could *he* do this thing to me?' I asked. 'I always thought he liked me.'

'You had a family row?'

'A row!' I laughed mirthlessly. 'A bust-up to beat all rows! But not with the Prince. I wonder where he is.'

'Why not at home?' asked Umberto. 'Isn't that the most likely place?'

'My God, you could be right. I'm going there—now!' I made the sudden decision. 'How *could* she get married to some damned Spaniard, a complete stranger, without at least writing me?'

As though struck by a sudden realisation that he had not thought of before, Umberto, his worried face wrinkled with concern, asked without warning, 'So it is your child?'

'You bloody well bet it is,' I cried. 'Look Umberto, I'll see you when I do. I've got one call to make on a friend in the Via dei Campi. Do you know where that is?'

'Sure. Can't miss it. Just behind the Piazza della Signoria. What on earth are you going there for?'

'Nothing. I just promised to say hullo to an old friend,' I lied lamely. In fact I had promised Access on my word of honour to report at my drop address

223

the moment I arrived. This was it, and all I had to do—how stupid it all seemed—was to ask, 'Would you like to buy a painting?' If he said yes, I had a message. If he said no, I would return the following morning.

As I had arrived in Florence in the early morning after taking the early train, it was even now only half past eleven. I could be at Settinano in a quarter of an hour after checking on the drop which was, as usual, a tabaccheria who said that no thank you, he was not in the market for paintings today. Perhaps later—

There were a lot of Germans in the streets but I thought nothing of them. Umberto had given me his spare key with a curious last phrase, 'See you get back—if you can, if not, to the next meeting—a presto!'

From there, and after checking the drop, I ran to the bus station behind the Duomo. I had to wait ten minutes for a No. 9 but it came and I jumped off at the Ponte Mensola and strode up the flower-lined road leading past BB's villa to the iron front gates and pulled the bell, thinking of those last attempted kisses through the grille in our final moonlit scene, after which the bottom had tumbled out of my life.

'Married! On the rebound, I suppose.' Savagely I vented my anger on the ancient bell, pulling it again until Enrico shambled out crying, 'Signor Johns! I didn't know that you were here. Welcome back.'

'Is the Prince here?' I asked without preamble.

He nodded assent.

'And the Principessa?'

'No, Signor. She is in Switzerland.'

'Good,' I cried. I had just wanted to confirm Umberto's news, to make sure he had been right.

'Let me in please. I want to see the Prince.'

After a moment's hesitation, he undid the lock, swung the gates open and I crunched forward along the cypress-lined gravel drive to the front door, still guarded by its haughty terracotta dogs sitting on either side of the steps. I knew that when Enrico let anyone through the gates he pressed a bell in the lodge to alert the servants, and I waited for Fawkes to arrive and usher me in.

'He's gone back to England,' wailed Maria, one of the young maids who helped in the house, 'it is very sad. I will announce you to the Prince.'

★　　　★　　　★

He was on the large balcony facing the garden, the long walk and the distant vision of the Indian pavilion fronting the calm pool in which we had splashed and swum and laughed so often. In a way, that beautiful view ahead of me had been my very first 'love glimpse' of Florence, blue in the distant haze like the backdrop of a romantic curtain behind the delicious foreground on which I now gazed.

'Ham!' cried the Prince. 'This is a pleasant surprise.' He held out his hand with a gesture of real warmth and obvious affection, so much so that I could hardly be angry.

Even so, I was too deeply upset to wait for the niceties. To hell with manners! I thought. I did take his proffered hand, though. But as I shook it almost mechanically, I blurted out, 'Is it true? Am I right in believing Fiamma is married? Why? Why?' In my anger I started shouting, almost in tears again, and finally cried, '*You*! I thought you were my friend.'

225

In a dry voice, slightly hardened, the Prince brought me up with a short sharp rebuke that crushed me like a cold shower.

'Of course I like you. But no father can expect to go overboard with joy when a penniless young artist makes his unmarried daughter pregnant.'

I gulped and felt myself blush.

'But I wanted to marry her! Nobody would let me.'

'I know, Ham. Believe me, I do know that—and I would have been delighted to welcome you as a son-in-law.'

'Then why didn't you give me the chance? Your wife knows I come from a respectable family. That's what I blame you for. Not giving me a break—not being fair. Just ignoring me like a bad egg.'

'I didn't ignore you,' replied the Prince sharply and, taking the matter into his own hands without asking me, called to Maria, 'Mr Johns will stay for lunch. Lay an extra plate. Yes, here on the terrace.' And to me he said, 'Let's have a glass of white wine and I'll try to explain.'

'No explanations can wipe out the fact I've lost the girl I love—thanks to you and your wife.'

'Let's leave me out of it, shall we?' asked the Prince with a smile.

'How can I?' I asked savagely. 'I loved that girl. I always will—and you regard her marriage to this *Spaniard* as a kind of joke.'

'Perhaps it is?' There was a question in his voice, but before I could fathom his puzzling choice of words, he poured out a glass of his own chilled local wine and then said, more gently than I had ever heard him speak before, 'Here. Drink it down. We

226

both will, and—dare I say it?—here's to you and Fiamma.'

Stupidly I muttered, 'I don't understand.'

With a long and tortured sigh, the Prince suggested, 'Sit down, Ham. Life is not always as simple as it seems.'

'It seems simple to me,' I retorted bitterly, sitting down on the swinging sofa where Fiamma and I had so often sat, swaying gently.

'It isn't,' reported the Prince shortly, almost bitterly. 'Let me tell you—since you seem to think so badly of me—that I do not have any money and so, if I like to live in style, then I must'—the bitterness in his voice increased—'more or less do as I'm told, more or less obey "orders". Usually I don't mind. They rarely conflict, because my wife is understanding of—and—well, I'm intelligent and discreet—and all this makes for a very happy life. And I'm fond of her. But if she makes up her mind when she's angry—God help the other side, my boy.'

He hesitated as if mustering words to suit the situation, and poured out another glass of wine.

'And when she saw your paintings of her daughters—and then learned about your—er—sex life, that was the end. She said she was leaving with her daughter at six the next morning, and if I didn't go with her, she'd denounce my private life publicly, and leave me. As flat as that.'

Shrugging his shoulders, the Prince added with another sigh, 'Of course I tried to argue. Said that BB admired you, that I was sure you wanted to get married. Fiamma was heartbroken. But there was the possibility of war in the offing and—'

'I understand that,' I said desperately, 'but didn't

227

you really try to fight for *me*? And what I can't understand is how Fiamma fell so quickly in love with another man. And while she was carrying my baby.'

'She didn't.'

'Didn't what?'

'You're very innocent in some ways, Ham. Have you ever heard of an arranged marriage? What the French call a *mariage de convenance*?'

I stopped swinging, sat up sharply. 'I don't understand.'

'This part is simpler,' said the Prince. 'My wife was determined not to have a bastard in the family. It would shame the family name, and you know as well as I do, she would bear the stigma for the rest of her life. And abortion would be completely impossible in a Catholic family. So, when we got to Rome, she arranged everything. She knows as many of the "right people" as I do—not always my friends, I hasten to say—but people who mix well, know their way around, have titles, but no money. Rather like myself,' he added sadly.

'I'm beginning to—'

'I thought you would,' he said. 'Once you had parted—and she soon found out that you had returned to England—you would stay parted until after the war if you weren't killed in the meantime. In which case, poor unmarried Fiamma . . .' He left the rest of the sentence unfinished.

'But I would have married her first.'

'Fiamma did tell us that your father had ordered you to go.'

'I would have disobeyed him. It wasn't an order—more advice of a wise move to make.'

'To us—even to me, I could see you in the front

228

line, perhaps dying before the marriage was arranged. And anyway, you can't just get married in a couple of days in Italy. It takes time.'

'So then?'

'My wife found a penniless Spanish nobleman—a very pleasant young man—and she persuaded him, for a consideration, a large one, to marry Fiamma, but never to touch her. That was the only stipulation that Fiamma made. No'—again he gave a wintry smile—'no bed and breakfast in *that* marriage. Just to give the child a name.'

I could not believe it, it sounded so absurd in one way, a contrived marriage in which the girl I loved was now living with another man—a very pleasant young man, the Prince had called him—living in separate beds, I suppose, but still—who could be married to Fiamma and never touch her? It was ridiculous.

'And the child?' Almost for want of *something* to say.

'The *boy*. A bouncing baby, nicknamed Ham after you.'

'A boy!' For a split second my delight made me forget everything else, before saying, more sourly, 'To be christened the Marquis of whatever he's called, and denied my name for the rest of his life.'

'Not at all. He won't be christened until after the war. By then I hope you'll be married to Fiamma.'

'But divorce. It's not permitted among Catholics.'

'Divorce, no. Annulment, yes. It's quite simple. I seem to be using the word simple rather a lot!' He gave his usual wry smile. 'And it's also perfectly simple because the marriage never *has* been consummated. It may look curious, considering

229

that Fiamma has borne a child, but the child has nothing to do with the marriage.'

'But you can't stop two people living together and not—well, if they have a few drinks or they're bored or never hear from me—or a thousand and one things,' thinking suddenly of the temptation that day behind the gooseberry bushes when Roz had asked me if I wanted to peep.

'You imagine too much,' the Prince said almost shortly. 'They'll behave.'

'Would they?' I asked myself. My heart gave such a bound I thought it would leave my skin, such a breathless manifestation of happiness that I could feel it pumping hard against my ribs. I might have to wait—but! I had begged her to wait when we said goodbye, so what was different now? I was still prepared to wait, just as I had promised her then.

'I only hope he treats her well—with consideration,' I muttered.

The Prince looked at me almost with outright astonishment, and then gave a huge laugh.

'What's so funny?' I asked angrily.

'My dear Ham, when people are paid for an arranged marriage, they don't *live* together, not even in the same country. The Marquis of Whatever, as you call him, returned to Spain the day after the wedding.'

'No!' The pounding in my heart increased until I thought it would burst, 'And Fiamma?' I had suddenly noticed that Maria was quietly laying out three plates on the loggia table, I hardly dared to think, or hope, or believe—

'Of course, Ham!' cried the Prince, reading my thoughts. 'She lives here. Where else? This is her home.' He paused and raised an eyebrow. 'My wife is still nursing her outraged sensibilities in Switzerland,' he said, 'and Roz is married to Kurt and living in Germany. But Fiamma—she has only gone into Florence to do some shopping. She'll be back for lunch.'

CHAPTER FOURTEEN

Faintly—and still hardly able to grasp what was happening—I heard the distant clang of the front door bell announcing—it must be!—that Fiamma was home.

'Can I go to meet her?' I looked at the Prince.

'Carry on,' he smiled. 'I can see you don't want to waste a second.'

'No *sir*!' I clattered down the steps into the drive.

There she was, her walk towards me suddenly erupting into a run, a cry, then a scream of excitement or joy from the blurred and distant vision of a thin pale fragile blue dress and a large Florentine straw hat which I had seen so often before, used as a shield against the summer sun. She fell into my arms without a word and we kissed each other over and over again.

Then she somehow managed to gasp, as she clutched me tightly, 'It's like a dream, beloved. Oh Ham!' She started crying—but unlike the last ones these were tears of joy. Finally, with the tears of happiness streaming down her face, I searched for my handkerchief and dabbed her cheeks.

'There!' I almost whispered as we walked slowly now, arms encircling each other's waists, towards

231

the lovely old villa from which even in April you could see Florence, the pink of the Duomo merging with the blue above the city. 'You're home now, and I'm with you.'

'For ever?' She smiled her question plaintively.

'Not yet. There is a war on. But I managed to get British permission to cross France and come and see you. And the Prince—while we waited for you to return—he explained a lot of things. So now,' I breathed in the fragrant air gratefully, 'I feel happier. I was so wretched, so miserable, until I knew something.'

'It's all right now, my precious Ham. If only you could stay here—no war, you'd be safe. Couldn't you?' she pleaded as we reached the door.

Shaking my head I laughed and squeezed her waist gently. 'Darling, what would the British do without me to help them?' She laughed too, a kind of tension broken, as though the war did not really matter or even exist. And did it, at this particular moment? I suddenly thought back to the time when we had made love so quickly behind the pool, and I felt the same urge now.

But—and in a way I am proud to admit this—I had an even more powerful urge: to see my son.

'The baby,' I murmured. '*Our* boy. I simply must see him, my darling.' I clasped her to me ardently.

'Of course. Our creation, darling Ham. Born of love and delight.' She ran, leading me with her hand linked to mine, towards the nursery.

It was a pretty room but I could hardly take it all in—the pale, spring-like effect of the walls, the curtains, and the bedspread—because a middle-aged nanny was watching the tiny bundle of

232

sleeping joy that was ours. I felt tears pricking my eyelids, not tears of sadness or joy, but simply of wonder. I longed to wake him, and tell him I was his father and how proud I was of him.

Fiamma touched my arm. 'He's just like his father, isn't he?! But sssh,' she whispered. 'Don't wake him.' She was the mother now, rather than the lover, being practical. And to the nurse: 'Thank you, Nanny, we'll come up again after lunch.'

'There!' Fiamma now squeezed me as we made our way downstairs. 'It makes me so happy to have you, and'—with a laugh—'also a carbon copy for when you have to leave.'

'So—you've all met then!' The Prince greeted us on the balcony saying, 'Let's go inside. And let's have a proper drink to celebrate this ...' he hesitated, 'this misunderstanding, which I'm, sure will have a happy ending. Maria, is there any champagne on ice?'

'Si, si, Signor Principe.'

'Bring a bottle here then, please.'

'Oh Papa, I'm so happy.' Fiamma put her arms round her father and nestled up to him. 'Thank you.'

'Don't thank me,' he said a little ruefully. 'Thank Ham for having the courage to come back, even when he's at war.'

After finishing the champagne we lunched quietly inside—Parma ham and melon, a modest Florentine steak and salad, followed by zabaglione; and after coffee the Prince said with an assumed air of innocence, 'So sorry. I have to go and see someone.'

For a moment I thought he was going to make a jocular remark on the lines of, 'Sure you two can amuse yourselves?' But his innate sense of manners made him keep the thought to himself. 'See you at dinner. I thought I might ask BB to meet you tomorrow evening. I'm sure he'd love to see you again. I'll phone him when I come home this evening.'

Had the Prince gently accentuated the last two words, 'this evening' as though to reassure us that we would be undisturbed all afternoon?

'Maybe,' said Fiamma as we sat on our old swing couch after the Prince had gone. 'Poor Papa was so terribly upset at what happened before—but he couldn't do anything about it.'

'I know.' I realised how much Fiamma loved her father, how upset she had been at the way he had hurt her. 'It's all over now. Come along, beloved, let's go upstairs.'

*   *   *

The warmth and the love of that afternoon were never to be forgotton.

I was hesitant at first, whispering anxiously, 'Is it, well, all right, so soon? I don't want—'

Tears glistened in Fiamma's eyes as she smiled. 'Of course. I had no complications, so it *is* all right.' She cupped my face in her hands. 'Thank you, my darling, for thinking so gently; and I know you will be gentle with me.'

All the tenderness in the world passed through us, a tenderness we had never experienced before, in which the physical act of love-making seemed to be just a gentle, floating experience of the brain, that we were indeed celebrating our love in a far gentler way than ever before. It was an experience brought about by the ultimate committing of our love. It is hard to explain; I had always loved this girl—a child I had called her sometimes—and it had never even smacked of a cheerful but unimportant 'affaire', let alone a quick 'fun thing'; there had always been a far deeper, spiritual feeling to our love-making, but never anything as deep as this was. I seemed to be—dare I say it?—on a higher plane. We spent a long time just lying together in bed on this afternoon, yet the time passed fleetingly. Life *was* fleeting in wartime—it was best to spend as much time together as one could. Later, we had a quick giggling bath together in the old-fashioned tub, and then dressed and walked downstairs.

During the afternoon I had once heard the bell ring—the signal from the lodge—waking me from one of our little in-between sleeps, and in my muddled thought I had wondered if the Prince had returned early, but that of course was nonsense. Enrico would never alert the servants because the master had returned. Or would he—just to put them on their guard? Still, I was relieved that he was not there.

Instead a telegram lay on the long Spanish-style table in the Tea Room—the first balcony, where letters and messages were always left. Neither of us gave the telegram a second thought until the Prince finally arrived about six o'clock and, before pouring out a drink, ripped open the blue-grey envelope, unfolded the flimsy piece of paper and then, with a look of astonishment at both of us cried, 'Well, bless my soul! The gathering of the clans!'

'What's the matter?' Fiamma looked up.

'Roz is arriving tomorrow.'

'Roz!' We both chorused our disbelief.

235

'Yes, Roz. With her husband. With Kurt.'

'Kurt!'

'Yes.' With his usual slightly ironic smile the Prince said to me, 'Kurt—and you—enemies meeting on neutral ground!'

'Don't worry,' I said hastily. 'I'm very fond of him.'

'I know you are, I was only joking,' the Prince smiled.

'Are they staying long? I must prepare a bedroom,' asked Fiamma, very much the loving, thoughtful Mrs of the house!

'They don't say. It just says,' he read, '"Kurt and I arriving tomorrow morning, love Roz."'

It would be nice to see Roz again. Of course I had had no news of Kurt until this morning when the Prince had told me they were married. When I left so hurriedly Kurt and I only had time for a brief farewell but it was a heartfelt one, and I had also the touching memory of Roz and me losing our loneliness in Florence that night, after Lella's wedding. I wondered how they were getting on. They had certainly been in love, and Kurt—such an exquisite musician—had certainly been deeply in love with her. But, as I knew, although all the girls had been brought up as Catholics, Roz was part Jewish. Her Jewishness did not matter to her, of course, but I knew how much she would feel that blood when in Germany. She would see the bestial way the Nazis were brutally ill-treating the Jews, and that, as Hitler had stated, they were determined to rid Germany of every single Jew that was left.

Ah well! I sighed, thinking, she is probably too

Italian by now to notice. I hoped that for her sake I was right.

I must have been wondering about the Jews in Germany—as almost without thinking I had asked the Prince over lunch, 'Is there a Jewish problem in Italy? I remembered some pretty stringent laws being passed. I mean for people like Berenson?'

With a sigh the Prince said, 'Not yet. Not officially. But unofficially—well, no Jewish music as you know, all books by Jews banned, and so on. But unofficially too the good ones—the Jews whom we like and who are generally liked—well, they're tolerated. But you have to be careful. Do anything wrong and you're in serious trouble.'

Thinking not so much of Roz as of BB, I asked, 'It seems so damned silly and petty. Vicious and nasty. Don't you agree?'

The Prince took the words right out of my mouth. With another sigh he said, 'Germany is much worse than Italy, and sometimes I worry about Roz. But you can never tell. The fact that both she and Kurt want to take time off to see us for a few days seems to indicate that all's going pretty well.'

'It's wonderful—not only to see her, but for her to see you,' said Fiamma happily. 'And to see that we two are both in love with each other. But'—with an anxious look at me—'you will behave won't you?'

'Of course,' I cried. 'I could never be the enemy of a man who plays Chopin like Kurt does.'

We dined very quietly, a clear soup, an escalope milanaise served professionally and swimming in a butter sauce, the corner professionally decorated with chopped white of egg and a few capers.

After dinner we sat and talked about nothing

237

specific and then went to bed early. Between them, the Prince and Fiamma had arranged that I should use one of a pair of spare rooms with connecting doors—originally part of the nursery complex with one room for the nanny. We used one room in which to sleep but I undressed in the other so that everybody might know or guess, but the proprieties were 'officially' observed.

★   ★   ★

Roz and Kurt arrived in Florence just before lunch, where Kurt stopped to see a friend at the Grand Hotel bar, and Roz went shopping. Then a taxi brought them to the Villa. When they actually reached the house, and we stood by the terracotta dogs to welcome them, Roz was the first to recognise me and shouted—almost screamed!—'It's Ham! Ham, darling, what are *you* doing here?'

As they neared the house, she ran forward almost ignoring the others and for a few seconds Kurt stopped, stood stock still as though finding it difficult to believe his eyes, as though I could not possibly be there. He was also in civvies. For what seemed like an eternity, he stood rooted, oblivious to the others. Roz ran forward, kissed her father and then, as she turned to Fiamma and me—wondering, perhaps whom to kiss first!—I ran down the steps crying, 'Kurt, this is terrific! How are you?'

The seconds of tension snapped as though someone had snipped a tautly-strung elastic band with a pair of ultra-sharp scissors, and then—friends or enemies, English or German—we threw our arms round each other and hugged each

238

other like the bosom friends we had been last summer.

'Still got time to play the piano?'

Two grins.

'Still got time to paint?'

Two shakes of the head. I had not touched a brush for months.

We walked up the steps, the Prince shaking hands warmly with Kurt—after all, I could not help reflecting, their countries were teetering on the edge of becoming allies in war as well as friends in peace. It was good to see him, though. You cannot break friendships just because politicians who do not know how to *avert* war (or who do not want to?) tell you to hate each other because one country has behaved unpleasantly to another; nor can you break friendships just because you are enemies meeting by chance in a neutral country.

As it was, everything went swimmingly from the first moment. It was a beautiful day, not yet warm, but with a crisp sun that seemed to light up the entire garden. The *parterre*, the garden of dwarf hedges, with a fountain in the middle, was lined with tulips, and the last fragrance from the land of the hyacinths wafted up to our large balcony above.

As the Prince uncorked some of his special Italian 'champagne for pre-lunch drinks, I stole a look at Roz when she did not know I was watching her. She was deep in conversation with Fiamma. I thought—imagination perhaps?—that she looked tired. Perhaps it had been the overnight journey, but no, it was not exactly tiredness, more a hint in her face of a kind of resignation. Or was that too strong a word? There certainly was the odd line on her face—anxiety perhaps, for the future? Or could

239

it be that she just missed the Villa Magari, as I did?

Kurt took my arm and said, almost shyly, 'Feel like a walk to the pool to work up an appetite?'

And as we strolled down the old tessellated path he said, 'What are you doing here?'

'Nothing!' I lied cheerfully. 'The war doesn't seem to be starting...'

'But you haven't joined up?'

'Not yet. No hurry. I will I suppose—if I'm needed. But I got a chance to come here, so I grabbed it. And you?'

'A lieutenant—on a few days' leave—special permission to visit Italy because Roz was a bit homesick.'

'Dare I ask what you're doing?'

Kurt laughed. 'No secret. In Intelligence—well sort of, more or less a glorified messenger boy and general factotum. I expect I'll be moved into something more active when the balloon really goes up.'

'Do you think it will?'

'We shouldn't be talking military strategy,' Kurt laughed again, 'but I wouldn't linger around Europe for too long if I were you.'

I made a non-committal reply, not thinking very seriously about what he was saying. It was only when we were talking after lunch and Kurt, after strumming for a few moments on the piano, started playing the gentle Chopin Nocturne in E-flat, a tune I loved—he had practised it so often in the old house—that he closed the piano with a snap and said abruptly, 'I think I'll go down the road to see BB. Coming along, Ham?'

I shook my head. All I was waiting for was to be with Fiamma. But what an extraordinary way Kurt had acted—so suddenly, so out of character. Instinctively I took a quick glance at Roz—and that provided the answer: what had they been talking about? The sad turned-down corners of her lips, the dew-drops of held-back tears at the corners of her eyes. And then a rather plaintive, 'Do you *have* to go now, Kurt?' followed by a sudden tightening of the mouth, an almost angry as well as resigned look. It all betokened a troubled love life.

Marriage not quite as idyllic as they had hoped for?

I wondered why. At least Fiamma and I, though not yet married, were still hopelessly, wonderfully in love. But perhaps I was being unfair. Surely they would still be in love, but no doubt living in Hitler's dedicated Germany was getting Roz down. By all accounts Nazism was even tougher than Fascism, Hitler a more fervent (and half-baked) paranoid than Mussolini. In the end, feeling sorry for Roz—and Fiamma making me realise that she wanted to talk to Roz alone—I called to Kurt, 'Hang on! I'll come with you. I would like to pay my respects to BB.'

'Great,' he cried.

'Back in an hour.' I did not want to stay too long away from Fiamma and, as it happened, I hardly stayed at all, for BB was away for a few days in Poggibonsi, up in the high hills behind Florence, in the 'country cottage' he had there.

'I'll stay on and play BB's piano if Mrs BB will let me.' Kurt had long since nursed a passion for Berenson's Steinway. He had practised on it whenever he could. 'That is if you don't mind?' he asked Mary Berenson politely.

'Our pleasure. Stay as long as you like, my dear,'

241

she laughed. It never gets used these days.'

So I returned alone—to a sudden twist in the drama. On the way up the drive—almost as I reached the front door—I passed the Prince going off in his tiny Topolino which had replaced his petrol-drinking Isotta Fraschini.

Winding down the window he cried, 'I'm terribly sorry, I've just been called to Rome. Ciano's sent for me. I'm going to the station now. I'll be back in a few days. Make yourself at home, Ham. Fiamma's just gone to have her snooze. See you soon.' With that he was off.

I was surprised, but on the other hand, as I knew from Access who had 'checked him out', he was working in Intelligence and if Count Ciano sent for him—well, that was the nature of the job. Curious, I thought, that all of us were in various Intelligence services but I did not, I admit, give the coincidence another thought.

For then, something else happened.

I heard a voice—it sounded like Roz speaking on the phone—and my heart nearly missed a beat, for though naturally we had all been talking Italian since we arrived, I *thought* I heard her intersperse her Italian with a single English word—'Si, si, Painter'.

Painter! Surely not. It was impossible. As I walked in through the door she was just putting the phone down and my heart gave another thud of fear.

'That was for you,' she said.

'For me? I thought I heard you talking about a Mr Painter.'

'Painter? The English word?' she laughed. 'Not me. But it was a man who would like you to phone him—he said it was urgent and that you would know him because he wants to buy a painting.' And quite innocently she added, 'I didn't think you were still painting.'

'It's one or two I did before my nudes. I thought I'd better try and earn a little money. Can't get any money out of England you see. So I've got to be terribly careful financially, or I'll have to go home. I've got my return ticket, thank God. But how funny. I could have sworn I heard the name Painter.'

'You're wrong,' she laughed. 'But it wouldn't be the end of the world if I'd used it, would it?'

'No, no,' I lied. 'It just sounded odd, suddenly, an English word like that.'

She smiled. 'You must have imagined it.'

She was right, I supposed. Still, I thought, as I climbed up the front stairs to our bedroom, it was odd. Yes, distinctly odd.

Fiamma was asleep, dead tired as the Prince had said. Though I desired her—just the sight of her there, blonde hair spread out as though by accident on the white pillows covered with occasional blue forget-me-nots to match the sheets—she looked so beautifully innocent that it almost broke my heart to think that soon we would have to be parted—and for how long, God only knew. For a long time I lay beside her knowing that soon I would have to go and see the tobacconist.

She woke first, and went down to the kitchen, to return with a pot of tea.

'I didn't forget,' she smiled. 'Best Ceylon, kept from our last meeting. Remember?'

I did. We had bought the tea in a special airtight tin from Procacci's in the Via Tornabuoni, and as we drank our second cup, I asked, 'Do you think Roz is really happy living in Germany?'

She shook her head firmly. 'No, she is not,' she said. 'She told me she hates it.'

'Do you think being—well half Jewish—' I didn't finish the sentence.

'Maybe it's partly fear, though nobody'll ever know, but she says she's seen some terrible sights—old Jews beaten up, and she's heard rumours that they're all taken to Concentration Camps and that they then vanish.'

'That sounds a bit far-fetched.'

'You think so? There *is* a war on, darling.'

'True,' I agreed. 'But then why doesn't Roz leave—come back to Italy for the duration? Your countries are allies, or almost—and Kurt could come over regularly, I'm sure. It's not the same for us. But Kurt and Roz—surely—' and again I left the sentence unfinished.

'She won't,' said Fiamma. 'She says her place is with Kurt. And perhaps *because* she's not wholly Jewish, I think she feels she can help some of the—well, the *oppressed* people. She says it's terrible there. She has to pluck up courage every time she goes walking in the streets.'

We did not talk about Roz any more for I had another subject to broach—and this time a sad one for both of us. I had to meet my contact. And I had to tread very, very carefully. I started by saying tactfully, 'Darling heart, I've got to slip down into Florence briefly but I'll be back in an hour.'

With a laugh she said, 'One moment it's briefly, the next it's an hour. Where are you going?'

'Just to—well, pick up a message.'

'I'll come with you.'

'Darling,' I said slowly, carefully, 'it'll only take a few minutes. Now be an angel, my precious Fiamma, and don't tell anybody.'

'Are you in any business?' she asked slowly.

'In a way. But not important, so don't worry your head.'

'Don't *worry*.' She kissed me gently. 'It all sounds so very mysterious. You're sure'—with her old mischievous smile—'you're not a spy?'

'Do I look like one!' I laughed. 'No, my beloved, but one thing you must remember—and then don't let's ask any more questions. Britain *is* at war. Not with Italy, thank God, or not yet. That's how I managed to get the permission to come here. But I was asked to do a favour for someone in return. And,' I spoke slowly, 'I may have to leave as suddenly as I arrived.'

'Oh no!'

'Maybe.' In my heart I knew that the message must be vital, almost certainly a recall for some job in Rome. 'If I do have to go in a rush, beloved, will you, here and now, swear to me, promise to me that, whatever happens, you will believe that I'm not running away from you. That you will always love me, that you will wait for me? All our lives if necessary. Will you promise?'

'I will. And you?'

'I will.'

'The same words,' she smiled sadly, 'as a marriage service. Oh, if only we could get married. The annulment's taking ages to come through. I suppose the church bureaucrats are affected by war like everybody else. Do you think we ever will be able to get married?'

'Absolutely! We will!' I spoke with conviction,

245

and I knew that my voice *carried* the belief that I felt, that I transmitted that belief to her.

'And I,' she pronounced, 'will never love another man, never look at one, never even think of anyone but my beloved husband-to-be.'

'Bless you, beloved,' I said. 'Now, I'm just off to Florence, then straight back. But I'm afraid—a bit afraid that I may have to leave tomorrow. But perhaps not. And not a word of this—I've just gone for a walk. Promise?'

'I promise. And I understand. Now off you go and pray God you don't have to rush away too soon.'

I took the next bus to Florence and made my way to the tobacconist and dutifully (though inwardly grimacing at the stupidity) asked if he wanted to buy any paintings today.

'A friend of mine does,' he answered slowly and deliberately. 'But he's in Rome. He asks if you can meet him tomorrow at six o'clock in the evening—and he *says* at the Cape of Good Hope.'

'I will.'

'And,' added the tobacconist, 'would you give Access this message?' He handed me a tiny shred of paper with a few words on it. I did not look at it but put it in my wallet and made my way to catch the next No. 9 bus back to Settignano. Well, at least we would have the whole evening and night together back at Magari before I caught the first train to Rome in the morning.

*   *   *

At the villa I told Fiamma I would be leaving the following day and she seemed to understand, almost to expect it. At least we could have one last evening of happiness. I charged her with the tricky business of explaining my sudden departure to the Prince, who was after all my host, and Roz and Kurt. 'But discreetly, darling. Remember our ... well, that you ... understand?'

She became serious, nodding conspiratorially as she realised the confidentiality of my mission.

'Of course. I'll tell them a telegram came ... trouble at home ... a family illness.'

'Clever girl!'

I reckoned they would accept that even if they did not believe it. Then I went into an upstairs lavatory, locked the door behind me, and took out the slip of paper to see what was written on it.

The thin, flimsy paper with faded letters looked like the tenth carbon copy of some message. I could understand two or three words but for the rest, it made no sense at all.

The cryptic message ran:

0905 AGPCLEEB MAGINOT STOP MAIN AGPARUNDSTEDT ARDENNES STOP

SECONDARY AGPBBOCK BELGIUM/HOLLAND STOP ENEMY 149 DIV US 136

OP AIR 1800 COMBAT US 3000

Returning it carefully to my wallet, I put it out of my mind. I had no idea what this gibberish meant. Decoding—or understanding—the contents was a job for Access. I had somehow become involved—how I did not really know—in carrying a few words, obviously from a German source, which

247

had been given to me. In short, a glorified messenger boy.

'Live for today!' I cried to Fiamma, 'and if I'm not able to return before the war's over, let us remember this last evening and make it the happiest of our lives.'

We did, making love very tenderly once again, and I set off for Rome the following morning, a new man, sad at leaving, yes, but refreshed in faith and spirit now that all my doubts and worries about Fiamma had been cast aside and I had seen Ham. Our future was resolved. I trusted her implicitly and that was all I needed until this wretched war was over.

★   ★   ★

Access was waiting for me at the Triangolo, and seemed quite different from our past meetings—almost nervous, barely shaking hands before barking in his great booming voice, 'Where is it?' I must have looked puzzled for before I could say anything he added, 'The message, dammit, the message. But discreetly.'

I had realised that the message must be important, so I had already taken it out of my wallet and it lay clutched in my left hand. Access had warned me of the dangers of counter-espionage. 'You never know when you're being watched,' he had boomed on more than one occasion. Adding with his touch of vulgarity, 'They could even peep through the keyhole if you're taken short and need to crap.'

Under the checked tablecloth I transferred the paper to my right hand then, hands on table, still

248

covering the message, I asked Access, 'Pass the sugar please.'

He did so. I raised my right hand, picked up the sugar bowl, dropped the message, giving him all the time in the world to take the message into his large hand.

'I'm off,' he said abruptly. 'Meet me tomorrow in the gardens of the Villa Borghese. A quarter to one. Near the Casina Valadier. Underneath the balcony. I'll take you to lunch. They have their own special Mozzarella in Carozza.'

He had not by the faintest hint given me any real feeling of the importance of this scrap of paper, but somehow he had transmitted a sense of its value and, the next lunchtime, after looking up and down to see we had not been followed, he led me up to a table on the balcony, ordered some wine, and said without preamble, 'Painter, you will go down in history as one of the unsung heroes of the second world war.'

'For what?' I laughed. 'For not killing any Germans!'

'Not that, sonny,' he boomed. 'For *saving* British lives.' Then switching conversation he said, 'Here they serve mozzarella in thick crusty French-style *baguettes*. Are your teeth okay?'

Slightly amused, I said, 'I can eat a crust, if that's what you mean.'

'Good. No false teeth? Good again. For that's what I do mean. Time is of the essence now. Vital, every second. This afternoon you go to the dentist. Here's the address. Five o'clock.'

'Hey!' I protested.

'And tonight—the last day of April—you leave for England.'

'England? Dentist? *Tonight*! What the hell...'

I must have looked confused for, without a word, he signalled the waiter and ordered some prosciutto, which would be followed by the mozzarella. And then suddenly, almost furiously, he said to me, 'And for Christ's sake stop asking so many fucking questions. Your job is to do as you're told. You've been followed. You've got to get this message to England. It could prevent us losing the war. I've got a man here who's a dentist. So you'll see him where I tell you at five o'clock. I'll give you the address. He'll drill a hole in one of your molars and hide a microdot message in it. That way no one can find it if you're questioned. Okay?'

CHAPTER FIFTEEN

When Access told me about the message that was to be concealed in my tooth, I muttered mockingly, 'The things I do for England!' But my inner feelings were more of anger than mockery, for I was proud of my teeth, which my mother used to say were 'one of your best features'. As a child I had had them braced to straighten them, and apart from a couple of fillings they were perfect and I certainly did not like the idea of some stranger tampering with them. Access merely sneered, and waved a hand in a gesture of indifference while he told me the dentist's address.

'He's American and neutral, but pro-British because of his—er—friendship with one of our ambassadorial staff in Rome, I understand. But you don't need to go into that. He's reliable.'

250

'I hope so,' I said. 'My teeth—'

'To hell with your bloody teeth,' Access said. 'He's reliable because he does what he's told without asking questions. And we've got his match in London who *undoes* what he's done. You follow me?'

Without enthusiasm I said, 'To get the message out again, presumably?'

Access gave a sigh of exaggerated relief, as though he had finally explained something to a dim-witted child. Then he waved me away. 'Get on with it.'

I got on with it.

The dentist's surgery lay in the fashionable Via Lombardia, and there was nothing amateurish or furtive about it. It evidently served a fashionable clientele. The receptionist was petite and auburn-haired, and as soon as she opened a leather-bound appointments book and I noted that the hour was ringed in red, she said, 'Please go straight in.' She nodded towards the door marked Surgery. A dazzling smile followed. 'You are expected.'

The dentist, who was called Dr Wilbur Rayment, was tall and good-looking in that rugged American way which reminded me a little of Steve. *Esquire* had been one of my favourite magazines when I was an undergraduate, and he might have stepped straight out of a Brooks Brothers advertisement.

'I'll fix you a drink,' were his first words. 'Got one right here in the icebox.'

We sat down on a leather sofa and I looked with amazement at the chair in which the patient would sit—or rather lie, for it had an extended leg-rest that made it look like a lounger which you might find in a catalogue of futuristic furniture. Dr Rayment noted my astonishment.

'Bit different from the old barber's chair with its pedal operating the rack-and-pinion mechanism to raise the patient, eh?'

I nodded.

'We're a bit more advanced in the States. Have to be. Cosmetic dentistry's much in demand—all these film stars whose teeth need capping or crowning, for the sake of the close-ups. Quite a business.'

'Must be profitable,' I laughed.

'Sure is. More than your little problem.' He, too, had a cheerful laugh. 'Let's have a look, shall we?'

He waved towards the chair and I climbed into it, finding it amazingly comfortable though the brilliant light directly above me made me close my eyes. He gave me a pair of black sunglasses—I had a fleeting memory of the effete messenger who had brought Ciano's letter to Magari—and hovered over me with a probe and a spatula. With my mouth propped open with wedges I could not say a word, only mutter incoherent noises. But he seemed to know exactly what was wanted, though of course he had to wrap it in the devious phrases of the undercover man. 'I understand that the matter to be conveyed is very small?'

I tried to say 'Yes' with my eyes. It was in fact extremely small—written with a very fine stylo in indelible ink on a tiny piece of thin silk that I had concealed in an equally tiny metal cylinder that had once held spare leads for a propelling pencil. A few moments later I fumbled for the cylinder in my pocket and handed it to him. 'It's in there.'

He took the silk from the cylinder and crushed it into a tiny ball. 'Not much bigga'n a pin's head.'

252

Released from his fingers, the scrap of silk sprang back into its flat dimension. 'Yeah, I guess we can hide that. That molar on the left—the one that hasn't been filled—has a good indentation on the top surface. Put a lid on it and it'll leave a space enough to tuck this scrap in.'

'A lid?' I queried, mystified, when he had taken the wedges from my mouth. 'Access said something about having a hole drilled—'

'Yeah, well, he's a bit behind with his know-how of dental progress. Y'know about plastics?'

'Well, I know what the word means: malleable, something you can shape—'

'Yeah, that's basics; but plastics is going to revolutionise dentistry. Vulcanite and ivory and porcelain are things of the past for falsies.' He turned and went to a glass-topped table from which he took some waxlike compound in a metal tray; before I knew where I was he had it in my mouth and was telling me to take a bite.

'Good.' He took the tray and returned it to the table. 'Now I've got the impression, my mechanic will make a thin hollow crown of acrylic resin to fit over the molar with this'—he indicated the slip of silk—'inside it. Cement the crown to the base of the tooth with amalgam and—' He waved a hand as if completing a conjuring trick. 'Come back tonight after surgery closes and we'll tie it up. Okay?'

And that was what we did.

I came back a few hours later, had the crown fitted on with only the slightest twinges of pain and then he gave me another drink, wished me 'Good luck, buddy!' and I was gone.

★   ★   ★

Now, with a tooth that felt uncomfortably large in my mouth, I had to get back to England as quickly as possible.

'They don't seem to have damaged your natural beauty,' said Access when I met him at the station at seven o'clock, and realising how proud I was of my teeth, added, 'What the eye can't see'—there was the suggestion of a leer in his voice.

'And now?' I asked, cutting short his pathetic attempts at humour which always seemed to be at my expense.

'England, home and glory! I wondered if we could arrange air transport but it's too tricky. If you could fly across France—our ally, after all—the buggers'd try to shoot you down just for target practice. They hate our guts, the frogs. Reciprocal, I must say,' he chortled. 'I thought of flying you to Lisbon, but it'd take too long. Might have to wait there for up to a week for a connecting flight. And we can't afford the time. This is the most urgent message you'll ever have to carry in your life.'

'So it's the train?'

He nodded. 'That's why we're here. To give you this ticket and so on to catch the Rome–Paris express tonight.'

'Tonight!'

He ignored my cry of surprise. I hadn't realised it was that urgent. 'The train leaves at eight.'

'But what about my clothes? Luggage?'

'Don't bother with luggage. Leave it in Rome.'

'But my clothes!'

'Bugger your clothes. Indent to C for replacement value. He'll understand.'

'You said as far as Paris.'

254

'Yes. At the Paris station you'll be met by a man called Monsieur Gaston. He'll have a car and take you straight to Le Bourget. Sorry to rob you of a night on the tiles with a floozie, but you'll fly across the Channel and be met at the airport in England.'

Well, I thought, that's that. Then another thought struck me. I might not have much in the way of luggage, but I did not want to lose it. 'Will you keep it for me until I return?'

'You won't return,' he almost sneered. 'Your job's done—or will be when you deliver. But'—grudgingly it seemed—'I have to say *well* done. So far. But I didn't want you tailed from your flat in the Via Margutta after the drop. So presumably you've got your passport and so on. Now it's "Home James, and don't spare the horses!"'

Then, without another word, not even a parting shake of the hand, this extraordinary man Access jumped up and in a matter of seconds had turned the corner, out of my sight.

*　　*　　*

I had no difficulty finding a first-class seat on the express which would take me direct to Pisa, then right along the coast to the frontier at Ventimiglia and Menton in France; after that, along the coast road past Cannes, then near Fréjus a right turn, so to speak, and up the main railway to Paris—and Monsieur Gaston.

In my compartment, which I shared with one other passenger, I examined the tickets thoroughly. Everything seemed in order. I could foresee no problems, and my fellow passenger and I enjoyed an excellent dinner and shared a bottle of wine in the restaurant car, during which time we stopped at Pisa, then trundled along the coast, while I dozed until, in the early hours of the morning, the train, with a grinding of brakes and a sudden flurry of noises and shouting, arrived at Ventimiglia.

I had no luggage, so no customs problems, not that there usually were any on these trans-European trains. And as always happened the immigration authorities came through the entire train to each compartment to make a cursory examination of people's travel documents.

There would be a lot of waiting, that I knew, heads popping out to look, passengers seeing if they could get a platform drink at three in the morning, heads peering through pull-down windows into the dimly-lit noisy, long, grey platform. Hard to imagine that in a few hours it would be light and that behind those same platforms—just a stone's throw away!—lay the placid blue sea, sitting there waiting for the first strollers to saunter in the morning sun, waiting for it to shine as it had shone, in memory anyway, so often on us.

Finally, the sliding door of our corridor was pulled back and a polite Italian voice asked, 'Passports, please.'

There were two officials. The man who seemed to be in charge examined the other man's documents, which included a letter which he read carefully, and which I imagined would tell him the nature of his business. Satisfied, he handed the letter and his passport back and with a smart salute gave me the same polite, if slightly fixed, smile.

'Thank you, sir,' he said in good English when he saw the blue and gold of my British passport as I

256

handed it to him. Then, as he saw my name, I noticed a curious change in his face. I felt my nerves suddenly twist with fear. Warm friendliness was replaced with cold aloofness. He whispered to his companion then asked, 'Mr Painter?'

'Yes,' I nodded, mouth suddenly dry.

'Mr John Painter?'

'Yes. Look, that's my passport, with my photo in it.'

'I can see that,' said the official, still polite but in tones as shivering as ice.

'Well then—I'm English—and I don't see why—' Anger started to replace fear. 'What's all the delay about?'

'There's no delay, sir. We're just examining—'

'You seem upset.'

'I'm sorry, sir,' he said less politely. 'But there's something I don't quite understand. Would you be kind enough to step outside for a moment. There are one or two questions we would like to ask you.'

'Ask them here,' I tried to bluster but it failed.

'Sorry, sir, but if you please—and your luggage too, sir.'

'I have no luggage.'

'No *luggage*?' He put a wealth of meaning into his words. 'Really, sir? This way, if you please.'

I hesitated. I did not want to go. To hell with them! Why had they picked on me? Why the suspicion? They didn't know about the message I carried, they *couldn't*, but they must be suspicious of something. Otherwise, why pick me up out of hundreds of other passengers? One man with a vital secret, desperate to reach London, travelling under an assumed name! But they couldn't know any of this! So why the suspicion? What were they after?

257

And then I recalled Access' words: 'You've been followed.'

The man I judged to be the senior official sandwiched me between him and his assistant. He went first, then me, then the assistant. It was impossible to escape, even had I wanted to. As we reached the steep exit door at the end of the coach, he called to two policemen, one of whom ran up. Without a word to me he handed me over to them, giving me my passport.

'This way, please.' The policemen were polite but firm. 'Just a routine check sir, we'll keep the train waiting if necessary.'

I was taken through the large main ticket hall and into a block of buildings behind and adjoining. 'Administration,' the policeman explained, perhaps to keep me quiet. A lift carried me up four floors, along a green-painted corridor, and then one of them knocked.

'Come in.' I was almost shoved into a room little more than a cell in size, cold and forbidding—its off-white walls, plain wooden chairs and a deal table, and along one side a shelf on which there stood several bottles and odds and ends I did not recognise. But the effect, the impression of cold hate, almost terrified me. Worse still were the two men who now faced me. Their style, manner, clothes, everything about them stamped them as Italian Secret Police agents.

Shades of that terrible lunchtime at Forte dei Marmi when the two evil men had beaten up poor Vanni! What had happened to him, I wondered inconsequentially.

Afraid, alone, nonplussed, I flopped on to one of

the chairs and asked, in Italian, 'Please, what's the trouble?'

'Who said you could sit down?' roared the obvious boss, a hulk of a man. 'Get up, *figlio di puttana!*'

I reddened with anger at the insult—and the manner in which it was delivered. Son of a whore meant much more in Italy than sonofabitch in America. Men had fought duels for less.

'Now,' he sneered as I stood up. 'Give us the message and it'll save a lot of trouble.'

I hope I did not show my real terror or go pale or flush.

'What message?' I faltered.

'Don't give us that shit. You were seen at the Café Triangolo exchanging a message with a stranger.'

A stranger! Access. Obviously they did not know *him*. Why then me? 'I don't know what you're talking about.'

'We can hurt people who don't talk—or won't talk,' jeered the big man. 'Hurt them in ways that don't leave a mark, just to make them talk a bit. Knees in the balls for instance. Ever tried it?'

Thinking of the way they had done it to poor Vanni—what a long time ago it seemed—I tried to speak but was unable to force the words out, only shake my head. This was unbelievable, incredible. How the hell had they seen me—why me?—pass a message? It was more than baffling, it was terrifying.

'Nothing to it,' said the shorter of the two men, who looked a little like Himmler, the same weasel face, the same rimless glasses. 'We watch all you bloody foreigners. Why are you travelling? And where's your luggage?'

259

'I haven't got any,' I managed to croak. 'Everything was stolen.'

'A likely story. Well, if you won't give us the message we'll have to search you. Now,' said the short man, 'strip! And double quick!'

I hesitated. I did not believe it possible. Then without warning, the big man kicked me in the crotch with all the agility that a Thai wrestler displays, and with all the force of a rugger player taking a vital penalty kick.

I let out a scream and the big man grinned, 'We *told* you to get a move on. Undress!' He almost screamed the word. 'We can't keep this train waiting all night. But if you don't take off your clothes, you'll be spending the night here.'

I let out a groan, half at the pain racking my testicles, half fury. Panicking, I felt I had to do as they told me, for I *had* to catch that train. In Paris there would be a plane waiting for me. A matter of life and death, Access had said.

I groaned again, doubled up with pain.

'Come on,' growled the big man. 'Or want another go?'

'I'll undress,' I panted, 'but I've got no message.' My teeth were chattering now with the pain as, still doubled up with racking twinges, I tried to take off my trousers, then shirt, then thin vest, shoes and socks, leaving me standing shivering in my underpants, trembling with pain as much as with fear, while the man shouted, 'Take off those pants. Come on, or I'll tear 'em off. Scared?'

And then, looking at me shrivelled up with fear, he jeered, 'Don't think much of that for a man-sized prick,' then lunged at me, though this time he missed, but I could feel that he had got what he wanted, the search, and being a professional he was not going to waste energy.

The smaller man was going through every particle of my clothes with a professional air, even turning my socks inside out, feeling for hidden lumps in the slightly padded shoulders, every section of my suit, the turn-ups in the trousers, ripping the pockets in case of secret compartments. Meanwhile the big man took a kind of chisel or thick knife from the shelf and prised open one heel of my shoes, then the next—but all in vain.

'Nothing,' grunted the small man. 'Not a thing.'

I heaved an inward sigh of relief. At least it was over now, and the pain was beginning to subside.

I spoke to myself too soon.

'There's only one possible hiding place left.' The big man gave me a grin. 'And you look a bit like a pansy, so you should enjoy it.'

Oh Christ! Not that! I squirmed. I would not let them. I would fight—yes, if it did come to a fight—if I missed the train—

'So,' said the big man, 'just relax and enjoy it.'

I could not. My determination forced me not to submit, but there I was, stark naked, shivering with pain and the horror of it all and anyway, the matter was taken out of my hands—into the big man's—literally.

With one big swipe of his huge hands, he hit me across the face and as I stumbled, half senseless, he gripped me round the neck in a kind of half-Nelson lock. I could not move anything except thrash with my legs. I tried not to choke, but each time I attempted resistance, all he had to do was increase the pressure and cut off my supply of air. He pushed me on to the table, the edge cutting into my

261

flesh, and then somehow, he turned me over on to my stomach.

Kicking and screaming—and not realising that the room was soundproof—I tried to fight, but each time I tried to squirm, he increased the pressure until I all but stoppped breathing. Then I felt the little man try to fasten my legs which were still kicking. He must have got a large rope, looped it under and round the table and pulled it taut. The rope cut into my legs like a knife, but I could not even scream. I could just hear him panting with the exhaustion, and then he grunted, 'Ready! Hold his head tight.'

Dreading what was going to happen next, half-unconscious, but trying to maintain some sort of grip on life, I saw out of the corner of my eye, the smaller man take out a rubber sheet about a foot square—I saw it because he dropped it and he said with a leer, 'I don't want to get my hands dirty.' Then he opened a tin on a small stool and took a handful of jelly that looked like vaseline and went round and smeared it round the entrance to my rectum.

I could feel his filthy hands playing around my bottom and then, with a grunted, 'Let's see now,' to his comrade, he pushed his longest finger into my hole, protected by the thin rubber sheet, at first gently but then somehow I managed a scream of pain as he pushed it right up. He moved the finger around, each movement an agony in itself. Almost passing out, I heard him say, 'Nothing there.'

The big man swore and said, 'Must have got the wrong man. Come on, we'd better rush. Can't keep this train back much longer.'

All that had happened seems in the telling to have

taken years—certainly I lived a whole tortured life in that agonising spell—but it was only a few minutes, maybe half an hour, I never really knew, before I managed to stand up, but crouching with pain. With the help of the two men I stumbled about as if half drunk as they tried to put my clothes on, or at least assist. When that was finally accomplished, one of them had the gall to say to me with a grin, 'No hard feelings. All in the cause of duty.' Then the two policemen, who had waited at the end of the corridor, half dragged me to the platform and the comfort of the train.

'Put him in the guard's van. Can't put him in first-class until he feels better,' one shouted, ordering the guard, who was anxious to be off, to help me.

No sooner was I lying groaning on the floor, dumped on a mound of empty mail sacks, than I vaguely heard the whistle blow, the rumble of slowly turning wheels, and the guard muttered to me, 'Swine! They deserve to be killed for treating people like this.' He managed to give me a sip of coffee from a Thermos flask and a nip of something strong, rather like brandy.

I did not *look* any different, except that I seemed ill, as though I had been vomiting, and the one livid bruise on my cheek where he had hit me hardest must have shown.

Panting with exertion at every slight movement, I tried to make myself more comfortable, to fit myself into the creases and nooks and crannies of the hard canvas mailbags. My anus hurt atrociously, so did my face. And that devil's work with his probing finger seemed to have rearranged all my insides so that suddenly I was seized with panic as I tried to

263

get to the toilet in time.

The French guard, who had taken over from Italian when we entered a new country, was even more sympathetic. Somehow I managed to control myself, and with his help and repeated imprecations of 'Les salauds!' I just made it, seeming to empty myself of everything inside me. And when I wiped myself, the basin was covered with blood.

I staggered back to the guard's van but later, after I had liberally tipped the guard, he brought me hot coffee and brandy and then, with his help, I managed to make my way to the nearest vacant seat in the next compartment. It was a wagon-lit with two bunks which had now been transformed into two couches and after one astonished look at my face, the other occupant tried his best to ignore me.

The agony began to fade from reality to a solid, but dull pain, my rectum from a scream of pain to an equally dull sore. And above all, there was one *good* thing—the unwelcome yet welcome irritation of having one extra-large tooth in my mouth. And *that* gave me a slow, strange feeling. The agony and shame I had suffered in the spirit as well as in the flesh, slowly began to be replaced with another emotion, a kind of tattered pride.

Never mind what those bastards had done to me! Goddam it, I still had the vital message, and I had defeated those two lumps of shit who had been unable to find it!

Next stop Paris!

264

CHAPTER SIXTEEN

The trip by RAF plane from Le Bourget to an unnamed airfield in southern England was uneventful and I arrived around lunchtime where an ancient-looking Austin, driven by a pretty young WAAF, was waiting to take me to London.

'You know my address?' I asked her.

'Yes, sir. Broadway Mansions.' She consulted a slip of paper. 'To see a Mr Morris.'

'No, no. I don't live *there*,' I explained. 'I really want to slip home and have a wash and brush up before I—er—present myself,' and though I did not say so, to try and repair some of the damage to my face.

'Sorry, sir.' She really *did* seem sorry. 'But my orders are—'

'Don't worry,' I sighed. 'If my boss doesn't mind my looking a mess, why should I worry?'

It took us a good hour and a half to reach Westminster and as the WAAF opened the back door of the car she sympathised, 'I do hope it doesn't hurt too much, sir. Your face, I mean, it's very swollen.' She did not ask any questions.

Nor did Mr Morris when I made my way to the end of the corridor-like passage with its sign 'Other Business'.

'Good morning,' he said. 'Miss Pilbeam is waiting for you on the fourth floor,' and as he waved me towards the lift, added almost enigmatically, 'Good to have you back, sir'.

Miss Pilbeam was quietly efficient and after expressing concern at the bruising on my face said,

265

'The same drill as usual, sir. C is most anxious to see you. As soon as the green light shows up, please go right in.'

She closed the door to her office quietly, and almost immediately the red light switched off and the green came on. I knocked and C stood up from his desk, looking just the same, wearing the same blue suit, I could swear, shook hands and said, 'Welcome back. Sorry you had a bit of a fight. But Access was delighted with your message.'

I made some non-committal remark, and he asked me a trifle anxiously, 'The face looks badly swollen. I hope it doesn't interfere with the—dentistry.'

'It's the other side,' I cheered him up.

Almost with a visible sigh of relief, he cried, 'Good! Then we'd better send you right away.' He pressed a button on an intercom set and the disembodied voice of Miss Pilbeam asked, 'Yes, C?'

'Get a car and take our friend Mr Painter to Wakeford, the dentist. It won't take him long. Tell the driver to keep the car, then it can take Mr Painter to his home. And at the same time, send a second car to Wakeford, and tell him to take one of our men and wait until Mr Wakeford gives him a small packet and bring it straight to me. I'll wait here until it arrives.'

When Miss Pilbeam had switched off, he turned to me and added, 'It won't hurt at all. All over in ten minutes. Won't even need a whiff of gas. And as a bonus, Wakeford might be able to do something to ease the pain in your cheek. I'll phone him. Then you go home, while I wait for the microdot film. Like to have a bite of dinner with me tonight? You would? Good. Meet you at the Savile

266

Club at seven o'clock, and then maybe I'll be able to answer some of the questions that I know must be puzzling you.'

'Well, I *am* baffled by lots of things—how and why the message so conveniently arrived in Florence when I was there. That sort of thing, you know.'

'I do know. Right.' C seemed in a hurry. 'You go off to the dentist, no. 1A Upper Wimpole Street. See you this evening.'

* * *

The London dentist's surgery was very different from the one in Rome. The area round Wimpole Street had received isolated bombs and, once smart, it hinted now of seediness. The overwhelming air attacks had not yet started, but the docks were being regularly subjected to sneak attacks. The surgery was up a flight of stairs that were dusted with plaster from an isolated, no doubt jettisoned bomb, and the old-fashioned chair was a bit lopsided in its anchorage. But the dentist was a perpetually cheerful man who seemed to thrive on misfortune. (Why are dentists usually so cheerful?)

'Never mind, eh? Here today and gone tomorrow, that's life. Well, isn't it?'

I had to admit that it was.

'Take some of my suppliers. May & Baker for instance: can't keep up with the demand, lab experiments, always the search for the unattainable. See what I mean?'

I could not see how it related to the work to be done, but he had me in the chair while he jabbered on, with my mouth open—hurting like hell—and

267

my eyes staring at laths through the torn ceiling plaster. I tried to indicate the tooth that needed attention, but there was no need.

'Okay, old chap. Won't take a minute. Nasty knock on the cheek. But as for the tooth, a little solvent round the base, lift off the lid, and hey presto! Something to be found inside, I gather, no questions asked, the last thing I'd do anyway. Well, the war must go on, as they say. Might sting a bit as I spray the gum, but no undue pain. We're all brave soldiers now—hey!'

I could feel his deft fingers, very gentle as they probed and massaged with a cottonwool bud, then a cold feeling as of menthol applied to a feverish forehead. Then it was over and there was the false cover, inverted like a tiny white top hat, and the microscopic ball of silk already springing open after being confined in its oral protection.

'Mission completed,' the dentist said with a laugh.

The mouth felt curiously empty—an odd feeling even after only one day with the larger tooth.

'Now let's take a look at this face of yours, and see if I can do anything.' Feeling the bruised inside of my cheek gently, he said, 'They certainly gave you a hell of a swipe.' I nodded, unable to speak.

The dentist took a good look at my teeth themselves. No damage, he told me, none loosened, and feeling around carefully, announced that there was no sign of any permanent damage to the jawbone. 'And that's the single most important thing. There's only one thing I can do.' He rang for the girl and asked her to bring in a bottle, the name of which I did not catch.

'This is special menthol spray for the armed

forces,' he explained as I got out of the chair. 'Just spray it in the mouth. It helps to heal the bruised inside flesh remarkably. The best I can suggest—just spray your mouth thoroughly twice a day and it'll help.'

And that was that.

But it wasn't, quite. 'Felt the deadening, did you, when I sprayed? Yes. Well, that was temporary—for the moment, see, while I probed out the amalgam. But it'll be a bit sore when the gum recovers its feeling. So I'll give you a longer-term thing.'

I could see he was busy with another spray. 'May as well use the relief nature provides. Donkey's years old, this one. Ancient Egypt, the Greeks, the Chinese. It's the basis of that stuff you had for the probe, menthol. *Mentha piperita* in the pharmacy, peppermint oil to you and me. Peppermint camphor, some call it. Either way, you make it by blowing steam through the leaves of the common peppermint herb. Used in toothpaste, coughdrops, chest rubs, inhalants for colds in the head ... there we are. Your mouth will feel like it's got a gobstopper in it ... never see 'em nowadays, do you? Well, c'est la guerre. Any problems, come back. But I guess you won't have any.' As I rose from the chair he gave me a friendly poke in the ribs: 'That's a good set of dining-room furniture you've got there'—and he roared with laughter.

*   *   *

When C greeted me at the Savile Club that evening and steered me towards the bar he cheered me up with the words, 'There's one thing you can still get
269

here, your fair share of whisky. In the pubs it's getting very short.'

We sat in the dark bar-room overlooking a small patio; deep leather armchairs and sofas, a few pictures on the walls, a bar at one end—a general feeling of homeliness, as though to say, 'Don't change anything. We like it as it is.'

'I prefer to come here to talk shop,' C confessed, 'because no one ever knows why we're even talking, let alone what we're talking about, I'm just as well-known in the City and no one ever asks me for Stock Exchange tips. But let's have a spot of dinner and after that, over the port you can fire away if you want to ask any innocent questions.'

I did just that after a quite reasonable dinner in an almost empty dining-room near the blue-ceilinged ballroom. 'Empty because of the problem of getting home at night,' explained C. 'The blackout's done enormous damage to evening drinking at clubs!'

'I'm sure the first thing that fascinates me, the first question I'd love to ask—is harmless.'

'That's a relief. What is it?'

'How the hell does this microdot business that Access was talking about actually work?'

'Oh that! Well, it's not difficult. There's a boffin in Dresden—Zapp, his name is—who's dreamed up something called "Mikropunkt". It's a system using cameras and microscopes; and the essence of it is that, instead of using an enlarger such as you use to make a snapshot into pictures to hang on the wall, you use a *reducer*. With that you can photograph an ordinary foolscap sheet of paper covered with typing and reduce it to the size of a stamp.'

I was tempted to ask if that was why 'Privitera,

270

Filatelico' had been chosen to act as a 'drop' in Rome, but that would have been too frivolous. C was not a frivolous man.

'Having got that far in the reduction scale, Zapp figured out that a microscope would be needed to bring it back to size. Well, that doesn't need much figuring out, does it? Then he had the brainwave. Why not apply the same principle to the microscope as to the reducer. Photograph the reduced image through a *reversed* microscope. Get me?'

I pondered. 'Well, if you got it much smaller it would be microsopic—'

'Precisely. Mikropunkt. As tiny as the dot on an *i*. Then the negative has to be coated with some stuff called "collodion", a sort of plastic you get from cellulose, and you've got your message pinpoint size. All you have to do then, if you want to, is write a perfectly innocuous letter about the state of the weather, lift your microdot off the negative with a finely pointed needle and transfer it to the letter where a full stop or a dot on an *i* should be. At the receiving end of course you reverse the whole process and bring your secret message back to readable size. Pretty simple, eh?'

'But to the layman like me, fascinating what you *can* do!'

'I suppose it is. Now, what next?' asked C with a slight smile.

'Something you won't answer.' I tried a lopsided smile of my own. 'What *was* this vital message all about? It's a bit irritating to be beaten up, have your teeth messed about—and not have the faintest idea why.'

'I sympathise.' C really did show his sympathy. 'But it isn't easy. How can I tell you a bit of the

271

biggest secret of the war!'

'A hint?'

'Yes, a hint—or two, perhaps. Let's start by saying that in nine days, on 10 May'—he spoke carefully, with great deliberation—'life as we have known it in your short spell will cease, completely, until we've won the war.'

I felt myself go pale. The intensity he put into the words was frightening.

'On 10 May the balloon goes up. The whole of Europe will be in flames.'

'How can you be so sure?' I blurted out.

'You!' he said drily.

'Me? The message?'

He nodded gravely. The Sandpit, as the coffee room was called, was empty. There was no way our conversation could be overheard. 'Just that. The message contained complete details of Hitler's overall strategy for a massive three-pronged attack—the roles of the German leaders, their positions, the first attack against the Maginot Line, a second in the Ardennes, a third against the Low Countries—Belgium, Holland, and Luxembourg. An enormous superiority in air power will devastate any chance of opposition. That about sums it up, and thanks to you, the cabinet is meeting tonight.'

For a few moments I did not know what to say and, realising the sense of despair—almost of fear—at such knowledge being given to such a young man, he patted my shoulder and suggested, 'Let's go straight on to double Scotches.'

When the glasses were in front of us, he told me that since all the military chiefs would know most of the details the following day, he thought it only fair to let me into part of the secret.

272

'You earned it—and were badly knocked around. And'—a trifle portentously—'after all, you are a member of the SIS.'

'I'll never breathe a word to anyone,' I promised him fervently. 'Never.'

'Let's say, just for nine or ten days,' said C drily. 'After that your secret will be common property.'

'It's terrifying.' I sipped my whisky. 'Thank God I *did* get through.'

'Thank God, indeed.'

'But how you must have worked to break the code so quickly. It was all double Dutch to me—the message of jumbled figures I carried.'

'We're lucky. I can't really say much about it, you'll understand that I'm sure, but we do have vital German knowledge about their cryptology— and have had since before the war. It's ...' he hesitated, 'it's a kind of machine, and our friend Hitler hasn't the faintest idea that we know all about it.'

C paused as if wondering whether he should reveal more. 'I thought you'd ask about the codes, "crypts" as we call them. I can assure you that we're very well advanced in the science of cryptology—thanks largely to our workers in the firm—the firm in which your service gave you some amusement, I believe.' [*It was not until many years that I realised C had been referring to the fact that throughout the war we knew the secrets of the German 'Enigma' encoding machine—christened 'Ultra' by us because of the ultra-secrecy involved. A Polish spy had contrived to get hold of a German machine and two copies had been reproduced in Poland, one of which had been given to an SIS man in July 1939. The Germans never knew that we had the machine which*

273

could decipher their most secret messages.]

'It's fantastic—and frightening,' I said. 'And when you think of all the luck involved in being in the right place to get the message.'

'I don't quite understand,' said C.

'Well, how *lucky* I was to be in Florence when that story broke. What a break for me. Seems too good to be true.'

'Luck?' C stared with a faraway look at the ceiling of the Sandpit.

'Well,' I used the word again. 'I might have got you what the newspapers call a scoop. But what a fantastic break to have me so handy to take the message to Access.'

'Really! Lucky?' C's pretence of innocence was studied.

'Well,' I used the same word a third time, perhaps to cover my increasing irritation, 'wasn't it? Are you going to pretend that it *wasn't* lucky?'

'My dear chap,' said C, not quite patronisingly, 'we don't *like* the word luck in the service. We don't like to trust in luck.'

'I appreciate that. But if it happens to fall in your lap?'

'It might—but only if you've conveniently placed your lap in the right place.'

Perhaps it was the fact that I could still feel my sore face—I *had* taken quite a bashing—that made me say, almost crossly, 'I *am* tired, C. Too tired to try and understand people who insist on talking in riddles.'

'Sorry.' Almost absently and without asking, he walked through the large division between the Sandpit and the bar and ordered (without asking me!) two more large whiskies and carried them over to our table.

'Ham Johns—you're home now, so we can use your real name—let me say first that you're still a member of the SIS, but the fact that you've been recognised by one group of Italian secret police poses a problem. In fact your duties may soon be drastically changed—and even more dangerous. But first you're baffled by what happened in Florence, and I feel I owe you an apology.'

'For what?' I felt slightly amused.

'You were,' he hesitated, staring into the glass as though searching for words. 'How can I put it without being offensive?' He sighed. 'There was no coincidence involved. You were—er—set up.'

'Set up!' Astonished, I echoed his words.

'Well, kind of.' Then he added even more drily, 'You didn't really think we'd take you on as a secret agent just because your father told us you're a good chap? Even though he is'—with a discreet cough—'in the Foreign Office. But at least we were short of operatives in Italy after Venlo so when your father told us that you had been working for a famous man like Bernard Berenson—though I'd never heard of him—it gave us a point at which to start checking on your past. Especially as Florence was a weak link because most vital messages were passed to the man who almost became your father-in-law.'

'The Prince!' I cried.

'Exactly. Messages arriving from Germany were often sent to him for immediate transmision to Ciano in Rome. And though we had a strong operative in Germany, somehow we didn't always intercept the messages.'

My mouth started to drop as I listened

275

spellbound. 'A vital source.' 'A weak link.' What was it all about? I was about to blurt out something or other when C held out a hand, as a kind of warning.

'Once we knew all about your involvement in Settignano, your habits, your—er—love affair with the daughter of the Prince—well, *that* was the reason we recruited you. We already had a faithful contact in Germany, and we heard *rumours*—only that—of major war plans being hatched by Hitler and we told Access to let you go when you asked for a holiday in Florence, something that normally would never be granted in work of our kind. Leaving an operative on the loose! Tut, tut. But in this case it was different. You seem to have fitted in perfectly.'

'Then why did you send me to Rome ih the first place?' I was bewildered by the sudden revelations.

'Didn't want you hanging around in Florence until you were needed, so I suggested to Access that he keep you in Rome until you *were* needed in Florence; and let *you* suggest that you'd like to visit Florence. But Access was only to agree when we heard from our Berlin contact that a message would soon arrive in Florence from Berlin.'

'The message seemed nothing but a string of figures and letters—it meant nothing to me.' I had to say *something*, if only to cover my stupefaction at the thought that all this had been one minor cog in a Europe-wide operation in which nobody except the men at the top really knew that I would be in just the right place at the right time to pick up a drop. And this, I sensed, was only the start of my involvement. The Prince I could understand. But who else?

But who would deliver to the drop. It would have to be the most unlikely of all persons. It *couldn't* be—yet it *had* to be. It must be Roz, the flirtatious but evasive Roz ('secret', Fiamma always called her) who, as i approached the villa, had cried out the word 'Painter', and then denied using the word. And how understandable it was that C, after finding out about my connections with the Prince and his daughters, would grab at the opportunity of recruiting someone on the inside, so to speak, then letting him—me!—act as a simple dupe caught up in a tangled web of which I knew nothing.

'Quite clever,' I had to admit, if a little sarcastically. 'At least I feel better now I know the message was worth it.'

'It certainly was,' said C. 'Now, all we can do is wait and see.'

Our conversation did not, though, clear up all the questions in my mind. How had I come to be followed back to Rome from Florence? Could it have been through Kurt, who had said rather vaguely that he was in 'Intelligence' and may have suspected I was too? Or might it have been through Roz? Could she have been playing a double game?

These questions, and others, remained unanswered for a very long time.

INTERLUDE

FORTUNES OF WAR, 1940–1943

CHAPTER SEVENTEEN

So far I have tried to tell the story of the strange involvement in my life—and the lives of my friends—of the beautiful daughters of the Prince Caeseri. Now I must explain the changes in my own life until the moment, some three years later, when my path again crossed with one of the girls—in, of all places, an accidental meeting in the midst of war in Regent Street in London.

But first, in brief, the intervening months and years. Hitler's massive attack, of which my message had produced such early warning, took place, as we all know, tearing Europe into shreds, causing the evacuation of Dunkirk, forcing France, to say nothing of other countries, into humiliating defeat after Paris had given in with hardly a shot fired—shades of heroic Warsaw!

The Battle of Britain followed—this was at least a glorious victory when the RAF shot the Luftwaffe out of the skies. Then followed the blitz, the sustained bombing of London, the massive raids on dozens of cities like flattened Coventry, devastated Plymouth.

I was angrily idle at this time, though in touch regularly with C at Broadway Mansions, waiting for what many of us felt would be the next stop—the invasion of an ill-equipped England. The only vaguely good sign was, at long last, that the neutral Roosevelt, treading carefully, did order conscription in the United States. I wondered what Steve was doing.

Father had told me 'not to mope' (his words)

because now I *wanted* to join up—a pilot in the RAF was my first choice—but it was my father who made me hesitate.

'C says hang on a bit. He may have a special job for you,' he said.

★   ★   ★

A week after that meeting with Father, the 'call to duty' finally came—in the form of an urgent request to meet C privately at his flat in Queen Anne's Gate. The flat, which backed on to the Passport Control Office in Broadway Mansions, was linked with it by a secret corridor which led straight into C's office on the fourth floor; but there was a great deal of difference in the comfort and furnishing. The threadbare carpet and tatty Ministry of Works furniture had been replaced with deep armchairs, excellent paintings on the walls, an elegant walnut wine table, and a drinks table glittering with crystal decanters and shining, polished glasses.

C poured two glasses of pale sherry. Light twinkled on the facets of the crystal and the amber liquid. 'I hope you will enjoy the next job I have in mind for you.'

I think I looked suitably eager as I sipped my sherry—a very good *fino* it was. I promised, 'I'll do my best.'

'Let me explain. Winnie's set his heart on the formation of a new team of specialists; and when Mr Churchill sets his heart on something he's inclined to get it. The group's very much concerned with sabotage and clandestine operations to help Resistance organisations in countries where the Boche has got a hold'—he noticed my raised

282

eyebrows and went on—'exactly. Just what we in the SIS have been doing. But I understand the activities of this new group—which is, by the way, called Special Operations Executive or SOE for short—will be rather more boisterous—less concerned with disguises and secret meetings.' I could see he thought of the new group in rather the same disparaging way I had come to view SIS. Professional jealousy, no doubt.

'I see, sir,' I said. 'And I'm to join?'

'You are indeed. The first recruits are now undergoing special training in your home county, Yorkshire. You entrain the day after tomorrow for Darlington, where transport will be waiting to take you to Catterick. After that'—his gesture was one of dismissal, almost as if he washed his hands of me and the rival organisation; then, relenting, he added, 'Let's have a last drink to your success.'

★   ★   ★

I have very little memory—certainly few happy ones—of the months I spent training in Catterick, for though we were officers being seconded for special, and secret, training, we had to do our weeks of square-bashing as privates in an OCTU—Officer Cadet Training Unit. Catterick camp was a vast spread of monotonous barrack buildings more or less on the site where the Romans camped their legions, calling the place Cateractonium. For the first month I was square-bashing on the parade ground that was big enough to muster a whole brigade. The RSM carried a pacing-stick and was heavy on sarcasm: 'Mr Johns, *sir*, can't you get it into your 'ead, *sir*,

283

that in the attention position the thumbs is 'eld in line with the seams of the trousers, and not wandering round as if you want to scratch yer privates. Is that clear, *sir*? Right, then. Atten*shun. Sir*.'

Much of the training had to do with explosives and could not be carried out near buildings. So our training HQ was soon transferred to Richmond, five or so miles away on the River Swale. From there we made forays out over the moors. We constructed mock bridges away from prying eyes, had supplies dropped by parachute, learned the hard way to endure bitter cold (Swaledale is often under snow for three months of winter) by building snow fortifications and learning from medicos about the mortification of the flesh in frostbite.

We laid down lengths of railway, drilling the sleepers to insert explosive charges at the weakest spots where the rails joined, marched over the moors with hundredweight loads packed round our bodies, and inspected transport planes from which, after several weeks' training, we started practice jumping. As another subaltern I chummed up with said, 'It's rich full life, Hammy boy. Exhausting, though. I planned a snogging session with a girl last night and I didn't even have the energy to get my hand up her skirt.'

In quieter moments we listened to lectures about the nature of explosives that had chemical names so long they had to be abbreviated to forms like Tetryl, PETN, Hexogen, and Pentolite; and our heads buzzed with instructions about making fuses, primers, and detonators. But there were not many quiet moments. For the most part we were trying to cross the fast-flowing Swale River on rafts made of

284

bits of stunted shrubs, or climbing the keep of the Norman castle with grappling irons, and 'blacking up' our faces and hands for night raids. We bivouacked in the disused warehouse that had once been the Theatre Royal and were frequently awakened by cunningly timed alarms that ensured the minimum of sleep and the maximum of discomfort.

Our commandant was a brigadier who had the build of an ox and a bullying nature that he assured us was 'for our own good'.

'You're not going to find the natives friendly when you're trying to blow up their power stations and wreck their trains; so it's no use letting you get soft. Your lives, and the lives of a lot of other people, are going to depend on whether you can go without sleep and food, or run, jump, swim ... in short, *resist*—in the physical sense as well as the moral. Got me?' he asked.

We got him all right.

Six months later—fitter than I had ever been, and filled with eagerness, having changed (I hoped!) code names for real action, I went on my first mission that lasted for month after month.

A two-seater Lysander with a range of only six hundred miles landed me in Italy—with only a few gallons of fuel to spare—then flew back across the frontier to refuel in neutral Switzerland.

In northern Italy, and disguised as an Italian peasant, I was guided to my landing spot with blinking flashlights in the countryside near Alba, not far from Turin. I brought with me a large supply of explosives and all the necessary equipment for large-scale operations.

My job was not only to link up with a waiting

band of partisans and teach them what I had learned in Yorkshire—how to blow up trains, bridges and all the rest of it—but to *lead* them in what turned out to be a highly successful series of partisan exploits, culminating in a major explosion at the Fiat works.

To the local Italians, who hated Mussolini and even more the increasing authority of the Germans, I became something of a folk-lore hero, although I do not think I did anything really spectacular or dangerous. But when the pick-up Lysander landed in a deserted field, and we re-fuelled her with stolen aviation fuel and we left, I was loaded with bottles of Chianti and grappa.

I spent a good two years, loving every moment of it, and if I do not tell all the details it is because half of me was, in a sense, dead. So near and yet so far from Florence, and without any knowledge of my darling Fiamma. I did not even dare to phone, because in no way could I disobey orders. Nor dared I sneak off and make my way to Florence on my own without permission—which would never have been granted. I would have been court-martialled on my return to England, and rightly.

By the time I did land back in England in 1943 the war had become global. The Germans had carried massive offensives deep into the heart of Russia. But their attempt to take Stalingrad had failed and they had been defeated. In the Far East, citadels like Hong Kong and Singapore and Batavia had of course been quickly over-run by Japanese who at Pearl Harbor had brought the might of the United States into the war. By the time I returned to a well-earned leave—and promotion to

Captain!—London had become a completely different place—cosmopolitan to a degree it had never known. There were Free French and Polish and Dutch troops, even some Russians in their odd greenish uniforms, and Chinese sailors in the black and gold of their navy; there were Czech airmen, Canadian nurses in their elegant grey, and, of course, the Yanks, as they were for the most part chummily known (though not always so chummily tolerated when they 'acted big' in the pubs and consumed most of the drink). The first contingent of GIs—nearly three thousand of them—who had landed at Belfast on 26 January 1942, received a blaze of publicity in the press. Hardly a soul in England had failed to register that GI meant 'Government Issue', and sweet-starved kids had adopted the importunate phrase 'Got any gum, chum?' at the first sight of any American soldier, and did a brisk trade in jam jars among frustrated drinkers who found the supply of irreplaceable glasses in pubs getting low.

It was all a great sight.

Then I saw another great sight—one which nearly stopped my heart with the shock of it, and this is what brings me back to the mainstream of my story.

It was a lovely afternoon in early August 1943 and—just to pass the time more than for any other reason—I was strolling along Regent Street, day-dreaming—there was little to buy without coupons—when I bumped into a woman.

Apologising profusely, I took off my peaked cap, stretched back to pick up her handbag which had fallen, and then, astounded at the unbelievable, we both cried out so loudly that people around us stopped and gaped.

'Lella, darling! What are you doing here?'

'Ham, darling. I've been searching all over to try to find you.'

For a split second I stood there, unshed tears of excitement smarting behind my eyes and then, very unsteadily, I said, '*You*, Lella! Oh! If you know what it makes me feel like, just to see one of the family!'

Equally unsteadily, she laughed, 'Yes, it *is* a family reunion!'

'But *how*? Come on, Lella, let's find a place to have a drink?' I bustled her towards the sandbagged Piccadilly Circus—minus its statue of Eros—and we crossed and went into the Trocadero.

'But *how*?' I asked again, putting my cap and swagger cane on an adjacent chair. 'What's an Italian lady doing strolling along Regent Street in the evening sun?'

Almost with a grin—and really she *did* have an infectious laugh—she puffed out her chest ostentatiously and in an exaggerated American accent said, 'Listen, buddy, I'll have you know that I'm a bona fide citizen of the *U*nited States and a member of her armed forces—here to win the war for you, and I kinda take exception'—then she almost dissolved into gales of laughter and spluttered in Italian—'don't you remember? I'm an American citizen. And when Steve joined the US Air Force, he's a bomber pilot, I managed to get posted as a WAAC, helping to run the Stars and Stripes Lounge—a huge place just behind Marble Arch, overnight bedrooms, baths, pool tables, a bar, card rooms. It's got everything.'

'And Steve?'

288

Her face clouded. 'When he was flying from England, it was fine—well, nearly fine. On lots of nights I lay awake, but always the next morning he phoned. Then suddenly, at a moment's notice, he was posted. The entire unit. From the subtle hints he makes in his letters, I can only feel that he might be in North Africa. That's where all the action seems to be. But the letters only come through the Army Post Office in the States, and of course they're censored.'

'You must, well, miss him terribly.'

'Agony.' She put a wealth of misery into that one word. I ordered two gins and tonic—at least they seemed to have a good supply of gin. Sometimes it was hard to get specific drinks, but easier if you tipped in advance. 'I stay at the club,' she explained, 'gotta nice room with my own bath'—the way the Americanisms like 'gotta' had crept into her vocabulary amused me.

'And of course,' I teased her, 'there must be so many pretty girls in the place—and so many husky men—guys I suppose you'd call them.'

'I don't date,' she smiled, 'if that's what you mean. Oh dear, doesn't it seem an age since we were all swimming together in our lovely Indian pool at Magari. And just when we were so happy, that awful business of you and Fiamma. Darling Fiamma, I haven't heard a word from her since the war started. Isn't it terrible to think of Fiamma and me as *enemies*. And you've never even seen her since our wedding day!'

I hesitated. After all, it *had* been in times of peace—and in Italy. And yet my secret trip to Italy had been the start of an enormous adventure so long ago. I would have to tread carefully.

'Actually I did see Fiamma once—just for a few hours. In the spring of 1940.'

'During the war! *You actually met*?' She put her glass down on the table, looking so astonished she seemed afraid she might spill it. '*You actually met her*!'

'Just before Italy entered the war,' I corrected her. 'I was so—so damned worried about Fiamma that I got a sort of special dispensation to go for a few days. I saw your father too.'

'You did!'

'Yes, and of course I learned that Fiamma was married. It was the first thing he told me.'

'Poor Ham! It must have been a terrible shock.'

'Well—the Prince did explain everything—'

'Mama was horrible to put you into such a position. She has a wonderful capacity for righteous indignation—part of her forthright Yorkshire upbringing, I suppose.'

I was not placated, and least of all as a Yorkshireman. No excuse of character was going to mitigate the separation she had forced on us. I said with heavy sarcasm, 'Well, I hope she enjoys her spell in Switzerland recovering from all the trouble she's caused. It should take a long time.'

'She's got some friends in Interlaken. If my guess is right she'll stay with them until'—she made an all-embracing gesture—'all this is over. That way she won't be an added responsibility for Papa, who's always tied up with his ... government work.'

'Whatever it is,' I said thoughtfully.

'Whatever it is,' she echoed. 'I've never really known.' She touched my hand sympathetically. 'But not so much about Mama—more of the other mama. You have a baby son! Is he beautiful?'

'Just like me, according to Fiamma,' I said proudly. 'Of course, when I saw him, he was only a few weeks old. Now he must be quite a toddler—he's three-and-a-half almost. I wonder when I will see them next?'

'At first I heard all the news. You see,' she explained, 'until Italy was at war, we could write letters from America, we could even phone at times. That was when we learned about Fiamma marrying that awful man—'

'Awful?'

'To Fiamma all men must have been horrible compared with you!' She leaned over and touched my hand. 'And then, once the war started—even though America wasn't yet in it—we were never able to phone each other. Still,' with a sigh, 'that's war. And you, Ham, what are you doing?'

'Oh, bits of this and that,' I lied evasively, wondering what astonished comments she would have made had she known that I spent two years or more *living* in Italy—without, alas, ever getting as far south as Florence. But I did not dare. Discretion was the basic price of my job. And I was so overjoyed to see a member of the family again—any of them except the mother!—that nothing could disguise my sense of sheer delight. Lella looked very much the same. That mischievous smile was still there. She not only had a beautiful figure and smile, and wonderful legs shown to great advantage in her khaki-olive green uniform, but she looked so—what was the word I was searching for!—so *inviting*. Yes, that was it.

'Tell you what,' I said suddenly. 'I'm waiting for a posting. Could come any day, literally, or else a month, you never know. But one thing is certain—when I go, it's usually at twenty-four hours' notice, even less, so I was wondering'—impulsively—'shall we go dancing?'

'Dancing! In war time?'

'Why not?' I asked recklessly. 'Who knows when we'll ever meet again!'

'You're right. Why not? Where? When?'

'I'll pick you up at eight this evening and we'll go to Parkes's Club. *Very* sophisticated. You'll love it. I'll come and fetch you in my old Ford. Dinner at the club first.'

'Air raids?'

'Hopefully very few. There are sporadic raids, but the docks still get most of them. The odd bomb might drop somewhere else, but don't worry, Parkes's has the choicest air raid shelter in London. You'll love the place. And wonderful service. My father made me a member after my last—er—mission and lets me sign the bills, so we can't go wrong.'

'And you'll fetch me in your car?'

'Of course.'

'Good. I hate the black-out. I get so scared.'

* * *

We reached Parkes's in one of the small streets off Shepherd Market, not far from Curzon Street, promptly at a quarter past eight. These were times of early dinners. Even the theatres started at seven to encourage people to get home early.

I knew that Lella would love Parkes's. The cost of a dinner was limited to the statutory five shillings (the maximum price for any meal in England) plus a liberal tip, usually paid in advance, as I had done at the Trocadero. The size of the tip usually determined the quality of the meal. A headwaiter just offered what he thought the tip—a disguise for part of the meal—was worth.

Parkes's, I was sure, had excellent stocks of food that was unrationed, but which was consequently in short supply—such as fish, and including lobster, poultry, venison, game. All vegetables were unrationed, though of course you never saw imported items like bananas. Still, given the right opportunity, you could still have a wonderful meal, and Parkes's had some good wines.

Lella, dressed in a newly pressed American uniform, looked so pretty that she immediately drew appreciative eyes from the galaxy of waiters. Especially attractive was her hair beneath a snappy forage cap, the hair flowing over the back of her neck and the top of her shoulders.

She fell in love with Parkes's. What made it so attractive—apart from its exclusivity—was what I can only call its 'homely' atmosphere. You went upstairs for pre-dinner drinks in a room which might have come from a larger version of your own sitting-room. Deep sofas faced each other, separated by a large, long coffee table, one couple on one sofa, complete strangers on the sofa on the other side of the drinks table. You did not talk to each other; it was not a 'get-together' club; but you were all part of the strange family, for the room contained no set pieces of neatly arranged chairs and tables, just corners filled with sofas, some with tables, some not. And when we had two very dry martinis—a drink which Lella had newly discovered—Paul, the tall imposing restaurant

293

manager to whom I had already offered a tangible 'insurance' against a bad meal, did not present a menu, but made suggestions, mentioning in a confidential whisper, 'We just happen, Captain Johns, to have a couple of very attractive lobsters, or if you prefer, one of our members has sent us a few brace of partridges to allow members to celebrate what used to be called the Glorious Twelfth'—he somehow managed to invest the last two words with capitals.

'I'm famished,' cried Lella. 'That's fine by me. Lobster and partridge.'

'I'm sorry, madam,' Paul coughed discreetly, 'but government regulations stipulate that diners can only have one main course. Lobster *or* partridge.'

'It's the rule darling,' I explained.

'Oh!' She looked baffled for a moment, then smiled at the waiting Paul. 'I'm so used to eating in the club, where nine out of ten men shout for "seconds"—anyway, lobster for me, please.'

'And for me,' I agreed. 'We'll come down in half an hour. A bottle of club white, and then if you can find a bottle of champers, put it on the ice for later when we go down to dance.'

'This is a heavenly place.' Lella looked round the dark-coloured walls, papered in a beautiful dark red semi-floral design, covered with paintings, mostly of animals—any, from dogs to horses.

When we descended to the dining-room on the ground floor, the room had the same pattern of old-fashioned wallpaper and paintings covered the walls here too, but the tables, more formal now, of course, were well spaced and on them napkins were stiff, the silver gleamed, the plates sparkled.

'It's all so *beautiful*,' Lella almost sighed, but with contentment, 'like it used to be at home. If only our lives could be as beautiful, and as peaceful.'

'Ah! That's asking too much.' I tasted the cold white table wine and nodded to the sommelier.

All went well at first, but then I cried, 'Damn!' just as we had finished the lobsters. It was the sirens. They started to wail their up-and-down piercing of the night. 'A raid,' I said to her. 'Nuisance value!'

All the same, the government was still very strict about air-raid precautions or, as they were always referred to, ARP.

'I'm afraid, sir, we'll all have to go to the shelters.' Paul looked apologetically towards Lella as he made the rounds of the tables.

'Do we *have* to?' Lella instinctively whispered.

''Fraid so. You'll just have to do without your mouse trap.'

'Mouse what?'

'Ghastly cheese. Now it's downstairs.'

'This way, please, ladies and gentlemen.' Paul stood at the top of the circular staircase. Vaguely I could hear the sound of dance music. It sounded like 'Smoke Gets In Your Eyes'.

'Where are you taking me?' Lella looked positively alarmed as, with the descent, the sound of music took over from the wail of the sirens.

'This is the shelter. A genuine shelter. With, as it happens, a band,' and to Paul, 'You kept a table?'

'Of course, sir. This way, madam.'

'It's not possible,' cried Lella as she took in the imtimate dance room, with its small circular floor surrounded by tables and, near the exit, a cloakroom and lavatory, and opposite the stairs a platform on which the band led by Dixie Dixon and his Blues, famous for the way he mingled his blues piano arrangements, and his three other instruments. Dixie specialised in producing soft, warm tender music, none of your strident so-called 'modern' tunes.

We danced, drank our champagne.

'I just realised,' I said, 'I've never danced with you before.'

'Am I as good as Fiamma?'

There was the heavy boom of firing which, I thought, must be the guns in Hyde Park.

'Ah!' I said. 'Not the same. You never dance in quite the same way as you do with the girl you're in love with.'

'True. Steve always says the same.'

The interesting thing was that Lella herself seemed to have quietened down since her marriage. The old days of teasing me seemed to have evaporated. She was certainly the most attractive girl in the room but—perhaps because of Fiamma—she was less sexually aggressive. Perhaps she sensed that I would quickly rebuff any overtures on her part.

All the same, the evening was a stunning success—until the All Clear sounded just after one o'clock. We had both agreed to go home as soon as the raid, which had obviously been small, ended, and I had left my car halfway along Curzon Street.

At the welcome sound of safety, I signalled to Paul to give me the bill to sign, and for the porter to get my cap and stick. It was a warm night, we had no overcoats, and had just reached the front door and were breathing in lungfuls of clean night air, and I had just reached my Ford and was about to look for the pocket torch I always carried because I needed a light to peer into the bonnet of my car to replace the rotor arm—that small but vital component which, to make it unusable, you had to take out of your car every time you parked it—a 'relic' of early invasion fears. At that moment the sirens started to wail again.

'Oh! Damn and blast!' I cried (partly because I was tired!), 'I bet I know why. A stray German plane has got lost on its way home.'

'Does it make any difference?' Lella clutched my arm, showing signs of fear. She had never been through the *real* night-after-night blitz, of course. What a long time ago *that* seemed. This was nothing—unless you had never experienced worse raids previously.

'We'd better go back to Parkes's, at least it's comfortable as a shelter.' In the dark I took her arm but almost slipped on the pavement edge.

'You okay? These bloody sidewalks!'

'You Americans!'

We were only five yards from Parkes's. To this day I cannot describe the moment of terror in which our world seemed to die. We had just got to the club entrance when some instinct—a swoosh, a sound, some reason—impelled us as one to dive into the entrance to the club with its two comfortable chairs where guests waited for members and which had a tiny glass-partitioned cabin where, in cold weather, the attendant answered phones, fetched coats or took messages. Yet at this moment, in which I registered all, it was as though terror had struck us—all of us—dumb. The night was silent but for the sirens and the

297

beginnings of a rushing wind. No shouts, no sign of panic, only one cry, 'Put that bloody light out!', not directed at us, but maybe at a sliver of light from somewhere.

Then—the awful thing is that there's *nothing* to describe. There was an unholy bang that almost burst my ears and Lella seemed to be hurled into space in the small room and then fall, but I could not see her. My lungs were choking with the beastly dust of plaster and fumes, so intense that I had no time to think how lucky I was to be alive, nor for the first moments to think of Lella, I was so convinced that the overpowering sense of choking meant that I was about to die myself—choking to death! I can remember the flashing thought: what a way to die!

Though I had fallen, miraculously jarring only an arm and leg, the pain did not matter, I was suddenly afflicted with one other worry, my choking forgotten. Where was Lella? All the lights had of course been obliterated from that brilliantly lit social scene and now in the blackness I tried to shout 'Lella!', terrified that it was she, not me, who had died. The cellar below must have collapsed. The bomb must have gone down. In fact I heard cries from below. But Lella—I tried to cry out, to shout her name, but my voice was no more than a croak. She seemed to have been hurled across the room. In the direction of the stairs? Oh God, the staircase must have collapsed, but my mind refused to think of the carnage below.

Gingerly I tried to move. Nothing seemed to be broken. I found that, though seized with an almost overpowering dizziness, I could just stand up if I gripped some support. I tried to feel my way round the room, finally managing to cry out, 'Lella! Where are you?'

Silence.

I had a sudden thought. I had forgotten my tiny pocket flashlight. I fumbled in my pocket—but there was no pocket, nor my valued flashlight. Not possible! I felt again. Not there! In place of the pocket was my bare skin, covered with a strange wetness that seemed to stretch all the way down to my knees.

The odd factor was that though I did not seem to be hurt, I could *smell* blood. It could not be mine. I waggled my toes and amidst the debris tried to bend my legs. No problem. Oh God! I thought, I hope it isn't Lella's blood. There was, odd though it may seem, little in the way of screams, only the occasional cry of someone in pain, or cries of hope, but not a sound from Lella.

Then an ARP warden with a flashlight burst into the chaos of the small reception room, waggling bands of light, and the first one fell straight on the corpse of a girl who had been lying across me. The blast had stripped her of every vestige of clothes. All ripped away like my jacket pocket and half my trousers. But she was not only nude, she had a gaping wound in the small of her back, from which blood had poured over me as she died instantly—yet I, a hair's breadth away, was alive. How was it possible that the blast which had ripped every stitch of clothing from her, and half (it seemed) from me, had landed in such a precise way that on its passage to the hell below it had spared me but not her?

'Come on, sir,' the warden tried to console me. 'You all right?'

'I think so.' Though I did feel a mounting depression, an overwhelming desire to be sick as I was forced to inhale the filthy dust and smoke. 'My lady friend,' I managed to gasp.

And then, I heard a faint cry of 'Ham!' I yelled with a sudden burst of vigour, 'I'm here. You all right?'

'Think so!'

'That's the girl, Warden. Can you flash a torch and see if we can spot her?'

Warily he turned the wavering beam and there, on the other side of the small room, near the entrance to the dining-room, at the foot of the stairs leading to the bar, the light rested and I saw her—I was as excited as though finding someone from the dead.

The mess—the carnage—separating the two of us was horrific. Bodies everywhere. Pictures askew or smashed, fallen beams that had miraculously missed us while killing others. And, I was thinking, this must be nothing compared with the disaster below. After all, the bomb had just missed us—this was only a kind of fringe damage compared with the shattered remnants below.

A loud voice from the top of the stairs called for quiet. It was the imperturbable Paul, his immaculate clothes tattered, his face blackened, who was crying out, 'Quiet please.' And when the noise subsided, he announced, 'I'm afraid that most of the people on the dance floor have been—there's little hope. But a few have been saved, though they're injured. We know this because though the main staircase collapsed on the dance floor, the kitchen stairs at the back are serviceable—just. Some people are badly hurt. The ARP will bring them up. But first, we must clear this reception area if we are going to be able to take the wounded to hospital.'

It sounded difficult, but that was only because none of us, perhaps aided by the warmth of the night air, though still shivering with fear, realised that the bomb had blown out the entire front of the club. In no time wardens were tearing out huge chunks of the mess—beams, fallen walls, dragging everything out into the street, taking out the bodies and reverently laying them in a row on the pavement a few yards distant.

The All Clear sounded soon afterwards, and then the flash lamps began to light up the scene more vividly. Someone carried out the girl who had died next to me. A man beside her was also dead. And on the other side, with the bodies all around, was the glass 'cage' where the receptionist normally welcomed guests and answered phone calls. It was tiny, the shards of its glass windows were everywhere, and yet on the tiny desk with its telephone and appointment book there also stood a bottle and next to it a glass of beer, half empty, standing upright as though waiting for the porter's next drink. But the porter was among the dead. He had been out of his cubbyhole, poor devil.

Once the debris had started to be removed ARP men were able to lift Lella over the remains of the debris. Miraculously she was uninjured.

'Oh, Ham,' she sobbed. 'Thank God you're safe.'

'Thank God *you're* safe.' I managed a tremulous laugh. 'Let's go!'

She walked quite steadily as I said, 'Let's hope the car's safe.'

'It was like a miracle,' she answered. 'I was lifted

301

by unseen hands and then gently landed in the opposite corner as though I'd been carefully deposited on sumptuous cushions.'

Outside the street still resembled what I suppose it really was—the aftermath of a battlefield.

One woman recovered consciousness to find someone holding her hand—to comfort her as she thought. But it was one of a gang of looters who specialised in removing rings and riffling through the handbags of the victims.

Napkins and tablecloths were used as bandages and wounds were washed in champagne. There were muddles over the ambulances and some took nearly an hour to arrive. Stretchers were improvised from screens and the many doctors and nurses who were present, enjoying an evening off, helped magnificently, setting broken limbs with wooden spoons and chair legs. Taxis were also used as ambulances, but some drivers refused because they did not want blood and filth in their cars.

'Come on, Lella darling.' I put an arm around her shoulders. 'Let's have another try at reaching the car. It's time to take you home.'

'I can't,' she faltered, looking really frightened. 'Yes, I *am* terrified.'

'But it's over now. And if I hand you over safely?'

'Look at yourself—you're covered in blood, and half naked.'

'Nothing a shower won't wash off.'

'No, I'm too scared to go home. Let me spend the night at your place. Have you got a spare room, or a divan, or something?'

'A divan, yes, but my studio is so small,' I began doubtfully. 'You should go to your club and at least

302

have a check up with a doctor.'

'I'm all right, I tell you.' She was shivering, teeth chattering. And then suddenly she burst into sobs so loud and racking they sounded as though they hurt. 'I won't go home,' she cried, wiping the tears with the sleeve of her uniform. 'I'm scared. Tonight I just want to sleep and be comfortable—a reassurance that it's not going to happen again tomorrow. I want to obliterate the night. Please help me!'

I was so sorry for her, she looked on the edge of screaming with fear so finally I said, 'All right.' I squeezed her arm, 'Come on home, poor Lella.'

'I'm not poor.'

'Yes you are. It's been a hell of a shock. I'll take you home. I've even got some Scotch.'

★   ★   ★

It had seemed like another world, a million years ago, when we had first set off for Parkes's night club. So happy, so excited at our sudden meeting from the past when the present was anything but really happy. And yet we had set off in such high spirits, so filled with the joy of life, casting aside all doubts of possible death or destruction or *anything* that was not joyous, a moment of exhilarating memory that we wanted to celebrate.

And now—dust to dust, ashes to ashes, there could not have been a truer phrase, mangled bodies wrapped in shrouds of thick layers of dirt. But at least we two were alive—and soon, because I had had the rotor arm and car keys in my other pocket, home.

Having lost my flashlight—still in my missing

pocket, I wondered?—I had to guide Lella carefully through the grey garden walls of Fulham Road, a thick, forbidding solid British wall, with the even more solid walls of Stamford Bridge football ground behind, with, in between, a hidden corner of Italy. On the right we passed the pear tree, then reached the corridor and the door of studio H.

I pushed the Yale key into the lock, opened the door, and not until I had guided Lella inside the room and closed the door behind me, and knew that no chinks of light could escape, did I switch on the light.

'I need a Scotch!' I said without preamble.

'Me too, please.' And looking round, she added, 'How pretty you've made this. But,' suddenly, her face aghast, she looked at me, then herself and cried, 'What a bloody mess we both look!'

Looking at *her* I laughed ruefully. 'We were all so covered in blood and dirt, everyone there, that we didn't seem to notice ourselves. Everyone was the same.'

I had poured out two very large whiskies—neat—and then suggested, 'It's half past two. Would you like a quick shower? Then I've got some cocoa, or hot chocolate mix, and you can make that while *I* have a shower.' Then I added, 'It's your chocolate anyway.'

'Mine?'

'All of you. Your people started sending us food parcels soon after the war began. They've been a godsend.'

'I'd love a bath. I'm too dirty to use the divan bed, the way I am now.'

One end of my high studio had been walled off to make a tiny kitchen, an adjacent tiny bathroom, and next to it a dining-room for four. Above these three tiny cubicles of rooms was the only bedroom, with its sloping roof, an extension of the studio roof.

'There you are.' I handed her a clean towel, soap and showed her how to work the shower. 'Or would you rather have a real bath—soak in it for a bit?'

She nodded. 'A tub?'

'If you prefer the American word,' I smiled, memories flooding back of the way Steve always called a bath a tub. 'I'll fill it up for you.' I turned on the taps. Then I ran up the stairs—flat and straight and wooden against the end wall and leading into the bedroom, and returned with a pair of pyjamas and a spare dressing-gown.

'These'll do for tonight,' I said. 'Bit big for you but—give yourself a good scrub first.'

'Bless you, Ham. Mind if I take my Scotch with me?'

'If you can find anywhere to put it,' I almost laughed. 'I'm going into my bedroom to take off these filthy things,' I said. 'Then throw 'em out of the window. When you've had your bath, give me a yell and while you're drying you can run a bath for me.'

'Will do.' She closed the door behind her.

When she had finished her bath fifteen minutes later and emerged into the studio, I laughed outright, she looked so attractive, pyjama legs turned up over and over, and the sleeves of her pyjama top hanging out over her hands, while the silk dressing-gown nearly reached her feet.

'Look at yourself!' She laughed back and I realised that we were both a little tipsy. Not drunk, but cocktails, white wine, champagne, and then

305

above all, the emotion and the terror. No, not really tipsy, but also exhausted.

'I've got a terrible confession to make,' I said as I made for the bathroom. 'I've got no blankets for the divan sofa. You'll just have to share the bed with me. It's large, but it's the only one.' And remembering the past, the nude I had painted, I added almost cheekily, 'You don't have to be afraid. I couldn't do anything tonight if you gave me a million pounds.'

I knew I was right—or thought I was right—because when I had cleared off the last of the blood and wiped the bath as thoroughly as possible I crawled into bed, the light had already been switched off and she was fast asleep. Within a minute I, too, was fast asleep.

*   *   *

How do these things happen? How is it possible that two people who deeply love their partners in life, and who are almost dead with exhaustion, who find themselves unexpectedly in the same bed, and then—

I must have been asleep, not a thought or nightmare blundering into my subconscious, and I suppose that when, twisting and turning, I switched on to my right side she, without waking, turned her back to me just as Fiamma had always done during that glorious month when we shared a bed in Forte dei Marmi.

Fiamma had called it 'fitting into the curve', saying it with a laugh, and here again, lying on my right side, Lella had automatically fitted into the curve—every nook and cranny of it, and almost

306

without thinking and almost as though I did not know what to do with my left hand, I did what I had always done in the past, flung it across the bed on the side of the girl who shared it. And who had obviously found that my too large men's pyjamas were uncomfortable, for she had kicked them off.

And so my hand fell on warm, naked flesh and without knowing at all what I was doing I automatically slid my left hand upwards and it ended under her pyjama top, just cuddling her breasts; then, exhausted, I slept. For how long? I have not the faintest idea.

It was dark. I was still in one sense in a state of shock—but the truth is never an excuse—but what did wake me up in the first few seconds was the way she turned over towards me ending up on her back, still very close to me, bodies touching, still no words, with each of us still drugged in half sleep, and then as though inviting me, moved her legs apart and without realising what was happening, I rolled across her and then, inside and only half waking, now realising for the first time what I was doing, a picture of Fiamma flashing before my eyes, I made a gesture to withdraw. It was not total. That was *my* sin. Lella dug her two hands into the flesh of my buttocks hard, pressing them, forcing me to stay where I was and whispering, 'Don't stop, Steve.'

It was all over in a few minutes—seconds even—and, crazy though it seems, I cannot for the life of me remember falling asleep, but it must have been instantly, for the next thing I knew was being wakened by chinks of light showing through the side of the curtains and I sat up, switched on the bedside light, looked at my watch and shouted,

'God! It's half past eleven.'

At this Lella, breasts showing through unbuttoned pyjama top jumped on the bed, a vision of beautiful legs and long mane of hair and cried, 'The Stars and Stripes! I told them I was going to Parkes's dancing. They'll think I'm dead.'

Not once—at first—did we mention what had happened. She just asked, 'Can you give me a lift? Urgently?'

I nodded.

'I'll have a bath later.' I nodded and started to put on my clean underclothes and my second uniform thinking, 'I suppose I'll have to pay for a new one myself.'

At that moment the phone rang.

'Miss Pilbeam here,' answered a prim voice from the dead. 'Could you please come round to see Mr Morris at two o'clock this afternoon?'

'Me?'

'Yes.' I could almost visualise the faint smile on Miss Pilbeam's face.

'But I thought—'

'See you this afternoon, Captain.'

Lella cried from the bedroom, 'Anything wrong?'

She had found an old mackintosh to cover her tattered uniform. Unlike me, of course, she had no change of clothes.

'Odd,' I said, and led her to the car outside the heavy gates and the grey wall of Fulham Road respectability. 'I know those sudden calls. It sounds as though I'm going to be posted. So if I have to dash off without letting you know, you'll understand it's not because I'm upset about—' I could feel myself colouring as I pushed the Ford into gear—'what happened.'

'She rested her hand on my knee as we drove towards Hyde Park Corner and then up Park Lane.

'It didn't mean anything.'

'It *did*. To me. I feel dirty and ashamed. Betraying a girl I love and my best friend's wife.'

'Don't ever talk such bloody nonsense,' she almost shouted. 'You betrayed *no one*. Neither of us was even properly awake. It was the natural reaction of two old friends in a state of shock. If we'd sneaked off when you were painting me in the nude—ah! That would have been different. But this—both of us needed help. All right, that's too much, but we couldn't help it. We needed warmth—and a little love. And now, it's all forgotten.'

Soon we had left Park Lane behind and then we were at the Stars and Stripes Club behind the Cumberland Hotel.

'Thanks for the lift.' She kissed me gently. 'And don't *ever* give a second thought to what happened. If you ever feel guilty, just remember what the alternative might have been—both of us killed.'

* * *

Three days later I was on my way back to—to Italy! Yes. Not only Italy, but of all places, *Rome*! I could hardly believe my good fortune. And not for SOE. Well, not quite.

When I arrived in Broadway Mansions,—I had scarcely thought ever to see him again—C gave me a slight smile and said briefly, 'I've arranged with SOE to borrow you. Now, here's what I want to tell you. You're bound first for Switzerland to meet your SOE chief in Geneva. A WAAF will pick you up at your flat tomorrow morning at half past eight and take you to your aircraft. Once in the plane, you'll be given a sealed envelope. Open it. Digest the contents. All problems after Geneva—they'll be looked after. Good luck, Ham. Let's see if we can pull off a double—as good as the last one you did.'

Fine! Excitement galore ahead! But was I bewildered? Baffled by being promised a sealed envelope, not to be opened until airborne, with no chance to whet the appetite of my natural curiosity?

No, I was not.

And for why? I asked myself. Because I was dancing with delight and excitement for another reason.

Almost as an afterthought, C fingered a small piece of paper.

'We got an odd sort of message for you,' he mused, while I looked astonished. 'Came from the Embassy in Berne who handed it on to Nelson of the SOE who of course knows all about you. Someone in Italy who's friendly enough to know our ambassador must have given it to him. Nelson sent it on to me. Told me to destroy it if I suspected a code. But I didn't. I knew who it referred to.'

'What on earth—?'

'Just a couple of words,' C smiled and handed the paper across his tatty old desk. I read:

OTTENUTO ANNULLAMENTO

I gave a whoop of joy. There was only one way to translate 'Ottenuto'—decreed, or even better, granted.

It meant that Fiamma was free.

310

PART THREE

ROME AND CASSINO, 1943–1944

CHAPTER EIGHTEEN

I left from Croydon airfield and, as I approached the plane even I knew enough to recognise that I was climbing into an old Anson twin-engine trainer.

'How far is this old kite supposed to take me?' I looked at the Anson incredulously.

'Less than an hour,' the pilot grinned. 'Fastened your seat belt?' I sat in one of the emergency seats just behind the navigator, and as soon as I could I tore open the sealed envelope. On top of papers, passport, and the wads of money was a slip of paper. It was brief and to the point:

'You are flying to Belfast. You have tickets etc to travel by train to Dublin where you will be met. You will then fly by a neutral diplomatic aircraft to Switzerland and await further instructions.'

I examined the rest of the packet. It contained an Irish passport made out for Mr Eamonn Byrne, Overseas Director of MacManus & Co, importers, of White Street, Cork. Visiting cards confirmed this. So did a letter on the firm's letterheading signed by the Chairman, Terence MacManus, requesting business assistance 'for one Mr Byrne' who wished to buy a hundred gross of Swiss army penknives if the price was right. The letter was folded into an unsealed envelope addressed to M. Theodor Kordt at the Coutellerie du Mont Blanc, Geneva; and I gathered that, having read it, I was to stick the flap down. A thick wad of well-used Swiss francs completed the package—but no, not quite: there was also a clipping from some sort of 'Who's Who' of businessmen telling me something of the background of my new identity: Eamonn Byrne, born in Dublin, educated at University College there, unmarried, had been with MacManus & Co for seven years. Not much to go on, I could not help thinking.

Evidently I was expected to cope spontaneously with any problems that arose. I smiled to myself at the thought of the variety of tasks that had come my way—messenger, courier, stool pigeon, partisan fighter, explosives expert. And now businessman, ostensibly buying Swiss penknives! A rich full life, I thought wryly; but very different from that of the artist I had set out to become.

I had no trouble reaching Belfast, then Dublin where I was met by a Mr Kelly who told me that the diplomatic plane was leaving the following day and would I join him for dinner at the Grand Hotel? There, away from English rationing, we had a wonderful meal.

During dinner Mr Kelly explained how neutral states which maintained embassies in most countries did their best to guarantee safe passage for planes and trains travelling between two neutrals.

'You see,' he said, 'under international law neutral countries can't be deliberately deprived of supplies. Food and raw materials must go through under the flag of neutrality. In the case of land-locked countries like Switzerland trains or planes transporting goods and people across enemy territory are covered by the Red Cross. Every flight is arranged in advance, and the belligerent countries advised. Usually they obey, sometimes they shoot a plane down. But on the whole it's safe.'

'It sounds a little scary to me.'

'It *is*, but don't forget that both Britain and

314

Germany depend on Switzerland for supplies of scientific instruments, so there is a certain amount of surreptitious give-and-take. And of course spies often get in under the guise of businessmen.'

'Like me!' I said ruefully.

'You'll love Switzerland!' he said enigmatically.

*   *   *

To my surprise the Irish plane was nearly full, and included four or five Germans, one of whom sat next to me, talking all the time, and who, when I told him I was flying for the first time in war, told me in a heavy German accent, 'Do not be worrying. We are a priceless German cargo and all the way along the flight path German fighters and gunners have been warned not to touch us.'

It certainly seemed to work, for we landed at Geneva airport, with the lake on our left, without even the slightest incident.

And what a place to land after the drabness of war! The richness of life was evident in the most luxurious way; this beautiful city had shops filled with watches, jewellery, furs, cameras, fine embroideries and household linens, musical boxes, and crystal and porcelain. In this country, tucked away in the heart of Europe, it was difficult to remember that it was only two or three miles from the frontier with war-torn France.

I easily found the coutellerie where presumably M. Theodor Kordt would be awaiting me. It was in the Rue du Mont Blanc, opposite the English church, and had a glittering display of knives, swordsticks, baize-lined canteens of table cutlery, letter-openers, razors, and surgical instruments.

The proprietor's name written on the window was Rudolph Lendi, which puzzled me until I remembered that I was back in the SIS and on my own. I had to piece together dozens of snippets of an ill-fitting jigsaw and show a bland indifference to surprise.

A tall man in a grey warehouse coat stepped forward to greet me.

'Can I help you, sir? Some souvenir, perhaps? We have a great deal to offer.' He gestured towards the display cases. I took the letter from my pocket together with a visiting card and handed them to him. To play it straight seemed to be the only thing to do.

'Ah. Mr Byrne. You are from Dublin?'

'Cork,' I said, poking a finger at the letterheading.

'But you yourself?'

'Oh yes,' I said, 'I was born in Dublin.' I certainly did not intend to get tripped up so early in our acquaintance.

'I thought so. Very fine cities, both. A fine writer too, James Joyce, wouldn't you say?'

I was thrown again. There had been no mention of literary quiz games! But I realised that he was simply going the customary roundabout way to establish my Irishness. 'Indeed,' I said. 'Very fine. Also Dublin-born.'

Some customers had drifted in and the grey-coated man pointed to a staircase at the rear of the shop. 'The office is on the first floor,' he said *sotto voce*.

It was a small bare room leading off a stockroom whose shelves were filled with packages. An old-fashioned rolltop desk stood against one bare

316

wall and in front of it was a creaking swivel chair on a three-legged pedestal. The man seated in it turned noisily to greet me as I entered. He wore a plain black coat and striped trousers and a wing collar with a dark grey tie with polka-dots.

'Nelson,' he said, extending a hand. 'Air Commodore when I'm in uniform; but this of course'—he touched his lapels—'is the best uniform for a businessman in a neutral country.' So this was the mysterious and famous head of the Italian sector of SOE! He looked pleasant enough, though his steely grey eyes showed that he would stand no nonsense if crossed. He asked, 'Kordt, I take it, has arranged the formalities of your visit?'

'Kordt? I don't know. I—'

Nelson pointed a finger at the floor. 'Our man in cutlery downstairs. Rudolph Lendi when he's required to be. I'm sure you know how people assume different characters in this war game we play?'

'I certainly do,' I said vehemently. 'It's confusing to say the least of it.'

He nodded gravely. 'I understand you prefer the action side of the job. I've heard many approving things of your methods with the partisans. Earned yourself the nickname of *Il Mago*, the magician, I gather. Well, I may have a job that will involve you in some danger.'

I smiled. 'Danger? Nothing could seem more tranquil than Geneva.'

It was his turn to smile now. 'Did I say Geneva? No, no. Switzerland has its uses as a neutral country, where plans can be hatched without attracting too much attention. And with no secret police of either of our enemy nations to plot behind the façade.'

'And the plot is—?' I probably showed my slight irritation with the evasive conversations that always seemed to characterise the SIS.

Nelson pulled one of the lower drawers of the desk half out and perched on it. He indicated the swivel chair for me to sit in. There was no other furniture in the bleak room, and very slowly he leaned forward, his thin hands clasped together.

'I needn't confuse you with the finer points of military strategy; but you need a bird's eye view of the present situation and future plans. "Putting the troops in the picture" is, I believe, the phrase used by our esteemed General Montgomery.'

I nodded. 'Can't say I'm what you'd call *au fait*. The papers only report what their chaps see for themselves, and not much of that, being limited to one four-page sheet. For the rest, it's what the Ministry of Information feeds them with.'

'Exactly.' He paused, considering. 'Putting it at its most basic, the object in Italy is to make the most of her weakness and gain control of her airfields and the whole Mediterranean area. As you know, Mussolini got pushed out last month and Marshal Badoglio took over.' He looked at his watch. 'And at this very moment . . . the Marshal is seeking a vis-à-vis with our top men with the object of negotiating Italy's surrender.'

I gave a low whistle, but he dismissed my enthusiasm with a gesture.

'I don't doubt we shall have the surrender in our pocket in a couple of weeks. But the Germans are much more formidable opponents. There are eight divisions commanded by Kesselring, who is, as our American friends say, no slouch in the matter of generalship. Six of those divisions are down in the toe of Italy after withdrawing from Sicily, ready to ward off our next attack. The other two are around Rome.'

I said brightly, 'And our plan is to push from south to north driving the Jerries before us?'

Nelson smiled. 'Put at its simplest, yes. But the enemy will not be easily driven. Also, the terrain is in their favour—mountains, rivers, ground hard going if not impossible for attacking tanks. If they get the chance to dig in, their defences south of Rome could be virtually impregnable. Especially as they include Cassino and the monastery on the mountain above it.'

This time I was on familiar ground. 'I know it. I went there with a friend before the war.'

'Ah.' Nelson unlinked his fingers. 'Then at least you know the ground. From the information we have at the moment we know that Monte Cassino is likely to be the hinge of the German defence line if they get the chance to dig in. It is also at the heart of what is likely to be our main approach to Rome.' He coughed, almost apologetically. He might have been a shopkeeper deprecating the fact that he was out of stock of the customer's requirements at the moment. So his next words were the more unbelievable. 'We need nothing less than for you to penetrate the German designs for the defence of Monte Cassino.' Now he smiled, as if pleased at causing a sensation. 'You can't deny there's an element of the danger you seek in the assignment?'

For a moment I looked almost aghast at the—not the *impossibility* of it all, but the sheer *impertinence* of it. What a bloody cheek was my first reaction,

319

and in keeping with my character I resorted to sarcasm:

'Is that all?' I asked sarcastically; but my sarcasm was wasted on Nelson.

'There will of course be other things. But for the moment—'

'I see,' I said. 'I just nip off to Berchtesgaden, or wherever Hitler's HQ happens to be at the moment, and purloin the plans in the best tradition of the superspy.'

Nelson gave a pale smile, but there was a glint in the grey eyes that warned me not to trifle with him any more.

'There will be no need for histrionics.' He leaned forward again. 'And I have to remind you, Captain Johns, that I outrank you by several degrees. No, no,' he added as I was almost about to rise, 'there's no need for formality; but it's as well to know how we stand.'

'Of course.' I hope I looked to some extent contrite. 'But I think you'll agree it's quite an assignment.'

'I know,' he nodded with a touch of sympathy. Then almost as an afterthought, only it was not, he added, 'You'll discover very quickly in Rome that there's an old friend of yours who is now your enemy.'

'I'm going straight there?' My pulse raced with excitement. 'And I know him?' I looked surprised.

'You do indeed. Before you became *Il Mago*. You met him in Florence when he was taking a message from Hitler to Count Ciano—a message we believe may well have concerned the German offensive against the Low Countries and France.' He shifted his position uneasily. 'And that message must have involved another friend of yours, the Prince

320

Caeseri. But it's the German friend I'm thinking of particularly.'

'You mean Kurt von Schill?'

'Exactly.'

'Good God! he's the friend I went to Monte Cassino with! What's *he* doing in Rome?'

'Quite a lot. He's deputy commander of the German garrison.'

I whistled. 'Quite a big job,' I cried, 'and with power.'

'Yes. He'll be worth watching. Well, that's in the future. First I'd like you to return after the shop closes tonight and make arrangements with Kordt.'

I said, 'Ah. And where exactly does he fit into the pattern?'

'You do well to ask.' Nelson rose from his uncomfortable seat and with a gesture suggested that we should change places.

'He's to be trusted: that's been proved many times. Under the grey warehouse coat he's sort of liaison man—has ways of making contact with people.'

He had indeed, as I discovered that evening. Like his coat he was grey and unmemorable. Apart from his being tall and thin I doubt if I could have given a description of him five minutes after I left. He was a chameleon character who would melt into any background—ideal in a 'liaison man'. He knew my problem and quickly solved it.

'I understand you have to get to Rome.' He made a statement of it, not a question.

'So I gather,' I began.

He broke in. 'I know: an assignment. And Rome is where you'll be able to carry it out.' The hand sketched a gesture of uncertainty. 'Now: your

321

present identity will be useless. You can't enter Italy as an Irish businessman; but you can travel as a non-combatant messenger for the Red Cross carrying surgical instruments for the General Military Hospital in Rome. Fortunately'—I could not be sure because his face was in shadow but I think he smiled—'we have such a consignment ready for despatch. As you know, the Swiss make the best surgical instruments in the world; and, being neutral, we can supply them to either side of nations at war. Fortunately also,' he went on, 'the headquarters of the Red Cross are here in Geneva, and I have a contact in the British Embassy who will—shall we say "Arrange"?—for you to be issued with a new identity. You speak fluent Italian, I believe?'

I nodded.

'From tomorrow morning, when you will visit the embassy and contact Dr Philip Cornwell-Evans, you will become Emilio Bardi of the Italian Military Medical Corps. You will wear a Red Cross brassard and drive a small van loaded with this consignment and painted with the Red Cross insignia. Your journey should be simple if you act with what the Italians call "senso commune", Supplies for the German occupying troops in northern Italy are coming in at Trieste. Then they go to Bologna. Your journey will be down the west coast. The worst you are likely to meet there is some partisan activity. They tend to blow up bridges, you know.'

'I know,' I said ruefully. 'I taught them how to do it.'

★　　★　　★

In the event, Theodor Kordt's plan worked like a

charm. At the embassy Dr Cornwell-Evans (he was a Professor, I gathered), who headed an internal department devoted to forgery, had prepared a passport and papers that would see me across the frontier, and permits to pick up the vehicle from Red Cross HQ, collect the already packed crate from the Rue du Mont Blanc, and be on my way.

'I'm sure you will be able to cope with any problems as they arise,' Dr Cornwell-Evans said. 'But everything is in apple-pie order. The goods are genuine surgical supplies—scissors, scalpels, that sort of thing—and the container is not sealed, so examination at each checkpoint shouldn't delay you unduly.'

As he said, there were no snags. My load was examined at the frontier, but there were few other delays and I made the journey in three days, and saw little of any warlike activity.

Once in Rome I had to deliver the instruments to one of the hospitals where I was to contact a surgeon, Dr Galdi. It was not difficult. After all, I already knew the city fairly well, and Mr Painter had a good memory!

Delivery of the instruments was little more than a pretext for meeting the doctor, who was the surgeon-in-charge, and who sat gloomily in an annexe to an operating theatre where white-uniformed figures moved stealthily about beneath brilliant arclights, trundling trolleys and presumably awaiting the next patient.

He stood up, extended a hand. He did not introduce himself, merely said, 'Thanks for the delivery. Have any trouble, did you?'

I shook my head. 'None really. The usual checkpoint inspections. But since I had nothing to conceal—'

323

He raised a quizzical eyebrow. 'Except ...' I could have sworn he meant to add 'yourself'; but he corrected it to 'Emilio Bardi, is it? Good. Like to know names. Especially of our—suppliers, couriers—couldn't do without you.'

'Rudolphi Lendi,' I said, and sensed at once that I had hit a target. The doctor smiled.

'Exactly. Very fine firm. Wasn't quite sure—'

'I see,' I said. 'But you are now?'

He shrugged. The shrug said in effect that you can never be sure. 'But I'm confident enough to give you two addresses. Here is a room with a bath in a small hotel called the Hotel Torino where you can stay. And this'—he gave me a keen look—'is where you can drop messages, a pick-up which will take the messages to be transmitted not to London but to wherever the command post happens to be. There's the address.' I read the piece of paper.

'The Triangolo!' I cried. 'I know *that* place.'

'Now I know I can trust you,' he smiled.

*　　*　　*

The visible proof of Air Commodore Nelson's remarks about Kurt von Schill screamed at me from *everywhere*—on posters, on unused windows, on derelict houses, on lamp-posts, mostly announcing restrictions. Everywhere I looked I saw Kurt's name as deputy head of the German forces. They all ended:

Gauleiter, Roma
durch Stellvertreter
Kurt von Schill
Oberstleutnant
324

and underneath in Italian:

Comandante, Roma
Deputato
Kurt von Schill
Tenente colonnello

which of course meant Deputy Commander Rome, signed by Kurt over his rank of lieutenant-colonel.

Kurt *had* come a long way since he was playing the piano at Berenson's soirées. Since I did not know where to discover any information about possible defence plans for Cassino, I felt that at least Kurt, in his high position, would know *something*, and I might start by finding out his habits, the way he lived and worked. Who knows? There might be a weak link among those who worked for him.

The Gauleiter's headquarters were in a fine building near Trajan's Column, the 170-foot pillar with its marvellous sculptured reliefs of scenes from the second-century emperor's battles. Normally, it would have been easy to mingle with tourists and watch for Kurt. But the Column had been completely enclosed in a timber stockade to prevent bomb damage; and apart from a few residents who went to pray in the flanking cupolaed churches there were few people around. Traffic down the Via dei Fori Imperiale was mostly official, and the municipal gardens had become air-raid shelters. I briefly wondered what 'disguise' I should adopt, but then the obvious solution occurred to me.

Though I had long lost touch with brushes and easels I was still, professionally, an artist, sustained so often through the dreariness of war by the memories of those wonderful days of sun and

325

delight at I Tatti and Villa Magari; and there were no laws, even in wartime, to stop anyone sketching in public places, so long as they were not sketching official establishments. The two churches flanking the Column, though not remarkable architecturally, were pretty enough to paint, so I found a seat in the municipal gardens with a view of the churches and the HQ and went sketching daily, letting my beard and moustache grow enough to give me an untidy 'artistic' appearance.

On the third morning, just after six o'clock, I saw him. I was a good hundred yards distant from the HQ's doors as I gazed upwards in a pretence of studying the church cupola, when Kurt arrived, acknowledged the salutes of the sentries as they presented arms, dismissed the beflagged Mercedes at the kerb, and went inside.

He did the same thing on two more occasions and I was puzzled by one thing: why did Kurt seem to arrive so early, before any of his staff? Was it because he had not spent the night at home and had to leave early to be discreet? He would not have been the first German to have an all-night mistress, yet somehow that did not seem to fit with his fastidious nature.

I decided to try and find out a little more about his personal habits. I knew he lived in a suite at the Hotel Excelsior—where else for the second most important man in the city?—but what was the real reason for his being an earlier-than-early riser?

CHAPTER NINETEEN

By now I had also acquired an ancient two-stroke motor-cycle of the sort that was popular among boys in the 1930s. Mine must have been at least ten years old for Italy manufactured nothing of that sort any more. With this I could (unless it packed up, which it did frequently) follow anyone. I decided I would follow Kurt.

Just before six o'clock the next morning, beyond but almost out of sight of the ornate and huge portico, I stationed myself at the Excelsior—which reminded me of a big Roman arch, where drivers of flashy cars drove in on the downwards slope of the Via Veneto, deposited their human cargoes and then drove straight on and into the streets.

About a quarter past six—early, I thought!—I saw Kurt come through the swing doors and stand, a rather lordly figure, his arrogant appearance making him look twice his normal size. He clicked his fingers to an obsequious doorman who scuttled from the portico into the bright morning sunshine on the pavement of the Via Veneto and gave three short blasts on the whistle normally used to summon taxis.

Immediately an open touring car, painted grey and with a Swastika flag fluttering on its bonnet, drew away from the kerb and turned into the huge darkened archway.

The driver jumped out almost before the porter reached for the door, saluted smartly, and I was able to hear Kurt ask him the German equivalent of, 'Got everything?'

327

The driver pointed to a large tea chest type of package, the open top of which had been carefully covered with a ground-sheet to conceal the contents. Contraband goods I thought, though that too seemed to go against Kurt's nature.

Returning the salute, Kurt jumped into the back seat, sitting next to the package. Then the car roared off with much klaxoning as though to assert German authority. It was not difficult to follow. All I had to do was be careful not to get too close because the streets were empty. German drivers—always a little nervous of big-city bomb attacks—were highly skilled at watching through rear mirrors. But my previous two years of working in Italy had taught me a few tricks too, such as swerving a motor-bike out of the line of sight of the rear mirrors ahead.

He turned right out of the Excelsior and drove towards the Borghese Gardens—shades of my first mozzarella!—and from there finally made for the Parioli area, that part of the tree-lined avenues on which almost every wide road is named after a country.

Towards the end of the Via Lisbona, an area of large ostentatious houses converted into spacious flats, Kurt's driver slowed down, obviously searching for the number of a building—difficult to descry because a double line of trees flanked the entire street on the roadside edge of the pavement. That and the small front garden between the trees and the building made it difficult for a motorist to see numbers and obviously Kurt and his driver had no desire to alight from the grey Mercedes.

We had almost reached the end of the road, where the Via Lisbona forms a right angle with the

Via Lima when the driver finally stopped and pointed.

The driver jumped out and Kurt descended, the driver pulled out the tea chest, held it for a moment—it looked quite heavy—and stood as though wondering what to do. His behaviour made it obvious he did not want to be seen.

Finally Kurt pointed to a spot between the trees where the package could be hidden. Then I saw him gesture to the driver, telling him to move the car round the corner into the Via Lima and wait. I saw him look at his watch, and then hold up two fingers, as though saying, 'I'll only be a couple of minutes.'

As the car moved out of sight Kurt took a look down both sides of the broad, empty Via Lisbona and then ran through the trees, into the small garden and lightly up the marble steps two at a time. Then he peered for the right flat button to press. I saw him press one, talk into the brass voice plate. He waited. A girl I could hardly see opened the door gingerly. I saw Kurt point to the package. She smiled her thanks and then, after a quick kiss on the cheeks, Kurt walked quickly down the steps, past the garden, turned left, then left again into the Via Lima, and I heard the car drive away. Not a soul had witnessed a thing—except me, and the girl.

Carefully I watched the front door of the flats. I did not have long to wait. The young woman—at first unrecognisable through the thick curtain of trees—came down, looked anxiously from left to right, then went over to the tea chest. It looked a little heavy and cumbersome for her to carry and she was puzzling what to do. Then she looked up, and I saw her face for the first time.

For it was when she looked up that I recognised her. My mouth must have fallen open with the sheer astonishment of what I saw, but could hardly believe. I could actually *feel* a kind of shooting pain in the area of my heart—a gasp of agony, gone instantly—the agony of a love that has lived for years only in the mind suddenly materialising into reality, as though a magical fairy, stars twinkling, had suddenly touched an invisible wand transforming an impossible dream into reality. It could not be possible! It was a dream. The apparition would vanish as quickly as magic had given me a moment's sight of her.

Or was it real? It had not come about by incredible chance, but by plodding army detective work, following a prime German suspect, just to see what he was up to. Routine. But not luck. It was Kurt who had led me to her—I looked again as she hesitated. Yes, it *was* her.

Anxious to make sure that she did not have a heart attack or scream if I crept up nearer and surprised her, I called, but not too softly, 'Fiamma! It's me!'

She spun round, almost tottered as though hit by an invisible force, an impossible dream that suddenly spoke words, looking for a moment up to the skies as though seeking the answer to some vast miracle. Then, almost stumbling with shock, but realising that the miracle was true and just, she presented a picture I shall never forget as long as I live.

One moment, dumbfounded, it looked like the end of the world—the unseen figure behind the trees suddenly stepping into reality. As she saw me she gave a cry of love—I know no other word to describe the sound. She stood there, tears on her face, and made that most beautiful of all gestures—she stretched out her arms, waiting to receive me.

'Oh Ham! My beloved, it's really you! It can't be!' she sobbed, but half-laughing, 'You certainly do give me terrible surprises. Oh, you darling man,' and as I wiped the tears away, she added, 'This is the single, most wonderful moment of my life. But how, how on earth?' I chose not to answer that, suspecting that she, in her heart of hearts, did not really wish me to—I could feel her trembling, almost with fear, perhaps with joy. 'Come inside, come please. This is my flat.'

'Shall I bring the loot?'

'It's for you—well, in a way. It's food for your baby. He's been ill, needs nourishing. You saw who brought it?'

'Yes, Kurt.'

'He's been a good friend. I *hate* having anything to do with the Germans. I don't care for myself—a crust of bread, a plate of pasta—but Ham Two, as we call him, he's yours, darling Ham One, he needs everything. I thought he was going to die—'

'I understand. Come on, let me in. I'll carry it.'

'It's not for me,' she repeated. 'You do understand, don't you? It's for Ham Two—he's a big boy now. Oh Ham! It's like a miracle.' Then suddenly laughing, almost hysterically, 'That wispy beard!' She followed the words with an almost nervous giggle. 'I'm not sure I like it. When we go inside'—we were walking up the marble steps—'I'll kiss you and see if it tickles!'

'I can't wait,' I too laughed. 'Let's get inside. I

331

want to see Ham Two.'

'He's waiting for you. He's a big boy now. We've got nothing in the way of toys these days, only a few old family ones'—she opened the front door and I carried the heavy chest in first—'so he spends most of his spare time daubing old newspapers with paint. Takes after his father.'

The first thing I saw in the lavish entrance hall was our picture—'The Blue Nude'—and I nearly dropped the box, I was so astonished. Not for the life of me could I imagine how Fiamma had come by it. I had left all my canvases with Umberto before I dashed off to London.

I suppose she must have seen my bewilderment for she laughed gaily. 'Simple, darling, really. I just went and asked dear old Umberto if I could have it—with your authority. I suppose I piled it on a bit—telling him it was something to remember you by and that you could not get there because you were swallowed up by the war.' She kissed me again. 'Feminine wiles! That's what did it! But he was willing enough. I think he has a soft spot for young lovers.'

I nodded. 'And it was his idea too.' I added jokingly, 'You'll be able to sell it for the value of the frame and canvas if you're ever on the poverty line.'

'You don't think I'd ever sell it—*our* picture?' she reproached me. 'Our love picture?'

I must say that gave me a flood of real pleasure, and partly because, after all these years without seeing it, I realised that it was not at all a bad picture. 'I'm so glad you kept it. After all these years.' And I could not help asking, with a touch of jealousy, 'Has Kurt seen it?'

Colouring slightly, she looked at me, again
332

reproachfully. 'Of course not. He's never been *in* the house. Apart from anything else, he knows that if the partisans see him being too friendly with an Italian he—or I—stand a good chance of being shot. But he's helped us.'

'Us? Do you live here alone?' We had walked into the large and beautiful marble-floored, elegantly furnished living-room. 'How did you meet Kurt?'

'By chance. Normally, we rarely go anywhere. There's a curfew until six every morning. But every now and again some high-ranking Italian officer, who's close to Papa, invites us to an all-night party—it has to be all-night because of the curfew. It's all very prim and proper—don't worry!—but at least we can get a drink and a square meal if they have a buffet supper. It's all very harmless, but it makes a change.'

'Including Germans?'

'Inevitably a smattering. They're very polite. They provide the food and drink. That's how, when I attended a party given by one of Papa's friends, I met Kurt. About a month ago.'

'It's a big apartment.' I was anxious to change the subject for, much as I had always liked Kurt, I hated the thought of Fiamma mixing socially with Germans.

'Don't be silly.' Reading my thoughts, she looked almost cross. 'It's a friend of Papa's who's begged us to use it because he's been posted to Switzerland and he knows that, if it's empty, the Germans will requisition it. I share it with Signora Stefano. She looks after the baby, and her husband who goes out every day, working at the gas works. They are a very simple, kind couple. I pay the modest rent to protect Papa's friend and Signora Stefano looks

333

after the baby as a sort of nanny-help.'

At that moment Signora Stefano came in leading such a sturdy looking boy of three that I began to swell with pride.

Fiamma introduced us, me as the father, without any embarrassment even after I had whispered 'Don't mention my name', and then I bent down to hold the boy. He did not protest.

Signora Stefano seemed a good, kind sort of woman and Ham Two obviously adored her. But of course I was really looking at the boy. What a fine little chap he was!

'Mamita, who is this man?' he asked Fiamma.

'Come on, I won't bite.' I gathered him up into my arms. He came willingly when I added, 'You wouldn't bite if I gave you some chocolate, would you?'

'No, never. And what's this?' He tried to tug the wisps of my beard.

'That's your papa trying to prove that he's a man,' giggled Fiamma, her face radiant with happiness doubled by my unexpected arrival. 'And darling,' she turned to me. 'We have one other live-in-guest who has a key and comes and goes more or less as he pleases, but he's not here at the moment.'

'And who's he?' I asked suspiciously.

'Vanni.'

'*Vanni*! Good God, I thought he'd be dead. What's he doing here?'

'You may well ask. He's not in the army, but he's fighting the Germans. He told me he was inspired by some strange legendary Englishman who was fighting with the partisans and was so daring that he became known as *Il Mago*. Vanni said he was the

334

bravest man in Europe and looked like you. What *have* you been doing all this time?'

'Being a magician.' I laughed off that remark. 'Any idea when Vanni's coming back?' I could do with all the help I could get.

She shook her head. 'He just seems to pop in and out for a meal and sleep. But at least he seems safe. And of course the Signora looks after the baby when I'm away.'

'Away? What do you mean? You go away? Away? Where? When?' I must have sounded shocked. 'Leaving Ham alone?'

'Shall I take Ham Two to play in the park?' asked Signora Stefano tactfully, and also indicating pointedly that we might wish for the privacy of lovers.

'Yes, you do that,' agreed Fiamma. 'You'd like to go for a walk, darling?'

'If Papa comes with us. Can he?'

'Another time,' I promised. 'Then I'll take you to the park.'

'*This* time.'

'Next time. Today I have to get some sweets for Ham Two.'

'Now?'

'Just one piece of chocolate. If you're a good boy.' It was amazing how easily I slipped into the routine of bribing a child!

As he prepared to go I said to Fiamma, 'Ham Two looks happy but'—I found it almost hard to think of him as our son—'is he getting enough to eat? He seems desperately anxious to get hold of that chocolate.' Fiamma was rummaging in the box of supplies brought by Kurt and found a small bar.

335

'There you are,' she said. 'Say thank you to your papa.'

'Will you come again—and bring me some more chocolate?'

'I will,' I promised. I added to Fiamma, 'He looks a bit thin.'

'He has been quite ill, as I told you. I managed to get some drugs from the hospital, but really, darling, it's Kurt who has helped, with the food.' As she waved to Signora Stefano and Ham Two at the door she added, 'For though the German people are suffering, I'm sure, the big-shots do all right and they get lots of supplies from Switzerland and they take all our best meat—our veal, our Florentine steaks—and some of it has been handed on to us by Kurt. In three weeks or so it has built up the boy's strength.'

'Well,' I was looking at the large living-room, 'I'm hating the Germans more and more, but I suppose Kurt isn't typical. Fiamma, my love,' I kissed her again, 'is the coast clear?'

'Of course. This way.' She was smiling as she walked into the bedroom. 'Why do you think Signora Stefano left so quickly? Because she's an Italian.' Almost eagerly she started undressing. I noticed that her blouse had been mended in half a dozen places. Poor darling, she was not the only one who was finding it hard to clothe herself.

She must have seen me look at her blouse.

'Don't worry about that,' she smiled, that wonderful warm smile of pure love, 'that's my housework dress...'

* * *

We made love the first time with the tender
336

gentleness and the need for physical as well as mental fulfilment of a young couple long parted, an exercise which, though the product of a long shared love, made us finish together at the final half-minute and left us both, I am sure, without saying a word, enriched beyond words.

Then we lay in bed, waiting, stroking, kissing. What bliss it was! But one thing I had to ask her. 'You said you went away and left Ham alone with Signora Stefano?'

'Yes, I'm a trained nurse,' Fiamma said quietly. 'I'm on a week's leave at the moment, but I work in the military hospital in Cassino. It's not far from the top of the mountain. You remember you went there once.'

'You a *nurse*! And at Cassino. That's the place I want to know more about.'

'Like Kurt,' she said. 'He's *very* interested in Cassino.'

'Why, for goodness' sake?'

'Oh, nothing really, I suppose, but when I told him I worked at Cassino he remarked, quite casually, "Well, we might meet there," and when I asked him why, he said one of his major jobs was to co-ordinate all the various plans for the defence of Cassino against the expected Allied attack.'

I was thinking like mad. Whew! What would I not give to know about those plans. But it was forgotten as passion stirred again, and not until that was over did we get up and dress—just before Signora Stefano returned, after which Ham Two demanded most of my attention.

Then, taking the rest of the day off—it was still only the middle of the morning!—we went for a walk in the park after which Signora Stefano made

337

us a plate of spaghetti with a Bolognese sauce made from Kurt's tinned meat and some tomatoes. We sat and talked and I told Fiamma about my chance meeting with Lella in London and our narrow escape (though I did not tell her *everything*) and how Steve had become a bomber pilot, probably now posted in North Africa or even southern Italy.

'Darling, how awful, that bombing. Poor Lella, poor *you*!'

'It was. But after a while—well, I don't have to tell you, you're dealing with the results of horrors all the time and you become anaesthetised to them. A sort of crazy nonchalance takes over.'

'I know. We get them in the hospital sometimes—"bomb happy" cases they call them and they have to go for treatment at mental centres.'

It was not fair to impinge on the happiness of our reunion, but I couldn't suppress a memory of bitterness. 'The sort of place your mother needed. Coming between us like that.' Then I added with hasty contrition, 'No: I shouldn't have said that; it was cruel—to you, my darling.'

She smiled, gently forgiving. 'It's all right. I understand. She was awful, but'—her fingers touched the corners of my lips as if encouraging a smile. Irresistible. My bitterness cleared in the warmth of her affection.

'*But*—but she is your mother. *I* understand too. Do you ever hear of her?'

She shook her head. 'Hardly at all. Letters are impossible with the censorship, and smuggled-out messages are too dangerous, even if there were a contact. This friend of Papa's I pay the rent to, he used to send me an occasional post card with "all

338

well" written on it, and I took it to mean that he'd seen Mama and had been asked to reassure me. But since Italy's surrendered I haven't received any more. But I am sure she's still in Switzerland.'

'And the Prince?'

Again she shook her head. 'His government work—I don't think even Mama knew what it was. We girls certainly didn't. He was quite high up, knew the king as well as Mussolini and Ciano, and had some kind of diplomatic passport which gave him privileges. But that was before the war. After ... everything, everyone, drifts apart. Signora Stefano tries to comfort me, she's always asking me if I've any news of him—'

'Signora Stefano?' I was suddenly intrigued. 'Why? Why should she be interested?'

Fiamma snuggled up close to me on the sofa we were lounging on. 'Oh, I don't know. Just maternal concern, I suppose. And of course she's terribly impressed because I'm the daughter of a prince. I think she believes Papa is terribly powerful but is probably being held by the wicked enemy so that he can't exercise any power. Like in a fairy story. She's a dear old thing but quite simple-hearted. Does it matter?'

'No, I suppose not, not really.' I dismissed the idea from my mind for more than half my brain was ticking over with another thought.

It was Fiamma's remark about Cassino. It kept pushing everything else from my mind, now that our physical needs had been satisfied. It was the nature of the German defence against the attack on Monte Cassino and its priceless monastery, the great obstacle in the way of an Allied advance up Italy.

Was there any way Fiamma could help? After all, she was a friend of Kurt's and a nurse at Cassino. There must be *some* things she could discover, some details she could squeeze out of Kurt if they met again.

'Well, Kurt did ask me if I would like to go to an Italian party this evening,' she admitted. 'But now you're here, I will phone him at the Excelsior and put him off.'

'Don't,' I urged her. 'You know we love each other, that I'm mad about you, that I hate you *ever* being with another man—but, well, put it this way. I'm sure the work you are doing in the hospital is magnificent and I'm proud of you. But if you can just find out any trifling thing that will help, it would be a million times more important. The right knowledge of Cassino at the right time will save thousands of Allied lives.'

She looked almost bewildered. 'I have only a week's leave, Ham, and you've only just arrived, and on our first night we should be in bed together, loving each other. Yet you ask me to go out and spend it with Kurt.'

'Beloved, I must tell you everything. I'm in daily touch with the Allied armies in the south. There! I've told you my deepest secret. We will have to take Cassino if we want to free Italy. But we've got to climb that great hill, with the Germans up there swatting us like flies, killing every man who tries to inch nearer the summit. We *have* to find out where the Germans are going to station their men so that we can attack somewhere else. In other words, how do the Germans plan to defend Cassino? That way maybe we can bring peace to Italy. Between us we can help to do it.'

340

CHAPTER TWENTY

It sounded simple enough: now I knew where my beloved was, surely we could pick up—as Steve would have put it—'where the action was'? But nothing in life is that simple, ever; and the complexities of war only pile on the difficulties.

There were troubles enough at the top level. Not the least was the incessant rain frustrating the Allies' advance and bogging them down in mud. That mud was holding up the supply convoys and turning the battlefields across all of central Italy into a quagmire. My roving commission as a secret agent had its advantages in that most of the time I was able to keep to the highways—the main motor roads that linked cities; and my Red Cross brassard and my old motor-bike offered enough concealment of my real identity to amount to a sort of anonymity that disarmed the challenges from recce parties of Germans or guards at checkpoints. As Emilio Bardi I was no more important than a messenger carrying urgent supplies of drugs from one field medical post to another. And as myself, in my real job as a courier and undercover man, I seemed for months to have little to do that was vital to the flow of the war. From time to time Access would turn up at the Triangolo or meet me quite openly at the Hotel Torino, and then we would go through an elaborate pantomime of old friends meeting and talking over old times which could hardly have convinced anybody; but as he said in his rasping voice, 'Transparency is itself a cover up.'

In spite of the apparent pointlessness of much of

my job, it was by no means easy to visit Fiamma. For one thing, frequent visits would have been even more suspect—or at least I imagined they would, which came to the same thing. Undercover work does not stiffen the sinews. Also, message-bearing to command posts often involved quite long absences from Rome. And as luck would have it Fiamma's duty hours as a nurse often conflicted with my presences. So we were, like any other loving couple parted by war, longing for each other physically (more than anything!), and mentally, but constantly frustrated by time or distance.

And as for gaining information about Cassino, nothing was coming of Fiamma's efforts. The Germans she met socially remained as tight-lipped as Kurt, and the gossip she heard in the hospital was little more than trivial, though once or twice she came up with the identification of a regiment that fitted into the overall Intelligence jigsaw.

'I'm afraid, darling Ham,' she said during one of our rare breathless embraces, 'I'll never make a Mata Hari.' She pouted and pulled playfully at my straggly beard 'Any more than you will make a stage artist like old Umberto.'

'Umberto,' I said sadly. 'It's like an echo from centuries ago. I wonder ...' But I had to bring my thoughts back to my need for important information. 'I wonder if Vanni ...' I began.

She shook her head. 'It's so long since I saw him last. He just comes and goes—'

—'and always with drama.' I completed the sentence remembering his sudden appearance at Forte dei Marmi and the ugly scenes that followed.

'Oh Ham!' she said, holding me at arm's length, her eyes brimming with tears. 'This war! Why is everything so ugly ... and everybody hidden behind, behind ...' She broke off almost petulantly, unable to think of the right word.

'Walls,' I suggested. 'But more like boxes really, Chinese boxes that fit into one another, everybody burying their personalities inside other personalities. Like me.' I twiddled bits of my beard into spikes and made a grimace, which at least turned her tears into giggles. 'Being Emilio Bardi, Painter, Eamonn Byrne ... never Ham Johns, myself.'

She put her arms around me. Her strength was like balm to my frustration. 'Don't say that, Ham beloved! You're always the only, the *only* Ham Johns to me!'

'No!' I said with mock seriousness, tilting her face upward so that her blonde hair fell away in a golden curtain. 'Don't forget Ham Two!'

'Could I ever! He's part of you, of me, of our love.'

As if on cue Signora Stefano entered, the boy clasping her hand and looking at me as if I had the solution to some problem that bothered him. 'You're like my Jack-in-the-box,' he said. 'You pop up and then down, you come, you go. Why can't you be here all the time?' His brow furrowed and I thought how peaked he looked. 'Is it the war, Papa?'

'Yes,' I said, 'it's the war. But when the war's over I'll be around all the time.' I dug into the depths of my Red Cross pouch and produced a tin of Nestlé's sweetened condensed milk which I had bought on the black market. I saw Signora Stefano cast a covetous glance at it. At least, I thought her glance was covetous at the time and was not

343

surprised—the rationing system in Rome never seemed to work. But later I was to wonder if it was something else.

'Here,' I said to the boy, 'this'll do you good—make you big and strong so you can look after Mama.'

He took it with a puzzled glance, weighing it in his hands. 'Is it to play with on the floor?'

'No,' I laughed, 'it's to eat. It's delicious. But you've got to open the tin first.'

'We'll go and find a tin-opener,' Signora Stefano said sensibly, leading him away to the kitchen. I was glad of that, because it was time for me to go and it was bad enough saying goodbye to Fiamma without the additional burden of seeing the boy's tears.

*   *   *

It was true what I said about Vanni's exits and entrances. They were always dramatic. After Christmas, which I spent in some godforsaken place where Access sent me, he laughed disagreeably when I told him it had been a false lead which led me to no more than a sprained back after my motor-bike plunged me into a bomb crater while I was driving along a pitch dark road. 'Too bad,' he smirked. 'All's fair in love and war.'

But I had managed to steal a few hours with no commitments to duty. This time it is love, I thought; not war. And I made my way to the Via Lisbona, wondering if by the devil's own chance I had chosen a day when Fiamma was at the hospital. But no, lover's luck held for once and she fell into my arms with all the pent-up ardour of years of

344

absence, though it had been no more than a few weeks.

'My precious Ham! I've been starved! I—'

Anxiously I looked down at her upturned face, tears of happiness glistening on her cheeks. Did her body, always slender, feel featherlight for lack of food? She sensed my worry. 'No darling, not *that* way! We get special rations at the hospital—when they're able to get them through; the nurses aren't too badly off. I even manage to smuggle a few bits and pieces out for Ham Two,' she added with defiant pride. 'And Kurt still helps when he can. No: it's the food...'

'Oh love,' I prompted. We paused as if by appointment to look at 'The Blue Nude', which seemed a little out of position.

'I have to keep it higher on the wall than it ought to be because Ham Two keeps wanting to ... improve it!' She snuggled her head into my shoulder and put her arms around my waist. 'Don't let's wait a minute longer!' She leapt ahead, her long bare legs gleaming as she pulled her dress over her head.

After the privation of weeks I can only say that our love-making was sheer ecstasy. We could not linger or wait to caress each other. It was as though we were poised on a brink over which we plunged without hesitation or thought.

'Couldn't hold back,' she murmured, her eyes closed, her breasts with their nipples thrusting like fingers against me as she reached across my body to search my groin. 'But now, this time...'

I took her hand from me and gave it a tiny slap, as if reproving a child for stealing sweets, then distanced myself teasingly from her until I felt

345

myself grow and could no longer bear the burning desire to unite our bodies again in love and delayed passion.

I suppose the world went on in its timeless way while we loved each other through the winter afternoon. The sounds of war were beyond our hearing. Out there men were being killed and children were being born; but sleeping and waking in naps like kittens we were as if endlessly cocooned in ourselves. Once, Fiamma whispered, 'Oh! If only—' A look of longing completed the sentence for her. But we both knew that such things as the need to stretch to avoid cramp were also part of bliss—if only to provide a contrast and the time for a restorative cup of coffee. Fiamma went to the kitchen to make it while I lay, my hands linked behind my head, in the silence of rapture. 'Typical man!' she taunted as she entered bearing two chipped mugs of what then passed for coffee (I think it was made from acorns). 'Lying back while the woman does all the work.' She let the old fluffy dressing-gown she had decorously draped herself with fall from her shoulders.

'I like that!' I responded, matching her decorum by virtuously drawing the sheet up to my waist. 'When . . .'

But any sly hint that my exhaustion might be justified was interrupted by the sound of the street door slamming.

There was nothing for us to feel guilty about; it was more the nameless fear that gripped us all during those years of uncertainty that made us tremble. Then I relaxed. 'Of course,' I said. 'Signora with the boy.'

But it was not. It was Vanni.

346

He looked vastly different from the last time I had seen him—beaten up, cringing with pain, starving, and on the run as he vanished into the pine woods surrounding Forte Dei Marmi. Now he was in old but clean casual clothes, and he had the look of a man well pleased with himself.

'My dear Johns!' he said amusedly. 'I find you in good shape, I see!' He had glanced in at the door as he climbed the stairs to what I assumed to be his room; but he had the good manners to pull the door to and mutter an apology before disappearing.

It was more than an hour before we saw him again, during which time we had a tepid bath (the heating would not run to more), dressed, and Fiamma prepared a scratch meal of something approximating to minestrone followed by artichoke sprinkled with some rather stale Parmesan cheese. But it was filling and quite tasty, and there was enough for Fiamma to call out and invite Vanni to join us—which he did, contributing to the party with many flourishes and winks and a great air of mystery a bottle of Soave. 'Ask no questions,' he said, finger to lips.

'Wouldn't dream of it,' I replied, apeing the tight-lipped Englishman. 'But after your dramatic entrance tonight . . .'

'Not really dramatic. When I come to Fiamma's I think of myself as a businessman coming home after a day's work. Well, perhaps not "home" so much as a pied-à-terre.'

'But Vanni,' Fiamma protested, 'we don't *know* what your day's work is. In fact we don't know anything about you after Mussolini ordered your release. When you turned up here I was only glad to see you and didn't ask any questions.'

'Just as well,' interrupted Vanni as he lit a cigarillo. 'In these times the less you know the better. They always track you down in the end, you know, just as those bastards at Forte dei Marmi said. With me, the hand on the shoulder, the confrontation with the pursuer, came as suddenly and as unexpectedly as I'd always known it would: in a café actually, where I'd been standing at the counter drinking a cup of what passes for espresso these days. I turned and there was this policeman straightening up as if he had picked something off the floor.

'"I think you dropped this, Signor," he said. I'd dropped nothing, but he handed me an envelope and made his way out of the café without another word. I felt myself trembling—shock, I suppose. It was all so sudden and so casual. No arrest, no handcuffs, no pistol held at my back. And when I looked at the contents of the envelope I laughed aloud—hysterically. For what I'd been eluding all that time was my order of release, dated many months previously and signed by Ciano himself "By comand of Il Duce". Still'—he pointed the cigarillo at me—'the less you know the better, as I'm sure you agree, my dear fellow.' A pause. 'Being in the same line of business, so to speak.'

I was startled. 'How do you know—?'

'What you do? The work of *Il Mago* doesn't exactly pass unnoticed amongst those of us who are, well, against the Fascists.'

He shrugged. Peering through the haze of smoke I realised I had never really noticed Vanni before—after all, his appearances, however dramatic, had always been fleeting. Now I saw his eyes had that strange intensity that often goes with fanaticism, and I recalled the loathing he had expressed when he told us about walking away from the battlefield, his horror at the desecration of their comrades' bodies by his own countrymen, the sickening impact of war at its crudest. Such a man had a truly sensitive heart of hearts, however much he disguised it under braggadocio; and even during our first meeting, when he had dashed in for a meal at Magari and dashed away again to keep a 'date', he seemed disillusioned by what had been going on in Abyssinia.

'Yes,' he continued, 'you could say that. I'm with the partisans. I'm also with the Mafia, the Communists, the Allies ... as the need arises. My coat is of many colours. I'm even, sometimes, with the Germans. Not all of them are bad—as Fiamma has reason to know.'

A glance passed between us. I re-ran Vanni's comment through my mind. Maybe it was better the less one knew; but that did not stop us all half-knowing about each other's activities, even if we stopped short of prying. I recalled 'C' telling me that the Prince and Roz were both concerned with messages and 'drops'. In other words they were both, however vaguely, in Intelligence or on the fringes. And Vanni, it seemed, was also one of us.

'A double agent?' I queried.

'Double, triple—' he shrugged again, stubbed out the little cigar.

'You mean you're on whatever side's winning.'

'You could say that.' To his credit he did not take my remark amiss. 'But always on the side that's winning against brutality and persecution; not necessarily against a specified enemy wearing a particular uniform. I suppose, really, I'm a bit of an

349

idealist. It's a silly thing to be in a world flaming with war and megalomania; but in my small way I try to give a pull on the rope that's tugging against . . . subjection—of nations or individuals.'

We were all trying to do just that; but I suppose Vanni saw things in his own way, and in any case it was his activities rather than his philosophy I was curious about. Why did he, when he first came in, have the look of a cat who's been at the cream? As if in response he suddenly shook himself free of his brooding mood, moved over to an armchair, and began to tell us about his new-found freedom after being so long on the run.

'I don't mind telling you, I'd had so long as a fugitive that the hole-and-corner had become my natural habitat. When you know your every move can lead to capture, trial—trial of a sort—and death, you are very wary. You become a man of many disguises and identities, living on your wits always in the shadows . . .'

'I know the feeling,' I said drily.

'Then suddenly comes freedom and you're off the hook; but the habit of concealment is too ingrained to shake off. So you're what your American chum—Steve was it?—used to call a pushover for secret work. Soldiering had sickened me, but there was room enough in the underground organisations—the partisans, the Communists, the trade union agitators—it was easy to hire oneself out. So I drifted, a small operator, useful, gathering information and passing it on to the right quarter.' He gave me a sly wink. 'You know, eh? *Collaboratore*, eh?'

'But on which side?' I asked coldly.

Another wink. 'Ah, that would be telling.'

Fiamma gave a little gesture of incomprehension, which did not surprise me. The political situation had been unstable for months. The Allied invasion of Sicily had brought Italy near to economic collapse and Fascism as such virtually to an end. Its own Grand Council ordered Mussolini to concede his powers to the king; and the Duce's son-in-law, Ciano, persuaded the Council to force his resignation. Everybody thought that Ciano wanted power for himself, but he did not. The king appointed an army man, Badoglio, and Mussolini was arrested as he left the audience chamber—

'For his own good, so they told him,' Vanni filled us in. 'And they had a point. There'd been uprisings every day for weeks, and mobs of strikers at the factories were after his blood—not to mention his cronies, who had to scamper away to Portugal or Germany.'

'Yes,' said Fiamma, 'I remember. But we didn't know *what* to believe.'

'Exactly,' I confirmed. 'There was conflicting news on all sides. Nobody knew the truth.'

It was late now, long after curfew, and the only sounds were of the occasional armoured car patrolling the area and the tramp of the night police on their rounds.

'Musso got whisked off to a hideout in the Abruzzi mountains and held prisoner there,' Vanni mused. 'But Hitler wasn't having his Fascist partner chucked out and humiliated. Not likely! He got his commando leader Colonel Skorzeny to organise Musso's abduction. It worked too. Skorzeny and his commandos landed on a plateau and simply kidnapped Il Duce, leaving his captors wringing their hands in horror. It was about the

351

most daring act of the war. And of course he's at the head of this puppet government now. Was there ever such a crazy set-up?' He smiled cynically. 'The perfect set-up for a freelance agent, wouldn't you say?'

It was Fiamma's turn to be cynical now. 'And who are you selling your talents to now?'

Vanni gave a brief laugh. 'Not *selling*, Fiamma dear. There's no money involved, I assure you. I've always had a little income of my own—from my mother, you know.' I was reminded of something I had assumed but never really taken account of: that Vanni was the son of an earlier marriage of Giorgio Caeseri. 'My services are given freely—at the moment to the Allies, by way of the partisans, and they, through what you English call "jiggery-pokery", have manoeuvred me into a job, waiting.'

Fiamma's brow furrowed; mine too. 'Waiting for what?'

Another laugh from Vanni. 'Waiting *at table*, my dears. Any restaurant with off-duty officers dining is a wonderful source of information. A few drinks loosen their tongues. Which is why I am pleased with myself'—he broke off, looked at his watch—'this is the time for the official news bulletin; and I rather think I know what the main item will be.' He rose and crossed to the shelf where the wireless stood.

The voice of Radio Rome was guttural, as if gloating on its words: 'The authentic government of Signor Benito Mussolini announces from its headquarters at Salo on Lake Garda that the trial of the traitors who violated the constitution of the Fascist Grand Council and betrayed Il Duce to the puppet king was concluded. All the guilty ones, including the treacherous son-in-law of Il Duce, Galeazzo Ciano, were today, 11 January 1944, shot by a firing squad. Mussolini himself signed the death warrant.'

Vanni flicked the switch. 'Yes. I'd heard. The verdict—and the sentence—were expected. Planned, you might say. It's that megalomaniac Hitler who gives the orders, Musso has no power at all. The German army's in complete control, the Italian Generals can't even do what they like with their own forces. Kesselring, the German C-in-C, pulls the strings and the puppets dance for him. A deplorable situation. But one I hope to rectify—in my small way.'

I could not help thinking that eavesdropping in a restaurant was hardly likely to change the course of the war, and said as much.

'How can you tell? You will agree, my dear Johns, that some of your own activities have been small-time. But you don't know how they fitted into the overall pattern. Perhaps as easily as—shall we say?—a message fits into a tooth.'

Again I was startled. I had not even told Fiamma about it.

'So you know about that?' I queried.

His smile, once more, was typical of the cat that has been at the cream. 'I told you: the work of "Il Mago" doesn't go unnoticed.' He crossed his legs and lit another cigarillo. 'And very valuable that little assignment was. I doubt if anyone told you, though.'

I remembered 'C' and his grudging acknowledgement.

'One doesn't expect anything really. I don't

suppose you will if you hear anything "to your advantage", as they say, in some grubby little trattoria.'

He indulged in another stage wink. 'Something rather better than a grubby trattoria. No less than the headquarters of the great Field-Marshal Kesselring himself—at a very fine villa at Soratte up in the Sabine hills! He's a cultured, sensitive man, and he's kept the Italian staff to cope with running the villa, so it wasn't difficult to get smuggled in as an old retainer.'

'But Vanni,' Fiamma protested, 'you're much too young to look like an old retainer.'

He chuckled. 'There are ways. Maybe I'll grow a long beard like Johns here, or adopt a *shuffle*.' As if in demonstration he got to his feet and imitated a bent old man. It was a travesty, but I must say I was impressed; and Fiamma broke into a giggle, 'And anything—*anything*—that knocks that strutting cock Mussolini from his perch is worth while. And his puppet-master. I shall be all ears as well as beard and limp.'

At that very moment, as if the word 'ears' had acted as a signal, there was a knock at the front door.

It was not especially loud or peremptory, but it had the insistent note of a visitor determined to come in.

Fiamma gasped, her hand to her lips; the blood drained from Vanni's cheeks; and I felt my heart pumping wildly. A caller after curfew? It could only be some official. Someone on Vanni's track? Or mine?

CHAPTER TWENTY-ONE

We stood stock still for what it seemed an age but could scarcely have been more than half a minute. The knocking continued, insistent yet not impatient. There were short pauses, then the rat-a-tat, rat-a-tat, rat-a-tat would begin again.

Fiamma who was nearest to the window, was the first to move. Vanni and I both felt the release of tension as she went to part the curtains.

'Careful!' Vanni cried.

She was marvellously composed, considering the shock we had had. I rushed to the switch and turned off the single table lamp that had illuminated the room. 'Now!' I whispered.

Peering over her shoulder through the gap in the curtains I could see the big Mercedes that stood outside. The Gauleiter's flag. 'It must be Kurt!' I said with relief.

But it was not. The knocking had momentarily ceased and I saw a tall German officer back casually down the steps that led up from the street to the porch. From this vantage point he peered up at the house as if half-satisfying himself that there were no occupants. Clearly he was not convinced. He returned. The knocking began again, louder, as if he was saying, 'You can't fool me.'

'I'm entitled to be here,' Fiamma said breathlesly. 'You two . . . I don't know. Better go in the kitchen. Keep quiet. Perhaps—'

'Perhaps he's just checking that you're not roaming the streets after curfew,' I muttered, though I knew perfectly well that a lieutenant-

355

colonel would hardly bother with such a mundane chore. 'We'll stow away, keep quiet, listen. At least we'll be on hand if we're needed. I tried to make a virtue of our presence but I had had no time to plan any action. Vanni reflected my look of bewilderment. Quickly and silently we moved to the kitchen. Looking back, I can see we were acting like guilty schoolboys. It was ridiculous, really; I had been—and Vanni too—in many tougher situations, but the unexpectedness of the interruption was, in some strange way, more sinister than anything that cropped up in the normal turmoil of war.

We heard Fiamma open the door and a suave educated voice apologising for the lateness of the hour.

'I was asleep,' Fiamma said convincingly.

'Of course.' We knew that the officer had stepped into the entrance hall, we heard the swish of the blackout curtain as it fell into place. 'Your hours at the hospital must be very tiring.' His footsteps followed hers into the sitting-room we had just left, but the door was left open, and we could still hear him talking.

'Allow me to introduce myself, Signora, though we have in fact met before. You may perhaps remember a little party to which Colonel von Schill brought you at the Excelsior? No, perhaps not, there were many people there—'

'Yes,' we heard Fiamma answer, 'you were the Colonel's deputy. I remember.'

'Second-in-command.' We heard him click his heels as he punctiliously corrected her. 'Colonel Konrad Neumann at your service. But no longer second-in-command. That is the purpose of my

356

visit. Colonel von Schill has been seconded to special duties at the headquarters of the Feldmarschall. I am now Gauleiter of Rome.' There was a long pause during which he seemed to be letting this information sink in.

'This would be of small moment to you, Signora, but for one thing.' Again a significant pause. 'As Colonel von Schill's second-in-command it did not escape my notice that from time to time he robbed our gallant German soldiers of their rations to bring you food. No, Signora, do not bother to dispute it. But now—there will be no more food. I intend to obey orders. You understand? That is the purpose of my visit. I depart now. Auf Weidersehen, Signora. I regret disturbing your—your sleep.'

We heard the door shut and the Mercedes drive away. Fiamma, white-faced, ran to me and I put my arm around her shoulders. She was trembling. 'Oh Ham! I relied so much on that extra for Ham Two. And did you hear the sneer in his voice under all that correctness of manner?'

'We did,' Vanni said. 'There was a threat there too, implied if not stated. He might as well have said, "Be careful. I'm watching you. I know all about you." You agree, Johns?'

Fiamma broke in, 'You think he knows about you two, that you were here?'

I frowned. 'Can't say, really. Or even that he knows we exist. But he must have smelt the cigarillo, so it's possible. We'd better be cautious. I tell you what, though: he doesn't know he's given us valuable information. "Seconded to special duties" means Kurt's on Intelligence work of some kind at Kesselring's HQ.'

Vanni sat down, swung his leg over the arm of

the chair, and looked thoughtful. 'Yes. Could be useful. Being at the fountain-head—well, the spray falls on the ears of unobtrusive listeners sometimes. And it can be filtered back to the cistern—in this case you, my dear Johns.' He grinned at his apt simile; then the grin faded. 'But will Kurt recognise me? What do you think?'

Fiamma offered a measure of reassurance. 'You and Kurt only met once, surely?' she queried Vanni. 'And that was at Magari. Is he likely to—'

'That's right,' I interrupted. 'It was one afternoon when you were on short leave and dashed in for a swim and a meal before dashing out again. At Forte dei Marmi, when you were beaten up, Kurt was on holiday with Roz. So Fiamma's right. It *is* only the once you've met. Think you can get away with it?'

Vanni smiled. 'With a beard and my old retainer's walk? You bet!'

'I hope you're right,' I said.

*   *   *

Some weeks passed before I heard anything from Vanni. This was not surprising for the links between us were complex and not reliable—depending as they did on accurate timings for visiting 'drops' that were not always possible to keep, on coded messages on the partisan radio, on underground 'newspapers' that might be traced by the *Guardia Segreta* and destroyed, or on birds of passage like myself. One of my drops—the café in the Via Margutta above which I had had a bed-sit—had been closed down and the barman, Marco, had disappeared. There were ugly rumours about where he had ended up. 'Concentration camp, probably,' Access said, 'after loosening his tongue a bit.' He added with a sort of evil glee, 'Could happen to any of us.' Which was true. We lived from day to day on the edge of betrayal and discovery. It was impossible to know for certain who was friend and who was enemy.

When Vanni's first scrap of information came it was not on the face of it of world-shattering importance: 31 PARACHUTE DIVISION PULLING OUT. True, troop movements were a vital part of Intelligence, but there were dozens of them recorded every day. But it was supplemented a few days later by something more intriguing. One of Vanni's partisan contacts, a farmer whose farm lay alongside Highway 6, had seen a convoy of tank transporters heading for Cassino. This would not have been remarkable except that they were carrying tank turrets detached from Tiger tanks of the SS Panzer Divison, not the tanks themselves. Other teasing snippets followed. The forward HQ of the Cassino area was reported to be pulling back from Frosinone to Arpino; a line of gun emplacements without guns was appearing along a tributary of the Liri bordering Arpino; and the whole of the area was being sown with mines. Then came news that some strange steel 'boxes' with open tops had arrived at Monte Soratte from the railhead at Bologna on troop trains carrying 'thousands' of soldiers transferred from the Russian front. The final scrap from Vanni was that he was hearing the word 'Luder' spoken a lot around HQ.

I managed to contact Access by leaving the message 'Signor Bardi offers you a gindiano' at the bar of the Hotel Torino, and we met at the crowded

Triangolo, where the customers varied from high-ranking German officers to shifty-eyed nondescripts. It was always better to be among a mass of people than to meet furtively and attract attention that way.

'H'm,' Access said when I'd given him my bits and pieces. 'Interesting—some of it, anyway. What d'you make of it?'

'Maybe the bits belong to different puzzles. The one thing I do understand is that the turrets were without their tanks. They haven't been able to use tanks much in this campaign because of all the mud.'

'That's hardly new—or interesting,' Access said. He paused. The aroma of cappuccino and espresso wafted up between us. 'What *is* interesting is that bit about 31 Parachute Division. It's been defending Cassino since our first attacks. Very successfully too, working as infantry without their 'chutes. Now why the bloody hell should Kesselring decide to withdraw them just as he knows the big attack's building up—as he must do?'

'May be they're due for a rest,' I said, though it was rather a feeble suggestion.

'Rest my arse!' Access said. 'The Hun doesn't work that way. Too bloody well organised.' He stroked his chin as if calming himself. 'No. There's something afoot here. Is it a plant? How reliable's this boyfriend of yours—this Vanni?'

'He is not,' I said with as much control of my temper as I could muster, 'my boyfriend.'

Access airily gestured with his hand as if pacifying me. 'No, well, all right. Your girlfriend's brother...'

360

'Stepbrother,' I corrected.

'I don't care a bugger who or what he is. Whose side's he on? That's the question.'

'Ours. So far as I know. How can one be sure?'

He snorted. 'You're getting cynical, Painter.' The snort changed to a harsh laugh. 'Just as well perhaps. No good being trusting in this bloody set-up. Trust 'em with your balls and they'll have your prick off too before you can shout "snap".'

I did not bother to ask him who 'they' were. 'Reverting to the information,' I said drily, 'and assuming that it's not a plant—'

He was suddenly serious, even half apologetic. 'Sorry, Painter. You've done pretty well—or Vanni has. Let's try and piece this stuff together.' He ticked off the items on his fingers. 'We've got troop movements—a division pulling out and others coming in; tank turrets and steel boxes; gun emplacements without guns; mines being sown along a defensive line; and a code word, Luder.'

'What's it mean? My German's scrappy.'

'Luder? It can mean dissolute, cad, slut, carrion. I don't think we need bother with it, it's just a fancy name they've given an operation. The other stuff, though. Looks to me as if the steel boxes are meant to fit in the gun emplacements and the turrets with their guns inside them. But why the withdrawal of 31 Division and the pull back from Frosinone to Arpino? If they're strengthening the defences with gun emplacements and minefields there's no need'—he broke off suddenly—'wait a minute. I've just thought: there's another meaning to that word Luder! Yes, by Christ! *Bait, trap*. That's it. They *want* us to think we can trap their Cassino defences by going round in a pincer

361

movement and cutting them off from behind, whereas in reality-'

'They'll trap us?' I queried.

'Possibly. I'm no tactician, but I've got a nose for smelling out rats. And this is a stinker.' He laughed coarsely. 'A stinker we've got to hold under the noses of the top brass before it loses its stench. Got me?'

I replied, 'Yes, I get you. It'll be Eighth Army HQ that needs to know. They're dealing with the east side. I'll contact them by radio, do a code translation.'

He shook his head vehemently. 'No, too sensitive. Might get picked up. And you can't rely on the Hun not having our cipher keys. No, it's got to be done orally, nothing written, no chances taken. And since you're the man who collected the information you're the man to deliver it. No fear of any garbling then.'

'It's nice to know you have that much faith in me,' I said wrily.

He laughed mirthlessly. 'Get on with it,' he said.

★   ★   ★

But I could not go without seeing Fiamma. I had an intuition about the journey I was about to make; something—disaster, achievement? I had felt, in a minor form, something of the same apprehension years before at the Slade when I submitted a test drawing of a leafless twig that my examining professor had said should reveal 'the sap still coursing through the veins'. He nodded approvingly at my pencil drawing and I felt the relief quietening my heart. But my present apprehension was hardly on the same scale. What it amounted to, I suppose, was that I wanted to share my fears, be comforted.

At the Via Lisbona Signora Stefano told me that Fiamma was not due for any more leave for at least two weeks. 'She stays at the hospital, Signor. There is *accomodamento* for nurses there, and the boy'—she beamed—'he is mine, safely. You see him now, yes?'

'Not now,' I said, though I longed to. 'It's too disappointing for both of us, such a brief meeting.'

'Si, Signor.' She smiled her understanding. Then suddenly her round merry face changed its expression. 'It is so sad for you—' Her voice trailed off.

'War is always sad,' I replied, 'and cruel.'

It seemed cruellest to me when I reached the hospital after a hazardous journey along Highway 6 to find the place in turmoil. It was hardly surprising. During the journey there I had had to abandon my motor-bike three times to shelter from bombardments—whether ours or the enemy's I never knew, and it made little difference anyway. Shells are shells wherever they come from.

And now the casualties were coming in as fast as field ambulances, trucks, and any other available transport could bring them. There would not be a chance in hell of finding Fiamma, or of being able to talk to her even if I could. Her duty would be as clear to her as mine was to me, and it could not include snatching time for farewell embraces. In any case, I told myself, why should this parting be any more permanent than any of the hundred others we had endured? I was being childish. St Luke's admonition to the physician to heal himself crossed my mind. I had to shake off my intuition about impending trouble. Access's words echoed in my mind: 'Get on with it.'

Then came a minor miracle.

In my mud-streaked and dishevelled state I passed unnoticed among the equally battle-scarred casualties, stretcher bearers, and orderlies who milled about the hospital. I had decided to make myself scarce and continue my journey without even attempting to find Fiamma, when suddenly I saw her. She was hurrying along a corridor carrying a tray on which were a syringe, bottles and some surgical gloves.

'Ham! Darling, I—'

I fell into step beside her. 'I know. Ships that pass in the night. You're on your way to an emergency.'

She nodded. 'Yes. But—'

'Me too. Of a different kind. Eighth Army HQ. But I desperately wanted to see you before . . . in case—'

The colour drained from her face. 'Oh Ham! Don't!'

'No. Don't worry.' I tried to reassure her. 'It'll be all right. It was just that—'

I steadied her with a hand at her elbow as she seemed to stumble and with my other hand I grabbed at the tray. But the shock was momentary—a second or two; then the light of love returned to her eyes. In a swift movement she crossed herself.

'Please, God,' she murmured, her eyes briefly closed. 'My love'—she had recovered herself—'be safe, my darling, darling Ham.' She made to take the tray, then paused as she dug into the pocket of her dress for a letter. 'This came—from Roz. Take it.'

I stuffed it into my tunic ready for reading later—Roz was a long way from my thoughts. I barely touched Fiamma's lips with mine, but something in that brief kiss gave me the comfort I sought. The last sight I had of her was of her slender body passing through a swing door into a ward, her blonde hair folded neatly into a plait beneath her white starched cap. Misty-eyed, I stumbled through the doors and passages and out into the open, noticing for the first time some cavernous gaps in the rocky hillside in the lee of which the hospital stood. The sounds of distant shells and the crump of not-so-distant mortars filled my ears. Across the field of clover that separated me from the pitted road, I could see the bloated corpse of a cow, its legs ludicrously in the air, as if waving to me.

Then I was on my way.

*   *   *

With the battles for the monastery at their fiercest, movements of troops were so fast and confused that there was no certainty that the location of even an Army HQ would be static for more than a few hours. All the information I had was that the Army Commander, General Leese, who had succeeded Montgomery, had his headquarters in the region of Benevento, the best part of one hundred miles to the south-east.

A minor fear I had was of being commandeered in my capacity of Red Cross orderly to help with casualties. I had always run this risk but so far had

365

never been grabbed—just as well, for my knowledge was virtually nil. But now time was of the essence. If my information was to be any use, I had to make it to HQ with the utmost speed.

To say that chaos reigned is to put it mildly. It was nothing new: I had been in the midst of conflicts of one sort or another for so long that I was hardened. The sound of bombs and shells after a time seem to be no more than the noise of traffic when you live on a busy road. Fiamma had mentioned her 'bomb happy' cases, and I had heard of chaps who walked about regardless in the midst of heavy attacks, laughing madly, shrieking defiance at the skies as if they cared nothing for their own or anybody else's lives. I had never felt like that, but maybe I had neither the nerve nor the adrenalin or whatever to call on. This time, though, I was so tensed up that I began to understand how it could happen.

The landscape was terrifying. I was moving against the tide of slowly advancing Allied troops—some in the tatters of uniforms of Moroccan, Indian, Goum, Canadian, and Polish armies. Pockets of resistance had sometimes been overcome at terrible cost. The landscape testified: bridges had collapsed into streams that were coloured with the blood of the newly wounded, the skeleton of a crashed plane stuck grotesquely up from a shell-hole like a monster spoon stuck in a pudding basin, abandoned and burnt-out vehicles lay rusting in the quagmires and stinking pools that were an aftermath of the months of ceaseless rain. My eyes took in the scene as horribly like those depicted in the allegorical paintings of Bosch, Pieter Huys, and Brueghel with their visions of hell and

366

purgatory dotted with grinning skulls, nightmare reptiles, and rotting flesh.

'Christ!' I thought (and maybe I was not so immune to battle craziness after all), 'crossing no-man's-land on a death-defying errand. Whoopee!'

Then I calmed myself down. I had to. My motor-bike was hissing and spluttering as if uncertain of itself. It seemed to recover as I hit bumps, but after I made my way across a further half mile or so of rocky ground it finally wheezed to a standstill.

I primed the carburettor. Not a gurgle. I had run out of petrol.

By this time I had passed through a battle-scarred village with farm buildings still smoking from the strafing they had received from an air attack. I could see the black plumes still rising half a mile or so back. Would it be worth while wheeling my bike back in the hope of finding an abandoned vehicle? What alternative was there? Looking around I saw that I was on a scorched stretch that might once have been an olive grove but was now no more than a tangle of burnt branches and stumps criss-crossed by strands of fencing that had been mangled into the soot-blackened soil. Shell-holes pitted the road skirting the field and, beyond, it seemed to disappear. If it edged into an incline perhaps I could coast down it to another village? Astonishingly the noise of battle had receded. The torn remnants of the formation I had passed had evidently reached the smoking village and harboured there. I had second thoughts about returning and seeking help from them; but it was forward movements I wanted, not a retracing of my own steps. I pushed forward towards the incline.

I was in better luck than I feared. The incline was quite a long steady one. It twisted out of sight round a corner at the foot and seemed to disappear into a copse; and if my eyes did not deceive me there was a vehicle—a scout car or something similar—which had crashed into a ditch on the corner. Maybe there was a spare tin of petrol on board . . . ?

There was not, of course. The vehicle had been shot up by an anti-tank gun and the driver sat still behind the wheel, his body pierced cleanly by an armour-piercing bullet that had penetrated the steel visor. There was a placid smile on his face as if he had been thinking of something pleasant when he died.

But though there was no spare can of petrol there was some in the tank. If I could siphon some out . . .

It was while I was thinking about how to find some rubber tubing to do just that that I heard a cry:

'Halte! Là!'

I turned quickly. From the copse twenty yards away a tall officer—French if his strangely immaculate uniform was to be believed—accompanied by two nondescript soldiers carrying machine-carbines emerged. I smiled gratefully. Here was help at last. Or so I thought.

'Là!' he said again. 'Italian, yes?'

'Non,' I replied. I pointed to my brassard and made a gesture to indicate that I was carrying no arms. 'Red Cross. Non-combatant. Actually I'm British, carrying an important message to General Leese's HQ, and I've run out of petrol. Perhaps you could help me?'

In answer he ordered his two gunmen to prod me towards the copse with their carbines. I protested with as much vehemence as I could summon but he waved us on impatiently. 'Là. Là.'

He had a sort of hideout in the trees. It included a wired-in compound in which a few German prisoners were guarded by more men with carbines. I tumbled to what the place was: a temporary interrogation camp where prisoners were held until they could be got back to the rail-head.

'Come this way. We will see into this matter.'

'There's nothing to see into,' I said, 'except my lack of petrol.' I was angry—with myself for having been distracted by my farewell to Fiamma into overlooking practical matters, and with this jumped-up Frenchman, Intelligence officer, or whatever he was, for delaying me.

In the little cabin that was his 'office' the two guards flanked him as he faced me across a rickety table.

'This is ridiculous—' I began.

'Not so ridiculous. No!' He had cold fishlike eyes. 'Too many use the Red Cross to desert, to spy, to betray. You could be with the battle—ahead, to gain Cassino. But you are going opposite, away. Fleeing, perhaps, from danger you are tired of—' his thin lips curled in a sneer.

I held myself back with difficulty. 'Listen,' I said with strained patience, 'we're Allies—at least I assume you are'—I tried, not very successfully, to inflect my voice with doubts of his authenticity—'and should be helping each other. I've got *my* papers of identification—'

'Not worth a centime,' he broke in. 'Half the prisoners that go through my hands have papers to prove they're not Germans. Forgery is a very useful art to the spy, the deserter, the undercover man.'

Too late I remembered that the papers I carried were those of Emilio Bardi.

'But this message—this *vital* message—perhaps that would go some way to my belief in your claim to be a British officer.' He paused, a twisted smile crossing his sallow face, and ordered one of the guards to search me.

With the other guard's carbine pointing at my chest I had to submit, fuming. 'For God's sake,' I yelled, 'you don't suppose I carry messages of that importance written down, do you? It's in my head. And if it's to be of any bloody use in Eighth Army planning, and the outcome of this sodding campaign to capture the bleeding monastery—'

He made a fastidious gesture with his fingers: 'You certainly swear like a British trooper.' He cast a cold glance down to the little pile of stuff the man searching me had found, ignoring the things like keys, money, lighter, cigarettes. Picking my Red Cross pass up by its edges he nodded and smiled smugly. 'But your identification tells me you are Emilio Bardi of the Italian Military Medical Corps—*not* a British name, I think. And—ah! What have we here?'

I had completely forgotten the letter from Roz that Fiamma had pressed into my hand before we parted, which I had not even looked at.

Scrutinising it his eyebrows rose. 'And now another surprise. A letter from your wife, or perhaps a fiancée, in which you become her darling Kurt.' The smile on his face had become triumphant. 'Hardly an English name, wouldn't you agree? She wishes you to tell'—another downward glance—'*Fiamma* that Mama is all regrets and forgiveness. How very pleasant! A family quarrel healed no doubt. And written from an address in Lübeck. So you are a German masquerading as an Italian masquerading as an Englishman. It is all very complicated.' He shook his head in mock mystification. 'But not too complicated, I think, for higher authority.' Suddenly he resumed his ice-cold stare and ordered the guards to put me in the compound with the other prisoners. 'You will get your wish Kurt, Emilio, Tommy—whoever you are. You will be taken back to Eighth Army Headquarters.' He paused significantly. 'But not as the bearer of some so-called vital message. As a *prisoner*'.

*   *   *

I had never felt more powerless in my life, not even on the train back from Italy when the Guardia Segreta were searching me. I cursed myself for mishandling the whole situation; though on reflection I could not see what else I could have done. As I was pushed into the barbed wire compound I wanted to cry, 'She's not my wife, you idiot!' but I knew that would only get me deeper into the mire. The only thing I had overcome was the transport problem. Sooner or later I would be taken to where I so desperately needed to go. But God knew when; and as a prisoner who might well be kept for days, even weeks, before being wheeled before a higher ranking Intelligence officer with whom I would have to go through the whole business of identification again. And it would be

371

much too late. I almost wept with the frustration of it all.

Sometimes, though, luck is on the side of the angels. I had been in the compound for only a few hours when I and the half dozen German prisoners were herded out and into a three-ton truck, lashed together by the ankles like galley slaves and with two burly guards with carbines accompanying us. It was dusk by then and of course I could see little of the receding landscape as we moved south. Several times we halted, apparently to allow convoys of vehicles to move forward to the Cassino area. Most of the time I was lying on the floor of the lorry, but occasionally I eased my cramped position by half sitting up. In the moonlight the eerie phosphorescence of the bloated carcases of long-dead sheep reminded me of the bedside night-lights of my childhood. I was exhausted and no doubt a bit delirious.

It must have been in the early hours of the morning when we jolted to a halt. Shouted commands and some pretty rough handling by the guards as we were off-loaded, still fettered together, brought me painfully to full consciousness. An officer—British, I could tell by his Geordie accent—stood by with a clipboard comparing his list with the names on the cardboard discs stapled to our clothing. His tiny torch moved like a glow-worm in the dark I could smell the familiar stench of scorched earth, sweat, latrines, and smoke bombs.

Now my eyes could make out the outline of a large building—it could have been a villa or a barn. I realised this must be HQ. Impulsively I shouted, 'It's urgent—vital—for me to see the general—at once—!' Immediately I said it I felt ridiculous, like the hero in a Victorian melodrama.

The broad Geordie accent brought me back to reality: 'And who the bloody hell are you?' The little stab of light found my disc. 'Bardi, Emilio. You don't sound like an Eyetie to me.'

'I'm not,' I said, 'I'm British. SOE,' I added, as if the magic initials would solve all my difficulties. 'Captain Hamilton Johns. And I'm not kidding about the general.'

He must have had many prisoners attempting tricks of this sort, but I had to hand it to him that he detected some genuine note of urgency in my voice. He could hardly lose anyway: if I was some sort of nut he could have me dealt with appropriately; if not, he would get a pat on the back. He summoned a sergeant and handed over his clipboard. 'Get this lot into the interrogation compound; but unhook this one and bring him to me in the GSO wing—under armed guard. Understand, Sergeant?'

'Sir.'

To me he said, 'If you're feeding me a load of crap you'll end up a load of crap yersen. I tell you that for nowt.'

*　　　　　*　　　　　*

The GSO wing was grandly named; but it was no more than a corner of what had once been an elegant drawing-room in the villa. The only illumination was from hissing pressure lamps which gave off a stink as well as a harsh white light from incandescent mantles. The Geordie, I could see now, was a stocky major, unshaven, with a battered nose and bright black eyes and black hair.

373

It was Catterick, Richmond, and climbing the keep of the Norman castle that convinced him. He had obviously done commando training over the same ground himself. I could see the flicker of belief in his eyes when I mentioned the bullying commandant and the sarcastic RSM with his pacing-stick. 'Okay, Captain; let's have your info.'

He looked grave when I wearily came to the end of my hotchpotch of scraps. 'Jesus! It can only mean one thing. The Hun's got wind of our plan to cut Highway 6 and close round the monastery. By withdrawing that Division they're counting on giving us confidence to do just that. The tank turrets and gun emplacements are a lure—"Luder" is right!'—to convince us they're defending more heavily—'

'But if they're not in fact defending more heavily—' I interrupted.

'We'll push in extra brigades for a reinforced attack, believing they are; then we find the buggers aren't, sweep on beyond the Monastery Hill, and get trapped by 31 Division coming round in a pincer movement. It'll save them a few thousand troops defending Cassino in a final battle, and we'll lose those we intend for the big push on Rome.'

He banged his fist down on the trestle table that held chinagraph-marked maps. 'But by Christ! If they're banking on bottling us up, we've got an equal chance, now, of cutting off their escape routes through the Apennines!'

CHAPTER TWENTY-TWO

Since I was only one of the cogs in the smallest wheel of the machinery for the battle of the monastery—that key point in the Cassino battle—it is hardly surprising that I cannot give more than a sketchy idea of the final assault on Monastery Hill. The earlier assaults had stretched over months and the losses on both sides had been appalling. Whether or not the monastery itself should be bombed had been a vital decision. The moral issues were complex; the immediate practical question was whether the Germans would use the building as a virtually impregnable defensive position. On Allied appeal the Pope was said to have given permission for the bombing so long as the monastery was evacuated and the art treasures removed. The battle would thus be shortened and lives saved—or so the theory went.

I cannot really say either whether my journey to Eighth Army HQ had had the desired effect of changing General Leese's tactics. I did arrive in time, I know. Leese, and Mark Clark of the United States Fifth Army, shared the information; that much I was told by the Geordie major before HQ moved and I moved with it—more as an act of charity than anything else.

'Thee's neither flesh nor fowl nor good red herring,' Geordie said. And it was true. I was not 'on the strength' of any unit, I had no vehicle, and I had to rely on bumming lifts from any driver I could convince of my need—'a floating liability' as Geordie added cheerlessly. There were advantages though. With the battle situation as it was I found it easy enough to attach myself unofficially to any unit for rations, which in any case were unreliable with supply lines so often ruptured by bomb and artillery attacks. My non-combatant status was both a help and a hindrance. Stretcher-bearing was about the limit of my use in Red Cross guise; but my brassard concealed my 'Secret Agent' activities, as I suppose I was rather grandly labelled. (Not that there was anything grand about the pettifogging business of clandestine meetings and 'drops'; the cloak-and-dagger aspect always verged on the farcical.) Anyway, my intention was to work my way back to Rome to report to Access for further duties.

But it was a long time before I got back to Rome.

★   ★   ★

Of course in the confusion of so many happenings I had forgotten the letter from Roz. The French officer had never returned it to me and I could only guess at its full contents and how Fiamma had come by it. I would have taken a small bet that Vanni had had something to do with getting it to her; and at least it revealed that the Principessa had relented to some extent and that Roz was writing from Lübeck, Kurt's family home. So evidently no disasters had struck at the mysterious Roz. But when had the letter been written? I had no clue. It could have been months previously. Only Fiamma could enlighten me, and God knew when I would see her again.

By now the Italian summer was overtaking us and everywhere the quagmires of the prolonged

376

rains had been baked hard and contracted, leaving fissures like a network of veins. The American outfit I found myself attached to at one stage had a baby-faced lieutenant from Nevada who told me the scene reminded him of home. Tears glistened in his eyes as he said, 'Gee, them shapes is like prickly cactuses.' The 'shapes' were the twisted wreckages of burnt-out vehicles and gutted buildings. 'They always frightened me when I was knee-high to a ladybug and Mom used to kid me they wuz shapes God had planned and they ain't nothing to be frightened of. She'd've been scary herself if she'd been here.'

That night there was an hour-long artillery barrage. I holed up in a cave in the hillside—it was riddled with them, some were really tunnels and had been used to store ammunition. There were decaying bodies too, and the stench of death, and the reverberation of exploding shells as the barrage reached its peak. The lad from Nevada had herded his platoon into the cave like a mother hen with her chicks. 'Ain't no point throwin' lives away when you can't get nowhere.' It was the wisdom of an old head on young shoulders, a battle-weary fatalism.

Of course it is easy with hindsight to put together the picture of the final assault on Monte Cassino in that May of 1944, to realise that such-and-such a brigade or battalion advanced a few hundred yards or seized a key landmark, and that eventually the ruined monastery fell to the Polish Corps, after a week of terrible fighting, on 17 May. Their Commander, Wladyslaw Anders, was rewarded with the acknowledgement from the Eighth Army commander, Oliver Leese, that 'This notable feat will, I believe, go down in history as a mighty achievement of Polish arms.' But individuals like myself saw at the time only the immediate devastation surrounding them, the thick yellow smoke from Nebelwerfen, the fountains of dust and rock that rose and fell deafeningly as bombs and shells hit the cracked earth. I remember it as a sort of cinematic flashthrough in which the projector is running wildly and frames have been juxtaposed in mad disorder, so that the eye and the brain cannot reconstruct any logical sequence. Only the incessant tattoo of machine-gun fire stitches the scene together. There are faces too—of Indians and Moroccans and Frenchmen and New Zealanders and Canadians, remembered as grotesque and bloody or staring in death; and scrambled messages that the Germans were withdrawing from their defensive positions among the rubble of the monastery.

Somehow—I never quite knew how or why—I was in the midst of the advancing forces; and somehow, equally confusingly, the fourth battle for the key point of Monte Cassino itself was over. Except for what the army calls 'isolated pockets of resistance' the detection of their 'Luder' and their own subsequent fear of having their escape route cut off. As I said, I never really knew whether Allied tactics were changed on account of my race against time. And I did not much care. Exhaustion took over. And to match it there was the silence of the dead and a profusion of red flowers among which the burial parties of both sides carried out their sombre tasks.

*　　*　　*

Recalling events from so many years ago is always a tricky business. The memory tends to be selective, to grasp what the emotions dictate and discard or distort what is best forgotten, or was obliterated by exhaustion. So although I have said 'we were there', triumphant with the ruined monastery captured, implying that with that important chess-piece removed from the board the Allies would swing rapidly forward to checkmate the enemy, that was an over-simplification. The historical records confirm as much. There were not only many drawn-out battles preceding the capture of Monte Cassino but many counter-attacks after. Despite the withdrawal of the main enemy forces we were still within easy range of their air and artillery bombardment, and those so-called 'isolated pockets of resistance' were frequently major engagements. Stretches of ground changed hands with remarkable rapidity, sometimes within a few hours. And at one stage, even, a 'tongue' of ground stretching from the town of Cassino all the way to Rome was in enemy hands—and that was days after the fateful 17 May when everything seemed triumphant.

But I must return to my recollected emotions of the time.

Once the main battle had ended—as it seemed to me then with victory for us, defeat for the Germans—I had a strange feeling (I cannot really call it an urge) which began to persist most forcibly inside me. For a few hours Monte Cassino would be empty of everyone but a party of Poles acting as sentries of that wrecked abbey on a forlorn strip of land until the army leaders arrived later on a tour of inspection.

But I felt, remembering my visit to Cassino so

long ago, that someone else was there, someone as deeply concerned with Monte Cassino as I had been, someone who wanted to see me. And I wanted to see him. It was Kurt.

Why was it so strong, this feeling? Why was I so certain that an enemy officer would be there on Allied-held ground? I can only think that the successive battles, culminating in the final one, had been so overpowering that they had given me a slight case of shell shock. I do not really know. I felt fine, but perhaps I was not quite normal. Few of us were.

So I decided to seek permission to go to the top, where smoke and dust still hung in clouds over the ruins. I was urged on inside me by what I call my 'Kurt obsession'. But the seeking of permission is one thing and the acquiring of it another. True, as an officer of the SOE little was denied me, but communications were as chaotic as the struggles of the troops had been. 'Take me to your leader' was a jokey catch-phrase of the time, but the carrying out of such an order was less easy. One obstacle was the cosmopolitan nature of the Allied forces. Italian and French I could cope with, but the Indian, Polish and Moroccan troops posed insoluble language problems. Also, command posts—when you could find them—could be those of a mere troop or company who in the general chaos had lost touch with higher formations. I had no radio, and on the one occasion when I came across an immobile armoured car and its Canadian commander it was only to find that his radio had been 'kaputed' by enemy fire. But he did tell me that a few hours previously there had been 'a kinda HQ with a brigadier' on a hillock a mile or so to the east. He showed me the point on his map and wished me luck.

I found the hillock, and the brigadier too. He was happily drunk, swigging something out of a hip flask and would, I am sure, have given me permission to go on extended leave if I had asked. So when I explained that I needed to get a bird's-eye view of the terrain in preparation for the next battle beyond Cassino and towards Rome he gravely put a hand on my shoulder and told me to go ahead. 'It'sh all yours, my boy. Help yourshelf.' Then he fired a shot from his revolver into the air. 'Rome, Rome, here we come. Here we bloody come. Whoopee!'

I saluted smartly, went on my way, recalling that General Alexander, Supremo of the Allied forces in Italy, had explained how vital it was that, when we broke out from Cassino, we must not rush off to take Rome, but must bottle up the retreating German forces. Yet there were strong rumours that the American general, Mark Clark, was planning to disobey orders and make a dash through the Liri valley to Rome. I knew of this because I had received messages from Geneva via our Triangolo radio contact warning of just this. In fact Geneva had even quoted Churchill as warning Alexander, 'It is much more important to use forces to cut the (German) line of retreat. The story of the battle, already great, will be measured not by the capture of Rome, but by the number of Germans cut off.' So what was Clark up to?

It seemed the most sensible thing would be to take a look at Clark's army through powerful glasses from the top of Monte Cassino. The forces would be spread out like a bedspread below the south-west corner.

There is nothing like clothing a crazy adventure in legitimacy to give you an added confidence, for though I *was* going to see if I could spot any American troop movements, I was more intrigued by the possibility of meeting Kurt.

For one glorious moment—was it really glorious?—I stood on the top of the hill virtually alone. I had quickly climbed the lower slopes, and then clambered up the last few feet, and the Poles were on the far side of the ridge and left me alone after one had run across and threatened to shoot until I showed him my pass.

Everywhere was dust, smoke, smouldering fires, the remnants of a searing inferno, great piles of rubble and the gaping, sharp ends of buildings where walls had only been partially demolished and stood unsupported but as though held by an unseen hand when by rights they should have fallen. Most striking of all was the silence, the utter, almost eerie lack of noise after the ear-splitting barrage that preceded the final onslaught when four hundred guns had roared out at almost the same moment, their shells bursting into the ground barely five hundred yards ahead. Now the agonising din—almost at times like a human scream of rage—had been silenced, so that the Poles, the bravest of the brave, could storm the citadel after the guns had wiped the earth clean.

Now at last for the moment there was a kind of peace, though it was the peace of derelict wasteland in the ashes of a beautiful symbol of faith founded some fourteen hundred years previously.

Everything around us had been demolished by the Allied air forces and our guns into dust, the dust of a great charnel house, of a monstrous cremation in which the ashes of each individual could never be separated, one from his neighbour.

All this time I spent crouching, partly for safety's sake, but also to examine through my binoculars the valley below me to the south-west. There were enormous signs of activity, reminiscent of an army ready to move.

I was behind a pile of boulders even though by now the Germans had hoisted the white flag and surrendered. But I was not really thinking of *them*—just of myself. For *them* the war was over—or was it? With the Germans you could never be *quite* sure that their signals told the truth. The place *seemed* empty, but now and again mysterious rustlings from nearby bomb wreckage whispered strangely. The wind probably. But my time as a partisan had warned me never to trust anything—or anybody.

My fears had been accelerated by an increasing niggling conviction that Kurt was in the vicinity. He had been so deeply involved in the planning, had been so trusted by his superior officers, that he had been taken from his prestigious post in Rome to go to Kesselring's HQ Intelligence Staff and help superintend defences. And like with me, past and present were intermingled. There was no war now, and he had learned something of my work, and each of us knew we were attracted to this spot. I *knew* he could not be far away. Yet why did I feel so strongly? And did he? Was it desire on my part that had made me clamber up this rough, torn path? Yes, it was. The lure of past friendship, now able to laugh at the devils of war. At this very moment.

At first it was little more than a hiss from a

crumbling, windowless ruin of a building on the other side, opposite from where I was crouching.

It was!

'Ham!'

'Kurt! I can't see you, but I can hear. Don't come out or you might be shot!'

I was facing our troops, way down the hillside, so it was quite safe for me to run across to the shell-shattered building where Kurt was hiding. I did so, still doubled up, but silent.

Within the shadow of a shattered archway where I had seen him once outlined, a dark figure against the sunlight, we stood facing each other for a moment. Kurt—tall, face matted with dirt, wearing no tunic, but a revolver at his waist. For a second—no more—we stood there, bosom friends turned by war into enemies, yet still friends; then we fell into each other's arms, hugging each other, almost in tears, enemies cloaked in an old friendship, friends who had climbed this very patch of hill to study the frescos for Berenson.

'Oh Kurt!' were my first words. 'Men are bloody fools!'

'Yes,' he agreed sombrely, 'plain bloody fools.' Then his face broke into a smile. 'How are you?'

'Fine.' I held him out in front of me to get a better look at him then cried, 'Apart from your revolver, you're not in uniform! Why not? Those are old slacks.'

Almost shyly he said simply, 'I pinched them. I don't know why—but I had an uncanny feeling that perhaps—'

'You were right. I had the same urgent feeling.'

'And the war—oh, Ham!' cried Kurt. 'If only the accursed war would end! I'm fed up to the teeth. So

384

I pinched these clothes from a dead body in the hope that I could come and meet you again. Dressed like you.'

'My uniform,' I said drily.

'One reason I wanted to see you was that I knew someone was tailing me in Rome—and I also knew about the strange blond soldier whom the partisans called *Il Mago*. And then Fiamma, who at first had been terrified of being seen with a German, seemed to become more friendly,' adding stiffly in his very correct and proper German, 'nothing improper, of course.'

'Of course,' I could not help laughing.

'Of course.' Almost moodily he threw a loose stone across the mud and scrub. 'But I never connected the two of you at all. I was just so fed up with the bloody war—all this blood and guts for nothing'—he hesitated, searching for words— 'except a sort of personality cult. You can't take on *all* the world—America, Britain, Russia, China—and get away with it. Hitler's *kaput*. God! I'm so glad to be out of it.'

'But are you?'

'Yes, I am. At least I hope so. Cassino's fallen to the Allies. I was part of that defeat. Our main line of defence south of Rome has been smashed wide open. I know I *should* escape—I know you'd let me—you'd understand. But Ham, at first I fought with my whole heart—all of it—and then somehow, the excitement of war began to turn bitter. Roz was unhappy. Her heart was *never* in it. And Fiamma, poor dear, half-starved, with your little son ill. I did what I could for her, but she was so afraid to be seen with me.'

'Your own sister-in-law.'

385

'I know. That's what makes me so unhappy. One moment my sister-in-law is my friend, my ally. The next day she's my enemy. It's crazy!'

'What do they—your chaps—the rank and file, feel?' I sat down against the wall, suddenly tired.

'Some diehards will fight for ever. Some will be delighted to be prisoners-of-war. Those who fight on now will probably die. The prisoners—at least with luck they'll eventually see their wives and kids and sweethearts again. And I'll see Roz.'

'Poor Roz. What a time since we met.' I was thinking of when we *had* met—and she had passed on a secret message—without knowing it—to me!

'Well, at least you'll soon be able to see Fiamma. I suppose you know she's working in the hospital? It's only about a mile's walk down the hill.'

I nodded. 'Yes, she's at the hospital,' I said. 'And of course, being on the south side of Cassino, it's escaped the Allied shelling—I suppose it's run by German doctors? But now! Suddenly what was once a safe place is now in the direct line of fire for Germans fighting a rearguard action. I'm waiting till the coast's clear, then I'll go down. I don't know who's in charge now.'

'The Italians, I think. I do know that some Italian doctors were left in the hospital when the Germans were running it short-handed. We needed them.' Suddenly, and with an impulsive gesture, he cried, 'Come on, Ham! Let's go and find Fiamma! The fighting's all over now.'

'Okay, you're right.'

No sooner said than the truth became a horrible lie.

Without warning the rattle and blurred staccato sound of sub-machine gunfire almost burst my ear

386

drums. Worse still—all of this happening in seconds—I was bowled over, giving an involuntary shriek of agony, clutching my left shoulder with my right hand, feeling the wet of blood, the crunch of shattered bone. And within a few seconds as I lay squirming on the ground, seeing a couple of faces, men in German uniforms who had appeared from somewhere, the shouting figure of Kurt screaming something I could not understand in German as he whipped out his revolver and, as the man realised from his language that Kurt was a German officer, shot him almost at point-blank range.

All I saw lying there was a man who at one moment had a face and the next moment all the flesh from that face had been stripped away by Kurt's shot. The second man had scuttled down the hill as the Poles ran across to see what had happened.

*   *   *

'Oh my God.' Kurt was almost sobbing, trying to stem the blood pouring from my shoulder and now, as he tore off his shirt, also from my left arm.

'The bloody Schwein,' Kurt used the German, 'and we're operating under a flag of truce! Dammit!' Then to me, 'Here, Ham, rest on this.' He picked up a bundle of rags—in fact old German tunics—made them into the next best thing to a cushion and very gently helped me down.

'It's not too bad.' He tried to console me but the pain was hell and the blood seemed to be pouring out—though that I knew was imagination. I could not *see* anything and shirts tended to stick to bloodied skin and give the impression of a lot of

387

blood. My left arm was also hurting.

'The bastards caught your left arm,' admitted Kurt after a look at the torn flesh. 'I can't tell, but let's hope it's not broken.'

Standing up he muttered to me, 'I'll have to get you to the hospital. That shoulder needs urgent attention. But how the hell? I can't *carry* you. It's nearly a mile to the town—or what's left of it.'

'Maybe if I rest a while,' I managed to gasp out, 'you could help me walk.'

Four Poles had arrived. One cried, 'What the devil—?'

'I'm English. A sniper got me. This,' I indicated Kurt, 'is an Italian. He'll help to get me to hospital. Not far away.'

'We could carry you.'

'Thanks,' I gasped with pain. 'I'll be okay in a few minutes. This chap knows the way.'

'Well,' doubtfully, 'if you're *sure*? But give us a shout if you need help.'

'Will do. And thanks.'

As the men shambled off, I said to Kurt, 'I just wanted to be alone—if you can manage.'

'Me too if I can. Let me look around. The road towards the hospital is now nothing but a smashed-up track. I might find a makeshift walking stick—*something . . .*'

He did. One section of the old abbey had suffered a little less than the others, especially a large plot of land which the monks had used to produce much of their food. And in one corner, under a ruined wall, but untouched, was a large old-fashioned wooden wheelbarrow. This was just what Kurt wanted.

'I'll wheel you down to the hospital!' Proudly Kurt brought back the barrow and displayed it to me. 'That's the simplest way of getting you there.'

Poor Kurt! How bloody ironic the whole thing was! An enemy 'captured' by a wounded British soldier (in theory anyway) now doing everything in his power to get me to a hospital which a few hours ago had been in the control of the Germans, but was now run by Italians before British surgeons took over. It was madness, the whole war! Madness!

Gently Kurt pulled the old uniforms from behind my back and made a fresh pillow on the barrow. I thought I could easily climb in but, as I attempted it, I started to keel over. Loss of blood, dizziness, excruciating pain, I do not know what it was. Had Kurt not caught me I would have fallen on to the hard rocks and probably broken something else. As it was, he managed to drag my steps, legs limp, the toe caps pulled painfully over the stones and shale until I 'woke up' and muttered, 'Sorry, Kurt. Must have passed out.'

'That's all right. There you are.' He lowered my almost inert body as gently as he could into the hard wheelbarrow. 'Here? That comfortable?'

It was not, nothing could be comfortable except an anaesthetic, but I grunted, 'Fine, Kurt. Thanks for all the help.'

'You'll feel better when you reach the hospital and see Fiamma.'

Kurt had put me in the barrow facing him because the less angular shape of the front of the barrow would be more comfortable, leaning my head to the right, so as not to hurt the left shoulder. I was also able to stretch my legs out, resting them on the handle shafts.

I had always imagined I possessed a fairly high pain threshold—especially after my experience with

389

the secret police in Ventimiglia—but now I was not so sure. The downhill journey from Monte Cassino was hell, pure hell. The surface itself was atrocious. The barrow had a wooden wheel with an ancient iron rim. It seemed as though even the smallest pebble over which we trundled invisibly had been turned by a malevolent nature into a huge stone, placed there deliberately to make me yelp with pain.

There was no way in which poor Kurt could help me ease the pain. Finding the path too stony and too rutted, he tried the rough grass verge, only to run the wheel into an unseen hole that—on one occasion—jerked me straight into unconsciousness for a few blessed moments. What I really needed was a good shot of morphia.

The long agony lessened as we approached the first paved streets—paved in the sense that some were cobbled, while the roadway was pitted with bomb craters and mud which Kurt had to circumnavigate. But at least for the last part of the journey I was spared the agonising ups and downs, of crying out each time I was jerked. Part of the trouble, of course, was that I was lying over the top of the wheel so that Kurt had no way of seeing immediately ahead.

'Only a few moments more,' Kurt soothed me. 'We're almost there.'

The ruined streets were not empty but, from the little I could see now and again when Kurt stopped for a rest, there was an atmosphere of lassitude. Nobody seemed to notice—to be interested—even in the odd spectacle of a man covered in blood getting a lift on a wheelbarrow. What we must have looked like to the spectators! A tall man, bare-chested, muscled, wheeling me along wordless but grim with the effort. You would have thought *someone* would come closer if only to take a look. Not a bit of it! They might have been zombies.

But of course, I thought, in a way that is what they were! After an ordeal lasting for months, they had been reduced to pitiful apologies for real people with no thoughts for the morrow, only for today. Looking back now on that nightmarish ride, I do not think I have ever seen such despair or resignation in the torn agony of the human spirit, the lack of interest in life itself, surrounded by shops with broken windows or boarded up, the wrecks of buildings, in many ways the most heart-rending experience I can remember.

'Here we are,' Kurt shouted triumphantly, almost jubilantly, though of course I could not see as we rounded past a smashed-up row of buildings. I could not see because I *had* to hold myself in position with my right hand, gripping the wooden side of the barrow to stop myself from falling over on to my damaged shoulder or left arm.

A minute later, everything changed. White-coated men and women seemed to converge on the front entrance, and Kurt, his duty done, just sat down on the kerb and buried his face in his hands.

A stretcher appeared magically, tender hands carefully lifted me on to its blessed comfort—after the wheelbarrow it was like the world's most sumptuous bed, though it was only a strip of canvas. As they wheeled me inside, I managed to croak, 'Sister Fiamma?'

Puzzled looks of baffled men and women greeted my remark. Struggling to regain consciousness, I gasped in Italian, 'Fiamma di Firenze!' I did not

391

know if it made any sense, so I managed to add, 'Daughter of the Principessa!'

I could not see why anyone should know, but I was too far gone to give a damn. Almost in tears, and on the verge of passing out, I again cried out, almost screaming, 'Fiamma! Fiamma!'

I heard some female voice cry suddenly, 'Of course! It must be the nurse in ward six. The gorgeous girl from Florence!'

A man's voice barked brusquely, 'Get her!'

Somehow I struggled to stay conscious, though I do not know for how long. Around me a blur of voices, twittered words I could not decipher or even want to. Kurt seemed simply to have vanished. As for me, I just wanted to sleep—for ever if I could. Only the thought which Kurt had confirmed, that Fiamma was still working in the hospital, kept my wits from deserting me.

She *must* come! And quickly! No time to lose (all this jumbled thinking happening in a matter of minutes), I had to see her before I passed out! 'Be quick, be quick!' I found myself shouting.

By now I had been removed by stretcher to a small white room with a blinding light shining from above and two women were trying carefully to examine my soiled shirt. In fact the pain was so bad and continuous that they could have torn the shirt off and I would have hardly noticed.

But then all the pain, all vague premonitions of death, disfigurement—all the thoughts that drop into your mind at times like that—vanished as though by magic when the door opened gently, and then there was the soft tender voice of Fiamma whispering, 'Can you hear me, darling?' and then she leaned over and, carefully avoiding my

392

wounded shoulder, kissed my cracked lips gently.

But, try as hard as I could, I was unable to kiss her back, I could not return her kiss. She had taken the pain away. She had come to see me. I was safe now. That was all I needed. I sank gratefully into blessed oblivion.

CHAPTER TWENTY-THREE

Between spells of unconsciousness during which demons seemed to be pursuing me down corridors of horror and prodding at my flesh with fiery fingers, I was aware of someone cutting the dressing away from my shoulder. Fiamma! my half-doped consciousness said. Could it be? The fingers were determined yet gentle. But my eyes were closed and I was too weak to fight against the pain of opening them or against the harsh bright light that seeped through my eyelids.

'Cover his eyes,' a voice—a man's voice—ordered. It was not the voice that belonged to the fingers. *Those* fingers were now laying a cold compress across my eyes and forehead and again I knew the familiar touch. I wanted to reach out, my hazy thoughts directed me, to my darling, my Fiamma; but quite apart from the impossibility of moving my arms my whole body seemed to be wracked with pain, which was hardly surprising after that ludicrous journey down the mountainside over rocks and bog and shell-holes in a wheelbarrow.

I wanted above all things to have the bandage taken off, to see her; and she could evidently see my
393

struggle to get my right arm up to my forehead; but the pain was too intense and the man's voice—a no-nonsense voice—said, 'For God's sake keep still if you want to save me, and yourself too, a lot of trouble.' And to Fiamma (I hated him for using that tone of voice), 'Get that mucky dressing away, nurse. And put some orange juice in a feeding-cup and pour it into him to keep him quiet while I look at this shoulder.'

I could feel Fiamma's trembling resentment as she put the spout of the feeding-cup to my lips and touched my cheeks with her fingertips.

And then suddenly it seemed as if it were no longer necessary to have my eyes uncovered. She was there beside me. Like a child putting off the moment of excitement when a parcel is finally unwrapped I wanted to save the precious moment of my first sight of my love ... for—what? I was wandering again, my mind muddled. I could not recall when we had last held each other. All the terror of war and action seemed to stretch between us: London, Rome, the flight from Ireland, fighting with the partisans, the shop in Geneva, the shriek of shells as I battled my way to Army HQ ... and ... Oh God! The aftermath of the bombing at Parkes's, and Lella. Lella! I choked over the dribble of orange juice that was moistening my mouth. It was the choking of guilt ...

Oblivion again. For how long I did not know. I was delirious, sweating, pursued by nightmares. But when at last I awoke I felt better. I was terribly weak, but tranquil and cool. I seemed to have no anxieties except the discomfort of my stiff shoulder and my arm strapped to my side. Gradually I adjusted to the hospital silence—that peculiar low

394

humming of voices that seems to be separated from you by a curtain of cottonwool, a sort of underwater feeling as you open your eyes.

Recovering from one of those hazy spells I found Fiamma beside me. Behind her loomed the burly white-coated figure of the doctor. She was businesslike, released my wrist and nodded shortly to the doctor that my pulse was all right. Then she moved off, an unusual remoteness about her, as if I warranted no more attention than she would give to any of the patients in her care. Well, perhaps that was so. Anyway, she would have to give that impression. All the same...

The doctor interrupted my thoughts. He was squat with a head as round as a cabbage and short grizzled hair. He had a fierce look that matched his speech.

'All right, are we?'

'Hardly all right,' I began. 'If "all right" means—'

'Figure of speech. Part of medics' vocabulary. Means nothing except "listen to me".'

'Well, I'm listening,' I said impatiently. His manner irritated me; yet I trusted him.

Various non-committal grunts came from him as his fingers probed round my shoulder. The delicacy with which he touched me belied the curtness of his speech.

'Bullet went right through. Singe marks on your blouse when cut away. Heat of velocity of bullet cauterised wound. Fair bit of damage though, I wouldn't be surprised. Lot of bones there in the shoulder. Can't say much till I've got an X-ray. Scapular and clavicle both splintered, I'd say. Doubt if you'll be able to move humerus for a long time to come. If at all.'

I said innocently, 'I don't think it's humorous at all.'

He snorted. 'That joke goes back to my student days. Can't call it a joke really. Humerus: Latin, upper arm. Scapula: Latin, shoulder, shoulder blade to you. Clavicle: Latin, key. Don't ask me why key means collar bone. But it does.'

'Not a very good outlook, then,' I said ruefully. 'I might not be able to use my arm again?'

'Can't tell. Bones splinter. Bones knit. Plaster helps. We'll get that done. X-ray too. Transportable X-ray apparatus. Comes in its own three-ton truck with trailer generator. On its way now along Highway 6 from Leese's lot. Know 'em?'

'Only too well,' I said laconically.

'Yes, so I heard. Being re-routed, the X-ray thing is. Didn't want it bypassed to Rome. Chaos there. Fritz not cleared out yet. Can't see that he can hang on much longer, though. Not in the nature of things.'

'The war's not over yet, then?' I said with mock innocence.

'Not on your bloody Nellie. Still building up for the big bash, the Second Front. Won't affect you. You'll be out of action for a bit, whatever the X-ray says.'

So it was arranged. It turned out to be less complicated than I expected. The truck was fitted with a pedestal on which I stood in front of an upright screen, while the white-coated radiographer told me to stand still, breathe in, hold my breath, breathe out again while the machine took its pictures. Outside, the trailer, with its oil engine driving the generator that provided the power, hummed and clattered. A litter of cables wound round the pedestal and the general effect was of a Heath Robinson contraption. I looked a bit disjointed myself too. I had lost weight, and with the sling and strappings removed from my arm the bullet hole and bruising surrounding it glared ominously back at me from the ground-glass screen. But when the pictures were developed and interpreted by Dr Turnbull (his name suited him) he seemed pleased. I could not think why. Myself, I felt utterly depressed. Battle fatigue in general had added its toll to the pain and I felt certain I would lose my arm, or anyway the use of it. He joshed me out of that pretty quickly.

'Can't say you'll be as good as new. Scapula splintered too badly for that. It's a thin bone, not much surface, and it'll heal like a bit of cracked glass. Know what I mean? Punch a hole through glass and it shatters star-shaped, cracks radiating. But they'll join, mend. In time. Expect to have stiffness there. But you won't be incapacitated. Not if you're careful. First thing, we've got to get it into plaster again, give it a chance. And, for Christ's sake, stop looking like a wet week. War ain't all doom and gloom. You've got that nice little Eyetie girl around. Why don't you marry her?'

'Why not indeed?' I said. 'Thanks, Doc.' I felt a bit ashamed of myself.

'Yes. Well. Get her and an orderly to prepare you and we'll get you plastered.' He gave a loud snort. 'Wish to God we could! Ha!'

I smiled. 'And you ticked me off for making feeble jokes. You've got a nerve!'

He stumped off, the X-ray pictures held by a bulldog clip at their corners.

Marriage. Now that the doctor had suggested it, it seemed the most reasonable and sensible thing in the world; and yet of course the most impractical. It was ridiculous! To be married in a hospital in the middle of a war with distant gunfire instead of a congregation singing hymns! Yet the more stupid it seemed the more my mind hinged on the thought. I quite raised my temperature thinking about it. And Fiamma had two days off before changing from day to night shifts. I understood from one of the other nurses that she had gone to Rome 'to see a little boy'. She took my pulse and raised an eyebrow. 'You must be calm now, or I give you bromide.' Saucily she added, 'You are thinking naughty thoughts down there? Yes. But not to be. You must be calm, no excitement, not hot with too much temperature. Or I call Dr Turnbull. You understand? This is important, you be calm.'

'I give in,' I said. Although the good doctor had awakened the idea in my head I did not feel I could face his machine-gun conversation.

But when he came on his rounds the next morning I decided to ask what he had in mind.

'In mind? Didn't have anything in mind. Shot the thought at you, that's all. Looking like a wet week, you were. Shot it at you, that's all. Don't care two hoots myself. Got a kid, haven't you?'

'We have a son four years old,' I said with dignity.

'There you are then. Give the little bugger a proper father. Can't think why you haven't.'

'It's a long story,' I said.

398

'Don't want to hear it.' He waved his stethoscope admonishingly. 'Don't tell me. Boring, all long stories. Got to get on, others to see besides you.'

And there, I thought, the matter had ended so far as he was concerned.

But I had another concern. Fiamma. That remoteness, that *withdrawn* attitude I had noticed a few days ago. I had been delirious. God knows what I might have revealed about Lella. But she would understand, just as Lella had. Or wouldn't she? It had been a mutual comforting after the terrible experience at Parkes's, a 'nothing' in the passage of love—hers or mine. Yes, she would understand; and yet I felt a sense of guilt. No: not guilt so much as dishonesty. I should have told her. But there had never been an opportunity—or at least I could convince myself there had not. I worried myself into a knot over it.

Dr Turnbull had passed me as fit apart from my shoulder. I became officially a 'ward patient' rather than a 'bed patient', which meant I could get up and move around if I felt like it (which I didn't much), visit the 'therapy area', as a sort of annexe with pieces of exercise apparatus was called. It was there I saw Fiamma the next time she was on duty. We embraced briefly, in so far as it is possible for a man with only one arm in proper use to embrace anyone. There was no place we could go for the intimacies or the sort of conversation I wanted.

But it was not necessary.

Suddenly, as she made a pretence of adjusting the padding that kept my plaster-encased arm from my body, I knew that she knew—or guessed. It was all in her eyes: a hint of amused wisdom that she summed up in a few whispered words:

'Ham, beloved, whatever it is—and I know there's something—it doesn't matter.'

'You know?' I said guiltily.

She gave a little shrug. 'Something. I don't know what. Lella: you kept on about her when you were delirious.' Someone passed by and she said with brisk formality, 'Coming along nicely, Captain Johns. Keep on with the finger exercises; they'll help.' Then with a gurgle of amusement as we became Ham and Fiamma again: 'I expect she'll tell me sometime. Lella and I, we always confided in one another as children. More than Roz did.' Her eyes clouded slightly. 'But whatever it was, I know it didn't count. Separation for lovers is a terrible thing. And we're not united except as lovers, no . . . with promises too.'

Suddenly words came back to me across the years, a summer afternoon at Magari when we were discussing the Prince's 'affairs' and Fiamma had said, 'Of course I wouldn't *like* it—but I've always assumed that all men do that after a certain time and there's nothing you can do about it.'

I had replied with the genuine innocence of first love, 'Well if I married a beautiful girl like you—' and she responded wistfully, 'Ah! That might be different.'

And that was what brought the word, the idea, back into my mind. Marriage. Crazy; but the more I thought about it the more it tormented me. And as if there were some kind of telepathy at work the doctor slyly aided me.

He bounced into the therapy area one morning bringing with him a tall officer wearing Royal Artillery badges and a parson's collar.

'This is the chaplain. Captain Scofield. God

400

knows what battalion. Doesn't matter. Found him prowling about up the line and thought I'd introduce you. Know what I mean? He's due to visit this Godforsaken hospital anyway, give it a pep talk.' Then he vanished, smiling a crooked smile as if pleased with himself.

The chaplain had a rumbling voice that seemed to come from deep down in his chest. 'I have been conspiring with the doctor,' he said. 'One of his patients needed the therapy of marriage, so he told me. I intend to fill the need if that is the wish of the parties concerned.'

I was so astonished that I could find no words. It was unbelievable, as if some tiny piece of a complicated mechanism had suddenly fallen into place and wheels were turning with the precision of a clock, waiting for the hour to strike. My amazement must have been reflected by my open mouth.

The chaplain smiled gently—a smile that seemed conjured from behind a curtain of sadness. 'Don't be alarmed, my friend. If the good doctor is mistaken, if I have had a wasted journey, I shan't complain.' He tapped a small battered attaché case he carried. 'I travel very light.'

Somehow I managed to force my expression into something a bit less stupid. 'This is ...' I began. I was going to say 'crazy'; and indeed it was—five years of frustration and longing and absence honed down to a wedding in a battlefield hospital at a moment's notice; nothing could be more 'crazy'. My ears heard but my head could not grasp it. I managed, though, to grasp some vestige of humour from the situation. Instead of 'crazy', I said, 'This is so sudden!' like a blushing girl in a Victorian novel.

401

Presumably—I never knew and was too excited to find out—Dr Turnbull contrived not only to have the chaplain, so to speak, kidnapped, but also to wrench Fiamma from whatever duties she was on, for suddenly she was there, radiant, her eyes glistening with tears of happiness.

Still recovering from the shock I gave her my good arm, vaguely aware that other patients were gathering round the room like shadows. Or were my eyes, too, misted with tears?

'Captains of ships can marry people at sea,' the padre rumbled, 'but there's no provision for battlefield weddings. Not that I know of. And we're supposed to be on consecrated ground—which this hardly is, unless you think of it as consecrated by shot and shell. But I doubt if God had any particular place in mind when He authorised parsons to unite people in holy matrimony.'

He opened the battered little case and took from it a rather grubby surplice and a prayer book. 'Just the essentials,' he said almost apologetically. 'Communion, birth, marriage, death.' He slipped the surplice on over his shabby uniform and began the service, quite unselfconsciously, as if the farcical nature of the event had not occurred to him.

'Dearly beloved, we are gathered here in the sight of God, and in the face of this congregation, to join together this man and this woman in holy matrimony; which is an honourable estate . . .'

The figures round the walls were still silent, shadowy. Distantly the crump of shells sounded: leftovers from a finished battle, the enemy retreating defiantly.

'. . . First, it was ordained for the procreation of children . . .'

402

Fiamma's happiness gave way to a sob and I felt her tremble.

'. . . Secondly, it was ordained for a remedy against sin, and to avoid fornication; that such persons as have not the gift of continency might marry . . .'

The prayer book seems to have taken care of everything, I thought guiltily.

'. . . I require and charge you both, as ye will answer at the dreadful day of Judgement when the secrets of all hearts shall be disclosed, that if either of you know any impediment . . .'

We both shook our heads. At least we could answer to that. I thought with gratitude of that scrap of paper which C had handed to me confirming that Fiamma's shotgun marriage had been annulled.

The padre paused in his recital of the words and adopted a less solemn tone. 'Sudden and informal as this is, neither of you can have thought of the ring. And even if there had been time and opportunity it wouldn't have been exactly simple to get one. Not that it is essential. Indeed'—he lowered the prayer book—'indeed, to be legally truthful *none* of this is essential. I'm marrying you in the eyes of God, not of the Law, which requires you to sign your name to a register. I have no register and no answer to the problem of finding one or of issuing you with a certificate to prove your marriage. But since I'm a parson I believe God to be above the Law. The ring, though: I think I have the answer to that.' He slipped the heavy gold wedding ring from his left hand.

Fiamma gave a little gasp. 'Oh! We couldn't. It would be a . . . a sort of sacrilege. Like breaking up

403

your marriage—'

'There is no marriage,' the padre said, and seemed to hold his breath. 'Not now. We lived in Coventry, you know. And Coventry was bombed. I puzzled in my grief as to God's purpose. My secular anger overcame my sacred duty, for I was not even allowed to die with them, my wife and children. I escaped because I was serving with the Forces. Serving! An irony if ever there was one!'

He gave me the ring. 'Whereof this ring given and received is a token and pledge.' A smile crossed his face. 'I'd like to have it back sometime if ever we meet again. But don't worry about it. Now say after me, "I, Hamilton, take thee, Fiamma"—'

In this way, in the hospital at Cassino, with neither pomp nor the witness of well-wishing friends, nor even a ring to call our own, I married Fiamma, the youngest daughter of the Prince.

CHAPTER TWENTY-FOUR

Such a deep happiness took hold of me after the wedding that it was like a balm to my injury. I slept soundly and without nightmares for the first time since I had been brought in. The doctor had certainly applied the right therapy! And though I had no idea what had happened to Kurt, the meeting with him before I was shot had added to my feeling of happiness. 'The 'psychic' feeling I had had when the smoke of battle cleared, and which I put down to shell shock, had proved to be justified.

'It was like a miracle,' said Fiamma.

'It *was* a miracle,' I replied, 'but if only I knew what had happened to him now! I can only remember him collapsing with exhaustion and sitting there with his face in his hands.'

She said comfortingly, 'I expect he was—well, taken care of.'

'Taken prisoner you mean?' I feared it was only too likely.

'Not necessarily. There's so much muddle, chaos, everything happening at once. But he certainly isn't in the hospital. I've checked. He might have been ... what do you call it? Repatriated? Or, he might have repatriated himself to his army.'

I felt doubtful. 'He was too fed up—with the army, the war, Hitler, everything. He seemed—well, suicidal, or almost. If it hadn't been for meeting me...'

Her eyes clouded. '*That* was the miracle—him bringing you back to me. If you hadn't met—'

I tried a weak smile. 'Lovers' luck!'

In mock protest she cried, 'Not just lovers, Ham: *married* lovers!'

Another feeble effort at humour: 'Exactly how long have we been married?'

She glanced at the watch pinned above her breast. 'Two days three hours and a few minutes,' she said, blushing and looking at me through lowered lashes.

'I know,' I said in an aggrieved tone, 'and not yet consummated.'

'You're evidently better to be able to *think* of such a thing!' She was suddenly serious. 'Oh Ham, if only we could—' Her hand strayed under the bedclothes to my naked body as if straightening the

405

sheets. I felt a great surge of sexual energy. But nurses and patients were milling about; short of a public display of our desperate need it would have to be controlled. I attempted a return to po-faced conversation: 'This hospital, so unstained by time and war that it looks almost new.' It was too. There was a clinical whiteness about it which was unrelieved except for the scarlet blankets on the bed. ('Red because they don't show the blood,' one of my fellow patients had said knowingly.) There was no sign of the accumulation of grime that gathers round doors and windows and in corners.

'It looks new because it *is* new,' Fiamma smiled, taking up my strait-laced tone. 'The Americans built it.' She went on to explain breathlessly how it had all come in packages like a child's constructional toy—walls and girders and generators to supply electric power and was built into the lee of a hillside in a few days. And it was strong enough to withstand the weather if nothing else. 'The roof's painted with a huge red cross and at night it's outlined in red electric bulbs because, you see, it's a hospital for everybody—Italians and Germans and everybody who's in the war. It'd be no good for the Germans to bomb it, there's a lot of them here anyway, and English and Poles and Italians and French—' Her breath ran out and trembled into giggles.

'Be serious!' I admonished her, though I was on the verge of giggles myself.

She straightened the bedclothes in a businesslike way and moved off to give her attention to other patients. I watched her as she helped a lad with bandaged eyes grasp the glass of water on his locker, and whisper to another nurse as they met in the doorway leading to 'therapy'. Such humour as was to be found in the hospital usually came from that area—some of it rather macabre 'gallows' humour, as when one of the patients, after performing his ritual of exercises (so Fiamma told me, trying to cheer me up) had wandered through the wards and scrawled on the charts at the foot of the beds of some of the more serious cases needing surgery, 'Store in a cool place until opened.'

I felt relieved and peaceful again and drowsed off into sleep that was interrupted only when a sudden storm of rain and hail beat on the flat roof of the ward. It must have been made of some hardened metallic substance, for the hailstones sounded like machine-gun fire and my sleep turned to nightmares again—nightmares in which the outraged Principessa, the brutal attack on Vanni at Forte dei Marmi, BB sitting tranquilly on the terrace at I Tatti with his hands folded over the knob of his walking stick, the Indian pool at Magari ... I was sweating again and my shoulder jumped as if it were being jerked by an electric current. Through a haze I was vaguely aware of Fiamma again at my side and something—an injection perhaps—that gave me almost immediate relief. Once more I sank into merciful oblivion.

★   ★   ★

When I woke it was night and I was remarkably clear-headed. The ward was illuminated only with shaded lights and, rationalising, I knew Fiamma could not still be on duty. I was comfortable and did not want anyone else, so I drifted off into sleep again. I was so clear-headed that I knew exactly what I wanted to ask Fiamma and had forgotten up to now: what had been the full contents of Roz's letter and how was Ham Two? It seemed to me dreadful that I should have forgotten. 'In the morning,' was my last waking thought.

I was brought to violent consciousness by the familiar screaming sound of a falling bomb that I knew would explode nearby. I had heard too many of them not to be sure. And it was deathly close.

The whole world seemed to split asunder as there was a blinding flash somewhere, somewhere slightly outside my awareness, and a chunk of the ceiling collapsed with a deluge of dust that I could feel choking me. My own voice screamed . . . or was it someone else?

My bed was flung on its side, I felt myself scrambling about in splinters of glass and dust, getting my clothes on, my shoulder oozing blood that somehow seemed to be mixing with the dust in my mouth.

Opposite me a bed had been grotesquely upturned on to its end. I had a momentary sight of it, its red unruffled blanket like a bloody gash in the brilliantly white wall that had been torn apart behind it. Such are the farcical moments of disaster that the startled face of the man in the upended bed glared at me as if reproaching me for his undignified situation. And although I find it difficult to believe now, ridiculous really, it was in that split second that my painter's mind created a canvas of the scene—the blood red gash its focal point, the face of the man so tidily tucked into his upended bed, startled by the awareness of death. Even a name for the picture got fixed in my mind: The Last Battle.

Except for that second of clarity and—if you

like—inspiration, my mind was utterly confused. I was floundering about on the floor with enveloping clouds of dust, and debris, falling everywhere. There was a medley of shouts. It was daylight but a grey fog was obscuring everything. A scream from somewhere, a long moaning sound from close at hand. I managed to get myself upright and cling to a strut that had been wrenched from its mooring. Gradually the dust was settling and I could distinguish vague shapes. I made my way with great difficulty towards where I supposed the door to be. I was still muzzy and my shoulder and arm were hurting like hell. Someone—it must have been another patient—grabbed hold of my good arm and we moved like drunken revellers over the splintered floor. The door had been blown out and half the wall too.

'Bloody shambles,' my companion said laconically. 'No peace for the wicked.'

I muttered, 'I'd better see if I can give a hand somewhere', though I had absolutely no idea what, if anything, I could do. Blood was beginning to congeal on my shoulder.

'Don't talk bloody daft, man. Tha's in a reet mess.'

Even in my dopey state I recognised the accent; and when I rubbed some of the accumulated dust from my eyes I saw it was my Geordie major from HQ. The battered nose was unmistakable.

'You too?'

'Aye. Shrapnel after we moved forward. Not much to write home about, but it got infected. The Yanks have got some new stuff, though, for blood poisoning. Penicillin, it's called. Seems to've worked. I was due to rejoin HQ—wherever the bloody hell it is. Now this lot.' He gestured at the ruination surrounding us.

Some sort of order had emerged from the initial chaos. I could make out moving figures now and hear shouts for help and stretchers—though there was no knowing where they were to come from. And despite good intentions we both collapsed on a pile of rubble. Shock and exhaustion, I guess. I found it difficult to speak, my throat being choked with dust and grit which I kept trying to cough up without much success; but Geordie had no such trouble, he kept talking, sometimes sensibly, sometimes a bit hysterically, with raucous laughs punctuating his disconnected sentences. I gathered he thought the stick of bombs could have come from a crippled Allied bomber trying to offload to gain height. It seemed more likely to me that it was a retaliatory attack for our victory at Cassino; but a shrug had to serve as an expression of that opinion.

'You need to slake your thirst, lad; and get that arm seen to.'

If ever there was a statement of the obvious that was it. I contorted my features into what I hoped was a smile.

He gave a bellow of laughter and started ranting again—much of it seemingly senseless, though I dare say that in my own dazed state I could not have taken in much anyway. I caught bits of a jigsaw of words that to me were like a surrealist painting, spellbinding but irrational. The train of thought led me to BB's scorn of such pictures, and from that to the chaotic landscape in the middle of which Geordie and I sat like worldly-wise observers of Apocalypse.

His ranting was more insistent now, and some of

410

it was punctuated by phrases I could understand if not attach much logic to.

'No point being an Intelligence Officer if you don't know what's going on underground . . . casks in the catacombs . . . monks' brew, Liebfraumilch now shouldn't wonder, Jerries rolled it down the tunnels.' A pause, his eyes had a faraway look. He gave another bellow of laughter. He needed a sedative—even I knew that. My shoulder was stiffening with the blow I had given it being tipped out of bed. The plaster was broken and filthy and a sort of grey paste tinged with blood had formed in the cracks. I felt hopeless, helpless, and terribly alone.

He jerked his thumb downward at the rubble we were sitting on. 'Real warren of tunnels. All to do with the water cisterns the Romans built. Two bloody thousand years ago—or thereabouts. Huh! Don't hold me to bloody dates.'

I shook my head, assuring him I would not. I had the notion he was trying to convey information to me; but *why* was a blank.

'Of course the Jerries used them.' He seemed to be musing rather than ranting now. 'But so did Neri and his mob. Still do, likely. Plotting vengeance, vendettas.' An explosion of laughter. 'What a mob!' Suddenly he was quiet, confidential, his hand on my knee. 'That was Clark's fault, rearming them. All right in theory, get 'em on our side. But you can't trust a nest of vipers. Treachery—that's what you've got, right in your middle. Get me?'

'Not really.' Either his mind was wandering or mine was. The name Neri tinkled a faint bell, but the rest of it was nonsense. I hawked and spat out a

411

clot of grey dust. Then came the marvel.

Across the desolate ground loomed an army truck with Red Cross markings on its front and sides, and from it emerged a team of doctors and nurses.

'The day shift,' Geordie said calmly, rather as if an expected train had drawn into the station on time.

Oddly, he was right; and even more marvellous than the sudden (and to me unexpected) appearance of rescuers was the fact that Fiamma was one of them. She could not, of course, rush to me and give me all her attention. Indeed it was some time before she even saw me. But I was content to wait, half listening to Geordie rambling on about tombs and tunnels and Roman cisterns and the 'they' who behaved so treacherously after being rearmed. It was all over my head and—though I was sorry that shock had so disturbed his thinking—rather boring. I distracted him by saying suddenly, 'That's my wife—the blonde one kneeling down supporting the chap with the bloody head.'

He stopped his talking and looked at me with sudden astuteness, as if a fog had cleared from his brain. 'Tha's dazed, lad. It's all this'—he waved airily—'this commotion. A bit of a sedative is what you need.' He waved again, as if trying to attract the attention of a waiter. 'Injection needed here—'

'That's good coming from you,' I replied almost angrily. 'Talk about the pot calling the kettle black—'

But I was interrupted for the most wonderful of reasons. Fiamma had at last seen me. She could scarcely believe her eyes, I could see that. Her dress was torn and dirty, her hair untidy and falling about her shoulders, the clips holding it into a neat plait

412

having worked out in her rescue efforts. She stumbled toward us over rubble. Yards away I could see her eyes brimming with tears.

'Ham, beloved! You're here, all right, I thought, I thought . . .' the words poured from her in a flow of relief and love. She took an alcohol-soaked pad from her pocket and wiped my face so that she could kiss me. Beside me Geordie looked on in amazement.

'I'll be buggered! I thought you'd gone soft in t'head, lad. But tha's not so soft to collar yon lass. By—!'

Filthy as I was she pulled my head down to her breast as if comforting a frightened child. I could hear the reassuring beat of her heart. It was so wonderful that I reacted with hysterical sobs. I felt that she too wanted to react with sobs of happiness. But her practical training took over again. She was looking with horror at my blood-encrusted shoulder. 'The truck's going back to Rome, to the hospital there. You must go with it.' She paused, and her eyes studied Geordie. 'You too.'

'Me? I've got to get back to HQ. Don't know where'—his voice fell into a mumbling; his mind had clouded again.

Fiamma took his hand and held it for some moments, as if giving him confidence. 'Yes of course, we'll see you get back. But you've been terribly shaken. You've got to be'—her voice became wheedling as if to a child—'put to bed. To rest.'

Geordie stood in a comical parody of dignity. 'Ah'm a British officer, I'll have you know. And British officers don't rest in the midst of battle.' He paused and sat down again, adding reflectively with

413

a thumb jerked at me, 'Though I must say that idea of him and me in bed with thee in't middle'd go down reet well.' A saucy smile spread on either side of his battered nose. Even in the midst of disaster, I thought, there is a sort of comedy to be found.

But it was not to last.

★   ★   ★

There was no journey to Rome—not that day anyway. And the order of things in my mind is as chaotic as the situation after the bombing. It was simply another nightmare continuing after the others. The clearest picture I have is of a tall German officer suddenly appearing in the midst of the general hubbub of stretcher parties, shouted instructions, and piteous cries. Though he had never seen me, I had seen him and I recognised him at once; it was the lieutenant-colonel who had replaced Kurt as Gauleiter of Rome and arrived so disturbingly at Fiamma's flat. Oddly enough, I even recalled his name, announced as he clicked his heels together, 'Colonel Konrad Neumann at your service, Signora.'

Why, and how, was he here now! And how had he managed to get through the Allied lines? (I did not know then that the Germans had counter-attacked and recaptured the ground north-west of Cassino so that they held a narrow corridor between the hospital, the town, and Rome.) As for why, I felt in my bones that his presence was something to do with us—with Fiamma anyway, for he did not know me. It was a feeling of imminent danger and I wanted to warn her. But she was no longer with us—presumably she was looking after someone else or had gone to try and arrange transport to Rome for Geordie and me.

Surprisingly, it was Geordie who supplied the answer. He had staggered off rather unsteadily—I supposed in search of treatment, or perhaps just aimlessly, his mind wandering. His walkabout, though, was far from aimless. As I waited, still half overjoyed, half wool-gathering, he returned.

'His Excellency the bloody Gauleiter of Rome is here in bloody person,' he said viciously.

'I know,' I replied.

'You *know*?'

'I know.' I explained briefly.

'Ah. So that accounts for it. And was your wife's name Caeseri, the daughter of an Eyetie prince?'

I felt sweat break out my forehead. 'An Italian prince, yes. Why?'

'He's after her for some sort of spying activity. I don't know what. But he's looking for the doctor in charge to ask him to identify her.'

'Fiamma!' I exploded, 'she's never been involved in any spying in her life. It's farcical!'

'What name did you say?'

'Fiamma. She's a nurse and a mother—the mother of our son—'

'That's not the name he said. It was'—a pause for thought—'it was *Rosanna*. That's it—Rosanna.'

Roz!

My relief must have sounded in my voice. 'Then he's looking in the wrong place. That's another daughter of the Prince; and she's married to Kurt von Schill, the previous Gauleiter. The bastard can go jump off a mountain—and land in Lübeck. That's where he'll find Roz. As for spying—well,

415

she's always been a bit of a mystery girl. Who can tell? She's half-Jewish anyway—a different father.'

Geordie looked up sharply. 'Listen, lad. I'm pulling rank now, and I'm telling you—get out while the getting's good. And take your missus with you. Yon Gauleiter's out to collar some girl named Caeseri and he's not going to be convinced the one he's got isn't the one he wants. He's an ugly customer and he means business. It's only a matter of time before somebody identifies her for him. And then—*kaput*! Reckon you can keep going with that arm?'

I shrugged. 'Why not? But escape? Where to?' I looked around. What was left of the hospital amounted to the jagged edges of the fabricated walls that looked as if they had been ripped apart by some furious Hercules, the debris of beds and equipment, a portion of the roof mockingly bearing its Red Cross drunkenly standing like a hoarding, and the gruesome remains of bodies that were beyond care. The rescue team darted about like marionettes, among them I could make out Fiamma earnestly talking to a doctor who seemed to be trying to organise the priority cases for transport back to Rome.

'Where to? Don't be bloody stupid, Captain. Haven't I been explaining to you? Into the underground route of course. One arm of it links up with the cellars under the monastery, the other exits in Cassino town.' A hollow laugh. 'What's left of it. It's where the tourists used to start their sightseeing tour of the catacombs.'

Almost nostalgically he added, 'My pa had a picture on the wall in the parlour that used to fascinate me. A print, it was, and it showed the

416

Roman slaves digging out the tunnel that drained Lake Fucinus. Three and half miles long, Pa said, and took eleven years in the building even with thirty thousand men slaving away. He got it from Pliny, I learnt later when I did history at Durham, and a right snippet of useless information it was. But it made me wonder about the Romans. Like bloody rabbits they were, always boring tunnels and digging out catacombs. See a mountain, bore a hole through it, seems to've been their motto. And I'll be boring a hole through you, lad, wi'out I stop.'

He fumbled in the pocket of his tunic, handed me a small pen-torch. 'Here, take this. It'll give you all the light you'll get and it won't last long.' A thumb jerked over his shoulder indicated the cavern I had first noticed when I sped from the hospital on my journey to HQ. 'Get going—sharpish. Leave the lass to me—I'll send her along after you.'

★   ★   ★

He was as good as his word. Suddenly Fiamma was beside me in the tunnel, dishevelled and breathless. In the little light that filtered in from the mouth of the cave we tried to caress each other, to sort things out. I was so muddled and exhausted that comprehension was almost beyond me. 'But—'

'Beloved, it's all that matters, I can look after you. That nice major—'

'I know all about him,' I interrupted, 'but Gauleiter Neumann mustn't set eyes on you. He'll recognise you at once and take you for Roz, who's evidently been up to something. Though what the hell she could manage in the way of spying when she's married to Kurt—'

417

'Darling Ham,' Fiamma said, drawing back into the shadows of a niche in the dank limestone wall as there was some skirmishing near the entrance, 'it's a long story.'

I took her hand tenderly, noticing that the too-large wedding ring had been secured in place by a thick elastic band. I almost laughed, though my shoulder was throbbing like mad.

'It's no laughing matter,' she grimaced. 'All this time to get ourselves married and then I have to hold on to you with an elastic band. It's ...'

'I know,' I said, 'infuriating, that's what.'

Only a few seconds had passed; but suddenly the urgency of our situation gripped me. I was in no shape to take command, but we had to move before Neumann tumbled to our escape route and came in pursuit. And had he more knowledge of the tunnels, catacombs—whatever they were—than we had? One arm to the cellars of the monastery, the other to the ruins of Cassino town. But which?

As we stumbled forward the darkness became impenetrable. The feeling was of icy cold, vastness, terror reflected from the unseen. We paused, our arms round each other, hearing nothing but the beating of our hearts and ... very faintly, the regular rhythm of water dripping somewhere ahead of us.

In such circumstances one is often given some extra strength, an additional flow of adrenalin, perhaps; but fear is overriding, it dries the mouth and—I had read of it in novels but always thought it a wild exaggeration—it makes the hair on your neck bristle.

I had to use the little torch. It gave a light as small as its pencil size. I swept it round. Its beam fell a few feet away and faded. Rock. A niche that had presumably once held the coffin of a dead monk but was now filled with metal racks holding neatly stacked bottles of wine. I threw the beam upwards; the rock was arched like the transept of a cathedral; thick webs of dust hung like tatters of ancient banners and a bat stared down at us, blinking at our interference with his reverie.

Fiamma screamed. I clutched her. Seconds later the scream echoed back from the mocking walls.

I glimpsed her hurriedly crossing herself. 'Let's go back!' she breathed.

Strangely, I had recovered some of my composure. Perhaps I was fit enough to lead, after all? I stroked her hair, felt bits of plaster sticking to it. 'We can't, my darling. Only forward. We've got to—we've *got* to try. Keep hold of me. I think I can see some sort of junction where we have to choose. Wish to God I'd thought to ask Geordie which arm went where. I guess the one to the left goes to Cassino. It'll be shorter than the one to the monastery—if my guess is right.'

I switched off the torch. 'We've got to save it. Just a few seconds when we get stuck. If I keep my left hand on the wall as we move forward...'

Our progress had the eeriness I associated with the pea-souper city fogs of my boyhood, when it had been exciting to find oneself going round in circles, back at the gate you had left ten minutes before. But there was no excitement here—only the fearful horror of the unknown ahead, the inch-by-inch, foot-by-foot uncertainty, and the certainty of being caught if we went back.

It was easy enough to say 'keep my left hand on the wall'; but this was my injured arm and every

419

movement cut through me like a knife. Fiamma was clutching my right arm and we stumbled forward over the icy dampness of the rock floor. At first, I had no means of measuring time or distance; then I worked out a system of giving ourselves a brief flash of light with the torch every twenty footsteps. That way, I thought, we could conserve the battery. I recited aloud, 'One, two, three, four ... seventeen, eighteen, nineteen, twenty'. Then for the next stretch Fiamma would carry on. Once a huge rat scurried across our path, its pink eyes flashing briefly in the beam of light. She screamed again; and I froze rigid with horror, as much with fear that any pursuers would hear us or see us as with revulsion.

'Darling!' I said. I could not keep the reproach out of my husky whisper.

Her hand was clapped over her mouth. 'Couldn't help it! Ugh! That awful slimy creature—it ran over my foot.' I could feel her shuddering and tried to calm her with my good arm. I hoped it was my imagination, but I seemed to hear the sound of distant voices. We both stood stock still, our hearing attuned like antennae. Nothing, that is, but the mocking echo of Fiamma's scream and the persistent sound of water dripping.

As the pencil of light periodically showed, there were channels and cavities in the walls and runnels for drainage at their base. One niche held a stone sarcophagus, another a stone carving of a bearded monk's agonised face.

'Tourist attractions!' I said with a feeble attempt at a joke to ease the tension.

How many times we repeated our 'twenty' series of footsteps, I lost count, and time had no meaning anyway. But there came a moment when I halted and stared ahead in disbelief. Was there, could there be, a faint pinprick of daylight? How often had I read that cliché 'light at the end of the tunnel'? But here it was in real life. Never more real and never more of a relief.

'We'll soon be there,' I breathed.

Fiamma began to sob. I guess she felt the same relief seeping through her veins. I held her close, trying to still her racking sobs. 'Hush,' I said as if to a child, 'hush then; it's all right. Soon be over.' I was still fearful of pursuit.

Gradually she calmed down and I became less tense too. But the relief brought with it a return of the awareness of my arm and shoulder, the knife-thrusts which fear had anaesthetised.

We ploughed on, continuing our 'twenty' series of fits and starts. I reckon that we half-walked, half-staggered, rather more than a mile during which the distant light began to get stronger and safety more real.

And then we were out.

I say 'out' as if we had reached some marvellous haven where we could sink down into a deep bed and seek oblivion in each other's arms. But what we emerged into was the heart of the ruins of Cassino town. We held hands and blinked against what first seemed to be the brilliant light of day. But it was only the contrast with the stygian blackness of the catacombs. In fact dusk was already falling.

We looked around at the ruined streets, the piled masonry, the doorways to gutted houses which resembled blind eyes. Fiamma shuddered—not with cold but with exhaustion and the aftermath of terror. For a moment we clung together, finding some sort of peace in our bodily contact. Over her shoulder I could just read a notice streaked with filth and hanging askew near the cavern entrance. 'Guided Tour Begins Here', it said. I broke into hysterical laughter at the incongruity of it; and Fiamma too began to giggle.

The town seemed deserted, its ruins were already sprouting weeds—it was three months since Allied attacks had destroyed it. No doubt there were troops detailed to 'hold the fort' against any possible enemy attempts to recapture the ground, as had happened before; but we had neither the heart nor the energy to look for them. What we found, as dusk deepened, was the corner of the garden of what had once been an imposing house. A low stone wall enclosed it and the grass was soft and springy under our feet. There we sank down and I held Fiamma as tightly as I could with my good arm as she gave way once more to desperate sobbing.

After a while she quietened. I found myself comparing our state with the night Parkes's was bombed and, still with a tinge of guilt, how Lella and I had found comfort together. At least we had been able to bath first! Fiamma and I now were like scarecrows. 'It's a good job we can't see much of each other,' I said consolingly, 'we'd laugh.'

'No.' The word was no more than a whisper. 'My beloved Ham, my own ... husband ... though I still can't really believe it. Not laughter. Love.'

I did not quite cotton on. I began to say 'Of course I love you', but broke off, realising she had not been questioning me. It was the wordless need of two human beings for each other.

I am not sure how our union was contrived. I remember feeling myself swell with desire and

422

Fiamma, astride me, gasping 'Aaaaah!' at the climactic moment. Pain, the longing for sleep, hunger and thirst—all were overcome in those few fierce minutes.

That way, in ruined Cassino, on a June night under the stars, our marriage was consummated.

★   ★   ★

I slept almost at once. But before I drifted off I murmured to Fiamma, 'So much for you to tell me ... about Roz ... the boy ... Kurt ... everything...'

'Yes,' she murmured back, 'so much ... But in the morning...'

'Right,' I said. 'In the morning.'

When I awoke it must have been close to midday, for the sun was high.

But Fiamma had disappeared.

CHAPTER TWENTY-FIVE

My first thought was that Fiamma had probably gone off behind some bush for a pee. I even laughed at her observance of such social niceties in a deserted garden in a ruined town. But as I gradually came round, became less drowsy, the realisation hit me that she had gone. Then I panicked, stumbling about crying her name, calling haphazardly into gaps in walls that might have hidden her, acting completely distraught, mad.

Eventually, I tracked back to some logical grasp of the situation. There were just two possibilities:

423

either Fiamma had gone voluntarily for some reason, or she had been abducted. I considered the first. She might have crept quietly away in search of help, food, not wanting to disturb my healing sleep. As for the second, the possibility filled me with terror. Had we been pursued through the catacombs? Had we given our presence and direction away to Neumann? But if so, why had I heard nothing of the abduction—for Fiamma could hardly have been taken without protest, and surely they would have grabbed me too?

Eventually, though, the body took over, as it always does, demanding food, drink, and attention. I had to get a grip of myself, get my arm and shoulder attended to, and eat. Otherwise I would collapse. I could only begin my search after that.

When you take a long cool look at things solutions will be found. On this occasion, I discovered no answer to Fiamma's disappearance, true; but at least I got an answer to my main problem, survival. During the afternoon a Mobile Field Bath Unit arrived and pitched its tents in what had once been the main square in the town. The tents held a skeleton network of pipes with outlets that squirted water over fifty men simultaneously. The water was fed from a tanker adapted from a tank transporter, and was heated by some sort of calor gas apparatus. The unit carried with it stocks of clean underclothes, and there was a medical orderly travelling with it whose main job was de-lousing and treating impetigo with gentian violet; but he had enough medical kit with him to clean up my arm. There was a NCO—a sergeant—in charge of the whole outfit. I had no trouble convincing him that I was an English officer

424

but serving temporarily with the Italian medics.

'Bloody turncoats! First on one side, then the other. Never know where you are with the buggers. But medics—well, they're not on any side, are they?'

'That's the theory,' I agreed.

He told me his orders were to stay in Cassino, so he could not help me with transport, but for three days there would be truckloads of Allied troops arriving—'And one of 'em's bound to be able to take you where you want to go.'

I had a mind to tell him I did not wish to go anywhere, I wanted to find my wife; but I could not imagine a phlegmatic British NCO coming to any other conclusion than that I had gone off my rocker. Nor could I blame him.

Food was no problem. The sergeant had enough rations for him and his platoon of Pioneers to last for their spell in Cassino, plus emergency packs; so I was able to share with them a meal of tinned stew, bread and jam, and tea which was a veritable feast after two days with neither food nor drink. He also gave me, winking slyly, a tin of corned beef and an emergency pack with its survival tablets of chocolate and malted milk—'In case you strike any emer*gency*!'

'Any . . .' Oh, I see; emergency.'

'That's it: emer*gency*. You can never tell in the field, I always warn my per*son*nel that. Be prepared for any emer*gency*, I tell 'em.'

'Jolly good show,' I said with a straight face.

From the truckloads of troops who arrived for bathing and re-clothing I learnt something of the battle situation; but their versions were garbled and varied, though it seemed certain that the Americans

425

had entered Rome and held it. Clearly General Mark Clark had disobeyed Alexander's orders and rushed his troops through the Liri valley so that the USA could have their singular triumph in laying hold to the capital. How this had affected Leese's pincer movement, based on the information I got through to him, was not clear, though one young second lieutenant, who was as disgustingly filthy as I had been before the bath unit did its job, accepted my identity with some awe and told me he had heard that a whole German division had been trapped in the Apennines. 'But it may only be a rumour. I'm with the Catering Corps and we don't get to know much about tactics.' He smiled. 'Dehydration of potatoes—that's more the sort of stuff we learn about. Did you know you could get powdered soup in Queen Victoria's time?'

I shook my head. 'And I don't know where the nearest troops are with any transport. I've got to get moving.' I told him in a nutshell about Fiamma. 'So you see—'

He gave a low whistle. 'Good heavens! You must be worried stiff.'

'I am. And I've also got to get back to Rome to report.'

He looked glum. 'Can't help there. Wish I could. All this lot coming in to get cleaned up are heading for Manfredonia and embarkation. Back to England, refit, and then no doubt reinforce the Second Front. Can't say I'm looking forward to it—not the Second Front bit. I'm cheesed off with the bloody war.'

'You're not the only one,' I told him. 'Well, I'll have to make my own way somehow.'

He tapped his forehead as if opening a sesame of

426

information. 'There's some gunners holding the fort round Ceccano way. I saw them as we came in. Quite a way, though. Twenty kilometres maybe.'

I shrugged. It did not sound a lot; and indeed the early stages of the journey proved fairly easy, for I was fed and refreshed. I had no compass and I was moving across a no-man's-land littered with the debris of battle; but my training at Richmond had included navigation by stars and such basic stuff as that moss grows on the north side of trees. In any case, I knew the direction was almost due west and so headed towards the setting sun, hoping to make contact with the gunners by morning. However, I decided to bed down for a few hours in one of the numerous caves that studded the hillside—that way I would save energy and stave off hunger. Some of the caves still contained guns abandoned in the upward surge of attacks on the monastery. But I was fortunate. In the midst of that battle-scarred chaos I came across a bombed farmhouse with one wall still standing, and clinging to it were a few ripening peaches which I grabbed and stuffed into my pockets. Very refreshing for the second stage of my journey, I thought.

The cave I chose was less a cave than an alcove, for it penetrated into the rock for only a few yards. But at least it was dry, and a carpet of moss stretching into the entrance provided a more or less comfortable bed. After slaking my thirst with one of the peaches I lay down and fell asleep almost immediately.

When I woke I felt amazingly refreshed. My arm was still painful, but my weariness had overcome the pain. I lay with my eyes closed for a few minutes letting wakefulness overtake me slowly.

Suddenly a slight noise alerted me and I was wide-eyed. The figure of a man stood outlined against the sunlit entrance to the cave.

*　　　*　　　*

'I hope I haven't disturbed you.'

The man spoke in Italian but with a slightly guttural tone. It was a cultured voice, the voice of a man used to being obeyed. I was on my feet immediately.

'Not so fast, my friend. I have the advantage over you. I can see you more clearly than you can see me. I am pointing a Walther P.38 at your chest, and you have an injured arm.'

'You're telling me!' I said bitterly in English.

He seemed to consider this. 'Just come out into the sunlight, my friend.' He moved back and I could see now that he wore the uniform and badges of a Generalmajor, a German major-general. The uniform was torn and filthy but in some mysterious way it still upheld the dignity of its wearer. The jackboots into which once-shapely riding breeches were tucked retained patches of gleaming polish, and there was an elegance about the cut of his stained tunic. He had intensely blue eyes and a growth of reddish beard, and there was something languid about the way he held the revolver, as if in gesture rather than threat. 'Ah, I see you are of the Italian Medical Service, so of course you carry no weapon and I can safely put this away. But you speak English—and a phrase, I think, picked up from the Americans.'

'Yes, I speak English,' I replied defiantly. 'So what?—and that's another Americanism.'

428

He rubbed his scruffy beard. 'I too speak English—better than Italian, a beautiful language too good for the spineless lot once our allies and now our enemies. In fact I was educated largely at Cambridge and am something of an Anglophile, despite this.' He ran a hand over his uniform. 'The fortunes of war do not always have respect for our affection for other countries. I suspect you are less an Italian than you would have others believe?' A pause and a shrug, as if he had not really expected me to answer his question.

'I am General Baade, lately commander of 90 Division—now scattered and decimated by the united efforts of the various Allies. But they made a good showing. They were defeated, but not vanquished. And had it not been for a traitor within the gates, the outcome of the battle for Monte Cassino might have been very different.'

So this was it! I knew instinctively that the traitor within the gates must have been Vanni, aided by my own liaison with Eighth Army HQ. I felt Baade's piercing eyes summing me up.

'"Oh what a tangled web we weave when first we practise to deceive,"' he quoted, and I realised he knew I was in the business of deception myself. 'But it's of no consequence,' he went on, 'for the campaign is over bar the shouting; and the shouting is all in Rome. Victory, it seems. But for whom is never clear. War is a strange thing. One could spend hours discussing the philosophy of it.'

Somehow or other this strange, gentle man appealed to me. For he was saying in rather high-falutin' language what Kurt and I had been trying to say as we embraced amid the ruins of the monastery: war was senseless: there was no more to

429

the philosophy of it than that.

Baade and I sat together on a flat boulder outside the cave. He plucked a tiny flower from a crevice. '*Centaurea syanus*, the common cornflower, habitat wasteland.' He turned his piercing blue eyes on me again and I noted the resemblance in colour. 'I am what the English call—and love—an eccentric. I once captured a British officer and persuaded him to guide me across one of his own minefields and in exchange I gave him his freedom. What could be more eccentric than that?' [*Major-General Ernst-Guenther Baade was noted for his bravery as well as for his eccentricity and Anglophilia. He was wounded and died on the last day of the war in Europe.*]

He was a most extraordinary and compelling man, and one who invited confidences; but although of course I did not tell him who I was (not that he asked), I did tell him I was heading for Rome when I could find transport.

'All roads lead to Rome.'

'I seem to have heard that before,' I said surlily. But it was difficult to be enemies with him. There seemed to be a bond between us, as between long-distance travellers.

He chuckled. 'We'll make our way together, telling each other tales as we go to pass the time. And if we encounter our compatriots each can be in charge of the other. You can be my prisoner or I can be yours. How does that suit you?'

I thought it was mad; but as I said, he inspired confidence, and our very isolation seemed to tighten our bond. The sun cast our long shadows before us as we set off westward.

It was a fragmented conversation we conducted,

but it was profitable. In fact so much so that I felt a glow of relief seeping through me. Baade knew Kurt! Of course it was hardly surprising, for Baade must often have been at Kesselring's headquarters and Kurt was part of HQ Intelligence.

'A very fine pianist.'

'I know,' I said.

'You know him?'

I had to be careful. 'I heard him play—before the war.' I added as casually as I could, 'Have you seen him recently?'

'Just before our defeat at the monastery. Von Schill and I persuaded our High Command to give an undertaking that Florence would not be bombed, that its many fine buildings would not fall to German attack.'

I did not dare say much for fear of giving too much away; but at least Kurt had got back safely. 'Florence!' I said. 'One of the most beautiful cities in the world.' I gave Baade a carefully edited version of my story with emphasis on Fiamma's disappearance. Again I added casually: 'Of course you know Colonel Konrad Neumann?'

We were striding across an unspoilt field bright with buttercups. 'One would think the world had been at peace for centuries,' Baade said. '*Ranunculus acris*. It seems a pity to crush them with our great clumsy feet. Neumann? Yes, I know him. A fine soldier, though I deplore his involvement with Luciano Neri and his mob.'

Neri! It was the second time I had heard his name in a short while and I still couldn't remember—

'Neri?' I asked casually.

'Deputy Mayor of Florence,' Baade explained,

431

'and a Mafia bigshot.'

'But I thought . . .' I began. Then suddenly things began to fall into place. My mind harked back first to the day we lunched at BB's and the Prince had remarked angrily on the time the Mafiosi wasted on plotting their vendettas instead of preparing to fight their country's enemies; then I recalled Geordie rambling on about them being a nest of vipers whom Mark Clark had rearmed to fight with the Americans instead of leaving them powerless after Mussolini had suppressed them. 'Of course!' I said. 'I remember. But surely the Mafia . . . ?'

'Oh yes,' Baade said with contempt, 'General Clark brought them out from under the stones that were hiding them and gave them guns. Such an innocent! Thinking that by giving them guns he had their loyalty in return.' Suddenly he took his Walther from his belt and fired a shot into the air. It echoed from the rocky hillside. 'Ach! They will run with the Fascists, the Communists, the partisans, with anybody. But their loyalty is only to themselves. They pursue only their private vengeances, their vendettas. Ruthlessly and patiently, with undercover informers, using anybody, friend or enemy, to track down those who humiliate or betray them. It would not surprise me if your lady is being held captive for some wrong, real or imagined, that she or her family have committed.'

My arm was beginning to hurt again with the physical effort of walking across country, but I was trying to remember other things. There was the incident when Ciano invited himself to the Villa Magari and that dolled-up, mincing messenger on

432

the motor-bike whom the Prince had put firmly in his place by making him wait for a reply to Ciano's message. Of course! That man *was* Neri, hatred concealed behind his dark glasses; and he was just the sort of character who nursed grievances and felt humiliated by the Prince's exquisitely polite contempt; and if Baade was right that the Mafiosi, like elephants, never forgot anything, let alone an insult, there was a possible motive for abducting Fiamma—if she *had* been abducted. Yet there could have been little point in abducting her unless some ransom was being demanded for her return; but perhaps the Prince, wherever he was, had received such a demand; and perhaps (again!) Fiamma had not been abducted at all but had her own reasons for vanishing ... it was all so confusing.

Now my arm was giving me hell again. I saw Baade looking at me with concern. Suddenly the harsh landscape took on a shimmering appearance, as if viewed through water, my head began to whirl, and I felt myself falling.

*   *   *

When I came round the General was kneeling by my side. He had taken off his stained tunic and rolled it up to make me a pillow, and he was cradling my head in one elbow as he moistened my lips with one of the peaches from my pockets.

'I passed out,' I murmured.

He looked at me with amusement. 'A statement of the obvious if ever there was one. You are in a bad way, my friend. The human body is durable, but it begins to react to neglect. We must push on after you have rested. By my reckoning we should strike Highway 6 soon, perhaps two kilometres. No doubt there will be traffic enough to convey us to Rome.'

'*Us?* But—'

He tenderly squeezed more juice from the peach on to my cracked lips. 'Even among enemies there is compassion,' he smiled, 'just as there is honour among thieves.'

CHAPTER TWENTY-SIX

I have only confused memories of our step-by-agonising-step progress. From the confusion a town—was it Ceccano?—seemed to grow up around us. Then a journey in an army vehicle that was as painful as that in the wheelbarrow. Most of the time I must have been delirious. I believed I was in Fiamma's hospital again. 'The Last Battle' idea seemed to scorch my mind and I felt myself to be scrambling about on the floor amidst glass and dust with the deep bass of the chaplain and the machine-gun voice of Dr Turnbull carrying on a hammering duologue in my skull. But it was not Dr Turnbull whose voice addressed me when I finally regained a vague sort of consciousness.

'We meet again'—was there an amused hesitation before he completed the sentence?—'Signor Bardi.'

A hazy familiarity refused to yield to puzzlement. I must have looked blank.

'I am Dr Galdi. You may remember delivering a valuable consignment of surgical instruments...'

Of course. I had. A hundred years ago. But it was

only a few months since C had assigned me the identity of Mr Eamonn Byrne and the SIS task that had brought me to . . . this. Slowly I tumbled to the fact that I was in hospital again, this time in Rome.

'You've had a rough time,' Dr Galdi said as if giving me news. 'You were more or less dumped on the doorstep like an abandoned orphan. I don't know the full story, but apparently some high-ranking Hun—'

'He saved my life,' I said simply.

'Good for him. But there has been a great hue and cry for you from our . . . friends.'

'Friends? What friends?' I asked testily. I felt comfortable in a drugged sort of way, but in no condition to cope with conundrums.

The ache in my heart was for Fiamma, and it was intensified by my knowing that, this time, there was no chance of her suddenly appearing like a heavenly vision and then materialising into the flesh-and-blood girl I had loved and married; no chance of her bending over me and smiling, the scent of her hair drifting into my senses . . . Looking back, I realise that the ache was largely one of self-pity. I had been through quite a lot, and only a stunned hopelessness seemed to face me now. I gave a mocking laugh. 'Friends?'

'Oh, you have some still. We all have,' he added cryptically. 'One of them's coming to see you tomorrow.'

My heart leapt for a moment. Fiamma? But it was, as I might have guessed, Access who turned up at my bedside next day. Typically he snarled at me, 'And where the bloody hell have you been? Dodging the column, I suppose.'

'Then you bloody well suppose wrong,' I snarled

435

back at him—at least, it was as near a snarl as I could get; even that small effort seemed to set my pulse jumping.

His face twisted into a sort of cynical smile. 'A joke, Painter; a joke. Lost your sense of humour, have you? If you ever had one.'

I sighed wearily. The tiny ward in which I had my solitary bed was like a cupboard with Access' overpowering presence. But suddenly he changed his tune, reached out and touched the empty sleeve of my pyjama jacket. (One of the differences between this hospital and the mocked-up one at Cassino was that we wore pyjamas instead of just our shirts or birthday suits.) 'German sniper pipped you, eh?'

I wondered how he knew; then I remembered I had told Baade. Evidently he had filtered my story down to the hospital authorities.

'Anyway,' Access continued, 'you've earned yourself a bit of leave. I dare say you can use it.'

'Use it!' I said bitterly. 'Once out of here—'

'I know: you'll be looking for your lady-love.'

I wondered how he knew that too; but it was hardly so startling, for if the SIS was not a pool into which trickles of information ran from every direction it was nothing. Anyway that was unimportant. Or perhaps it was important. I said eagerly, 'I suppose you haven't any info?'

He shook his head. 'Everything's at sixes and sevens—'

'When wasn't it?' I put in.

'Huh! You can say that again. The supremos—Churchill, Alexander, Eisenhower, that lot—have all got bees in their bloody bonnets about the importance of Rome. Capture Rome and it's the

436

solution to everything. Well, we captured Rome—or the Yanks did, first—and what happened? Fuck all. The king abdicated, Badoglio resigned, and in comes some doddering old politician with a coalition of anti-Fascists. The Germans clear off to the north and establish a new line of defence with eight new divisions dragged from the Russian front, and Alexander's going to lose seven of his to the Second Front. Result—bloody chaos. On top of that, Alexander's ordered the partisans to disband because he's afraid they'll stir up a revolution and the Germans will take advantage of it.'

I thought of all the marvellous work the partisans had done to hinder the enemy and the lives they lost in the process. And now? But what about the Mafia element? Disbanding partisans, many of whom might be nursing resentments, seemed to be inviting trouble. But all this was high level stuff. I was only a small fish in a very big pond. I tried to tap the 'human' side of Access, if there was one, and asked him flatly for help.

'In what way?' The mask of cynicism and suspicion was beginning to slip back into place. 'I'm not running a private-eye service for tracing lost wives.'

'You're right in the middle of a network of information,' I said with a hint of indignation. 'Something relevant might come your way. I'm a bit hamstrung lying here.'

'You won't be here for long. Dr Galdi tells me they're going to turn you loose with your arm in a sling. Come into Out-Patients daily for exercises. Not much else wrong with you. Shock and exhaustion were the main trouble.' He rose and made his way to the door.

It was like him to fire a parting shot: 'They've got plenty of poor shot-up sods who need real attention. They don't need any malingerers poncing about.'

I did not deign to answer that. But I thought I would give him something to think about. 'While I was trying to find my feet again in Cassino after the bombing, who do you think turned up? Neumann. He was looking for Roz. I thought you ought to know.'

*   *   *

When I did eventually get out—with my arm in a sling as Access had predicted—it was nearly the end of June. Rome was a city, I found, where the signs of victory and defeat were curiously intermingled. Military vehicles were everywhere. Trucks were parked in the open space fronting the Colosseum, a convoy of tanks were crawling along the sidewalk leading to the Castel Sant' Angelo, traffic was being directed by American Military Police in their white helmets and gaiters, and in the Termini railway station troop trains waited with steam up while Allied soldiers in a dozen different uniforms were being shepherded aboard. Civilian traffic moved painfully, as if with the creakings of age and neglect; the shops were still decorated with the flags and ribbons of welcome (a bunch of French tricolors in the shape of a huge rosette was nailed defiantly to the wooden structure encasing Trajan's Column), but in the suburbs people queued for rations and children begged *biscottini* from burly American GIs.

And where was my son—*our* son? I thought.

Begging in the streets?

My convalescence had left me shaky and depressed and my mind reacted slowly to everything. In some ways I was a zombie, like the people in Cassino; and anxiety over Fiamma paradoxically prevented me deciding on what to do, or where to go, first. My state of mind was, though, in complete contrast to my appearance. Access had had me kitted out with a more or less new officer's uniform before I left the hospital—service dress too, right down to the swagger stick and green Intelligence shoulder flashes. Among the crowds of troops in battle or fatigue dress I felt ridiculous. Access must have used influence to get the uniform, but he could not resist pinning an unsigned note to the trousers: *Clobber for poncing about in on leave. Try the Villa Marsina for a drink.* I felt no more like 'poncing about' than flying in the air; and for a while the only way I seemed to be taking leave was of my senses. But after a while I adjusted, and my course of action then struck me like a blinding light. Where else should I go first but to the Via Lisbona?

Public transport was running in a sketchy sort of way, but I chose to walk to the Parioli area, wrily seeing myself as the young husband putting off in delighted anticipation the moment of reunion. Yet I knew that realisation of that dream was impossible. Or was it? If she were free Fiamma would have gone straight there. But—

The tree-lined avenue was the worse for military wear. The surface had been battered by heavy vehicles, tanks and tank transporters, while the marble steps of some of the grand houses were littered with broken sandbags.

439

I headed for the house and ascended the steps. Some of the windows were broken and chunks of masonry had fallen from the cornice into the short garden. The curtains of Fiamma's flat were dragged across the windows as if resisting intrusive glances and there was no answering ring when I pressed the bell I rubbed some of the grime off the glass panels of the front door and peered through.

On the other side of the glass a face peered back at me.

It must have been the dirt on the glass that distorted the features into a look of villainy, for when the door opened it was Signora Stefano's round merry smile that beamed at me.

'Signor Johns! How fine you look in your uniform!' Her pudgy little hands were raised in pleasure; then suddenly she became serious. 'But you are wounded, yes? The war, the war—ah, avversità!'

'Evil days indeed, Signora—'

'Come in, come in, you must tell me about the Signorina, the bambolo—'

I interrupted her: 'But it's *I* who want to know, Signora. I thought you might have news—'

'I?' she shot at me without hesitation as she waddled forward into the hall with its fine carpet and elegant furniture. 'But how would I know, signor? She is gone one day when I come back from the market, and the bambino too. And the picture.'

She gestured towards the wall. Where 'The Blue Nude' had hung was a space, a slightly discoloured surround to a blank like a mocking smile.

She led the way through to the kitchen, where a small birdlike man sat at the table eating pasta. I thought there was something a bit shifty about his eyes as he looked up, but he was civil enough as she introduced him as her husband.

'Daniele, his work is for the gas utility, he is an engineer.'

I knew that. But what else? I wondered. The shifty look bothered me a bit. My work with the partisans had brought me face to face with many shifty looks and evasive ploys. Mafia? It was a thought to keep in mind. If Fiamma had left suddenly and taken the boy and the picture with her, she obviously intended to leave permanently. But freely? Under duress?

'When was this?' I asked Signora Stefano, 'this sudden departure?'

'When? Ah—Daniele, you remember when you work the early morning shift and come back to find me distressed. Because no note—nothing. Just the picture—'

Daniele stopped cutting at his pasta and took a small diary from his pocket. 'It was 15 May.' He glanced at his wife. 'I had a cell meeting that night.'

Only six weeks ago, yet so much had happened! 15 May must have been when we were advancing for the final attack on the monastery. Why had Fiamma said nothing? Surely she had opportunity enough during my spell in hospital; even that night when we consummated our marriage? Well, perhaps not then, for I had had so many questions which I myself, lost in bliss, had failed to ask. But earlier? Duress, and an even more frightening word hammered in my mind—blackmail.

*   *   *

To say I scoured Rome for a lead would be to put it

mildly. The city was all haywire in its administration. The civil and military authorities were at odds. Merriment and tragedy seemed to collide at every street corner. Black marketeers sold illegal ration tickets in shops that displayed fabulously expensive jewellery; people of apparently irreproachable respectability fought for priority in queues for identity documents and travel permits; the Town Major's and the mayor's offices were besieged by people searching for lost relatives; and everywhere marooned service men were trying to find detachments of their own units. Yet because the curfew had been lifted to celebrate the liberation of the city, wild parties were the order of the summer nights, with lusty youngsters stripped off and bathing in the fountains, then wrapping themselves in flags torn down from battered buildings from which crowds poured forth to cheer every time an Allied tank or truck convoy headed northwards through the city and towards the fighting.

The Excelsior Hotel had been taken over as a leave centre for troops who had fought on to the verge of collapse and would be useless until they recuperated; and Access had wangled me a room there. The building that had been the Gauleiter's HQ had ironically become the HQ of the Allied Civic Administration. It was draped with Allied flags, but inside nothing had yet been organised, it was all piled-up furniture and puzzled officers to-ing and fro-ing clasping clip-boards and trying to communicate in unfamiliar languages. There was no information to be found there.

So I tried all the hostels for displaced persons, all the hospitals and police stations, all the nursery

442

schools that were still operating in case Ham Two should be in one of them, and even the office of the housing authority, which I thought might have knowledge of tenancy changes. But they had—or said they had—no record of the ownership by any friend of Prince Caeseri of any houses in the Via Lisbona.

'Return when things are more settled, Capitano,' said the little clerk, drumming his fingers on the table. 'At the moment it is chaos.' He trotted his fingers across the table in an expressive gesture. 'Everywhere people run, without much purpose. The Germans retreat to the north, but Rome is not the only flower in the bunch. There is Florence . . . They fight all the way . . .'

Florence! I thought. Ah, those long-ago love-filled days!

I had to stop myself believing that everyone was ganging up against me, deliberately withholding information about my beloved Fiamma, putting smoke screens and blind alleys between her and the boy, and me; otherwise I would have become completely paranoid. I told myself that the explanation, when it came, would be simple, not sinister; that it was only grimed glass that had turned Signora Stefano's smile into an ugly distortion; that the 'cell' her husband attended on the day Fiamma disappeared was no more than a meeting of his trade union; that Fiamma had simply been too entranced by our bedside wedding, and later too concerned with the bombing disaster and the drama of our escape to think of explaining to me something which was probably unimportant anyway. After all, if it was just a move to another flat . . . But no note to Signora Stefano—that was what was so puzzling. I simply could not get rid of my fears.

In that frame of mind I went to the Triangolo, but it had turned into a sort of soup kitchen where displaced persons, refugees from towns that had been bombed, were fed on the pitifully small amounts of food that the armies were releasing from their commissariats until supplies became more organised. There were many such places about, yet it made me slightly sick to know that some restaurants and bars got plentiful supplies 'for Forces only' while kids were begging for biscuits and the black market was flourishing.

I took my troubles to the place Access had mentioned, the Villa Marsina. It was near the Termini, was 'For Officers Only' and had a seedy sort of cabaret going. The room was noisy and smoke-filled and the dancing girls were doing their best to make contacts that might result in smuggled-out rations or money that could be used in the black market.

I found a table that had only one chair at it and ordered a gindiano. No cabaret could have cheered me up, but I discovered a gloomy sort of pleasure in watching the cosmopolitan crew of officers seeking relaxation. One in particular in the far corner of the room attracted my attention. He was half hidden by several of the girls who seemed to be dancing attendance on him, and there was something about the set of his shoulders that seemed to strike a chord; but I let my attention wander and finished my drink and ordered another before I looked again. This time the girls had moved away to resume their dance on the tiny stage and I could more clearly see his back in its olive green American walking-out uniform.

Surely ... it couldn't be? It couldn't *possibly* be ...

I upset the remains of my drink in my hurry to cross the crowded room amid pushes and shoves and reproaches, not all of them polite.

'Steve!'

He half rose, awkwardly, and a look of—what was it, pain or disbelief?—crossed his face.

'Ham! For God's sake!' He paused, then took my hand and pumped it vigorously. 'You old son of a gun! Where the hell did you spring from?'

I sat down and he called to a passing waitress to bring us more drinks. 'Boy! This we gotta celebrate!'

When the drinks came we toasted each other and tried to start a long-lost-buddies conversation; but the noise was overpowering.

'Let's get outta here—come round to my place.'

As he went to rise, putting his hands on the table and withdrawing his right leg from its stretched-out position I realised that his hitched-up trouser leg revealed part of a leg of metal and leather that terminated in a wooden foot.

CHAPTER TWENTY-SEVEN

We were making our way slowly through the crowd towards the goor, Steve with his gammy leg and me with my gammy arm, when one of the numerous power cuts of that time took effect, the lights dimmed for a minute and then went out. The darkness was the more intense for its suddenness, and in the general mêlée of tables being knocked over, laughter, swearing, and people stumbling into each other, we got separated. By the time I reached one of the Exit signs (which were still illuminated, presumably by gas or oil lamps) it was hopeless trying to find anyone. It was well after midnight and a cloudy sky anyway, with nothing but the illumination of the traffic to lighten up the darkness, and as the crowd spilled out of the Villa Marsina they mingled with the stream of passengers coming down from the Termini.

I was familiar enough with the city to find my way back to the Excelsior without any trouble and I shrugged off my disappointment at losing Steve. But he would be bound to go to the Marsina again and expect me to look for him there. There was no special hurry.

If only I had known then what answers he had to so many questions!

But next day events took a different turn.

★   ★   ★

'Something's come up right in your line of business,' Access said. He was, for him, almost jovial. 'Painter, my boy, you can justify your bit of leave and wear that poncy service dress at the same time. What d'you think about that, eh?'

'I don't know,' I replied. 'What is it?'

He started a long rigmarole, which I admit I was listening to with rather less than all my attention, about the progress of the war in Italy. I gathered that the Germans were still fighting tooth and nail against an Allied advance that was beginning to run out of steam as it pressed on north up Highways 3 and 4; that German engineers were slowing us down by skilfully timed bridge-blowing; and that Kesselring had been promised four more divisions as reinforcements. Also, the top brass in England were giving nearly all of their attention to the fighting in France and virtually none to the campaign in Italy.

'A bloody lost cause we are out here,' said Access. 'Only useful in so far as we're tying up Kesselring's divisions.' He drew his eyebrows together in annoyance as if he were personally being insulted by the Supreme Command's plans. 'Bloody brasshats. However, we've got a very much smaller baby in our arms. Our personal top brass—C—has asked us to look after Flo.'

I must have looked puzzled for a moment until the penny dropped. 'You mean Florence?'

'Of course I mean bloody Florence. Wake yourself up, Painter. You're getting soft with so much hanging about.'

I nudged my arm in its sling. 'Hanging about is not exactly what I'd call it.'

'Plenty of people've had more important things than that shot off,' he said vulgarly. 'Anyway, this is investigation, not activity. Quiet stuff, to do with art, not with exposing yourself to German snipers or getting lost in catacombs. Get me?'

'Not really,' I said. Though I recognised Access' abilities, his aggressiveness always made my hackles rise, and I found his half-hints annoying, a sneering attempt to make me appear an idiot. But I could do little but accept that the whole business of undercover work was riddled with veiled hints and dead ends and that it was no good griping about it. I said wearily, my native Yorkshire accent breaking

447

through, 'What's to do, then?'

'Those that don't fight, plan,' he said. 'And they're planning as if it's all over, we've kicked the Hun in the balls, we've had the dancing in the streets, and we're all living in a land fit for heroes.' His face twisted in a snarl. 'Like it was last time, remember? No, of course you don't remember. Bloody whippersnappers from Cambridge.'

'Oxford,' I corrected him.

He gave a short laugh. 'I know you think I'm a piggish old bastard; and I am. It's the way I've gone through life—fighting.'

For a moment I glimpsed the other side of the man, just as I had in the hospital when he gripped the empty sleeve of my pyjama jacket. He had started with some big chip on his shoulder in the face of the imagined superiority of others, and he never cleared it off. But somewhere there was a soft centre.

'Listen'—he continued, the old Access, the hard nut now—'the boss man and his Whitehall cronies are looking ahead. "Farsightedness", they call it. "Planning for the future." And the long and the short of it is, they want some sort of assessment made of the art treasures of Florence. There's going to be a Commission set up, and you're the man to be on it, or so they think. Tracing all the stuff that's been nicked—put into Goering's private hoard no doubt—and planning the restoration of stuff that gets damaged, buildings, bridges, that sort of thing. Waste of bloody time if you ask me. A bridge is a bridge and as long as you can cross a river on it it fulfils its purpose.'

I thought of the Ponte Vecchio, the Ponte alla Carraia, the Ponte Santa Trinità.

'Still,' he continued, 'I suppose it's a good thing to try to grab something out of the wreckage.'

'Of course it's a good thing,' I snapped. And I went on to tell him what Baade had told me about the German High Command agreement, given through neutral Switzerland, to avoid destroying the architectural glories.

He stroked his chin thoughtfully. 'Is that so? Doubt if it'll hold much water, though. There was an agreement not to bomb the Cassino monastery, implied if not actually given. Look what happened.'

'That was to save lives,' I said. 'And anyway warning to evacuate the place was given. Most of the art treasures were shifted to safety in the Vatican.'

He shifted impatiently, as if anxious to be rid of me and my frivolous concern with non-essentials. 'Well, you're on your own. Make something of the job if you can. It'll do bugger-all towards winning the war, so I wash my hands of it. But you know the drop if you want to get in touch.'

'I know it,' I said, remembering. 'The tabaccheria where I ask if anyone's interested in buying a painting today.'

'That's the one,' he said scornfully.

★ ★ ★

I had a go at contacting Steve before I set off for Florence, but he was not at the Marsina, and although the staff knew him well by sight they knew neither his name nor where he could be found. I scribbled a few lines and left them for him:

Steve: What a sellout, meeting like that and losing each other in the blackout. I saw Lella

449

briefly in London last year but she only told me you were a bomber pilot—no details of regiment or anything that would get this to you through the Field Post Office. But I guess you're a frequenter of this place. I'm just off 'on duty' to Florence (our happy stamping-ground!) but expect to be back in a few days. Then we'll hit the roof! I'll contact you here. Bestest. Ham.

I had mixed feelings about my return to Florence. 'Happy stamping ground,' I wrote glibly; but the question mark hanging over Fiamma's and Ham's whereabouts and the thought that their lives might be in danger amounted to tragedy, not happiness. Nor was my depression lessened by the present conditions. I recalled how Kurt and I had travelled on our trip to Cassino for BB. The journey this time was very different: there was no 'espresso', just some battered carriages pulled by a wheezing engine, and several times we had to be shunted into sidings to clear the way for military traffic. Also, there was still considerable fighting going on in and around the city, and Arezzo was as far as the train went. But my uniform got me transport in a convoy that was heading for Florence with supplies of—of all things!—boots, groundsheets, and woollen cap comforters.

Some South African troops had cleared the area south of the Arno and a couple of days later there was a big Allied push to cross the river and get control of the city; but the enemy was not giving up ground easily and it was a week before we could be said to be in command.

The green flashes on my epaulettes and an

450

explanation that I was on 'special duties' made things far easier than I expected in a fighting zone. The units I contacted were so used to the cosmopolitan set-up of Allied troops that they thought little of 'oddbods' who attached themselves willy-nilly and asked to be put on the ration strength. But Access' words 'You're on your own' could not have been more apt. I had no contacts, was completely in the dark about the starting point for my task, and felt that, with shells still falling on the northern parts of the city as the Germans pulled back to what they called their Gothic Line of defence, C and his Whitehall cronies were being a bit optimistic in their plans for an Arts Commission. But when I finally knew what it all involved, I was thankful that I had not been able to see ahead!

*   *   *

I tried the tabaccheria first. If nothing more, Access would hear that I had arrived in Florence.

The windows were boarded up—as they were in most other shops—but a rather grubby notice on the door proclaimed that 'The Grand Liberators were welcome'. It was written in three languages, as was the phrase beneath it: 'Business as usual, but no cigarettes or newspapers today.'

Like every other tabaccheria it was more like a general store and it sold (when it had the stocks) everything from pins to rather lurid religious prints that were suspended from wires round the walls, their corners curled and dusty. The proprietor was the same tall man I knew from my earlier assignments but, as was the rule, he made no

451

acknowledgement of recognition.

'I wondered if you were in the market for paintings today,' I said hesitantly.

'I'm not,' he replied; 'but as it happens I have the address of someone who is.' He went behind the counter, ferreted in a drawer, and returned with a vulgar comic postcard such as used to be sold at the seaside in England before the war. It showed a huge woman with breasts and buttocks like balloons inviting people to join her at Brighton—'where I get more than my fair share of the sun'. On the reverse was written in block letters THE ADDRESS U KNOW.

It was typical of the whole schoolboyish set-up that Access should choose this way of directing me to Umberto. I had never forgotten him—how could I?—but I did think of him as a victim of the turmoil of war, probably turned out of his flat, on the run, perhaps even dead. Now here was this hint from Access, who as always was more in the know than he admitted. I suddenly felt quite benevolent towards him.

I made my way out of the Via dei Campi and round the Piazza della signoria to the bus stop behind the Duomo. Of course no buses were running—the Allied liberation was far too recent for public services to be in order yet—but I felt a pang of nostalgia as I thought of the journey up to the Ponte Mensola and the flower-lined road leading past BB's villa to Magari. But this was no time for nostalgia.

As in Rome there was a mixture of sadness and joy in this most beautiful of cities: the war-torn streets with their sandbagged emplacements dribbling out sand; an abandoned armoured truck

452

halfway through a greengrocer's shop and ludicrously decorated with bunches of still green bananas; and flags and tinsel-decorated posters welcoming the liberation but with the painted words streaked with rain as if the gods had been crying over the desecration.

But there was bright sunshine now as I made my way to the familiar Lungarno Hotel in the Borgo San Jacopo and, beside it, the tall thin building with Umberto's studio flat at the very top.

The lift was not working. It had always been a bit rickety, and now its lattice gates had been secured with wire and a forbidding notice 'Guasto il motore' warned people that the motor had broken down. I smiled as I began to climb the stone steps. Refuse had accumulated in the corners on each landing and the windows were grimy and cracked. Everything's broken down, I thought.

I never expected the bell of Umberto's flat to ring, but it did; and after a few seconds I heard shuffling footsteps. Then the door was opened, cautiously, and Umberto's round face, more lined now than I recalled it, and topped with the ancient beret, peered round the jamb.

'Ham! My dear boy!' His face lit up, and the hand holding a stick of charcoal trembled. 'But what ...? At last!—Entra, entra! Come in, per piacere! Please!' His delight confused his speech and he flung the door back so heartily that it knocked over a lay figure that stood behind it. 'Ah! So, so ... this is the most happy time when my old friend the young artist returns to the studio, to his old teacher ...' He flung the charcoal among the litter of paint tubes and jars on the table, then turned and regarded me seriously, pointing at my arm in its sling. 'But what is this! You have been in the war? Yes, I see you wear the fine English uniform—*Capitano*, is it not? You are in the war, then?'

'You could say that,' I answered wrily.

'Of course, of course. Are we not all in the war? My *eccitazione*, emozione, make me too foolish. It is an enemy, then, that makes you injured? Ah, how sad! But it is not your painting arm! That is good luck!'

'Well, there is that,' I said ruefully. 'But it's about the only bit of good luck that has come my way.'

I made my way across the bare paint-splashed boards looking around at the familiar—but how long ago it seemed!—shabby sofa and chairs, the dais with its throne, the stacks of paintings standing against the walls, and the fat stove in the corner with the short spiral staircase behind it leading to Umberto's bedroom. The old memories came flooding back . . .

Umberto could scarcely contain himself as I spent the next hour or so telling him everything that had happened since last we met. He kept bobbing up and down, exclaiming 'Sacramento!' 'Dolore!' or whatever fitted his response to my narrative, looking for a cracked cup to pour a little rather sour wine into, and pushing his beret back and forth on his head.

But when I came to the latest development, my present task, he so to speak stopped in his tracks and flung up his arms:

'Ah! Now I am as you call it "in the picture"!' A bellow of laughter came from him. 'I too am your friend in this *iniziativa*, this *associazione*—' His paint-stained fingers wriggled in the air. 'I *know*. Si, si, I *know*!' He beamed. 'So much for you to tell me, and no chance for me to tell you what is good news. Si. Yes.'

'Sorry,' I said, 'I just kept rambling on. I can certainly do with some good news.'

He suddenly quietened dramatically, and leaned forward. 'So it is good news that I make my peace with your friend Berenson, is it not?'

'Good God!' I exclaimed. 'You and BB? Never! You think he's a charlatan. Or *did*.'

He waved his fingers airily. 'We still keep our opinions of each other to ourselves. It is I'—Umberto pummelled his chest—'I who am the charlatan to him. But it is of no matter. We both love art in different ways. But for the future of Florence we ... *riconciliarsi* ... ah! I don't know. You English say ...' he smote his forehead.

'Bury the hatchet,' I told him.

'Si! It is so!'

From his excited explanation I gathered that he and BB had been detailed as members of the Arts Commission to which I too had been assigned. It was typical of Access to play the fool and lead me to Umberto with his ridiculous U KNOW message. But I could not help laughing inwardly.

'So you've met Mr Berenson?' I queried.

'Of course, of course. He comes here from Poggibonsi, where he lives while I Tatti is occupied. But we meet in the Lungarno next door because here the *ascensore* no longer works and he is old, frail, he cannot climb the steps. So he comes—this is when the Germans are here, you understand? He comes with the Generalissimo and your big friend the musician—'

455

'Kurt!' I shouted. 'With General Baade! He told me—'

Umberto held his hand up. 'The Generalissimo, yes, and Kurt. But how can I tell you when you keep interrupting?'

'Sorry,' I said, 'but it's such good news. I—'

'So. These two gentle Germans, they see beyond the war, and a *riconciliazione* is made with the Allies in Switzerland that the war goes on but Florence is not blown up with guns and bombs. It is good news, no?'

'It is good news, *yes*,' I said; then I sighed. 'But not the *real* good news.'

The smile vanished from his round face as he caught my mood. 'Ah yes, and whatever I can do to help you find your beautiful Fiamma I will do now. Yes?'

'Yes,' I said, smiling bleakly. 'Yes, please, *please*.'

★   ★   ★

Nothing materialised before I returned to Rome, but I established with Umberto that I would contact him again as soon as I had further orders. Access had demanded my return via a message through the tabaccheria, but then only told me that I would have to wait until the military situation in the north had settled down a bit.

'All in good time,' he growled. 'The sodding arts have got to take a back seat when the Hun's still bashing away.'

'There's supposed to be an agreement,' I put in.

'Don't be a twat. I told you. Agreements aren't worth the paper they're written on.'

So, cooling my heels, I tried to contact Steve once more and visited the Villa Marsina again. Steve had got my note and left me one in return:

Sellout's right, buddy! I gotta go to England, a place called Roehampton, which is the limb-fixing center, 'cos my old pegleg's playing me up and they're gonna fix it. I'm being flown there and back on a hospital plane—they don't reckon to be more than a few days, so cross your fingers and contact me Allied Civic Admin, where I've got a desk job. V for Victory, as old man Churchill says. See you. Steve.

It proved to be rather more than a few days, for there were further muddles about his convalescence—so they told me in the now fully operative Allied Civic HQ—but at last we were facing each other across his desk which was piled high with files.

'Not my jazz at all, Ham. But somebody's got to do the clean work. I'm no Duggie Bader.' [*Group-Captain Douglas Bader, CBE, DSO, DFC lost both legs in a flying accident in 1931 but rejoined the RAF in 1939 and flew until captured in 1941.*]

'It was a battle wound, then?'

'You betcha. Tunisia, November '42. Flak came through like there was no tomorrow. Managed to get back to base, but I had half a leg and a bootful of blood. There was nuttin' they could do except chop it off at the knee. You ever seen the set-up of bones at the knee? Boy!—it's like an electric control centre! The only good thing was, I was outa the war for a while. Outa *this* war, anyway. They hospitalised me to Worthing on the south coast.

457

Nice quiet place with most of the air raids going over the top to Southampton and places like that. When the stump had healed over a bit I had to go to this place Roehampton, which is where they fix you up with fake limbs. But it was near London—and Lella.'

'I know,' I put in. 'I told you in my note. I met her quite by chance in Regent Street and she told me she worked at the Stars and Stripes. Marvellous for both of you—'

'Yair,' he interrupted, lighting a Lucky Strike. 'Only it didn't turn out that way so much.'

I had a dreadful feeling he was about to reveal some tragedy.

'No, no.' He flicked the ash from his Lucky Strike and I noticed his hand was trembling. 'Nothing to put the light out. But I guess it's doused a bit.' He shrugged, gave a twisted sort of smile.

'So?'

'So it's like this. She came down to see me at Worthing, got compassionate leave—the works. She hung around holding my hand, the real Florence Nightingale, and if she could have shooed all the nurses away and taken over she'd have been sky high. We were the two lovers reunited, real McCoy. But with all this'—he gestured down at his leg—'no dice! Not that I coulda raised a smile, never mind a ramrod. But we promised each other that when I'd got Tin-Pan fixed—Boy!'

'And?' I prompted him.

'It's not funny stripping off a tin leg as well as your underpants. Get me? She was marvellous about it, kept the light out so's I wouldn't be embarrassed, but I needed the light to unharness myself. Buckles and bows! You wouldn't believe! Like unwrapping a Christmas parcel. Lella, lying there in the Stars and Stripes bunk went white-faced, with the notice still on the wall saying walls had ears and Hitler might be behind one of them. I could see her wrapping up the romance in her mind and throwing it out with the garbage. I felt really sorry for her.'

It crossed my mind that he might have been more sorry for himself, which I could understand.

'Trouble was,' he continued, 'I opened my big mouth too wide. We resorted to conversation, screwing being outside my capabilities—you know, catching up on what had happened to each of us during the time apart. Not much of a substitute, but . . .' He gave a hollow laugh.

'I tried to keep it romantic, hang on to the shreds, how we'd learn a new technique—all that sorta junk. Mind you, I meant it, every word. She was always my baby, that Lella. You remember the way we sorted each other out that first time at Magari? Roz for Kurt, Lella for me, Fiamma for you. Undying love, all that—'

'So what went wrong?' I asked, puzzled.

'What went wrong was as I said. I opened my big mouth too much at the wrong time. There's Lella, waiting for a fix, and I can't manage it because of Tin-Pan here and the pain I'm in, and I go rambling on talkwise to try and ease the situation a bit and I let slip that earlier I'd had a coupla screws with dolls when the situation got desperate. Not whores, nice gals with husbands away fighting, like I'm one of 'em too, and there's the loneliness when you're grounded for two day' furlough . . . But she didn't see it that way. All that Italian temperament,

459

eyes flashing, claws ready to scrape my eyes out.'

'Lella?' I interrupted.

'Yair. Well, tumbles in the hay, wartime. They don't count, but she reckoned on them counting all right. Boy! Did she! Big deal. And the more I tried to explain that it wasn't a thing, just easing the lump in my pants, the more she went to town on the injustice of it. Keeping herself for me in the face of all odds, all the pressures she gets from guys in the Stars and Stripes—the usual guff, y'know? Mind you, I believe her. She'd hold out thick and fast if she'd made a vow of chastity, which is what she reckoned the marriage service is. But she couldn't take it that it isn't the same for men. You get me? You look like you've got your mind on something.'

'Oh, I get you all right,' I replied. 'It's just that . . . well—' But I couldn't get out what I wanted to say easily. I suppose I was half trying to ease my own guilt, half trying to get it over to Steve that there could be circumstances when the breaking of vows is justified. Or *seems* justified at the time.

I put it clumsily, trying to explain about the bombing of Parkes's, the tension, and the terrible need to gain release from it, the aftermath of comfort in each other's arms, the acknowledgement to each other that it was meaningless in the terms of love or even simple sexual desire. Yes, it was clumsy, the way I put it. Perhaps I should never have put it at all; after all Lella herself said 'It didn't mean anything. You betrayed no one. It was the natural reaction of two old friends in a state of shock'. But I never expected the reaction I got from Steve.

His face contorted into a mask that might have

460

been that of some hideous figure from a horror film. His lips were working soundlessly, as if he were tasting the strength of venom to be spat out. I saw the veins in his temples throbbing, his cheeks darkening with rage. Then the words came.

'You mean you laid Lella—'

'Wait a minute', I cried. 'No, you could not say that, and I explained it meant nothing to either of us. Like you said to her.'

'You lousy stinking bastard! I'll—'

With amazing agility he eased himself up and came round the desk. I half rose to meet his attack, but with my arm in its sling I was at a big disadvantage. I had no chance to parry the swing he made to the side of my head.

'Take that, you fucking swine, you pig-shit bastard!'

The blow connected undefended. I had no time even to shift my head round. A blood-red mist swam before my eyes as I crashed back against my chair and fell to the floor with files and a heavy glass ashtray from the desk collapsing about me like bricks from a bombed building.

The last thing I remembered before I passed out was a couple of white-helmeted Military Police rushing into the room and putting restraining hands on Steve as he prepared to lunge out at my crotch with his false leg.

CHAPTER TWENTY-EIGHT

'Bloody Yanks,' Access snarled. 'Over-reacting, over-emotional, over-sexed, over-sensitive. *And*

461

over here!' He laughed harshly at the old joke. 'No background, no history, that's their trouble.'

He was such a caricature of 'Disgusted, Tunbridge Wells' writing letters to the newspapers that I almost expected him to add 'Wogs begin at Dover'.

'Just because you poked his wife in the blackout,' he went rumbling on. 'Never known such a fuss.'

Because the Military Police had had to intervene there needed to be an inquiry, as called for by US Army regulations. It did not have quite the weight of a court-martial, but I had been questioned in camera by the presiding officer and Access had attended formally as Colonel Claude Dansey to give evidence of my character. His uniform with its red lapel tabs and cap band made him into even more of a caricature. He was muttering away about the waste of time and 'clowning around in full canonicals' when we should be getting down to business. As it was, Steve received a reprimand entered in his records.

'What business?' I asked. I was still feeling a bit shaky. Steve's lunge at me landed me in hospital again, but only briefly, for luckily I fell on my good arm and no further damage had been done; in fact the left one was now free of its sling, and both were stiff so I had gone back to wearing mufti because I could not salute properly. But as Access had lost no time in pointing out, 'the bloody holiday's over'.

The best news, though, was still to come. After all the frustrations and dead ends, the unavoidable feeling that some sinister mob was ganging up against us, I got my first clue to Fiamma's disappearance—not only her disappearance but to where she and Ham Two might be now.

462

Associations, suspicions, perhaps just the hunches one gets from undercover work, or a combination of all of them, insisted that I should now contact BB. After all, we were to work together on the Arts Commission, whenever it got started, and anyway we were old friends.

It was not hard to get an okay from Access. He gave me one of his twisted smiles which always added to my suspicion that he knew far more about everything than he was prepared to admit.

'It's best you should find these things out for yourself,' he said cryptically; and added, 'It's a nest of vipers you find yourself in, eh, Painter?'

That phrase again! But I had no time to ponder on it now. Poggibonsi, Umberto had said; and BB had often mentioned the refuge, the 'hideaway' he had there for times when the professors, the art students, and the tourists all became too numerous for him and he needed to escape into different, more austere, surroundings. 'Even beauty palls when there is nothing to contrast it with,' he had said, smiling; 'so even ugliness has its place in the scheme of things.'

Poggibonsi was about twenty-five miles south of Florence, and much of it had been destroyed by artillery fire. I found a kindred spirit in the Town Major, who had been on the staff of the arts magazine *Apollo* before the war and spoke of the tragedy of the church of St Lucchese, which had caught fire when a shell had hit it.

'I couldn't get over it for a while and asked for a posting into the front line. There were frescos in there six hundred years old and still bright as buttons, and a lovely triptych old Berenson had catalogued somewhere.'

Or *I* had, I thought.

The squat little house I found on the outskirts of the town was certainly austere, but it was comfortable, and what BB called the 'working room' was filled with paintings of a character I never thought would come within a thousand miles of his presence, for many were of the kind he attributed to 'the charlatan school'. There were Picassos, a Chagall, several Dufys, even a Paul Klee, for I remembered him remarking to me that, if there was one thing he agreed with the Nazis on, it was their inclusion of Klee's work in an exhibition of 'degenerate art' in Munich before the war. The pictures were not hung but stood in ranks against the walls. Some were in packing cases waiting to have the tops fixed, the canvases separated by corrugated cardboard. Labels on the wooden cases were addressed to *Reichsmarschall Hermann Goering, Karinhall*.

'His estate,' BB explained. 'He's the only one of the senior Nazis to have any aristocratic pretensions. Karinhall is named after his first wife.'

BB had been given advance notice of my arrival by the Town Major, who was too cautious to let me go there without checking that I had authority.

'I'm sure you won't take it amiss,' he said, 'but I'm making sure nobody with the wrong intentions gets near Berenson. It's easy to get the wrong impression.'

Indeed it is, I thought, eyeing the packing cases. But the reason was simple, and painful to hear...

★　　★　　★

'My dear colleague!'

464

He welcomed me with obvious pleasure and found a bottle of vermouth which he poured with the same thimble-sized measures I remembered. He was almost eighty now and the war had left indelible marks on him; his skin was dry and shrivelled and liver spots covered the backs of his hands—as might be expected; but there was also a sadness in his eyes that robbed them of their old penetrating brightness, the enthusiasm with which he would assess the technique displayed in the draping of a figure or the fall of light on a tessellated floor; and that was not merely age. Something less benign had taken its toll.

Sitting opposite me in a wing-backed chair BB told me his story. But his speech was hesitant, his narrative confused, and I have had to rearrange and present it as if I had been there on the day in June 1940 when what BB flatteringly calls 'the deputation' arrived at I Tatti.

There were four of them—three grim-faced men of the Guardia Segreta and one wearing black-tinted glasses who flaunted his effeminacy in a way that was exaggerated by the pale blue uniform he wore. There is an especially sinister quality about the colour of innocence when it is flaunted in the cause of evil.

'Allow me to introduce myself,' the blue-suited one said. 'I am Luciano Neri, Chief of Police. You understand?'

BB allowed a little smile to touch his lips. 'Certainly I *understand*,' he said in his carefully modulated voice, 'I understand your name and your—er—your occupation.' He inflected his hesitancy with a cool contempt. 'What I do not understand is why you have called upon me.'

465

Neri flicked one of his polished leather riding boots with the switch he carried. His cherubic cheeks and cupid's-bow mouth were like an obscene parody of a Botticelli angel. The dark glasses glinted like black flints. 'You will soon see, Signor Berenson.'

An icy chill touched BB's shoulders; but he remained calm, his hands folded over the handle of his stick. 'I am not Italian,' he said as if explaining to a rather backward child, 'and as I was educated mainly in England and America I prefer to be called Mister.'

'Your preferences are neither here nor there,' Neri said, 'and if I were you I'd forget about them. You are an alien.' He paused for effect. 'And a *Jew* alien, I understand.'

'A long time ago, and in another country, I was a Jew, yes; but I do not practise the persuasion.'

Neri crossed to the wall on which hung two fine Renaissance portraits with, between them, the mandatory picture of Mussolini wearing his tasselled cap and thrusting his chin aggressively forward. 'I understand this is some kind of joke—an *insulting* joke.'

BB paused to collect his wits. He realised he was on dangerous ground and played for time. 'A joke? I understand that it is the law that a picture of Il Duce should be displayed in every household.' Then he added with subtle emphasis, 'Its is no joke, I assure you.'

Neri could only take BB's words at their face value: subtleties were beyond him. But his suspicion that he was being taunted was inflamed. Unsure of his ground he sought the refuge of his minions, who had been prowling about the room,

466

like detectives looking for clues to some mystery. 'Found anything?'

'Pictures,' one of them said dumbly.

'I can see that, you fool!' Neri said. 'However'—he turned to BB with a false smile—'since the object of our visit is to discuss the subject of pictures we will go on from there.'

'Really?' BB said mildly. 'Well, I am said to be something of an authority. On the Renaissance period in particular. I do not intend to be falsely modest about it.' He allowed the little smile to play round his lips again. 'My fees, of course, are commensurate with my experience.'

It was Neri's chance and he seized it. 'Your fee, Mister Berenson, will be your ... shall we say freedom? Relative freedom anyway.'

Despite his self-control BB felt his face go ashen. 'I—I don't think I understand you.'

Neri came closer, the three thugs grouped behind him. The old man's hands trembled but he tautened them with an effort and reached for the tiny glass of vermouth on the wine table beside his chair. Holding it steady restored his nerve.

'You will, Mister Berenson; you will. Very clearly. You understand that you will understand?' The hand holding the switch came up and pointed, an extension of the fingers of which the nails, BB noticed, were painted red.

'Possibly, if you explain clearly. I am an old man, Signor Neri, and perhaps—as the English say—a little slow on the uptake. But I will do my best.'

'Good. Good.' Neri either ignored or failed to notice BB's hint of sarcasm. He strutted about the room while his minions stood threateningly with folded arms, timing his pièce de résistance to a nicety. It was a document which he flicked down on to a table with an air of sneering authourity. 'That will need little understanding. It gives the Council full possession of this house for as long as necessary. You have another house in Poggibonsi which you will move into immediately; and there you will remain until the Council or'—the full lips twitched in a grin—'or your *age* decide otherwise. And at Poggibonsi you will be in the service of our allies, the Fascisti of Germany, who will demand your evaluation of pictures and other works of art which fall into their hands during the course of possible hostilities. These will be kept in safe custody.' A pause. 'It is the policy of Il Duce to comply with Herr Hitler's wishes regarding the preservation of notable works of art.'

And in everything else, BB thought. But he let that pass. Shock was still seeping through his frail frame. To leave I Tatti! His priceless collection in the hands of God knew whom! He struggled to be philosophical about it, and his inner strength must have been far stronger than his appearance revealed, for he said to me now of the four war-torn years that had passed:

'I bore them with fortitude. After all, I wasn't in a concentration camp. I was under no more than a regime of house arrest, with guards who were at the worst indifferent and at the best kindly.' He touched his silky beard with a fine handkerchief where a drop of vermouth lingered. 'I had knowledge that was useful. This place became a clearing house for works of art that were plundered from the galleries, the churches, and the great houses of Europe.' He gestured with the ivory crook of his stick to the packing cases. 'Many of them to be handed over to that gross Nazi for his personal edification.'

I was puzzled. 'But why,' I asked, 'couldn't all this go on at I Tatti? Surely there was no need to keep you cooped up here? You weren't any less likely to try to jump over the wall here than at Settignano. Or were you?'

He smiled softly. 'No, no. It wasn't a matter of my escaping: it was a matter of commandeering a suitable headquarters for their undercover activities. The Mafia was still under Mussolini's suppression order at that time, and they had to move circumspectly. Where better than in premises officially commandeered for the extended wartime activities of the Chief of Police? Respectability epitomised!'

Thinking aloud I said, 'I begin to see how the nest of vipers was built. More like a cuckoo's nest really—the Mafia being hatched under Musso's very nose.'

'He—Neri, I mean—would have preferred the Villa Magari,' BB continued, 'for he had a score to settle there too. But I was necessary to his German masters to evaluate their thefts as they trampled over Europe—"relocating", as they called it, what they had stolen—'

'Magari!' I almost shouted. 'You've been there?'

He shook his head. 'No, no. But Magari was the scene of Neri's humiliation. Prince Caeseri gave him what our American friends inelegantly call the squelch—or so I understood from one of the guards who was a little less than discreet. And a Mafioso snubbed is an enemy to be feared.'

Yes, I thought. And not only had Neri been snubbed by the Prince but he had also been fired from his job as Deputy Mayor by Mussolini when the Prince reported the vandalism at Magari. But it would not have been difficult for him, with the backing of Mafia intimidation, to wangle himself into the job of Chief of Police, which was just as powerful. Probably more so. I wondered again if my hunch had been right. Had Fiamma become involved, been the target for Neri's revenge? I could not help shuddering at the thought of those blood-red talons hovering over her.

BB was getting tired, I could see; but he was anxious to hear what he called my 'chronicle of events'. We had a scratch lunch consisting of minestrone and tinned ravioli, for which he apologised; then he excused himself for his afternoon nap and reapppeared after an hour or so looking as spruce as ever. While he was listening to me, which he did without interruption, his eyes expressed inner emotions which I could not fathom and his hands lay limp in the rug that covered his knees.

'Who would have thought your work for me could have led to such terrible complications?' He gave a quizzical smile.

'Hardly your fault, BB. *C'est la guerre*—which is what everybody says to account for everything nowadays. But it doesn't account for Fiamma.'

'A very beautiful young woman. You scarcely did her justice in that head-and-shoulders sketch you showed me; but it showed, I thought, a certain grasp of form and structure. It was the spirit, the *essence*, that was missing. Her youth, her *femininity*.'

He means Fiamma's *eroticism*, I thought. But of course it was not a word he would think of. I was

470

startled. I had forgotten about the sketch I did as a cover-up for 'The Blue Nude', which I never dared to show BB.

'You asked me if I'd been to Magari.'

'Yes!' I said eagerly.

'I haven't of course. House arrest is somewhat ... limiting.' The little quizzical smile hovered round his silky beard again. 'But I know someone who has.' He slid the rug from his knees. Suddenly he had the air of a benevolent uncle who had planned a surprise for a favourite nephew. 'And we must be prepared to meet him. He comes under a flag of truce.'

He walked, upright but with hesitant steps, to the window almost at the same moment as a car drew up on the cobbled courtyard outside. It was a shabby little Opel, the nearest the Third Reich ever got to producing a 'People's Car', for the much publicised Volkswagen that had enticed 300,000 would-be-owner-drivers to order it in the early days of the war had never gone into production; but the Opel sold for roughly what an Austin Seven would have cost in England. This one was muddy and had dented mudguards and tyres worn to the treads, and out of its tinny door stepped a man in German uniform almost as shabby and with a look of careworn frustration.

It was Kurt.

*   *   *

Of course I should not have been so open-mouthed with surprise. Umberto had mentioned Kurt as one of the two 'gentle Germans'—Baade being the other—who through neutral Switzerland had

471

represented the German side in the agreement with the Allies that Florence should escape further bombing and shelling for the sake of its priceless antiquities; and with Umberto and me, he, and Berenson of course, would form part of the Arts Commission that would advise on the restoration of works that had suffered. Nothing, though, lately seemed to work out right for me and dead ends were two a penny. So Kurt's smile at my astonishment was justified. But we were quickly through the barrier and embracing each other with joy. As with our fated meeting at the summit of Cassino, hostility in the name of nationality was forgotten.

'Ham! My good friend!'

'But we're supposed to be enemies! It is ridiculous!'

Loosing himself from my clasp he wagged a finger at me. 'Each time we meet we say this. You remember?'

'Of course I remember! How could I forget? That ride in the barrow! Agony! And I passed out before I had a chance to thank you. Never even knew what happened to you except that I heard, in a roundabout way'—I paused, clamping up. I had become so conditioned to keeping my mouth shut and my ears open that names were always suppressed. But now it did not matter. In a world still at war we were part of a tiny enclave that had no concern with fighting.

'Baade told me,' I continued, 'of your efforts to win the High Command over to the idea that Florence should be spared. So I was sure you'd got back. But I never knew how or why.'

'How? Why?' he echoed. '"How" is easy. With

472

confusion all around a nondescript man passes unnoticed. I have feet, and after a little rest I could use them. And one man alone can much more easily avoid the scattering of enemies still around. It was a long way but I reached my regiment eventually.'

BB took us both by the hands as if we were children and led us to chairs. 'You will excuse me if I sit down. At my time of life ... well, you two are young but will not mind sharing the privileges of old age.' He settled himself and smiled.

Kurt went on: 'So "how" is easy; but "why"—there you have a different problem altogether. And indeed I have often asked myself, Why? But really it amounts to no more than that I am a good German but a half-hearted soldier. A tug-of-war between love and duty, you might say. Why go back? Nobody knew where I was, I wasn't wearing the Führer's uniform, I had "done my bit" as you English say, the war had shaken my marriage ...' He made an expressive gesture with his hands. I was reminded of how sometimes in a Chopin Nocturne they had hovered over the keyboard like butterflies waiting to alight. 'So why?' He shrugged. 'It is a difficult question, my friend. One so difficult I cannot answer it. Except that duty finally triumphed.'

I recalled Vanni and his disgust with his fellow countrymen looting from their dead comrades.

'Also,' he continued, 'I had seen and helped you—the third member of our ... what is the word? ... triumvirate, that's it, the triumvirate of our happy days at Fiesole, all of us swearing to marry the three daughters of the Prince.'

'Well, we did,' I said.

Kurt's smile was gentle, almost wistful. 'Yes, oh

yes. We married them. And they married *us*.' His smile turned hard, almost cynical.

I sensed a bitterness that I did not like, and which scared me. 'Of course they married us. What the hell are you getting at, Kurt? Have you got regrets or something?'

'Me? No, not me. But Roz—I don't know. Sometimes she must have, wherever she is.'

His expression was so stony now that I began to think he was trying to tell me that she had died. Shock ran through me—more, perhaps, because it hit me as a reminder that I had no idea where my beloved Fiamma was either, or even if she was alive. But of course Kurt did not know that. In fact, it now crossed my mind, that he could not have known anything about our bedside wedding. I had not seen him since he carried me down from Cassino. Yet he said with such assurance *we'd* married the three beautiful girls that he must have known about Fiamma and me. Or was he just counting our idyllic love affair as a marriage?

'Half a minute . . .' I began. Then I remembered. Of course! Fiamma and Roz had written to each other. Fiamma had given me a letter from Roz—the one I had never even read. 'Why do you say "*wherever*" she is?'I queried. 'I thought for a moment you meant—'

He shook his head. 'No, not that. At least, as far as anyone can ever be sure of life or death in this damned war.'

'Then why—?' I ventured.

'Why do I say "wherever"?' He glanced towards BB, who seemed to have dozed off. 'Because, my dear Ham, I simply do not know where she is.'

I smiled wanly. 'We're in the same boat, Kurt.

474

You don't know where Roz is; *I* don't know where Fiamma is. Or our son.'

He looked puzzled. 'But weren't they in the house in the Via Lisbona? Where I used to take them some spare rations?'

'Yes. And we were eternally grateful to you. But that all stopped when Neumann took over.'

'It would. Neumann was in everything correct, down to the smallest detail, and had no love for the Caeseri family anyway. They had caused him too much trouble.'

My mind switched back once more to that night at the Savile when C revealed that the Prince had been a link between Germany and Ciano in Rome and I had tumbled to the fact that it was Roz who had delivered the coded message to the drop. So there were two Caeseris who were suspect, possibly double agents, and Kurt, who had married into the family and had hinted when war broke out that he was in Intelligence, and myself (not then married into the family but too close to it to be ignored) with my partisan activities and my SIS guises: certainly there was more than enough potential trouble there for German Counter Intelligence. And even Fiamma had hinted that she might have been involved when, as we crouched in the tunnel fearful of pursuit, she whispered, 'It's a long story.'

It was a complex story rather than a long one, but I tell it now as Kurt told it to me, straightening out some of the corkscrew corners.

★ ★ ★

It started with Kurt's father. Dr Helmut von Schill, a metallurgist, worked for the Krupp armaments factory in Essen. The Krupps had supported Hitler in his rise to power, financing the Nazi party—'By putting a tax on employment,' Kurt said sourly—and getting rewarded with honours 'more or less of their choice'. 'Well,' he went on, 'they'd more or less *made* the Ruhr area in the four hundred years they were there mining and casting and making steel, building factories and constructing guns and ships and submarines and, after the Versailles Treaty, secretly rearming Germany; so I suppose they were entitled to privileges.

'It wasn't for me, that life of privilege. My father had known Alfred Krupp, the top boss, as a boy and he wanted me to go into Krupp's "for the glory of the Fatherland", as he put it. He took me to Essen on tours of the factories, but the furnaces made me ill with the heat and the clouds of smoke and grit—which came from the burning coke they used to increase the carbon content of the wrought iron—smothered everything with soot. But there was a spectacle too: the white-hot steaming metal, the millions of sparks from the furnace, the crusts of iron oxide peeling off the ingots—that was the place for *painters*. The colours! You'd have been in your element there, Ham. Pictures all around for you to paint. That wonderful portrait you did of Fiamma! I remember it now, seeing it for the first time, standing on the piano, all blue and a masterpiece of likeness even though it wasn't like a photograph. But you'd captured the *glow* she had, a sort of'—he paused, his forehead wrinkled—'it was like love with sex wrapped up inside it. There! I can't describe it. But then of course that was why it needed a painter to bring it out—because there
476

were no words.'

In his chair BB stirred and sighed, an old man dreaming.

'That's right,' I nodded. 'What words can't do, paint can.'

'Or music.' Kurt flexed his fingers as if playing inaudible arpeggios. 'That was for me. My father saw that there was no chance of my following in his footsteps, but both my parents helped me. They backed me in my musical studies and ... everything. Even with Roz when they met her for the first time on that holiday in Bornholm.'

'But why shouldn't they?' I asked perplexedly.

'When they knew she was half-Jewish they knew it would cause problems. The Krupps backed Hitler in his anti-semitism because once, years ago, the Rothschild bankers had lent the firm money when they were nearly bankrupt and they hated being beholden to what they called the *Judenschwindler*. It was a guilty hatred and everybody had to fall in line with it.'

'Like all the Nazis,' I said.

'Not only that,' Kurt added, 'Alfred Krupp was a member of the SS, so there was double caution needed over anyone even half-Jewish in our family.'

But there was a give-and-take side to it too—common in Nazi Germany. Particularly valuable Jewish workers—especially scientists— were 'arranged for' and escaped the pogrom. 'Impure Aryans' like Roz were tolerated when they came from Italy—Germany's ally—and had influential people like the Von Schills to back them. Her father had long since returned to his home country, America; but his record was on file in the vast filing system accumulated by Himmler.

477

'It was all kept at what they called an "honourable" level, the taint of her Jewish blood; but we were "regulated" under Himmler's anti-Jewish laws in case'—Kurt laughed bitterly—'we should taint the entire German nation.'

I reacted angrily. 'You mean you were forbidden to have children?'

'That is exactly what I mean, my old friend. It was a near thing that our marriage was not compulsorily annulled. If it had been, after America came into the war, Roz would have been an enemy alien—a half-Jewish one at that, eligible for the concentration camps.' He broke off suddenly, as if to escape the horror of the thought. 'But *you*, Ham ... little things I know, from Roz's letters, when they got through to me and Fiamma's got through to her. A marriage, I understood—very romantic, at the bedside; but after that—nothing. And Steve, that'—he snapped his fingers—'what is the phrase? *Unbekummert*, carefree—'

'Happy-go-lucky?'

'Yes, that happy-go-lucky American who shared our house at Settignano and married Lella.'

'No longer happy-go-lucky,' I said grimly.

*   *   *

As I finished bringing Kurt up to date with all that had happened to me since Cassino, BB, whose head had been resting on the wing of his chair, suddenly looked up. 'It is true I have been dozing,' he said, 'but my dozing is like that of a cat—alert to anything that is of concern to me.' His grey eyes took on a mischievous look such as I had seen many

478

times when he had been about to regale the company at I Tatti with one of his rather tedious stories. 'Such as painting.'

He rose slowly and surveyed the paintings stacked against the walls as if uncertain which stack held the one he sought. 'It may be in another room. Life in the ... prevailing circumstances is not as orderly as I am accustomed to and I get confused as to the location of certain paintings. Had you been with me, my dear colleague, better arrangements would have been made. But'—he gave a little shrug—'C'est la guerre, as you so aptly quote; and the war will provide adequate excuse for the disarray. Now let me see...'

Slowly he moved along the stacks, from time to time hooking a few pictures forward with the handle of his stick and murmuring to himself '... no, I think not ... among some nonsense by that rascal Picasso, I think, and unsigned.' He turned and gave us another mischievous look. 'Possibly because the—er—perpetrator wished to remain understandably anonymous.' A pause while he raked forward some unframed canvases. 'Ah! Eureka!'

He let the canvases fall back with a little thud, then said to me in a tone of mock reproach, 'You deceived me, knowing I would not approve. And you were right. The style!—atrocious, great slashes of thick paint like pasta, scraped on with a palette knife. But Kurt was right, in the way that those who lack knowledge can sometimes be right, intuitively, I mean. There is indeed a *glow* about the portrait, as if the essence, the *spirit* of the sitter had been imprisoned in those coarse slashes of impasto. A faint familiarity puzzled me when it came into my possession, as if I knew the sitter through veils of memory. But today, as I sat half dreaming there after lunch with Kurt, drew that veil back for me.'

He turned and with his stick slid the foremost canvases aside to reveal 'The Blue Nude'.

*　　　*　　　*

Any further revelations were suddenly banished by the arrival of an army truck, its tyres screaming to a halt on the gravel outside. There was a general scrabbling as whoever it was was challenged by BB's official 'guard'—one of the ordinary civil police. We heard a commanding bellow telling the man to stand aside and the Town Major entered. He was no longer the friendly ex-member of *Apollo* but a very grim down-to-earth field officer.

'Captain Johns, come with me at once.'

I was so startled I began to protest. 'I—'

'Captain Johns, I am giving you an order. Get into that truck immediately.' My training in the OTC and at Catterick had sunk in enough for me to know that there could be no disobeying an order without a court-martial. And anyway, even through my resentment I was curious to know what the panic was all about.

Once in the truck and hurtling (as it seemed to me) down the shell-pitted road towards Florence the Town Major seemed to soften up a bit; but I realised that he too had his resentments.

'Pestilential nuisance you turned out to be.'

'I'm sorry, sir'—this was a relationship that demanded terms of strict formality—'I don't quite understand.'

480

'Well, you could hardly be expected to. It's the interference I take exception to, the assumption that a Town Major has bugger-all to do except sit on his arse all day and deal with lost kids and refugees. "Root Johns out," comes this imperious message; instanter, immediately, if not before, yesterday in fact, personally in your own vehicle, *get him*. It's a bloody good job I knew where you were.'

I stopped myself reminding him that he knew because I sought his permission to see Berenson.

'It's these smart-alec outfits you work for,' he continued in his grouchy tone. 'SOE, SIS, all that lot, all high-and-God-Almighty, dishing out orders like bloody visiting cards, with authority from Army Commanders and Supremos and Prime Ministers and Presidents and the King himself, I wouldn't be surprised.'

I said hesitantly, 'I didn't think I was that important, sir.'

'Not you, you clot: the outfit—underpinning the war, levelling the ground, nosey-parkering into this and that, working the oracles. Or that's what they'd have us believe.' He suddenly seemed to switch into a better frame of mind. 'Still, people in glass houses ... I'm in a fairly cushy little number myself.'

I said, trying to avoid any hint of self-righteousness, 'I think most of our work's pretty fragmented, sir—probably doesn't make sense to those who are in the centre of things.'

As he did not respond I ventured to ask him, 'Any idea what it's all about, sir?'

'Me? Not a clue. Only this phone message, originated by the top Intelligence wallah and double-checked by me as to authenticity, to get you

481

to the station in time to get the Rome train—which has got special clearance.' His face set in a half-hearted smile. 'If you're not important you're not all that unimportant, evidently.'

A man of moods, I thought.

★   ★   ★

So it was Rome again. And Access of course, though the venue was different this time—nothing furtive or undercover about it; in fact it could not have been more public, for it was in the Allied Civic Administration building.

Access met me at the Termini station almost as if I were a returning holiday-maker; and not only did he meet me, he was almost apologetic in his greeting—though perhaps more mockingly so than I gave him credit for.

'Welcome back to the hurly-burly. Fresh from the country air, eh, Painter? Laying the lasses in the cornfields, what?' He jabbed at me with a stubby finger as we climbed into a small Fiat that had seen many better days but flew a small Union Jack impudently from its radiator.

'Since your summons arrived at the crucial moment when I was at last getting somewhere in my search for my wife and son, I don't much appreciate that,' I said. I probably sounded angry, and I was. Typically, Access sneered coarsely.

'Got a cock-stand merely at the thought, eh? And sulking now like a frustrated old maid!'

I did not bother to answer.

'Never mind.' He made a face as if soothing a fractious child. 'We're going to see your tin-leg friend. He'll make it all better. Some of it anyway.'

I had not seen Steve since the inquiry, and in the brief moments whenever he flashed across my thoughts I supposed that his 'desk job' was hardly likely to have been that of a mere clerk. But his rank of major in the USAF would have entitled him to something higher up, and so it proved. He was something called, in the style typical of Americans dreaming up impressive-seeming titles, a Co-ordinating Liaison officer, and his job was to link Allied Intelligence HQ with the army planning staff, whose 'war room' was tucked away in the recesses of the building behind the official 'front' of the Civic Administration. I doubt if anyone was deceived for a moment, for staff cars with the pennants of high-ranking officers flying from their bonnets arrived and departed frequently. But at this stage of the Italian campaign, with the Germans in retreat, that was probably unimportant.

The prospect of seeing Steve again gave me a similar feeling of anticipation to when I sensed Kurt's presence at the top of Cassino. We three, and the Prince's three daughters, seemed to be interlinked, sometimes joyfully, sometimes in the agony of parting, like a Chinese puzzle in which the rings, having been parted, defy all efforts at reassembly.

What I *was* surprised at, however, was his contrition. The most I expected was a hang-dog look of embarrassment, a sheepish smile, yet still mixed with hostility. But no: he rose uneasily from his chair and moved awkwardly round his desk. The smile he gave me was genuinely carefree, part of the old days.

'Sorry, old pal.' He extended his hand and I took it warmly. 'I easily get steamed up these days.' He tapped his leg. 'Old tin-pan's a right bitch sometimes, though I must say this new one they fixed me up with at Roehampton is a real hike-up; and when I've got used to having it around . . . well, who knows? Screwing as usual, eh?'

'Congratulations,' I said, and I meant it.

'Did you know, Ham,' he said with the sudden enthusiasm of a schoolboy, 'they've gotta name for these things'—he tapped the leg again. '"Prostheses", they call 'em. And they were invented five hundred years BC! Think of it! Some Greek guy got himself caught by the Spartans and chained up by the foot; so he escaped by cutting the foot off and getting a new one made.'

'Well, well!' I said, echoing Steve's innocent wonder.

'If you two have finished playing old-boys-together,' Access interrupted sarcastically, 'perhaps we could get on with the business in hand.'

*   *   *

The business in hand resulted from a piecing together of Intelligence reports which had filtered through by way of leaks from Kesselring's HQ (how many of them via Vanni, I wondered?) that, despite the agreement to leave Florence intact, the Germans were making a determined stand north of the city. This meant in military terms that the Allies could only be prevented from pursuing them in force if the bridges over the Arno were blown up. Already some of the old buildings round the Ponte Vecchio had been shelled and a counter-attack was threatened. This would have to be knocked out before it built up because we were in a vulnerable position on the south side of the city and could easily lose our foothold. We lacked troops—so many had been withdrawn to serve in France—and there was disagreement among the Allied commanders.

That was the broad picture—'the global view', Steve called it, and added that it was 'for the big-shots to work out the big strategy'. Our own mission was on a smaller scale but had a key role.

'Deceptive of course,' Access put in, 'which should suit you two.' He gave a sneering laugh, as if debiting us with more infidelities than we could be guilty of in a lifetime. 'Men were deceivers ever, as the bard says.'

'So who are we deceiving?' I asked tersely.

'Stupid question. The Boche. Who else? One doesn't deceive one's friends.'

I cocked a quizzical eyebrow at that but did not voice my thoughts. Sometimes the whole of life, all relationships, seemed to be one big deception. But with their masks and disguises down people reveal unexpected sides to their natures. Even Access had shown moments of tenderness; and the high-ranking Baade had proved to be a friend as much as enemy.

As if on cue Steve said, 'The Intelligence picture is that you have some pull with'—he glanced down at a file on his desk—'Major-General Baade, who's commanding this division that's making a stand. What we gotta do is kid him into thinking we're stronger than we are south of the Arno and that it ain't worth the bother. Because if we don't we're gonna bite the dust.'

I saw no point in trying to convince Steve (or anybody else) that I had no pull with Baade. I was

485

in his debt rather than he in mine; and in any case there had been a tacit agreement that Florence was to be preserved from destruction by both sides.

Almost as if answering me Access broke in.

'Whatever's been agreed on neutral ground doesn't count. That's for post-war, after the party's over.' He glared at me. 'The war's still on, you know, Painter. All the artistic considerations come later—restoration and all that bunk.'

I gripped the arms of my chair. 'But there won't be any need for all that bunk, as you call it, if the city's destroyed. That's the whole bloody point: to show that men have still got some feeling for their own past and achievement. Otherwise you might as well drop a bomb on St Peter's right now and call it a day.' I was almost exploding with anger and angry men are always easiest to deflate in argument.

Smirking—I loathed him when he smirked!—Access said, 'The "agreement", as you call it, isn't worth the paper it's written on. If it's written at all. Which I doubt. As I understand it—and don't forget it's two-sided, as much our say-so as the Hun's—we hold a flag of truce over *unnecessary* destruction. Which doesn't stop either side calling anything necessary if they feel like it. Be your age, Painter. Wars are for winning, by fair means if possible but for winning anyway. And this is a war, not a church committee organising a garden party for the steeple preservation fund.'

My anger was still vehement but more controlled now. 'Steeple preservation! It isn't only steeples that need preserving! It's the churches, the galleries, the bridges, the houses, the pictures, the sculpture—all priceless! Don't you realise that Florence is the birthplace of the Renaissance, that
486

Michelangelo, Petrarch, Leonardo, Giotto, the Medicis, Dante, Boccaccio, Brunelleshchi, all belonged here and that their works—'

Access' eyes turned upwards. 'For Christ's sake, Painter, spare me your catalogue of wonders. I can't out-call you in Florentine history, but I can in savvy; and what I brought you here for—with VIP treatment I hope you noted—was instruction.'

'Well, let's get on with it,' I said. I was still ruffled but not so ruffled that I could not give him a taste of his own phrase. 'If you mean the flag flying from the bonnet, yes I noticed it.'

Access grunted. 'That's what you'll have for your next assignment. Same vehicle, different flag—a white one.'

I looked at him with the astonishment I felt. 'The message I'm receiving loud and clear is that I'm to drive into enemy territory, pop in for a cheery drink at German HQ, and drop the hint to Baade that he'd better hold his horses because we've got faster ones and more of them south of the Arno. "Thought you'd like to know, old boy, so that you can re-jig your plans." Is that it?'

Access' eyes rolled up again. 'I can't believe it! I've got through to you first shot.'

I could not believe it either. It was what my Yorkshire mother would have called 'reet daft'. But reading my thoughts Access went on, 'Nothing extraordinary about it. Envoys have been going from one side to the other under flags of truce ever since war began. So what's biting you?'

'The pathetic faith you have in my ability to turn the course of the war,' I replied.

'You haven't done too badly so far,' Access said

with grudging approval—or was he just buttering me up?

'Damn right, he hasn't!' Steve suddenly exploded. 'His name's right at the top of the "hit parade". I got that from the big man, C.' He turned to me quietly. 'It isn't so crazy, Ham. And I'll be with you, backing you up. Besides'—his face assumed the boyish smile I remembered from so long ago—'there's a bonus, for both of us. Baade's at present at the German HQ, and that's at the Villa Magari! They commandeered it from the Italians a week or two ago. Like old times, huh?'

Magari! To say it was a morning of surprises was to put it mildly. I began to see the link between BB, Kurt, and the house of our golden dreams—dreams that had become war nightmares. 'I know someone who has been,' BB had said when I asked if he had seen Magari; and a moment later Kurt had arrived—where else but from Kesselring's headquarters? And now we were going there.

* * *

It is one thing to talk about entering the enemy camp under a white flag, quite another to do it. It smacks too much of surrender to be comfortable. I said as much to Steve as we drove north in the battered Fiat along stretches of the highway that in parts were so peaceful that orange and olive vendors had set up their stalls at the roadside, though God knew to whom they were going to sell their wares, the traffic being almost entirely military.

'Shucks, Ham,' Steve replied, 'don't take it thataway. No shame involved. We're going for a parley arranged by the top brass. Access is right: we're envoys, ambassadors, like in the old days. It's old-fashioned but it's not shameful. Anyway there's nix you can do about it. We're under orders, on a mission.'

A mission of deception, I thought. To a man who had saved my life. I did not like it, not one bit. Again I said as much to Steve.

He tapped his leg. 'And I don't like this much. Or buddies who lay my wife.' He waved my protesting hand away. 'So it's all right now. I blew my top and I apologised. Since this'—he tapped the leg again—'I've been what the docs call unstable, and that doesn't mean only on my feet. It's changed my life, my ... I suppose you'd call it my nature—y'know, fiery one minute cool the next. Not like I used to be, frisky all the time. I brood, then blow my top. Lella says I want fixing up by a trick cyclist.'

'Lella?' I said. 'You mean you've *seen* her?'

'Seen her? No. Not since—well, I told you.' He added cagily, 'We—er—correspond. And she reckons she's free, sex-wise. And she's some baby sex-wise. Remember?'

I remembered all right. Not the night after Parkes's, but her teasing gestures when I painted 'The Yellow Nude' at Forte dei Marmi; and her flagrant sexuality contrasted with Fiamma's, which was secret and loving. And Lella's nature, like her mother's and unlike Fiamma's, was not forgiving. The Principessa had had no qualms over taking Roz's father as her lover when she discovered that the Prince had a mistress. And I had no doubts at all that Lella would follow her example in claiming a no-holds-barred sex life.

I said sympathetically, 'It'll come out all right in the end. It did years ago with the Prince and

489

Principessa when he strayed soon after they were married. They adjusted. And they will again. So will you.'

I expected a caustic reply to that; but Steve looked grateful. 'You reckon? Hope you're right.'

The road slid back beneath the shaky little Fiat. The orange sellers and egg sellers and even flower sellers dozing by their stalls alternated with shell holes filled with scummy water, fire-blackened villages, rough burial mounds topped with crude crosses—the detritus of war. It was completely irrelevant, but my idea of 'The Last Battle' began to expand in my mind. The central upright scarlet rectangle, the horrified eyes facing death—that was the seed of my original conception; but now a foreground of symbolised rituals took possession of my mind's eye—flower sellers, grave-diggers, boots marching across a field of buttercups, the white surplice of a padre bereaving his finger of its wedding ring ... they were only images, nothing coalesced, they were just fleeting ideas that made me long to have a palette knife thick with pigment in my hand instead of the steering wheel of a Fiat. But the compensation was—ah!—that the battered little car was taking us to Magari. Magari, the syllables hammered in my brain. Then an absurd thought occurred to me, ousting both painting and Magari from my mind. I said suddenly,

'A small point we've forgotten—what are we using as a flag? My handkerchief's khaki. Underpants? Wouldn't be ... well, right for the job. Might be taken as an insult, get us off to a bad start.'

Steve shrugged. His leg was bothering him, I could see that; but the flag was not. 'I guess you're right. German humour doesn't go very far. But we'll detour and get something in Florence, a towel or something. Do a bit of looting maybe.'

'I've got a better idea,' I said. I pulled the car into a lay-by where an old woman sat in a deck chair with arms folded for all the world as if she were lounging on the deck of a luxurious liner. Branches of white-flowering oleander protruded from sawn-off jerricans at her feet. We could have had the lot for the single one of the five dollars Steve peeled from his billfold; and as we drove off I could see her in the rear mirror hastening away to declare her good fortune.

'That'll end up on the black market,' Steve said. 'And we'll end up in the nuthouse, driving into the enemy camp with a bunch of white flowers waving from the hood.' He gestured dismissively. 'Still, you're supposed to be the Baade expert.'

'I think he'll understand,' I said.

*   *   *

The Baade who faced us across a plain wood table in the Magari drawing-room was very different from the man I had last seen through a haze of pain when we travelled together across country. The stubble of red beard was shaved off and he wore immaculate uniform. He smiled, but his eyes had a glint of blue ice rather than warmth. His attitude was coldly courteous.

'You will remain standing, Captain Johns, but Major Price may sit. He has, I see, an honourable disability.'

'One of your Messerschmitts,' Steve said.

'One of your Boeings, no doubt,' Baade replied drily.

What Access had called 'the business in hand' was despatched briskly.

'I understand, gentlemen,' Baade said, 'that you are calling on me to honour an agreement—made ex-officio, as it were, through neutral powers—to avoid any unnecessary destruction of the city of Florence. And behind the appeal is the implied threat that breaking the agreement can only result in the routing of the *Wehrmacht* from tenaciously held positions north of the city by the enemy's superior forces. Am I right?'

'That's about it, General,' Steve said. 'You got it in one.' There was a satisfied note in his voice; but not in Baade, which hardened to match his steely eyes. He looked directly at me.

'My Anglophilia does not extend to betraying my country, Captain Johns, or to disobeying my commanding officer, or weakening my resolve to stand firm against enemy forces, however allegedly powerful.' He switched the piercing look to Steve. 'You will recall from your schooldays, Major Price, that when your country was embroiled in civil war, the commander of the Confederate Army, General French, sent a note to the commander of the United States forces, General Corse, by way of a messenger bearing a white flag. The note told General Corse that he was surrounded and called on him to surrender to avoid a needless effusion of blood. The reply was sent by the same messenger and said that Corse was prepared for the needless effusion of blood whenever it suited his opponent.'

He paused. 'The present situation is somewhat similar and the message in response is the same. I

492

make myself clear, gentlemen?' As if with a relaxation of formality he added, 'I can assure you that no more than *necessary* destruction will be ordered.' And to me: 'In the happier times we hope for, we may meet again. We are, I believe, designated members of an advisory committee on ... restoration.'

There was a bitter undertone to my voice as I replied, 'If, sir, there is anything to meet for.'

He smiled. 'We must be optimistic—and wary.'

Guards slammed to attention as he accompanied us to the door. It was all very civilised. We might have been leaving after a weekend at a house party. Steve managed the steps with awkward dignity, holding to the balustrade and giving an affectionate slap to the terracotta dog as he passed, as I had seen him do often before. A German soldier in gleaming helmet and boots opened the doors of the decrepit Fiat. The oleanders were already drooping from the radiator.

'A somewhat—er—ambiguous idea,' said Baade as if approving a child's well-meant gesture. '*Nerium Oleander*, a shrub with blossoms of beauty and fragrance. But the leaves when crushed give off the smell of death and are poisonous to man and beast. Did you know that?'

PART FOUR

FLORENCE AND THE VATICAN, 1944–1945

CHAPTER TWENTY-NINE

The weeks since Fiamma's disappearance had stretched into months. Weeks without any clues to her whereabouts, or Ham Two's; every end a dead end. The raw wound left by her flight, abduction or whatever it was, had become a dull insistent ache. I recalled an old aunt of mine who always included in her letters of condolence to bereaved relations the phrase 'Time heals'. Maybe it does; but the ache usually remains.

'Like this bloody arm,' I said to Steve.

'You're lucky, buddy.' He slapped his leg.

'I know. I ought to be counting my blessings. Sorry, Steve. It's just that—'

'Sure. I know.'

Our abortive mission to Magari had renewed my fears and worries. I tried to shut my eyes and memory to the heart-rendingly familiar scene—the villa itself, the gardens and Indian pool, even, I thought, a glimpse of Enrico somewhere along the rose walk, though it could easily have been a ghostly echo in my mind. Familiar, and yet brutalised by war and alien occupation.

Steve had had the burden of reporting our failure to his Intelligence Co-ordination bosses and I had the same problem with Access. Oddly, neither seemed perturbed or surprised, though Access showed his usual curled-lip response.

'Can't trust bloody amateurs. Anything to be done, do it yourself is the only policy.'

I shrugged. 'Well, you could have done that.'

'No good keeping a dog and barking yourself.'

I refrained from pointing out he was contradicting himself. He leaned forward. 'And don't come it with me, Painter,' he said threateningly. 'I'm bigger and older and uglier than you. And I hold all the cards.'

It was almost a repeat of the situation in Geneva when Air Commodore Nelson had pulled rank and warned me against sarcasm. I mumbled something that could be taken for an apology.

'All right. Dismiss. Piss off.'

'Sir,' I said tonelessly. I recalled the bullying sergeant-major at Catterick. He would have called it 'dumb insolence' and recommended the Adjutant to have me on Orderly Officer for a week. I had reached the door when Access called me back. His temperament was as changeable as Steve's had become since his 'tin-pan'.

'Life ain't all a bed of roses, but it ain't all a bed of nails either. You wanted info about your wife and boy—no, don't get excited.' He held up his hand to suppress the eagerness he could see in my face. 'I haven't got any. But there's someone who has, and she's coming here—in the call of duty, not just for your bloody benefit.'

'She!'

'Unless your sister-in-law's a man in drag—yes, she.'

I was speechless for a moment; then, 'You mean Steve Price's wife, Lella?'

'No, I don't mean Price's wife, whatever her name is. I mean the other one, the one who works for her father—and for us.'

I felt faint, yet so angry that I almost exploded. 'Christ! You certainly do hold the cards! Why the hell you couldn't have put some of them down—'

He was all smooth-tongued now, like an actor switching in seconds from drama to comedy. 'Simmer down, Painter. I don't want any apoplectic agents. It's bad enough having one who puts his little woman first.'

This time I did explode, while Access sat there with his eyes turned upward as if calling on God to grant him the patience to deal with a bad-tempered child.

'That's just about the bloody limit! You've gone too far this time, *sir*!' I could feel my shoulder nagging and sweat running down from under my arms. 'Another insult like that ... that'—I was stammering with rage—'th-there are places one can complain to about senior officers.'

He laughed raucously. 'Oh, don't be so bloody pompous, Painter. It doesn't become you and it's not in your nature. You're out of your depth. You've been with me long enough to know that I'm the one putting on an act, hiding my feelings, not you; you're the simple country boy who kills 'em all with honesty and marries the girl next door. Like *Mr Deeds Goes to Town*. Remember?'

His sideways glance was ambiguous enough for me to be uncertain whether he had just hit by chance on the film I saw in London that day I idled away a couple of hours, or whether someone along his line of informants had actually seen me visit the cinema. As if giving a half-answer to my question he said,

'Quis custodiet ipsos custodes? Who guards the bloody guards themselves, eh? Oh, I went to school too, Painter, though you might not think it. See what I mean? Now, if you've calmed down a bit ...'

It was true. He had taken the wind out of my

sails and I was almost tempted to laugh—at myself. And he was right: my anger had been dutiful rather than justified. It was just that my excitement had got the better of me.

'No offence intended,' he went on. 'We're in a tricky business, and the less we know about each other the less we'll get called on to . . . divulge.' His face had a grim look now. 'Remember the Venlo incident?'

I laughed shortly. 'Wasn't I sent to you to replace Best, the man who got kidnapped by the Germans?'

'*My* man, Painter. He ran his HQ in The Hague very efficiently. It was called the Continental Trading Company and Best was a well-known chap in Hague social life—monocle, spats, rolled umbrella, bowler hat—and he and his wife used to give parties and soirées musicales and all the city high-ups went.' He paused and mused. 'Rather like your chum Berenson, huh? Ah, that hits the nail on the head! There isn't much I don't know about one way and another.'

'I give you that,' I said with feeling.

'I thought you would. Best's house was at 19, Nieuwe Uitweg, next door to Mata Hari's, which made it ironical, for Mata was a German spy in World War One and Best's place was a teeming centre of anti-Nazi espionage in this one. Best's trouble was that he loosened up on his principle of keeping his agents ignorant of each other's existence, or anyway of their activities. Which is why he's in a Gestapo jail now. I wouldn't like that to happen to you, Painter.' He clenched his hands together, cracking the knuckles. 'You with a wife and family. So you only ever know enough for . . . well, immediate purposes. Get me?'

500

I had cooled down by now. 'Oh, I get you all right,' I said resignedly: 'with me it's always been a case of never letting the right hand know what the left hand doeth.'

'Ah! A biblical scholar too, eh?'

It was impossible for Access to keep a civil tongue in his head, I realised that. But there was no reason why I should not make my acquaintance with 'higher authority' clearer. So I said casually, 'Yes, I remember now that C hinted to me the Prince and his daughter were somehow concerned.'

'Did he now? H'm. Damned if I would have. But no doubt he had his reasons. We go in a lot for plants, misleading people, making "confusion worse confounded" as the saying goes.' He paused meaningfully. 'Surprises again, eh, Painter? I told you, I went to school too; a Latin tag, a quote from Milton—it's surprising what you can get away with. *Nothing* is what it seems, eh, Painter?'

I spread my hands. 'I give up. Are you trying to tell me now that Roz isn't coming after all?'

'Of course not. Large as life; and her princely dad too. They'll be here—or if they're not there'll be trouble.'

And I had to be content with that.

★   ★   ★

Of course I had intended to return to Poggibonsi to pick up the thread of how BB had acquired 'The Blue Nude'. I told Steve about it on the way up to Florence and he agreed we would make the diversion after our mission was finished. But in the event we almost unspokenly agreed that a time-wasting diversion on top of our failure would

501

not, as Steve put it, 'ante-up our image'. Then it turned out that the outcome was smooth, not rough—'Jeez, there's no understanding the four-stars,' Steve said with a gesture of dismissal—and I kicked myself for not keeping to our earlier decision. But now fate had taken a hand again and, as I put it to Steve, 'A dead end's been turned into a live one.'

'For me too,' he said cheerfully. 'Heard from Lella this morning. I think she's yielding. Coming out anyway.'

'Coming out *here*?' I said, astonished. 'To Rome?'

'Sure. Why not?'

'But she's based in London. She had a full-time job at the Stars and Stripes.'

'Had, that's the operative word. Once the Second Front was launched there were hardly any troops left in London. They're all beating their way through France. So she's fixed herself a transfer.' He added casually, 'Wound herself round some general's legs, that's for sure. But so what? If it brings her out here it's the heist.' With an effort (he was sitting in a desk chair) he lifted his false leg with his two hands and laid it on the desk. 'Funny when you gotta pick up bits of your body like girders. I'm practising this for the great reunion. My medic says I'll be okay for ballet if I can get more control over the joint between stump and tin-pan. So watch now.'

I watched as, obviously with a tremendous effort—I could see the sweat on his forehead—Steve inched the limb to the edge of the desk top and managed to let it descend in a more or less graceful arc without hand-held assistance. I made applauding noises.

502

'Sure. Well, it all helps with ... confidence. I don't want any farcical show like before. It's enough to turn any girl off.'

'But ... ?' I left the question unasked.

'Oh sure, sure. Take the damn thing off before starting the proceedings. A robot leg's no come-on, even if it's only from the knee down. I guess there'll be a whole new technique to learn.'

'You're looking forward to it, you randy old so-and-so!'

'You betcha!' He smiled as he dabbed his forehead. 'Phew!'

I silently made a little prayer that he would not be disappointed. His changes of mood were sudden and unpredictable but a happy reunion with Lella would ease the trauma which his disability and their separation had caused—well, perhaps not so much the separation itself (we all had to contend with separations, I thought grimly) as the *mood* of it.

*   *   *

It would be nice to be able to describe a scene in which the Prince and Principessa, their three daughters and sons-in-law, all met in a joyful reunion and, as Fiamma had long ago said to me of her parents' first reconciliation, 'lived happily ever after'. But as Steve said with a lopsided smile, 'Life ain't like that, buddy.'

He was, though, the first one to get anywhere near a fairy-tale ending.

Days passed in which I was detailed as a cipher officer at the Allied Civic Administration HQ piecing together reports from Allied units in contact with the enemy. From these it appeared that the situation was more or less static; but there were also hints that, over on the Adriatic sector, the Eighth Army was preparing a new offensive, and that in our sector the American IV Corps should be geared to match it in an all-out push against the main German defence line across Italy to the north of the River Foglia—the so-called 'Gothic Line'. It was a tedious job demanding a lot of concentration, broken hours, and no time off because reports could arrive at any time and had to be dealt with at once. But at long last I was off the hook and took my boredom to the Villa Marsina for a change of scene. At least it was noisy and lively and offered relief from depression and tortured thoughts. The so-called cabaret was pretty awful, but there was plenty of conversation of the off-duty kind with other men and women officers if you wanted it. I did not, particularly, not at first anyway. Later perhaps, when I had unwound a bit. For the moment I sat on a stool at the bar and watched the barman dealing with flurried officers who were trying to remember how many gins and tonic, how many pints of the thin sweet beer, and how many schnapps they needed for the table companions they had rashly invited to join in the round. The bar was tucked away in an alcove, which diminished the noise a bit, and after a couple of gins and tonic I felt more or less girded up for frivolity.

I was easing myself from my seat and putting a wad of small 'forces money' notes on the counter to pay for my drinks, when I felt soft fingers covering my eyes and heard a voice—soft as the fingers and familiar from the long-ago past.

'Guess who!'

Perhaps because Steve had mentioned her

504

forthcoming arrival my astonishment was the less. But I greeted Lella with real joy and held her at arm's length for a moment. It may have been my imagination, but the light of mischief in her eyes seemed brighter than even I remembered it.

'Ham, honey, you're the next best thing to m-a-a-m-a-a-a-n'—she chuckled at the parody of the Southern accent she had picked up in the States—'an' I just 'dore you.'

'Me too.' But I had to be careful. If things between her and Steve were getting straightened out there was no room for flirtation.

'Steve coming?' I asked casually.

'Sure. But you can keep a seat warm for him and hold my hand till he arrives. He's got some top brass conference.'

'Okay,' I said. 'I'll wait till he comes. Then I'll nip off and leave you two to fall into each other's arms. Meanwhile, what's the news?' She twirled the glass of Vermouth I ordered for her in her hand.

'Well, I got myself a posting out here when the Stars and Stripes business began to fall off. Same sort of job—at the Excelsior fixing leisure comforts for battle-weary officers.'

'There are plenty of those,' I said with a wry smile.

Suddenly her mood changed. The fleeting mischief slipped from her eyes and she became less the provocative, fun-loving girl I had known since before the war and more the serious-minded wife with a mission.

'I had to make some pretty tricky manoeuvres to get out here, Ham. Some of them I don't want to have to repeat.'

'Adjustments to army schedules?' I asked, raising

a casual eyebrow.

'You could call them that. I was due for a Pacific posting. But some of these big-boot generals are . . . well—'

'Easily led?' I suggested.

'Easily led,' she agreed. 'And in some funny directions.'

'Ah, the wiles of women,' I said with mock solemnity. 'What would we do without them in wartime?'

She was suddenly shocked. 'Oh, Ham!—I didn't mean *that*. I didn't go for secrets, sell them to the enemy, anything like that.'

'Of course not,' I reassured her. 'I was joking. You just wanted to fix it so that you rejoined Steve.' I squeezed her fingers. 'He's mentioned . . . well, the difficulties.'

'Darling Ham—you're like a tonic; or maybe I mean a comfort—like Mama when we were little, tucking us up and leaving a light on when we had nightmares.' She reverted to the nub of our conversation. 'Yes, there were difficulties, mainly my fault.' She put her empty glass down. 'I suppose we were too young to marry really, hadn't had our—what do you British call it?—our *fling*. But the war hastened everything up. Then separation. It was hard—oh, terribly hard to keep myself to myself. But I did, even though I was aching for love and . . . sex. You know?' Her eyes lit up with a hint of the old mischief. 'But there was only that once, in London . . . with you, darling Ham.' Her eyes met mine.

'That was comfort,' I said, 'like Mama leaving the light on to blow away the bogeyman. As you said yourself.'

'I know. Then when Steve told me he'd slipped up sex-wise as he called it—and so lightly, as if he expected me to take it as a matter of course—I was so hurt and angry I just didn't care any more. I felt free to be'—she hesitated.

'Your old fun-loving self?'

'Uh-huh. But it didn't last. I couldn't help feeling guilty—thoughts of Steve and his handicap and how different it made our love-making and whether it would be like that for always. They weren't nice thoughts. Ham; they were cynical and selfish and I deserved a good beating.' The smile suddenly lit her eyes again. 'But I managed to reform. Except...'

'Except for the big-booted general,' I completed the sentence for her.

'If I hadn't, I might never have seen Steve again.' She made a little gesture of resignation. 'Or you.'

There was an awkward pause. I knew what I wanted to say but I could not phrase it properly in my mind. In the end I botched it.

'There was ...' I began, and broke off. 'I think I ... it was me ... I ... well—'

Lella laughed merrily. 'You're like a schoolboy confessing to stealing the cookies. But I think I know what you're trying to tell me.'

I touched her hand. 'Not to *tell* you; I've done too much telling already. I should never have told Steve ... caused all that trouble. What I really want is to say I'm sorry. I really am.'

Her eyes glistened. 'I know you are, Ham. And I am too in a way. But in another way I'm not. Bringing it all out into the open has helped. There'll be a scar maybe; but only a little one.' She took a compact from her shoulder bag and dabbed her nose. 'And it won't show.'

At that moment Steve arrived. It may have been my imagination, but I thought his walk was less stilted; but then of course it would be. He was meeting Lella. 'I've kept the seat warm for you,' I greeted him cheerily. 'Have fun.'

'You betcha!'

CHAPTER THIRTY

It was typical of Access and his cat-and-mouse tricks that he should keep me hanging in suspense. I heard no more about Roz, or the Prince, for several days. I was fully occupied with routine work at the HQ. Most of it consisted of encoding and decoding and collating information from Intelligence reports and preparing 'situation maps' for the top brass in the operations rooms behind the façade of civic administration. I did the job conscientiously, recalling the rubric drummed into us at Catterick that 'the course of a battle can depend on a map reference'. But my heart was not in it. Once or twice I caught a glimpse of Steve in the warren-like corridors. He grinned broadly and gave me the thumbs-up sign, but we had no chance to gossip. His happiness delighted me, but envy gnawed at me too and I was beginning to feel very sorry for myself until I recalled Roz's admonition about self-pity. Yet even that could not entirely take the edge off my longing, always frustrated, to get at the truth—to get at so many truths—and find Fiamma and Ham Two.

Equally it was typical of Access that, when the

summons came, it had a whiff of melodrama about it. It landed on my desk in one of the pink inter-office envelopes used for confidential memos and was franked TOP SECRET. Inside I found a grubby scrap of paper that was actually the title page torn from a novel by Ruby M. Ayres, *One Woman Too Many*, and on the back was written in pencil *Be ready 0945 tomorrow in uniform repeat uniform. RV lobby Excelsior*. The Excelsior, with its partly restored grandeur to fit it for a leave-centre, was obviously the right rendezvous for meeting the Prince. But was there some grim significance in 'One Woman Too Many'? One could never tell with Access, whose humour, such as it was, veered between the schoolboyish and the outlandish. I knew it would be useless to contact him. He would only say: 'Wait and see, Painter; wait and bloody see.'

Which I did, seething with impatience, and sweating with a mixture of pleasure and anguish through the few hours of sleep I managed to grab.

By half past seven next morning I was ready. My uniform had been sponged and pressed by the hotel's valeting service and the sting of a close twice-over shave had been alleviated by a lime-smelling lotion provided 'with the compliments of the United States cosmetics industry'. I ordered a breakfast of hamburgers with scrambled eggs, waffles with maple syrup, and orange juice. Afterwards, I sat with assumed nonchalance smoking a cigarette reading *Il Messaggero*, which had the official war reports supplied by the Office of Information, together with pictures of cheery soldiers dipping ladles into dixies of tea, unloading blankets and kitbags from

509

three-ton lorries, and herding depressed German prisoners on to a train at the Termini station. But the main space was taken up by crudely drawn maps showing the advances in France, action shots of 'Supremo Ike' and his generals, and editorials criticising the Allied Occupation Forces in Italy for mishandling the food situation so that the citizens of Rome had to take to the black market. Adjoining pictures of the queues outside the Triangolo soup kitchen and the glittering scene inside the Ostaria dell'Orso, where wealthy Romans and top-echelon officers dined, were given the caption 'Gorging, Starving'. It was all very depressing but somehow remote from my feelings of anticipation.

Restlessly I rose and went into one of the lounges. There was a buzz of conversation but I avoided it and sat myself down in an armchair by an alcove of books stamped BOOKS FOR THE TROOPS FUND—LCC LIBRARIES. They were mostly paper-covered and *One Woman Too Many* with its title page ripped out was among them. I wondered if there were some coded message in the text—it would have been like Access to play a game of that sort—but there was nothing obvious. He was merely being juvenile.

I suppressed my impatience until 9.30. Then I made my way into the lobby where portraits of Roosevelt, Stalin, and Churchill stood on illuminated easels. They had been done by a skilful hack who had achieved photographic likenesses of the leaders but had little feeling for their characters. So much I noted with my painter's eye.

'Standing in judgement, eh, Painter?'

It was Access, dressed in his 'full canonicals'. I suppose I was expecting the Prince, and perhaps

Roz, to be with him; my disappointment must have been apparent.

'Patience, Painter.' He touched me on the shoulder with his swagger stick. 'It's a fact, I believe, that you're not even certain of the purpose of this'—a short laugh—'this masquerade.'

'No. But—'

'Good. The surprise will be all the greater, then. Follow me.'

Outside, a Humber limousine stood at the kerb. Its radiator carried a pennant but it was concealed inside a silk cover like a rolled umbrella. The chauffeur wore some sort of uniform and a peaked cap, and his companion, formally dressed in black coat and striped trousers, stood holding the door open and smiled in a dignified way as we took our seats. The door closed with the smallest of clicks.

'Grand, eh, Painter?'

'Very grand,' I confirmed. I knew he wanted me to question him but I refused to fall for the bait.

The footman—I can call him nothing less—had removed the cover from the pennant before taking his seat beside the chauffeur and I could see it now, fluttering in the breeze. It was silver and gold, emblazoned with crossed keys and the papal tiara.

'Ah,' said Access. 'You've spotted it, I see. The emblem of the papal state, Vatican City.'

'Don't tell me this is the Pope's car,' I said.

'The next best thing—the British Minister's. Know Sir D'Arcy, do you?'

'Me? Hardly likely. His Majesty's Minister to the Holy See moves in loftier circles than I do. I only know his name, Sir D'Arcy Osborne, and that he's vaguely related to Churchill.'

'Descendant of the Duke of Marlborough. Know

511

why we're in his car, do you?'

Drumming up respect for Access' rank, which I thought I had better do as we were both in uniform, I replied, 'No sir.'

'Because we're going to his flat, Painter; that's why. To meet your friend—no, father-in-law—the Prince.'

'I see, sir.' I knew it was useless to press the matter. 'I hope he's still my friend as well as my father-in-law.' But my eagerness got the better of me after all. 'Do you think he'll know anything about Fiamma?'

'We'll see, we'll see.'

Which was all I could get out of him.

*   *   *

We were moving down the Via del Tritone, and turning into the Corso Umberto. As we crossed the Ponte Cavour the dome of St Peter's loomed against a grey sky, vast in its magnificence. From whichever direction one approaches it, it takes the breath away.

We left the car and went up steps to enter the Vatican precincts along the Bernini colonnade. Beyond was the Sacristy and the square which contained the diplomats' residences. It was like entering another world. Nuns in veiled coifs trotted to and from a building which I learned later was the convent that also served as the commissariat where food was prepared for the residents, and the Swiss guards in their parti-coloured uniforms marched stiffly with their halberds glittering. They reminded me of nothing so much as the Beefeaters at the Tower of London.

512

'Just over a hundred acres of neutral country,' Access remarked as we climbed stairs to a luxuriously appointed flat. A butler dressed like the footman took our caps and canes and laid them on a walnut table next to a silver tray and a leather-bound visitors' book. The last signatures in the book, I noticed, were Giorgio Caeseri and Rosanna von Schill. My excitement, held in check in front of Access, mounted.

'This way, gentlemen,' the butler said. 'His Excellency has business at the Ritz, but if you will be kind enough to wait in the ante-room I will bring his other guests to you.'

'The Ritz?' I said, puzzled, when the butler had gone. 'It got a bomb months ago; it's been closed ever since.'

'Not *that* Ritz, you ass!' But Access closed one eye in a conspiratorial wink. 'The barracks where the Vatican Gendarmerie live. Known to all the escaped prisoners as the Ritz. They do pretty well there, it seems, with the Minister and the Yankee Chargé d'Affaires, Harold Tittmann, dishing out cash for their creature comforts.'

'The things that go on!' I said with feigned astonishment. I knew about the smuggling into the Vatican of escaped prisoners-of-war in the guise of tradesmen, clerics, and refuse collectors; in fact one of the partisans I had worked with was caught by the Germans while cutting telephone wires but escaped and worked his way to Rome and literally climbed over a wall into the Vatican, where he collapsed and was taken care of by one of the sisters of the convent. Like Switzerland, the Vatican was a hive of espionage, a local industry almost, and a strange haven where representatives of the warring

513

nations carried on a bland pretence of peace. Access had used the word 'masquerade' and it applied here too.

'Colonel! My dear Ham!' Prince Caeseri had entered the room silently like a grey shadow. A step behind him Roz, dark-haired, elegantly dressed in a cream silk frock that might have graced the pages of *Vogue*, stood smiling. Before I had time to do more than shake hands with the Prince and embrace Roz the butler padded in with a tray of fine china cups and saucers and a silver coffee pot. He was as dignified as Fawkes.

'His Excellency hopes you will accept refreshment. He feels sure you will find much to talk about until his return. He should not be long delayed. Coffee, Your Highness? Signora? Colonel? Captain?' He busied himself serving us and withdrew after indicating the bellpush that would summon him if needed.

There was a moment's silence. Then—

'Much to talk about!' I exploded. 'That must be the understatement of all time!' I could scarcely control my laughter.

'Hysterics, Painter,' Access put in, 'do not fit the situation.' He was acting my Commanding Officer now, hinting I was disgracing my uniform, that a note might go on my confidential file.

The Prince smiled gently. 'I must say I have some sympathy with—er—Captain Johns, Colonel.' Was there a hint of mockery in his tone, something of a royal reproach? 'After all, it is a long time since he and I met and ... went our various ways and family ties were—well, severed. And he is a family man as well as a soldier and a British agent.'

Access had the grace to look contrite. 'Sorry, sir.'

'Agent,' I echoed. 'Not much more than a carrier of messages.' My tone was perhaps a bit sour.

The Prince carefully put his coffee cup down. 'But *vital* messages, Ham. Or so I understand. There were other things too, well-known to the anti-Fascist fraternity—a supply train that failed to reach its destination, a factory that suddenly had its production halted when a mysterious explosion occurred. The exploits of your partisans have not gone unrecorded.'

I shrugged. '*Il Mago*. But there was nothing much magical about that. It was just passing on what I learnt in my own training. They took the risks, got caught sometimes and were tortured—even children, who were very good at letting the air out of tyres of German army vehicles.'

Roz shuddered. She was still beautiful, but the strain of her undercover work was beginning to show beneath the poised exterior. Once or twice her hands trembled and her coffee cup tinkled in its saucer. My mention of torture must have set off a train of thought in her mind. As if half-releasing pent-up reminiscence she told us how she had feared her Jewishness was a threat to Kurt and his family.

'His father's scientific work was more or less indispensable; but Kurt wasn't. He was just a German officer doing his duty; he didn't want to do any more. His heart wasn't in it.' (Kurt's own words!) 'And mine was with his. When the war actually started and the Gestapo began to show signs of furtive interest I knew I'd be more hindrance than help; so when Italy was in the war too, I made my way back. We had a pact, but the
515

parting was agony.'

'Don't I know it!' I said feelingly.

'I know. Poor Ham! But I was always able to put on an act—and Papa found it useful.'

She turned to the Prince, who was sitting with his legs crossed and his long fingers steepled together. Access had moved to a chair farther away from us, as if he were a watcher on the sidelines.

'Oh yes—most useful, indeed,' the Prince confirmed. 'There were so many organisations—anti-Fascist, anti-Communist, anti-government, anti-almost-anything-you-like-to-name, that I knew Roz could help me in my Royalist stance—and, paradoxically, with Mussolini over the Mafia—so I put her on my pay-roll at once.'

As Roz smiled ironically he added, 'Figure of speech—the pay-roll, that is. Not the service, I and my . . . associates . . . discovered a hidden talent in Roz. All little girls love pretending—to be mothers, nurses, brides; but when I look back I seem to recall that Roz was usually quite serious about it. Perhaps it was a talent she inherited from . . . her father. Her mother and I didn't encourage it. Probably I was a little jealous, her mother fearful she might end up a strolling player.'

'Yes,' I mused. 'I remember Fiamma telling me years ago that Roz had a secret side to her.' I could have added that her challenging sexuality was a mask for the personality she wanted to hide, but I did not. 'I replied that she would make a good spy.'

'It was a useful talent,' the Prince continued, 'for undercover work—spying if you like—is not much more than deceiving people. But of course a woman has the additional advantage of her . . . femininity.'

I felt a sudden surge of shock. The Prince smiled

516

blandly. 'No, no. Don't misunderstand me—'

'It wasn't necessary,' Roz put in, 'for me to sell my "favours" to the other side.' She seemed amused at the idea, not shocked like Lella had been. 'But I had a lot to do with money all the same. All those "anti" organisations Papa mentioned—they needed money. Not always for themselves, but for equipment. Your partisans, for instance: their explosives, their radio transmitters, their secret printing presses, their forgers' tools—they all had to be bought with *pourboires* and pay-offs to factory workers who had to look the other way or who risked arrest by smuggling out sticks of gelignite secured inside their trouser legs. And they in turn needed money for the black market—'

The Prince interrupted her. 'I don't think you have to tell Ham that even the lower reaches of war are an economic whirlpool.'

'But money has to come from somewhere,' Roz resumed, 'and the somewhere in this case was Switzerland. Papa had little difficulty in persuading the Papal Court and the diplomats appointed to the Holy See to give me *my* appointment as *courrier monétaire*, as they quaintly called it. Like the Red Cross ambulances, the Vatican vehicles are allowed free access across war zones to other neutral states. It's international law. At least, that's the theory. But they're always suspect—well, naturally; it's a privilege too easy to abuse. Even some Red Cross vehicles—and hospitals and neutral ships—get shot up sometimes.'

'You're telling me!' I put in.

'And as for suspected spies, short shrift! But I was a nun, you see, from the convent here, and I

517

carried a letter of authentication from the Holy Father. Also, a priest, Father Renato, travelled with me, though in another vehicle. He had a portable altar and he could hold Mass or serve the dying anywhere along our route, for any of the soldiers, whatever side they were on. Sometimes we had Americans and English and Italians and Germans all at the same Mass, at the roadside with planes and shells flying overhead. When the blessing had been said they melted away and went back to their fighting. At least, I suppose they did. What else could they do?'

'What else indeed,' I repeated. Everything she was saying was fascinating, but there were other things on my mind.

'I think I played my part pretty well. Make-up made me look older, and the habit and the wide-winged coif all helped. Even Mama didn't recognise me at first.'

'You mean—?' I began.

'Oh yes. She was still at Interlaken, staying in her friends' flat; and I was able to get there quite easily. Geneva was the Diplomatic base. And once you were there it wasn't hard to fix diversions. There were no restrictions on travel and the Swiss trains were as efficient as ever. It was like being in another world. I left the Papal Convoy, as it was formally called, in Father Renato's charge and went off on one of my missions—as they were *politely* called. I had contacts to make and messages to pass. Luckily an elderly nun in the robes of the Sisters of St Vincent de Paul—the convent down in the square there—doesn't attract much more than respectful glances. And the churches and confessional boxes are ideal places for posting information and anything small that clandestine operations might need. It was easy too to keep in touch with couriers returning to Germany. That way I could get my letters to Kurt posted in Lübeck. Misleading, deceptive!'

Access chuckled. 'I keep telling Ham that! A life of lies—that's what we lead!'

The Prince made a gesture of acceptance. 'What you say is true, Colonel. Even in my own sphere of operations there was a good deal of deception.'

I realised he was going to tell us what he had been doing in the war, and that I would have to wait still longer for any news he had about Fiamma and Ham. But as it was all part of Access' 'masquerade', I kept quiet.

★   ★   ★

The Prince's job was at the highest diplomatic level. His ranking as the equivalent of a British Privy Councillor stationed him midway between the king and the statesmen of the involved countries. Victor Emmanuel was in fact a thorn in the flesh of all parties. He had supported the Fascists by giving the premiership to Mussolini in 1922 and then repudiated them when the dictatorship had allied Hitler with Italy. And during the war he had become discredited and a target for the Communists. Hitler was indifferent to his fate so long as he kept out of the way, and Churchill had called him 'petulant and interfering and a damned nuisance'. The Prince had had the delicate task of trying to persuade him to abdicate.

'It was persuasion disguised as advice; and if that was deception I deceived even my own royalist loyalty; for it didn't work. His Majesty was obstinate, even when the Allies' invasion of Italy began. The best I could do was to get him away from Rome to Brindisi, where he was more or less happy studying the Roman antiquities. I remained his link with toppling figureheads—Mussolini, Badoglio, Ciano—and with the triumphant generals as they came and went; and, even more important, with Sir D'Arcy here. The British Minister to a neutral state is in a finely balanced position—juggling with peace and war, almost. He can smooth things or—what's that quaint phrase you have in English, Ham? Something about boats—?'

'Rock the boat?'

'That's it: rock the boat.' For a moment he seemed to be recollecting something agreeable. 'Yes. In those early days at Magari my wife used to call you all "Three Men in a Boat".' He passed a hand over his thick grey hair. 'But, as I was saying, Sir D'Arcy has many powers—among them, the power to legalise marriages.'

My face must have reflected my puzzlement; but my heart gave a leap.

'I understand,' the Prince continued with a smile, 'that you and Fiamma were married in somewhat ... well, shall we say "clandestine" circumstances; which fits the aura that surrounds us.'

My heart was really pumping now. If the Prince knew of our hospital marriage he could well know ... I was on the edge of my seat in my eagerness, my hands clenched over the arms of the chair. 'You mean, you know about Fiamma and me and what's happened to her and ...?'

'Calm down,' Access put in. 'I've told you before

520

about your tendency to fly off the handle.'

I ignored him. 'Fiamma—' I began again.

Access gave one of his sneering laughs. 'Works in the middle of the bush telegraph and doesn't realise what news buzzes along it!'

The Prince of course was much more gracious. He nodded consolingly. 'I understand your anxiety, Ham. And certainly we knew where Fiamma *was*: she was here in the Vatican, being cared for by the convent sisters after escaping from the Gauleiter and his Mafia bully boys—'

'You see, Ham,' Roz put in, 'they thought Fiamma was *me*.' I was about to interject, but Roz went on. 'Somewhere along the line my disguise as a nun had been penetrated and reported to the head of the SS here in Italy, General Wolff, and Colonel Kappler, who ran a branch of the Gestapo. They were after *me*.'

'It was partly my fault,' the Prince said. 'I'd heard from the friend of mine who lets his flat in the Via Lisbona to Fiamma that she was nursing at the field hospital at Cassino, and I suppose I mentioned it in general conversation somewhere. Unwise. There are always ears to the ground, devices on the telephone. You know, Ham, how one has to converse in a sort of nonsense language; but mine wasn't disguised enough.' He looked grave. 'But even if I'd guarded my conversation better there were those who had an interest in passing on information. Fiamma's ... er'—he snapped his fingers in annoyance, unable to capture the word he wanted. At last it came. 'Fiamma's *nursemaid*, that's it. Yes—'

'Signora Stefano!' I said with astonishment. 'But

she was an old darling—she simply adored Fiamma, and Ham Two.'

The Prince shrugged. I suddenly remembered the Signora's husband, the small birdlike Daniele and his remembering a cell meeting the day of Fiamma's disappearance from the flat. Perhaps the illusion of villainy I had sensed through the glass panel of the door had not been an illusion after all . . .

But my thoughts, my unimportant thoughts, and the conversation, were interrupted by the soft-footed appearance of the butler. 'Your Highness, His Excellency has returned and would be glad if you would join him in the drawing-room for drinks.'

★   ★   ★

Sir D'Arcy Osborne was a man of immense dignity and calm. If I had been asked to paint his portrait I would have been tempted to enclose him in a sort of nimbus to convey his tranquillity. But behind his gravity there was the echo of a smile, as if long ago he had heard a joke about something and still cherished it. At his feet was a small cairn terrier with a constantly wobbling tail, perhaps informing the company that anyone approved by his master was all right by him too. Whenever the Minister moved, the dog remained in the shadow of his feet. He stepped forward to greet me, his handshake dry and firm.

'Captain Johns, how do you do? I scarcely need to introduce myself to anyone else, but we, I think, have not met.'

He was a man to whom one could be nothing but

as courteous as he was. 'No, sir, I haven't had that pleasure.'

'No. But your—your exploits'—he invested the word with charm rather than heroism—'are well known to me, and indeed to a great many people who are appreciative of them.' His steely eyes wavered momentarily to a fine portrait of King George VI that dominated the chimney breast over the tiled surround of the fireplace. 'But of that more anon. We will enjoy an aperitif before we go into lunch, and then I hope we can discuss the things that are on all of our minds.'

CHAPTER THIRTY-ONE

The things on our minds! Another understatement? My own mind was writhing with questions. Access was not far wrong when he rebuked me for flying off the handle; I was having the utmost difficulty in controlling myself. For the Minister to turn to my 'exploits' when all I wanted was to continue listening to the Prince's story since it seemed to be leading to Fiamma, was frustrating in the extreme. But it was all part of a pattern—the pattern of my war life: half-smiles, veiled disclosures, hints, betrayals, gains, losses, jagged edges everywhere ... and here we were drinking cocktails in the pleasant drawing-room of an ambassador to a neutral state in the very heart of a world war! Was there ever anything so crazy? Somewhere Somerset Maugham says that life is a mass of untied ends, nothing like novels at all; and at that moment I completely agreed with him. Maugham had worked in the secret service during the 1914 war and, if his experiences were anything like mine, I thought harshly, he had every reason for saying it.

But with men of my upbringing conventional behaviour tends to take over even in the most bizarre circumstances. I remembered Geordie's comical parody—'British officers don't rest in the midst of battle'. And of course I behaved conventionally now, looking at myself mockingly from the outside, so to speak, standing and accepting a drink in a fine crystal glass, like an actor in a Noël Coward comedy.

We circulated, the butler discreetly hovering, keeping his eye on our drinks. The conversation was small talk, reminding me of peace-time occasions when my parents had guests for dinner and the pre-prandial murmurings were of the weather, holidays, and the merits of this or that prep school.

'Any minute now,' I remarked to Access, 'someone's going to say the evenings are drawing in. No wonder Somerset Maugham said life's full of loose ends.'

'Maugham?' He expressed momentary interest. 'Knew him slightly in the Kaiser's war. Another thing he said was that an agent's work is monotonous, a lot of it bloody useless.'

'Amen to that,' I said, holding out my glass for a refill of gindiano.

*   *   *

Strangely once we were seated around the gleaming walnut table with its place-settings of fine china and crystal and crested silver cutlery, my depression and exasperation seemed to wear off. Sir D'Arcy had placed Roz on his left and the Prince on his right, with Access next to the Prince and myself beside Roz. The butler withdrew after quietly assuring the Minister, 'Everything is to hand, Your Excellency.'

The meal was buffet style, with a cold collation on silver platters spread over a damask cloth covering the sideboard. Consommé gelé, cold poached salmon, salads, fingers of thin toast spread with caviare ('From our Russian friends,' the Minister smiled), wild strawberries that reminded me of those that grew in the untamed part of the garden at Magari, Roquefort and Gorgonzola cheeses, and celery in tall glasses. The corks had been discreetly drawn from bottles of Laurent-Perrier champagne. It was all very English upper crust; and it was typical of Access to be vulgar about it.

'Come and get your rations, Painter, Good-o!'

Overhearing him, Sir D'Arcy said with exquisite courtesy, 'Rather better than the Army Catering Corps can provide, perhaps, Colonel. But then, their facilities are rather more restricted.'

When we were seated Sir D'Arcy raised his glass. 'To a successful outcome.' Outcome of what?, I thought rather irritably; but I could tell there was no diverting the man from his planned path. As though to confirm this he went on: 'It has always seemed to me sensible to take first things first. My dog has the same idea.' He spooned a little of his consommé into a bowl and put it on the floor. There was an answering thump of tail.

The Prince smiled gravely, Access more vehemently. 'Of course, Minister.'

'Yes. Well, I think that as Captain Johns and

Frau von Schill are rather less informed than'—a nod towards the Prince and Access—'the others of us, I may as well follow the King's advice to the White Rabbit and begin at the beginning.'

The beginning—so far as concerned whatever the Minister was leading up to—was Churchill's, indeed Britain's, reluctance to treat Rome as an open city. He quoted Anthony Eden as saying that 'The British have as much right to bomb Rome as the Italians had to bomb London . . . and we should not hesitate to do so . . . if the course of the war should render such bombing convenient and helpful.'

'Signor Mussolini,' Sir D'Arcy said with a tiny smile as he took a sip of champagne, 'declared that we British were a race of brigands who had brutalised a quarter of the human race.' He paused and set down his glass. 'No doubt suitable retaliatory replies could have been made and probably were. But a constant stream of appeals went forth from the Vatican via Geneva. The Holy Father pointed out to Mr Churchill and President Roosevelt that Rome belongs to the world, to all mankind, and not to Italy alone. But the replies were always the same: military expediency must come first. The Germans had to be driven from Rome, and if their communications and military installations had to be bombed in the process—'

'I know,' I said. 'C'est la guerre.'

'The universal answer,' Roz put in with a smile. 'But I must say I felt rather important when some of those appeals from the Holy Father were given to me to carry. Me!'

Sir D'Arcy looked slightly put out by the interruption; but he continued with an acknowledging nod to Roz, 'You were indeed important, my dear. But in the event the Eternal City turned out to be as vulnerable to the exigencies of war as London or any other capital in the path of bombs. Six of them fell here in the Vatican—oh yes, our tranquillity was—er—disturbed. They were small bombs, but they damaged some precious relics in the tombs near Santa Marta. Air Chief Marshal Tedder is said to have wired General Alexander, "Sorry to say some of the early Popes went airborne this morning."'

'Jolly good!' Access roared; then, seeing the Minister's eyebrows rise he added apologetically, 'I mean the joke of course, sir, not the . . . violation of the tombs.'

'I'm sure.' A few flakes of salmon were put on a saucer and lowered to the dog. 'But your observation is timely, Colonel; because it is of the preservation of precious things that I'm concerned to inform, particularly, Captain Johns.'

'If you mean the Arts Commission, sir,' I responded, 'I do know about that. Colonel Dansey was the first to tell me; and since then I've been in touch with Mr Bernard Berenson, Signor Umberto—'

'Yes, yes,' the Minister interrupted, a trifle impatiently, 'we know about that, and about your abortive visit to General Baade.' He smiled as he spooned lobster sauce on to his plate. 'In fact the whole plot was hatched here after a great deal of regrettable reluctance on the Allies' part. The same argument over and over again—military expediency. So long as the Germans kept a foothold in Rome the city was a military target. We know the result—five thousand civilian deaths, some irreparable damage. President Roosevelt kept assuring us that he was committed to a policy of avoiding damage to religious shrines and historical monuments to the extent possible in modern warfare. Then he put the onus on His Holiness to persuade the Germans to withdraw so that bombing could cease. An impossible task. The Pope himself was in danger—the threat of a plot to abduct him and deport him to Germany, which Hitler and Mussolini hatched, had never really been removed; and perhaps for that very reason he wanted to set the scheme rolling. I enlisted Prince Caeseri's help, and the King, Baron von Weizäcker, the German Ambassador, and Mr Tittmann all joined me for a meeting in the Pope's private library. We drafted an agreement. Rome had been violated and we wanted to prevent the same thing happening to Florence—' he paused and looked from Access to me—'with results you know.'

'Only too well, sir,' I replied. 'General Baade also put military needs first. He did promise, though, that there would be no *unnecessary* destruction.'

The Minister nodded. 'But the situation has changed. I scarcely need to tell you the disposition of the enemy forces.'

True, of course. For days I had been collecting and collating Intelligence reports in the Operations room. Kesselring's forces were making a desperate fight to hold ground north of Florence before withdrawing to their well-prepared Gothic Line. Our strategy for misleading them into thinking we were stronger south of the Arno than we were had evidently failed. Interrogation of prisoners now revealed that there was a possibility—even a probability—of their planning a counter-attack to

528

regain Florence. It was this that had created a crisis for the Allied army chiefs. With Kesselring aware of our forces' thinness on the ground some deception had to be planned to change his mind about the counter-attack. It was to discuss this that Access and I had been summoned.

'These concerns are not really mine,' Sir D'Arcy continued, 'but as a diplomat your chief in London—C, I believe you call him—has asked me to play what part I can in linking together what he calls "the component parts of an infernal machine". One of them has still to join us—a prisoner-of-war whose release from the Gendarmerie barracks I was able to arrange this morning. It was a matter of confirming his identity—a simple one since his father was on hand.'

The Prince smiled and acknowledged his host as more champagne was poured into his glass; then he looked at me and smiled again at what I guess was my open-mouthed astonishment.

'Yes, it was Vanni. He had been caught by the Germans, a spy who had got into their headquarters as a waiter. There was the threat of Gestapo torture to discover what he knew, and, of course, death or the concentration camp. But he managed to escape with the aid of some partisan friends—I don't know the details.'

'I thought the partisans had been disbanded by General Clark,' I said in surprise.

'No doubt,' the Prince replied, 'but disbandment in theory and in practice are two different things. A party of them ambushed the car in which Vanni was being taken to the interrogation centre, and he managed to remain in hiding until the Allies had fought their way into that area, and then make his way here. But the Gendarmerie were not going to take any risks by releasing a man who merely *said* he was the son of Prince Giorgio Caeseri. Happily,' he smiled, 'I was able to confirm his story!'

*   *   *

Pleading that he had 'diplomatic business' with the Prince and Colonel Dansey in the afternoon, the Minister sent Roz, Vanni and me back to the Excelsior in his limousine. Vanni had joined us at the cheese stage and more champagne was opened. He looked shrunken inside his clothes, as if he had been ill for a long time; and he had the furtive look of all hunted men.

Access gave a gloating grin as we left the Minister's flat. 'Jigsaw coming together, eh, Painter?'

'No, it isn't,' I snarled back. '*Sir.*'

'It will, Painter; it will.' He nodded towards Vanni and Roz who were halfway down the stairs. 'You've got the right companions. See you later.'

'Sir,' I said. My impatience was giving way to resignation. If there was a conspiracy to keep news of Fiamma from me I had to fight it calmly. Of course there was no conspiracy, but my anxiety increased as each curtain seemed to be partially lifted and then dropped down again tantalisingly at the point of revelation.

I too was halfway down the stairs when he called a parting shot: 'And get out of that uniform and into something sensible. There will be work for you to do before long.'

'I never doubted it,' I retorted.

'Kurt should never really have been a soldier,' Vanni remarked. 'He's not the type.'

I nodded agreement. We were in my bedroom at the Excelsior. The rooms had been partitioned in order to double the accommodation and there was not a lot of space. Vanni was lounging on the bed, his hands behind his head; Roz was in the Lloyd Loom basket chair, and I perched on the dressing-table stool. Its mirror had sustained a crack from some nearby bomb explosion.

'We weren't warlike types—Steve, and Kurt, and I. We just wanted to enjoy the world, and use what talents we had. God! How innocent we were!'

'Me too,' Vanni replied. 'I volunteered for the army, thought of myself as a dashing warrior, the idol of all the girls. I hadn't bargained for the filth, the cruelty, the—' He broke off. 'Well, you know my story. So, when *this* war caught up with me I opted for the undercover stuff. Cowardly, you call it—keeping out of the shot and shell—in theory anyway.'

'I don't know that I've ever found it particularly lacking in danger,' I said mildly.

'Touché!' Vanni eased himself up, swung his legs to the floor and lit a cigarillo. 'I wasn't meaning to belittle your exploits, my dear Johns. I meant—' He stopped. I could not tell whether he was weary, embarrassed, or fearful there was a listener the other side of the partition. But I was able to reassure him: I had noticed the room was empty as we came by.

He smiled wanly. 'No, it wasn't so much that, though I know what you mean about the feeling of

531

being watched, overheard. No: rather, it was—well, guilt, I suppose.'

'I don't follow. You were leading up to something.'

'Yes. But guilt got in the way.' He looked shame-faced.

'Guilt about *what*, for God's sake?' I shouted. 'Why the hell can't you, can't everyone, stop talking in riddles? I'm on edge enough over Fiamma, over my work, over the pains in my arm, over whether I shall ever be able to paint again, over every bloody thing, and you start blethering on about guilt—' I got up, stumbling over the stool as I did so, and felt myself losing control, sweat trickling down my back and into my eyes. I had not realised just how much on edge I was. But now Roz stood up, clasped me to her—a surrogate sister, even a surrogate wife; I felt her warmth, her comfort, her sympathy. For a second or two waves of intimacy passed between us. I could believe, I almost did believe, that for those few seconds Fiamma's arms were around me. Roz took the handkerchief from my sleeve and dabbed my forehead with it. I kissed her in response. It was a delicious kiss—firm, friendly, even sensual. But not Fiamma's.

Across Roz's shoulder I could see Vanni, full-length on the bed again now, his eyes closed, the nearest he could get to withdrawing himself from the intimate little scene he had brought about.

'Thank you, Roz,' I said, giving her an affectionate embrace. 'You are a wonderful comfort—like your Mama leaving the light on when you were little.'

She looked at me quizzically. 'You knew that?
532

Oh, of course, Fiamma will have told you.'

'No, not Fiamma: Lella.' I was calm again now, my sense of proportion in its right place. I said, almost facetiously, 'All the daughters of the Prince have come to my aid in time of trouble—Fiamma when I was in need of repairs, Lella when I was reacting to bomb-shock, you when I am feeling so desperate and frustrated.'

She was suddenly serious, almost reproachful, as she held me at arms' length. I caught the glint in her eye.

'I know,' I said. 'Cardinal sin: feeling sorry for myself. You've told me before.'

She turned away, smiling now. 'Well, you're not the only one feeling frustrated.'

Nor was I. Roz, too, had lost contact with Fiamma while she was being cared for by the convent sisters. 'But you did see her?' I asked anxiously.

'Oh yes, I saw her. She was sleeping the sleep of utter exhaustion and so, of course, when the sisters said she shouldn't be wakened, I agreed. Apparently she'd sought refuge, the guards at the check-point passing her through because she was in nurse's uniform; then she collapsed as she was crossing the square, and was taken in unconscious.'

'Not injured?' The mere idea turned my lips dry and the palms of my hands sweaty. But no, Roz assured me, the sisters had said nothing about any injury and there had been no sign—it was just exhaustion, and perhaps malnutrition. After that single sight of Fiamma, Roz had been assigned to one of her *courrier monétaire* journeys and was away for over a fortnight while the Prince was down in Brindisi with the King, trying to prevent him from

533

'rocking' the diplomatic boat. So it was simply a matter of logistics that neither he nor Roz were around while Fiamma was recovering. And when Roz eventually returned Fiamma had gone.

'Gone?' I said. The tension was making me clench my hands. '*Gone?* Just like that—*gone!*'

But no, it was not that she had just disappeared, vanished into thin air. So far as the sisters could make clear—and Fiamma herself was hazy with weakness—she had returned to wherever she had come from, saying something about 'the villa by the sea'.

Forte dei Marmi!

Every other thought flew from my head. I must get there! I decided to keep my uniform on, for everyone in civvies in the Allied liberation area was subjected to spot checks at road blocks and railway stations, and although I had my Emilio Bardi identity papers and other documents that would clear me, I did not want to risk any delays. The uniform would clear me, anywhere this side of the actual fighting line. And that was north of Florence, three hundred kilometres away.

My excitement of course was obvious. This was something positive! Action I could take! Within a few seconds my gloomy frustration had turned into overwhelming joy—but it was joy spiked with fear. Who was holding Ham Two? Why had Fiamma left him? The first question had only one answer: enemies—though into which category they fell was impossible to tell. The second had alternative answers: either she had been forced, which seemed unlikely if she had managed to get to Rome; or she had left the boy happy with someone she knew. Signora Stefano? But had the Prince not suggested

534

she was linked with the Mafia? Or had I just assumed that myself? My mind was in a whirl, in turmoil, I could see nothing clearly except that I must get to Forte dei Marmi. I made for the door, muttering excuses, but suddenly Vanni was on his feet and shouting.

'Hey! Hold on, I haven't yet said what I came to tell you—haven't had a chance with all that lovey-dovey going on between you and Roz—'

'To hell with it!' I cried. 'I don't want to know. I'm on my way to Fiamma!' I flung the door open.

Framed in the doorway stood Access.

'Not so fast, Painter. You're not going anywhere except where I send you—and that is not to find your lady love. And get that uniform off, as I ordered you. There's a job to be done and it comes under the heading of duty, not love. Get me?'

CHAPTER THIRTY-TWO

Outwardly I managed to retain my composure; but inwardly I crumpled, a mass of conflicting emotions.

Access came on belligerently, with that half-grin that showed how he enjoyed baiting me.

'Told you I'd see you later, Painter,' he smirked. 'And here I am. Enlightened you, have they?' He nodded towards Roz and Vanni.

'Vanni was telling me about his guilt and Roz was telling about my wife,' I said flatly, 'and then you burst in.'

'And you tried to burst out.' He was suddenly apologetic—or what with him passed for apologetic.

'Sorry about that, Painter. But something's come up. That was the diplomatic business HQ was on about. He's been on the phone via Geneva to London and confirmed what I suggested to him: C wants you to do the job. You and these two between you'—he waved a hand at Roz and Vanni—'but you will direct operations.' He smiled the satisfied smile of a producer who has at last assembled the cast for a play. 'No, no,' he continued as he saw my anger, 'calm yourself. Don't want you flying off the handle twice in one day. You'll do yourself a mischief.'

I realised at that moment that, when I opened the door to find Access standing there, my instinct had been to hit him, to give him a knockout blow, like the hero of some *Boy's Own Paper* story. But it is strange how, at emotional moments, problems seem to sort themselves out—or perhaps we just imagine they do. It is a bit like making love: the excitement and tremendous build-up of energy give way to warm lethargy, a peace in which nothing seems to matter; you are in a cocoon where you have been purged of anxiety, and the problems melt away. In my mind the conflict had been straightforward— Access had even used the right words: 'love', 'duty'. And his call to arms had won.

'Let's get down to it,' I said—calmly now.

'Right.' Access was eyeing me piercingly. Had he understood my treacherous thought? I hardly think so; I had scarcely been aware of it myself. 'Brass tacks. The enemy counter-attack on Florence is now a certainty—not a probability, or a possibility, but a certainty.'

'I'm not surprised,' I said. 'It was always pretty dicey trying to fool them we were strong south of the Arno.'

'Wait a minute,' Vanni put in suddenly, 'I'm not sure that was the reason. Remember, I was at Kesselring's HQ, and Kurt—well, Kurt and I became good friends. He more or less adopted me as his personal waiter in the HQ mess and used me as a messenger sometimes; and of course he was at all the planning sessions with the Field-Marshal and the divisional commanders; so he knew what was going on.'

'And a lot of it leaked out,' Access said with a nod in my direction. 'As we know, since Painter collected some of it.'

A nod from Vanni. 'Strange business, treachery. Makes you feel uncomfortable, guilty.'

'But you were helping Italy, not betraying her,' I protested.

'*I* was, yes; but aiding and abetting Kurt—some of the guilt rubs off—' He shrugged, as if inwardly resolving a conflict. 'But as I said, Kurt isn't a natural soldier. He was sick of the war, he wanted to get away, just as I did that day in Catalonia when I saw the looting going on. And he *is* opting out.'

I could not believe it—Kurt a traitor? No, he had always said he was a good German but not a good soldier, true. But a traitor? Of course he did help Fiamma and Ham, but that was hardly betrayal.

Access interrupted. 'Shocked, eh, Painter? No matter; traitors have their uses—to the other side. In this case, us.'

I turned round, saw my face in the dressing-table mirror, white, stricken.

'Then the opportunity came,' Vanni continued. 'Kesselring was ordered to Hitler's headquarters— "Wolf's Lair" they call it—in the forest of Rastenburg in East Prussia. The Führer was mad

537

because, over on the Adriatic sector, Leese's Eighth Army had caught them on the hop and crossed two rivers, the Metauro and the Foglia, in a big push towards the Gothic Line, and Kesselring had had to transfer the best part of a division from the Gothic Line north of Florence. Mad! Hitler was in one of his violent rages, shouting and banging his fist on the table and demanding a new strategy, including the recapture of Florence. When Kesselring returned, Kurt was at the briefing. Kesselring was so depressed he was almost ready to resign his command. But the Führer ordered him to bring the division back from the Adriatic side and use it to attack Florence—a tactical manoeuvre Kesselring knew was crazy. Not only that, he had been persuaded by General Baade that honouring the agreement to leave the city virtually untouched would be a moral victory.'

Access chortled. 'What the hell do the Boche care for moral victories? Sod all!' He gave a half-apologetic nod toward Roz. 'We're only rough soldiers, my dear. Forgive us our trespasses, eh?'

Roz nodded and rose, straightening her dress which had revealed a lot of well-shaped thigh as she sat in the basket chair. 'I must go and make some arrangements here if I'm to be involved in this ... job. It shouldn't be difficult. After all, Lella's more or less running the place. And I know what Vanni's going to tell you.'

'Classy piece,' Access said, as Roz closed the door behind her.

'What do you expect?' I said. 'The daughter of a Prince.'

Access merely guffawed.

Then: 'Carry on, Vanni.'

'Yes, well, as I was saying—the time came for Kurt to make up his mind when he knew that Florence was going to be attacked. He could not forgive his own countrymen for destroying one of the most beautiful cities in the world.'

I nodded seriously. 'It is that to all three of us—Steve and Kurt, and me.'

Access for once had the grace not to chip in with one of his scornful asides.

'Yes, I can imagine.' Vanni paused as if collecting his thoughts. 'But Kurt didn't see what he planned to do as real treachery. It would save lives as well as save Florence. He made photocopies of all the documents relating to the counter-attack—movement orders, map references, everything. Then he smuggled the copies to me with instructions to get them to Rome, knowing that if the Allies had the information they could plan in advance—counter the counter-attack, so to speak.'

'But you got caught?'

'I got caught,' he repeated derisively. 'I forged a pass to get me past the guards; but I didn't forge it well enough. I was arrested and found myself on the way to Gestapo HQ. I hadn't been searched—that was a job for the specialists—but I knew that, if the papers were found on me, they'd be traced back to Kurt, and he'd be arrested too. I was trying to think of some way to get rid of them before we got to Lucca. The best I thought of was to plead I needed to crap and use the paper that way. But the two camp police, who were guarding me with Schmeisers, just laughed and said they'd put up with the stink if I shat myself.'

Vanni paused and lit a cigarillo, an echo of the strain he had felt still lingering in his eyes.

539

'There had been a lot of fighting around Lucca, still was, with the Americans partly in occupation of the town. But fate took a hand—offered it to me almost. A funny thing, but that vehicle we were travelling in had a lot to do with it. It was one of those old Daimler-Benz five-tonners, lightly armoured but bulletproof and used before the war for carrying bullion. In the war they were used by German fitters going to the aid of broken-down tanks, and the structure had been weakened by dividing the inside into compartments for storing spares. So ... The roads had been heavily mined as the Germans fought their way out and we struck one of their Tellermines as we tried to avoid a shell hole; it had been cunningly placed and it blew the back off the truck and the door with it. The guards were just blackened corpses like branches of burnt wood; but I was forward, just behind the driver, and he and I were no more than hurled to the floor with the blast—bruised and covered in muck but miraculously surviving, though God knows how long it took us to come round. When we did, I saw him looking at me and trying to gather his senses together enough to make a lunge at me. Quickly I bashed my boot into his skull. I heard some bones crack but I don't know if I killed him.' Vanni gave a twisted grin. 'I didn't wait to see.' The grin resolved itself into a look of self-loathing. 'Strange how anyone who is sickened by the brutalities of the battlefield can indulge in such—inhuman acts. Not that it was the first time; and I don't suppose it will be the last.' He shrugged.

'In the last resort—animal instinct—self-preservation,' I mumbled.

Access interrupted, on cue. 'Quite the philosopher, this Painter.' He cleared his throat. 'Well, it's obvious you escaped, presumably with the help of the Yanks?'

Vanni completed his story. He laid low until dark, recovering and waiting for the ringing in his ears caused by the blast to die away. A lot of shelling was going on and a nearby village was on fire. He could just make out an orchard with the trunks of shell-blasted trees sticking up like spikes. He made his way to an out-building where a farmer and his wife were sheltering. They had escaped from the village just before their roof fell in. All the farmer said was, 'What are you doing here?' He was beyond being surprised by anything. His family had been arrested for helping Allied prisoners and only he and his wife were left. After a moment, still dazed, he asked, 'How did you get here?'

'*Mago*!' Vanni said.

'The word acted like magic itself,' he went on. 'They thought I was you! "*Il Mago*!" Even when I explained that I wasn't "*Il Mago*" but did know him they couldn't do enough for me. They knew roughly where the partisans had an outpost in Lucca and told me how to get to it without getting entangled with retreating Germans. After that—well, it was straightforward.'

'Except the counter-attack order,' Access said ominously. His voice was rasping, a danger signal. 'It's useless now. Obviously when Vanni was arrested the news would have got back to Von Schill and he must have thought the document had been discovered, and he was for the high jump, a Court Martial—only there'd be some painful extraction of information first.' He made a mime of pincers and fingernails.

541

I shuddered. Kurt, whose hands were made for music ... 'So now—?' I said faintly.

Access groaned. 'What now? Think about it, Painter; think about it, for Christ's sake. There's Von Schill at the heart of the German planning headquarters, not knowing whether we, the Allies—the enemy to him—have got the counter-attack order or not. He can't say anything without revealing his own treachery; and he's sick of the war and anyway feels in his bones that the Boche has lost.' He turned to Vanni. 'Didn't he say so to you?'

'Many times. The signs are clear enough. Over on the Eastern Front the Russkies are winning; and after only three months of the Second Front Hitler's best armies are being forced back across France to the German frontier. Where's the sense in going on? Unless you're a born-and-bred soldier, which Kurt isn't. So what does he do? He does what I did—he walks out. With a price on his head.'

I was stunned, confused. 'But you can't *know* this,' I protested, 'I mean, about Kurt ... deserting.'

Access snorted. 'We can and *do*. The Vatican, Painter, is like a bloody colander—full of leaks.' He laughed at his own feeble joke. 'Wolff, the SS man who liaises between Kesselring and the Vatican, gets the message and drops a hint to Kappler, who's king of the Gestapo here. Then the German Ambassador goes to a party at the Portuguese Embassy and the waiters serving the drinks overheard threads of conversation and join 'em together. Know what I mean?'

'If Johns doesn't, I certainly do', interposed

542

Vanni. 'At Kesselring's HQ I gave the impression I was deaf or stupid. Very useful. Not that it saved me in the end. I really *was* being stupid then, forging a pass in so much of a hurry.' He stubbed out his cigarillo. 'We live and learn.'

'So we know,' Access continued. 'And that's where the job comes in. Work out your own method. Use him'—a nod at Vanni—'and the girl if you want, if they can help. But get Von Schill; and bring him back here. I told you, traitors have their uses. As hostages maybe; or sources of information that can be—ha!—coaxed out. Maybe his wife *can* help, eh, Painter?'

For a moment I tried to absorb all that had been said and half said. I was far from certain of my mission—even more uncertain than when I was detailed with Steve to go to Baade. And I hated the idea that Kurt was a deserter even more than my orders to go and apprehend him.

I said with forced sarcasm, 'I gather I'm supposed to comb Italy for Kurt von Schill, arrest him, and bring him back?'

Access snapped his fingers. 'That's it, Painter!' He beamed like an indulgent father.

'And have you a clue where I start looking?' I asked.

Casually he replied, 'Oh, didn't I mention it? Sorry, Painter. Must be getting feeble-minded in my old age. Ha! Yes, well the last reliable information we had was that he's in Florence. *Florence*, Painter! It shouldn't be much of a task to winkle him out from there, now, should it?'

★　　★　　★

543

I had to make some sort of plan. It was all very well for Access to say that if the field was narrowed down to Florence it would not be difficult to winkle Kurt out. To me it sounded well-nigh impossible. In any case it was only 'the last information' Access had had, and it was not necessarily reliable. Where, whom, had it come from? The more I thought about it the more I thought about wild-goose chases and needles in haystacks. But I had to do it. Both friendship and duty demanded it.

There was no point in taking Vanni. He was ill and exhausted, and no doubt still on the 'wanted' list of the Gestapo. He was safest and best looked after in the 'Ritz' gendarmerie.

But with Roz it was different. She could help—I felt sure of that, though I could not figure out what her role might be until she reminded me reproachfully that, after all, Kurt was her husband and she longed to see him and was that not a good enough reason?

'Don't forget, Ham, you and Fiamma weren't the only two who fell in love in Settignano and haunted Florence.'

Which was true of course. All lovers are selfish in the way they imagine their awakening love to be exclusive, shared by no one else. Enraptured with each other, they cocoon themselves in their rapture and give only the briefest thoughts to the raptures of even their closest friends. And so it had been with us three boys and the daughter of the Prince. Our shared days at Magari, swimming in the Indian pool or drinking aperitifs on the terrace with the Prince and Principessa, were a delight; but what, for Kurt and Roz, and Steve and Lella, had been the equivalent of the matchless days Fiamma and I spent in Umberto's studio when we vowed our love and gloried in each other's bodies until exhaustion and sleep overtook us? What, for them, matched our bubbling delight as we sought luck by rubbing the golden snout of the boar in the Porcellino market or giggled at the solemn tourists queueing to see the masterpieces in the Pitti Palace? These were intimacies not to be shared with us any more than ours were with them.

Roz interrupted my thoughts. Her eyes were brimming.

'Oh Ham! A marriage of desolation—that's what ours has been! I know it's the same for thousands in this war, but knowing about others' heartaches doesn't make your own any less.'

I conjured up a look of stern reproach. 'And what about self-pity, that cardinal sin?' I reminded her.

She smiled weakly, brushing the tears away. 'I know. Father Renato used to hear my confessions many times when we were on the road with the Vatican convoy. He was harsh and gave me severe penances for the good of my soul. But I think he understood. He knew there was a lot more worldly love about than the spiritual kind.'

'Sensible man,' I said.

Then it struck me how Roz *could* help: if Kurt was 'on the run' he would seek hideaways he could be sure of—which was partly why he was making for Florence. Like Vanni seeking refuge at Forte dei Marmi he would make for the familiar—some house where he was known and no questions asked. As I knew only too well, Resistance personnel and undercover men like myself relied on such 'safe houses' and 'drops'. And who would be more likely to know such a house in Florence than Roz—some place that also had romantic associations to which Kurt might return?

When I tactfully asked she looked puzzled at first. 'Oh yes. You had your studio where you painted "The Blue Nude"; and we—well, we had our favourite cinema where there were armchair seats to hold pairs, proper love-seats, and discreet usherettes who never showed more than one couple into the same row if you went in the afternoon when the audience was thin. And there were little trattorias where they knew that lovers wanted to be in quiet corners—we spent hours in them lingering over two cappuccinos; or we went up to the Fiesole hillside where there's a half-circle of those old stone benches arranged like in a Greek theatre. Terribly uncomfortable, but who minded? And when we'd made love we looked out over the valley spread out below and the mountains in the background. It was heavenly, we felt we were the only two people in the world.'

'As if you've never been alive before,' pausing and smiling as I matched it in my memory.

'That's it.'

I hesitated before jolting us both out of our memories. These were not places Kurt would return to as a refuge. Was there anywhere, I asked, more sheltered, more solitary, with people he could trust and with no questions asked?

It was Roz's turn to hesitate. Her dark hair fell across her cheek as she pondered. I was not sure whether she was reluctant to tell me or whether her memory failed. Or was this just the secretive Roz playing another part? But she answered that question without my having to put it.

'There *was* another place, Ham. I didn't mention

it because it's sort of … sacred. We made a pact we'd keep it to ourselves—not that there was anything dramatic or top-secret about it. It was just that—' She frowned in puzzlement and I could see a fleeting likeness to Fiamma when she found the strain of modelling a bit too much and I had thoughtlessly been engrossed in wielding my palette-knife without realising she needed to rest.

'I know,' I responded. 'Something like a treasured souvenir that you keep in a locked box, like Victorian ladies used to keep a locket with a loved-one's hair.'

Now Roz's frown changed to a look of astonishment. 'How did you guess?'

I shrugged. 'I didn't really guess. I was imagining myself in your place.'

'But it's exactly right, Ham. Well, *almost* like in that game "Animal, Vegetable and Mineral" we used to play as children and you got within an ace of the object … it's like second sight, or whatever they call it!'

'I haven't got that. I wish I had,' I said ruefully, though I could not help remembering how, on reaching the top of Casino and the shattered monastery, I had been certain I would meet Kurt among the ruins.

She went on to tell me how in the spring before the war she and Kurt had taken the No. 9 trolley-bus and gone on what they called an 'expedition' to Florence.

'Kurt was in a lavish mood. He'd had his first cheque for a recital he'd given on the radio and he wanted to celebrate. We had a fabulously expensive lunch at the Baglioni Roof Garden and afterwards we went window-shopping in the Via Tornabuoni and on the Ponte Vecchio—you know?'

I nodded. How could I forget that night after Steve's wedding party when Roz and I had comforted each other and watched the sunset-flecked Arno framed in the space between the shops on the bridge? And it was into one of those shops that Kurt had led her.

'Almost as if it was destined we should go there. Kurt wanted to buy me what he called "some token"—nothing as elaborate as an engagement ring, which he thought would be much too grand and formal; and we didn't yet feel that way about each other. It was much simpler—more like one of those boy-and-girl romances we'd seen curled in our love-seat in the cinema, I can't explain better than that.'

I understood completely. 'Just one of those *magical* days.'

She nodded, closing her eyes as if recalling it all. Then she touched my hand affectionately. 'Dear Ham! You are *the* most understanding man. I'm sure I couldn't explain all this to anyone else in the world.'

In the shop, which sold *gingilli*—trinkets—rather than elaborate and expensive jewellery, the shopkeeper had welcomed them with old-world courtesy and then had looked at Kurt with astonished recognition. He had been among the audience at that first public performance of Kurt's in a concert of the Florence Academy which his teacher had arranged to give him extra confidence and experience.

'Such beautiful playing,' he said, gesturing with his hands. 'I have heard all the great ones—Paderewski, Rosenthal, Mischa Levitski,

Pachmann—but your F-minor Ballade of Chopin, it was of an excellence that they would have acknowledged. I *know* it. I felt the music intensely—Chopin speaking to me from his heart through your hands. Ah!'

There could have been no better augury for the magic of their day, it was spring, they were in love, and Kurt had had the thrill of being recognised and congratulated—'Just as if he were already famous.'

The shopkeeper—'the little jeweller', Roz called him—was Jewish; but he had been granted Italian citizenship because he had been born in Florence and had not been turned away like the immigrants who sought refuge from Hitler's pogroms. He caused no trouble and had been left alone; and his name, Benvenuto Galletti, aroused no suspicion.

'I told him about myself,' Roz said, 'and also that I had been raised a Catholic, like Kurt, and we spoke for a while of the terrible things that were happening in Germany and the threat of war. And that seemed to lead naturally to the token Kurt wanted to buy.'

It was a trifle, a novelty in the form of a tiny gold cross of which the upright and the cross arms were detachable and each had a thin gold chain so that they could be worn by two lovers and joined in their cruciform shape only when they were together. And on each arm was engraved a syllable of the Hebrew word 'Mizpah'—'The Lord watch between me and thee, when we are absent one from the other.'

The little jeweller smiled benevolently at the couple he had, so to speak, 'adopted' in the magic of the day. Then he leaned across the counter on which the two arms of the cross lay gleaming on a black velvet pad and whispered conspiratorially, 'It

549

is a melding of the two faiths as well as of two young lovers—is it not so?'

Now I watched Roz as she unfastened the top buttons of her dress. The two halves fell apart. She wore no bra and the fine gold chain holding the tiny gold crossbar had slid across her breast to embrace one erect rosy nipple. 'You see?' she said provocatively.

The urge to take her in my arms and caress the beautiful symmetry of that breast was almost irresistible. But I resisted it.

'Yes,' I said, 'I do see.'

*   *   *

But the expedition had not ended with the purchase of the *gingillo*. The little jeweller had been so touched by what he called 'the melding' that he had gone on talking about the threat of war, shaking his head sadly as the afternoon advanced and tourists passed to and fro across the Ponte Vecchio. He spread his hands in a typically Jewish gesture of resignation.

'Troubles, troubles, always troubles,' he said mournfully. He stopped, his bright eyes seeming suddenly to visualise some future in which his adopted couple might need help. 'Always here there will be a friend,' he said. 'It is not often I am given the chance to seal young love. I shall remember; but perhaps ... you ... will go away and forget. And of course it is right for young lovers to forget all but their love. It is the way of lovers.' He sighed. 'But perhaps not ... ?'

Kurt had bowed formally but without hiding the emotion in his voice as he said, 'We shall not forget,

550

Signor Galletti; I promise you.'

'If the little jeweller is still there on the Ponte Vecchio,' Roz said to me now, 'that is where Kurt will go.'

CHAPTER THIRTY-THREE

The train Roz and I travelled on to Florence was full of troops returning from the Rome leave centres to the front. Most were Americans and there were plenty of wolf-whistles as they eyed Roz in her elegant dress.

'How on earth do you manage to be so well turned out?' I queried.

'This? Mama always wanted to splash out whenever I visited her. I think it was her way of assuring herself that I was still her daughter, that I wasn't finding a vocation and drifting away into a nunnery. "So depressing seeing you in that nun's habit," she used to say, "Buy yourself a pretty dress when you get back to Geneva." I suppose it was also her way of expressing a continuing link with the family she'd been cut off from by the war.'

'Possessiveness, more likely,' I said grudgingly.

The train rattled along, sometimes stopping unaccountably between stations while the troops made caustic remarks about being able to pick flowers from the embankments and the civilian passengers sighed or dozed off with their mouths open and their stomachs rumbling. Those who were awake looked greedily at the slabs of chocolate and cookies that were being consumed by the Yanks—who, I must say, were generous with their offerings—but it was a painful reminder of the tricky food situation, with soup kitchens and black-market luxury highlighting the ugly contrast of a war-torn land.

As we neared Florence Roz broke into my thoughts. 'Possessiveness,' she repeated in a musing tone. 'Yes, perhaps you're right. I think maybe it was a compensation for Mama's insecurity, marrying a Prince and being overawed . . . and of course being separated. She's got friends in Interlaken, but it isn't the same. Then the boy came along and she felt once again part of the family—secure.'

'What boy?' I asked irritably. I was not interested in the Principessa's loneliness: I had enough of my own, and in my mind she was the cause of a good deal of it.

Roz looked at me in astonishment. 'The boy? Why, *your* boy of course—Ham Two.'

I felt the blood drain from my face. My mouth went dry and the beating of my heart sounded in my head. It couldn't be—it simply *could not be*!

'I—I—' I stammered. I wanted to say 'I can't believe it', but the words would not come out.

At that moment the train clanked and squeaked to a standstill and shed its cargo of troops and weary civilians on to the platform. My heart racing, I gestured through the noise and bustle to Roz to stay in the compartment until everyone else was out. Then I pulled the door shut. We were in a tiny world of our own. Breath obscured the windows, the fuggy air clung to us like a mist. I said at last, 'I can't believe it!'

'But surely Fiamma told you?' she replied, as if to a dim-witted child. 'I wrote to her at the

552

hospital—'

'Told me *what*?' I said angrily. I wanted to shake words out of her. I passed a hand over my damp forehead. 'For God's sake, Roz, I must know. Don't you understand? *I must know!*'

As I said it I had a cloudy memory of the letter Fiamma had thrust into my hand that chaotic day when I briefly saw her at the hospital as the casualties came flooding in and I was on my way to Eighth Army HQ. Whatever it was Roz thought I knew about must have been in that letter—the letter I had never read.

'And so it was,' she confirmed when I told her about the confiscation of the contents of my pockets by the officious French Intelligence officer.

'But what *was* it?' I sounded brutally harsh, even to myself.

What she told me was harsh too—though the background to it I knew only too well. The rationing system in Rome had broken down because of the Allies' constant attacks on the German supply lines and the conflicting political elements of the Italian administration; and with Kurt, of course, no longer bringing packages of additional supplies the effect on Ham Two was becoming dangerous.

'It was plain and simple malnutrition, Ham. He wasn't a strong child—he'd had several bouts of illness—and what food there was had very little nutrition in it. Most of the bread was made from chickpeas, maize, the pith of elm bark, and mulberry leaves; and meat and milk were practically unobtainable unless you had money or influence in the black market.'

So I had not been far from the truth when the thought had crossed my mind, during my search for

Fiamma in Rome, that our son might have been begging in the streets, pleading with victorious GIs to give him biscuits. *Victory*! I thought bitterly: it has a sour taste.

'So that was where "The Blue Nude" came in,' Roz continued, jerking my thoughts back to the present. 'Fiamma sold it to buy food for the boy on the black market, but hadn't the heart to tell you when you were convalescing; because she'd once sworn that whatever happened she'd never sell it.'

'For Christ's sake!' I exploded. 'It was only a bloody painting! Did she think I'd mind when our son's life was at stake?'

But in my heart of hearts I knew *she* would have minded—deeply; and I minded too. For there was something revolting in the idea of the picture, that expressed the dawning of our love, falling into the hands of strangers—perhaps even the monstrous red-taloned Neri—who would find it merely titillating and laugh coarsely. By sheer good fortune, though, it had been channelled via the Nazi loot route into BB's care; but I felt it had been soiled by other hands. But in the depths of distress I realised Roz was still talking.

'—I had the answer, though. And it wasn't too difficult. Mama was beginning to regret her treatment of you and Fiamma. She wanted to make amends. And how better than to take Ham Two into her care? Food and doctors were all available in plenty in Interlaken, and nursery schools too; and above all he'd be safe and a great worry would be taken off Fiamma's mind. I managed with Father Renato's help to get Fiamma to agree to put the boy into the care of the sisters in the Vatican convent until I could smuggle him in one of our convoys to

Geneva and she could return to the relative safety of Forte dei Marmi.'

I shook my head, trying to disperse the fog from my thoughts. The great thing that shone out clearly was that Ham Two, at least, was safe. But Fiamma—?

Suddenly a porter opened the door and asked sarcastically if we realised that the train had finished its journey and did we want to be shunted into the sidings with it?

'All change,' I said to Roz, and out we got.

*　　*　　*

An atmosphere of menace hung over Florence. It is difficult to describe—menace is a feeling, something that gets into the bones and the blood. A war-torn city is always menacing. The apparatus of war is visible and audible: sandbags, road blocks, boarded-up shops, the sudden diminishing lights as power fails or is reduced, the distant drone of aircraft, the clatter of military vehicles and the voices of their crews as they make their way through to distant venues of engagement. And there is the day-to-day traffic too, with people trying half-heartedly to assume some appearance of normality, as if the war were something to be shrugged off as a tiresome episode.

But as we walked out into the city, it seemed that this was more a personal menace, almost as if I had been singled out for its threat. Stupid no doubt but real enough for me to remark on it to Roz.

'It's the weather,' she said reassuringly—and indeed it was grey and humid, with rain drizzling down almost continually and the Arno turgid and muddy and slicked with oil.

Yet it was more than that, and more than I could shrug off.

Accommodation was not difficult to find. Roz went to her old convent school, which was being used as a transit camp for displaced people and those whose houses were casualties of the fighting. I was welcomed by an American liaison officer, Bill Vine, to whom Steve had given me an introduction. He had a comfortable billet near the Palazzo Riccardi, which housed the civilian admin- istration—the Prefettura—and was barely a mile from the Arno and the Ponte Vecchio.

'Looking for a fugitive, are you?' he queried.

'You could say so,' I said tersely.

'Buddy, you sure have a tough assignment there, a real hard make. The city's full of 'em. And it's gonna get fuller. You seen this morning's communiqué?'

I shook my head. I had not seen anything, nor did I wish to see anything or anyone—except Kurt. And my Fiamma.

He flourished an official news-sheet from the Prefettura. It was from Kesselring's HQ: 'Everything possible has been done to deprive the Anglo-American adversaries of every pretext for the bombardment of Florence. Thus the fate of the city rests entirely with the Anglo-American adversaries.'

I smiled wryly. 'They have a neat way of putting the ball in the wrong court.'

'Sure, sure. Typical of Kesselring; he's a cunning bastard. But he's dead serious with his plans. My lowdown is that he's moving his artillery forward and that he's personally been in touch with Goering to boost his Luftwaffe strength. If you ask me,

556

buddy, we're in for some heavy action hereabouts.'

*   *   *

Our search for Kurt, seemingly hopeless as it was, had to begin somewhere; and although I had my doubts about pledges given five years earlier, when war clouds were beyond the horizon, Roz was insistent that Galletti's shop on the Ponte Vecchio should be our first contact.

Everything in the famous arcade was shabby and neglected. Grimy windows half concealed what little merchandise the shopkeepers had for sale. The goldsmiths and leatherworkers had managed to get together a few items of their work for sale mainly to the American troops who had the money to buy them; but it was a pathetic attempt at recapturing the stylishness and luxury of pre-war days when tourists and cognoscenti used to stroll across the bridge, fancying they heard, in the gallery above their heads, the ghostly trot of sixteenth-century hooves as Grand Dukes and Princes of rival factions crossed the Arno on assignations of love and death. The only echoes from above in 1944 were of another kind of death—fighter planes screaming across the sky in pursuit of bombers relentlessly droning on their errands of destruction.

I was not hopeful of our visit, but I was wrong. Partly, anyway. I had not even expected Signor Galletti to be still there.

A drab curtain was lowered almost to the bottom of the window, leaving space only for a flyspecked sign with the words *Gingilli/Souvenirs*. I laughed harshly. 'Souvenirs!'

The door opened squeakily and Roz and I entered.

The shop was a litter of tawdry gewgaws —brooches and tiepins on cardboard rectangles, cheap beakers imprinted with pictures of the Palazzo Pitti and Ponte Vecchio, cheap fountain pens held to display-cards by elastic loops, brassy medallions on neckchains flecked with verdigris—I felt Roz's fingers tremble in mine, as if with a reflex of memory.

Signor Galletti sat behind the counter, his eyes startled at the entrance of customers. His skin was white and unhealthily pappy, like that of a washerwoman whose hands have been too long in hot water. He wore the yarmulke—the Jew's embroidered skullcap—on his thinning hair.

His eyes searched our faces. For a moment he could make nothing of us. Then some recognition of Roz dawned in his eyes.

'Signorina! From so long ago!' He eyed me cagily. 'But this is not—?'

'No,' Roz confirmed as she drew the gold chain from the neck of her dress to display the tiny gold bar. 'But a very good friend. And we seek the other—to complete this.' Light glinted on the gold.

'The other?' Clearly the little jeweller was suspicious of improper liaisons. 'Your husband?' Clearly also, though he recognised Roz for her beauty, his memory was hazy as to when and how.

'My husband—yes; but not then. He bought me this keepsake to hold us together even in absence.'

Galletti pushed his glasses higher on his nose and peered. Then came an explosion of memory. 'Of course! The Mizpah cross. The young man was to become a great pianist. Such playing!' He paused and sighed. 'But I suppose the war—'

We explained briefly, Roz reminding him of the words he had used: 'There will always be a friend.'

He nodded gravely. 'Yes. He was then a friend. But the war made him an enemy—an enemy of my people.'

'And of you too?' It was a loaded question.

A shake of the head. 'Music is not for enemies. Wagner hated Jews, but can one hate his music in revenge? It is superb. No, Signora, if he is sickened of war and is a fugitive he would not be refused sanctuary by me. But he has not sought it. I have not seen him—though I have seen others who need help.'

He told us that the occupying German troops had treated him as a figure of fun—an attribute he had encouraged by cultivating eccentricities. He rode a tricycle about the city with a notice on the handlebar demanding everyone to 'REPENT FOR ATONEMENT IS NIGH'. He would repair the troops' watches free, recommend bordellos with 'special services', arrange guided tours of the city's architectural glories for off-duty officers, and teach Italian. He gave away pseudo-religious tracts explaining Armageddon and told fortunes by astrology—always predicting German victories. And he was an unofficial poste restante for messages and a clearing-house for bribes and black market goods. 'Every city has its eccentrics and I was one of them. My guilelessness gained me the Germans' confidence. I was considered mad but useful.'

But his uses were double-edged. The Germans and their Italian allies were not the only ones to avail themselves of the little jeweller's many services. Resistance workers, partisans, agents of political splinter groups, the civil police, even the suppressed Mafia called on him. He played them off one against the other with considerable effect, secretly congratulating himself on causing a good deal of trouble without bringing much to his own doors—'Though there were occasions when I feared for my life—as when the Chief of Police—'

'Neri!' I almost shouted the name.

'Yes. An evil man, hand-in-glove with evil. He came in one day—'

But I did not want to hear about Galletti's encounter with Neri. Had Neri happened to mention anything about a prisoner, a hostage, a nurse—'This Signora's sister, and my wife?'

The little jeweller shook his head again, and by the glint of tears in his eyes I knew he longed to be able to help. 'But no, Signor. It was a moment of fear only, he was trying to trace some documents which had disappeared from the Prefuttura—documents that had indeed been through my hands. Fortunately I deceived him with chutzpah, what you English call cheek, and he went away unsatisfied. But of a nurse hostage—no, nothing.'

Then the city had been liberated by the Allies' advance, Neri had been replaced, 'And I could resume my status as a Jew'—he touched the yarmulke on his head—'and my business as a merchant.' He sighed. 'Though I have nothing worthwhile to sell now.' He gestured towards the shelves. 'You could have everything here for a few lire. Worthless, worthless.'

We were just about to leave the shop when the little jeweller gave us a ray of hope.

'No. I know nothing of any hostage; and Herr von Schill has not sought refuge here.' He paused. 'I am old now and my bones creak a little. But I feel

560

in them that he will come.'

It was little enough in all conscience after all we had hoped for; but it was better than nothing.

★   ★   ★

The menace that lay over the city took tangible form a few days later. The intermittent rumblings of gunfire and sporadic attacks by German bombers that had done little damage except in the suburbs south of the Arno—rather as if the enemy were respecting the 'preservation pact'—ceased and their absence was alarming because we knew it meant, as Bill Vine, my American contact, put it, 'the Kraut's drawing the bolt back and taking aim'.

Suddenly there was great troop activity. I was out of touch with Intelligence sources but it was obvious—from the profusion of armoured vehicles, anti-tank guns, and ack-ack equipment invading the gardens and squares—that preparations were being made to meet the forthcoming counter-attack. Overnight the city shed its aura of rehabilitation after the bonds of battle. Once again it was a city at war. The ancient buildings brooded through the murk of rain, the narrow streets resounded to the grinding tracks of tank, in the parks towering coils of barbed wire rose like rusty trees, waiting for the engineers to construct barricades from them.

Although I was in the midst of the build-up I felt remote from it—'shamefully so', I admitted to Roz as we saw a company of weary GIs establishing themselves in the Via Tornabuoni. 'A soldier so-called, and I've never fired a shot in anger.'

'You've done plenty,' she retorted. 'I can't believe all your work with the partisans wasn't dangerous. And being an undercover man isn't exactly without its risks. Don't belittle yourself.'

I shrugged and quoted mockingly, '"They also serve who only stand and wait."'

'*And* get beaten up when carrying vital messages in their teeth, *and* make breakneck dashes to Army headquarters, *and* help girls escape through the catacombs of Cassino ... It's not a bad record, Ham.'

Perhaps it was not, and I smiled gratefully in response. But I could not help feeling inadequate, even for the complex but passive task ahead. To find Kurt! Kurt—escaping from his own forward-marching compatriots, seeking refuge with his enemies. The irony of it! But where? I had gone through the motions of searching for clues. The Town Major commented acidly on how, whenever he saw me, as at Poggibonsi, I seemed to be searching for someone, and no, he had not had any information or orders about any Kurt von Schill, and it seemed to him that, with the balloon about to go up, 'Intelligence wallahs' should find something better to do. He was not in one of his sympathetic moods. Bill Vine, on the other hand, was helpful. He arranged for me to draw a jeep from the vehicle pool, which eased my transport problem. Roz suggested there might be friends at the Conservatorio where Kurt had studied who might have kept in touch and even given him refuge. But the place had long been closed down to become sub-offices of some government department.

Umberto? Kurt might go there hoping that the old artist knew of *my* whereabouts or could give him sanctuary, a hiding place. I imagined him thinking that, once the counter-attack began, there was a better chance of his being lost and forgotten in the confusion of the fighting, but that meanwhile...

I drove the jeep round to the Borgo San Jacopo with the beginning of wishful hope warming me. But climbing stone stairs to Umberto's studio (the grimy notice still warned that the lift was out of order) I felt sure the studio would be empty, and so it was. This time even the bell did not ring and when I banged on the door and put my ear to the panel the only answer was a hollow silence. As I descended an old crone emerged from one of the landing doors and told me the Professore had gone—she knew not where. 'Perhaps to the south, to Rome, where there is no war.' She made a gesture of resignation. 'This is a bad time, Signor. Fot all of us it is a bad time.'

'You're telling me!' I echoed the GI idiom with a harsh laugh. She merely looked puzzled, so I went on my way.

Another dead end.

As I got into the jeep my hopes were at their lowest. I wanted to abandon the whole cockeyed assignment, let love conquer duty, and drive straight to Forte dei Marmi. A knight in shining armour to the rescue of an imprisoned princess! Such romantic nonsense!—I could even hear Access' sneering guffaw.

Then, as the engine burst into life, a different throught struck me—so forcibly that the shock of it seemed to travel down my spine like an electric current. Perhaps that rapport, that had seemed sometimes to link Kurt and myself and had brought us together at the summit of Cassino, was the cause; I do not know. But it occurred to me that he might—if he could get there—make for the little

563

villa 'over the road' from Magari which we three young men had shared. There at least he might be safe from his pursuers for a brief respite. Of course, my mind, grasping at hope, was grossly over-simplifying matters. I did not even know what his route would be; and *he* certainly would have no idea whether the house was empty or in enemy hands. For that matter, nor had I. Since I had driven to Magari with Steve to see Baade, the Germans had been pushed north as far as Prato (fifteen miles north of Florence) on the western flank and as far as the tiny republic of San Marino over on the Adriatic sector, leaving the Fiesole hillside, with Settignano nestling below it, clear of enemy. But with the counter-attack planned, how long would it remain so? No use delaying. The notion clutched at my mind, an idée fixe. 'Get on with it, Painter,' I seemed to hear Access say.

I took the road to Settignano at furious speed.

*　　　*　　　*

I lay flat on the hillside peering down through binoculars at the little villa. The avenue of cypresses hid Magari, but I could see our house clearly. It looked battered and forsaken and the surrounding fields showed no sign of life either. But my training reminded me that an apparently lifeless landcape was not necessarily a safe one. I decided to wait until dark.

The rain held off but thick black clouds billowed in the September sky and a cold wind blew from the north. I shivered and felt doubts creeping in. Surely I was mad? But I clung obstinately to my hope. I had driven the jeep off the road into a copse and

564

now sat in it, dozing fitfully. Gunfire sounded and occasional orange flashes lit the sky. 'It was like that on the Somme,' I remembered my father telling me, 'a few fireworks and then the big bang, the calm before the storm.' I shivered again, noting, prosaically, that my stomach was rumbling with hunger.

Around nine o'clock I judged it dark enough to make my way down the hill. It was raining again and the house loomed like a derelict hulk through the autumn darkness. There was a smell of wet leaves as my feet trod the soft ground bordering the road. In the copse where I had left the jeep an owl hooted eerily.

Silence.

I recce'd round the walls, getting entangled with the creepers that, neglected, had grown over the windows.

One window—the one into the sitting-room where the piano had stood with 'The Blue Nude' on top of it—was broken. As I put my head through the frame the smell of wet leaves mingled with the stale air of a long-shut house; and a very faint sound, as of sharply indrawn breath, came to me.

I knew then my hunch had been right.

'Kurt,' I called in a loud whisper into the room. I heaved myself up, then through the window and heard my feet creak on protesting floorboards. 'Kurt! It's me, Ham.'

There was a scuffling and the figure of a man lurched out of the darkness. In the instant of his rush it flashed through my mind I could be wrong, that I had disturbed an enemy, that I had nothing to defend myself with except my hand.

But I was not wrong. It was Kurt.

He embraced me, sobbing with relief—and joy. 'Ham! My good friend—you!' I thought how idiotic this was—a colonel in Hitler's army crying like a child in the arms of his enemy.

We said little as we made our way, stumbling, up the hillside to the copse where I had left the jeep. Kurt was exhausted, I could tell that from the way he walked, clinging to me and frequently pausing to get his breath. God knew what he had endured; but the tale could wait. I was anxious only to get him to safety, to avoid for the time being the formality of arrest and interrogation.

Where?

The Prefettura, the Town Major, the army tactical HQ—all would be concerned only with passing him back to Rome as a prisoner-of-war; but I wanted him to be reunited with Roz first, to recuperate to face his ordeal.

Where?

Slumped in the seat beside me Kurt gave me the answer himself.

He had been living rough, like Vanni escaping from the horrors of Spain, and making for Florence and refuge with . . . the little jeweller. Roz had been right; we had simply visited Signor Galletti too soon.

'So much history repeating itself,' I said as we approached the outskirts of the city. 'Vanni sickening of war, then you; you taking me to safety . . . and to Fiamma . . . in a wheelbarrow; now me taking you to safety . . . and Roz . . . in a jeep. You must admit, Kurt, that life does have its little ironies.'

But he did not even smile. He was asleep, exhausted.

566

No doubt I could easily have contacted Access; but I did not do so. It was convenient to let him think I was still combing the city for my quarry. When Kurt and Roz had been reunited would be soon enough. I would then send a triumphant two-word, two-fingered message, the equivalent of Churchill's V-sign: 'Success. Painter.'

The delay was a decision I have bitterly regretted ever since.

★ ★ ★

Even now I find it difficult to write about the reunion of Roz and Kurt without recalling my own heartache. What favoured them, I wondered, when Fiamma and I were still parted? In truth, of course, nothing did; but all I could see then was them together, myself alone.

Conveniently, Bill Vine was on a tour of duty that took him away from the billet—'Going liaising, pal,' he said as if he were going on a fishing weekend—'keep the place hoovered'. He buckled on his revolver, smiled cheerily, and was away.

So I was able to give Kurt a bed and let him sleep—which he did solidly for twenty-four hours. When he awakened, shaved, and cleaned up a bit he looked a new man, more like the Kurt I had known.

'You'll be safe here,' I told him. 'Relax. I've got some arrangements to make.' I was being deliberately mysterious.

'You mean . . . Roz?'

'Wait and see,' I said. It was strange how, in a city preparing for attack, I should be mainly concerned to re-unite these two. If anyone deserved it Kurt and Roz did. But I wanted their reunion to have an element of drama about it, not be just a casual meeting in my billet.

Thinking back, I can see that part of the pleasure I got from 'arranging' it was vicarious, a reunion for Roz and Kurt, yes, but to my imagination acting as 'stand-ins' for Fiamma and me; but at the time I was conscious only of a feeling of happiness that I had the power to find these two a brief peace in the turmoil of war. Kurt would have to be handed over as a prisoner—and a defector too, which would gain him no respect—and Roz would return to duty. But for a day or two at least...

I walked through more drizzling rain to the Ponte Vecchio. There was an atmosphere of tension. GIs in improvised ponchos, and Moroccans in bedraggled kepis, huddled in groups awaiting orders. One group had created a brazier from a jerrican and set it on the Dante stone. Thin smoke rose from whatever it was they were burning, and as I passed one of them was saying, 'He wrote "The Divine Comedy"—huh!—and a bloody fine comedy this is!' His was a thin reedy voice, as ludicrous as the brazier defiling the stone.

It was all so depressing; but in contrast unalloyed pleasure awaited me at the little jeweller's. He was overjoyed that I wanted him to reunite the lovers of the Mizpah cross. *Of course* they could stay with him. There was a little store-room behind the shop and a pallet bed—'Not very comfortable, you understand, but...'

He kept raising and spreading his hands and

568

murmuring 'Oy, oy, oy,' in an attempt to express the great happiness that had come to him.

The next morning I took the jeep and collected Roz from the school. Her eyes were bright with joy and anticipation. 'Oh Ham! How *did* you manage to do it?'

'Never mind,' I said putting a finger to my lips. '*Mago!*'

She snuggled her head on to my shoulder. The rain had stopped, and strands of her dark hair blew across my face. 'Hey!' I said, laughing, 'You're obstructing my view.'

The Ponte Vecchio was deserted. 'No customers—not even for my rubbish,' Signor Galletti said, looking with distaste at his wares. 'People hide, they feel threatened. They hide in the crypts of the churches, the air-raid shelters.' He sighed. 'Oy, oy, oy—nowhere is safe. But here now—' He opened his arms as if to embrace Roz. 'You shall see.'

We went round the counter, through a low doorway, and into a room stacked with dusty boxes—presumably full of brass tiepins, thick beakers and cheap rosaries—with a bottle-glass window through which you could see the distorted surface of the river. 'When the sun shines,' Signor Galletti said, 'it strikes back from the river, through the glass, and—' he mimed a man blinded by sunshine through the magnifying effect of the glass. 'Wonderful! But now, in the rain, not so good. Never mind. The sun will come later. And it is for the nights you must be comfortable. There!' He gestured towards the pallet bed on the floor. Over it lay a patchwork bedspread. 'The nuptial couch!' And behind a hand discreetly raised he said in a confidential tone: 'The—er—*ritirata* is through the door to the left behind my desk—*là!*'

I smiled. The intimate detail of the situation of the lavatory clear, I left Roz with the little jeweller and went off to get Kurt.

*   *   *

My sense of guilt begins to take command here. The ifs and buts crowd in. *If* I had done my duty and driven Kurt to Rome instead of to the little jeweller's ... *If* I had not been so sentimentally insistent on seeing him and Roz clasp together the two tiny units of the Mizpah cross ... *If* I had not savoured the joy of seeing them in each other's arms before passing through the low doorway, their heads silhouetted against the bottle-glass windows ... *But*, the counter-argument usually wins, because it is easier to justify one's actions.

The German counter-attack had begun at dawn two days after. It was clear that their artillery was aiming for the bridges to prevent the Allies crossing the Arno for a confrontation on the north side; but we were already across and massing to repel the attack. The German gunners' aim was terrifyingly accurate. The bridges to the east and west of the Ponte Vecchio were hit one by one, some damaged irreparably. The shells exploded on the banks and in the river, raising great gouts of water that carried with them bits of iron and masonry and timber that reminded me of gigantic versions of the drawing-room 'bombs' of my childhood from which party gifts would be showered into the air when the touch-paper was lit.

The gunners obviously intended to make the

Ponte Vecchio the principal focus of their fire and I hurried to warn Kurt and Roz. They had probably run for it already, but I wanted to make sure.

There were small terrified crowds of people huddled against the walls of the Palazzo Vecchio as I doubled through the streets where ack-ack gunswere spitting their shells against a lone Heinkel that was droning away somewhere above the clouds, and the church in the square just north of the bridge was blazing.

The thunder of our answering guns was deafening. Thick smoke blew along the arcade from a fire at the south end of the bridge, but so far no damage had been done to the shops. From the north end of the Ponte Vecchio to the little jeweller's shop was perhaps thirty yards. The door was open and then I saw Roz making her way out through dust and smoke. Kurt must be behind her, but there was no sign of the little jeweller. As they emerged there was a tremendous explosion some distance away. (This, I learned later, was the bomb that destroyed so much of the heart of the old city around the Palazzo.) There was a shuddering underfoot.

I shouted. 'The south end's safer—and I don't think the fire's serious', and Roz ran, her hair streaming behind her. As Kurt followed her there was a splintering noise overhead and a great wedge of masonry fell, spraying a huge, choking cloud of dust.

Kurt was directly beneath it.

Roz turned and screamed and rushed back to Kurt. I remember the two of us with a sort of superhuman strength shifting the heavy wedge of masonry away from Kurt's inert body. And I

571

remember her gazing down at his glazed eyes and back into mind, hopelessly.

A sudden, tremendous blow then stunned me, and I collapsed. It was the last thing I remembered.

CHAPTER THIRTY-FOUR

Somewhere outside myself I was thinking, quite objectively, as if considering the matter as the subject for a medical thesis, that the body is a strange mechanism. It was dark in that detached corner of my mind, a windowless cell in which a phantom person was living and trying blindly to clinch with the corporeal me—two mis-matched elements trying to come together. Then blackness, like an engulfing sea.

Pain.

I think I screamed, the sound somewhere remote in that detached corner, a protest against such mis-matching.

Then there was a sensation of moving in darkened corridors, water dripping, crescendo, each drop a blow on a brass gong, another scream (my own?), pinpricks of light, footsteps, eyes peering from the darkness, talons dripping blood, a questioning face above a scarlet blanket in an upturned bed . . .

The nightmare was timeless, interminable, or perhaps—as the phantom in the dark cell was matter-of-factly observing—only of a few seconds' duration. Most dreams are, anyway. Strange mechanisms, the body, the mind.

Pain . . .

The first face I was aware of through the screen of pain was distorted, a *liquid* face, molten wax being poured into some sort of mould, but having a strange memorable beauty which the nerve-ends of my mind tried to grasp. It was feminine. And its features seemed to swim moistly together, a kaleidoscope under water. I think I tried to reach out and touch it, with, at the back of my mind, the idea of assembling the shapes—the eyes, mouth, nose . . .

The answer to that was a blade of agony that cut through my whole being.

Consciousness vanished, and the face spiralled away into nothingness.

*   *   *

'You've had a nasty wallop on the head' were the first words I could make out from a colourful harangue of voices. Faces, like the voices, swam into my vision—faces doubly defined like faces through a hangover. Two of them. One, the face belonging to the 'wallop on the head' voice, thin, with rabbity teeth and smooth centre-parted hair. He wore a short white coat and was holding my wrist; for a moment I could not think why. The other face was seemingly disembodied, suspended in space and surrounded by a strange darkness. A woman's face, the face from my nightmare, but familiar from real life . . .

Fiamma! I thought, yet I knew it was not. But I had startled myself into movement and the pain wracked me. I cried out.

'Lie still, Ham.' Another voice, a gentle feminine voice. 'Completely still. Or it'll hurt.'

573

'True enough, old man,' the rabbity-toothed voice said. 'You've done your back a bit of no good too. Complete inertion, that's what we want.'

Then it came to me. I was like a slow-witted child building the C-A-T bricks into a word: hospital, doctor, nurse. Only it was not a nurse, it was Roz, her face disembodied in its dark surround because she was wearing the black wimple and robe of a nun.

'Full canonicals,' I said mirthlessly to myself. It was all I could think of. Then I lapsed again into unconsciousness.

*　　　*　　　*

Everything fell into place in due course—'due course' being the early days of my recovery.

They had flown me back to Rome in a Dakota fitted out as an air ambulance for the more serious cases—'And yours was one of those, old man,' the little rabbity-toothed doctor said. 'No doubt about that. We thought we were going to lose you. There could easily have been some brain damage—in fact we think there was, you were in a coma for a hell of a time. A clot of blood, you know.'

'I don't, but I'm prepared to believe you,' I replied.

'Then there was the damage to your spine—one of the vertebrae pushed out of alignment—'

'You don't have to tell me that,' I interrupted. By now they had fitted me with a sort of steel corset that kept my spine rigid, but there was still a lot of pain.

He nodded. 'That was why we suspected brain damage. At first you weren't responding to the

574

pain, it wasn't signalling itself to your brain; and we had no high-powered neurological unit or neurosurgeons here. We could only stitch up the wound in your scalp and hope the concussed brain would resume its function. As soon as you shouted with pain we knew it had.' His lips closed over his prominent teeth as if he had come to the end of a story.

He had not, of course. But I had to piece it together—like the voices and visions in the nightmare—from what was told me by Roz and Access (who made snide comments about my 'spending more time in hospital than in the field').

The German counter-attack had failed—or, rather, its success had been limited.

'A combination of circumstances,' Access explained. 'One of them may have been Baade's genuine reluctance to damage Florence unnecessarily; your truce visit with Price may have been more successful than you think, Painter. Another was Kesselring's contempt for Hitler's strategy, which he saw as militarily unsound and followed only to a limited extent.' He paused, numbering points on his fingers. 'Then there was Von Schill's defection, which made them think we had the counter-attack plans—'

'Stolen by Vanni,' I put in.

'Exactly. They're not slow on the uptake, the Boche. But what they did not know was that we'd crossed the Arno in strength and were in place ready to counter-attack the counter-attack.' He rubbed his nose with a thick forefinger. 'We did well on planting misleading info. Sir D'Arcy was quite shameless about it. Useful man, eh, Painter?'

'Certainly,' I said with a marked lack of

enthusiasm. I was heavily sedated and inertia was the only alternative to the pain my back was giving me...

The lassitude persisted for weeks. So did the pain. I had frequent visits from the doctor and an osteopath whose manipulations were sometimes more agonising than the original pain; but the X-rays, I was assured, showed things were going well and it was 'only a matter of time', though the steel corset might have to be a permanent feature of my underwear.

'Very cheering,' I said morosely. 'I'll relish wearing a chastity belt.'

I was assured facetiously that 'that side' of my life would not be affected. I was one with Steve there, I thought: a couple of war-wrecked husbands.

And a third dead.

It was Roz who completed that tragic story for me.

Her brief appearance during what I came to think of as the 'nightmare days' was not repeated for at least two weeks—I lost count of time in a haze of semi-consciousness and dope—and when she arrived she was still wearing her nun's garb.

'Working girl?' I asked her, thinking of the Vatican convoy, 'or have you taken the veil?' It was a silly question and a cruel one. I had not realised how cruel until her brimming eyes reproached me.

'Oh Ham! At least you don't *know* about Fiamma. You haven't had her die in your arms. You'll go on looking for her and in the end...'

'Maybe.' I took her hand. The Sisters of St Vincent de Paul wore white mittens as part of their habit. Hers covered her wedding ring like a shroud.

'I'm sorry, Roz; I truly am. If I could move I would kick myself.'

'Don't worry. At least it is a help to talk about it.'

And as she talked it seemed as if I was living again through the horror, re-enacted through her eyes.

'It was such a mockery, Ham. The Ponte Vecchio was never hit directly at all. It was the explosions at each end that made the arcade ceiling come down. I could see it as I ran back—a huge flat slab with jagged edges. I remember thinking, as I ran, that I'd never looked up and seen that ornate ceiling before with all its gilt scroll work and tiles. And Kurt—I screamed, choking on the dust and filth in my mouth. And you, running . . . it's like one frame of a film repeating endlessly in my mind.'

'And then?' I took her hand, held it, trembling.

'He died instantly, Ham. His head—the blood poured from it into my lap after you pulled the masonry off him and then collapsed yourself when another wedge fell. People came running through the fog and dust. It was chaos, Ham. I don't really know . . . Signor Galletti was there somewhere . . . and the guns in the distance.'

Silence fell between us. There was nothing to say. I hoped that somehow it was a comforting silence, and that my understanding crossed it. I wanted to say to her that I was glad I had known Kurt, that he was a good German and that he died for his country as much as any soldier who fell on the battlefield. I wanted to erase the thoughts of betrayal that must have been in her mind—in both our minds. I wanted to point to how the stupidity of war put people into hopelessly wrong slots and then left them to work out their own destinies. And I wanted to add something about how, in the act of betraying his country, Kurt was being loyal to a higher ideal—to civilisation. I also wanted—selfishly—to remind her of my own despair. But Fiamma was her despair too—a sister in all but parentage. The thoughts raced through my mind—perhaps some of them were conveyed to her. But I could not tell. My mind was fogged up with effort.

'So you're back on duty,' I said to break the silence, my eyes on her nun's garb again, 'on the Vatican convoy.'

She nodded, a tiny smile around her lips. 'Even under false colours work is a comfort. But you may have been right, Ham ...'—she hesitated—'well, partly right, about the veil. The Church is a great comfort too.'

*　　*　　*

The days dragged into weeks with agonising slowness. The war passed me by. There was still fighting going on near the Gothic Line, which the Germans were desperately defending after the Florence counter-attack had been repulsed. To tell the truth, though, I was indifferent to it. The sense of ennui was overpowering. And Access was leaving me alone—I would have been no use to him anyway. There were whispers that I was to be invalided out, but I was as indifferent to them as to nearly everything else. My head had been shaved to enable the surgeons to stitch my scalp wound, and by Christmas the hair was growing thickly again so that I could at least face myself in the mirror without shuddering; and I was able too to move about and, with a lot of gritting of teeth, have a

578

bath unaided. But my spirit was at an all-time low.

'Down in the dumps, are we?' the rabbity-toothed English doctor said.

He was a good and caring doctor but the clichés fell from his lips relentlessly. There is a limit to the number of times one can answer 'How are we today?' and 'Pecker up, old man' without snapping, and I snapped back several times. He took it in good part though, 'Join in the fun, old man. That's what we need—a little raising of the spirits, eh?' He closed an eye conspiratorially. 'Maybe I'll give you an injection of yeast?'

'Ho, ho,' I said.

The 'fun' he referred to was playing chess, dominoes, and cards with the other patients; but none of it appealed to me—nor did my sullenness appeal to them.

It was of course the inactivity that was getting me down. I had too much time to think, to turn inwards on myself. The doctor added—but only half-jokingly—that if I did not 'pull myself together' I would become a psychiatric case.

Then, quite suddenly, fate played a different game altogether, dealing her best cards into my hand, as if with a mocking disregard for her past misdemeanours and an echo of Access' favourite phrase, 'Get on with it'. And no doubt she also added *sotto voce*, 'you won't get this chance again.' But I heard.

★   ★   ★

I had persevered with therapeutic exercises worked out by my osteopath and the orthopaedic surgeon to strengthen my back. They were boring and

579

consistently painful, but they were effective; and by February 1945 I was able to walk—with the aid of a stick, it is true—for fair distances without feeling more than ordinarily tired. The doctors were pleased with my physical progress but continued to worry about my depression.

'Only you can conquer it, old man. Why don't you take up a hobby—something to get the old brainbox working?'

'Like knitting?' I replied.

Then came the fateful first card of the deal.

My wanderings about Rome had no special objective beyond exercise. That was part of the aimlessness of my mind, my listlessness of spirit. But one day, in the Via Condotti, I was sparked into interest. I had just passed the Café Greco from which a GI was emerging, his arm around the waist of a pretty Italian girl.

'Gee, Honey,' he was saying, reading from a leaflet in his hand, 'd'you realise that all them great guys from the past—Byron, Shelley, Goethe, Keats, Gounod, Bizet, Gogol, Wagner, *and* Mark Twain—used to go there for their chow?'

I have no idea what she said in reply, for suddenly my eye caught sight of the name over the shabby shop next door to the café.

Sangallo.

Sangallo? For a moment I could not place it. Then it came like a bright light into my mind: Sangallo was the Florence dealer in artists' materials where Umberto used to shop for his paints and brushes and canvases, never paying but always swapping them for paintings. This must be the Rome branch.

The name gave an immediate lifting to my

spirits—the happy past linked with the sombre present through the catalyst of a name! And if Umberto had escaped from Florence to Rome there was nowhere he was more likely to go than Sangallo's. They might even know where he was living.

'Of course, Signor,' the elderly manager said. 'Certainly we know the Professore here. A charming man, a little "eccentric" perhaps; but of firm opinions. We have some of his paintings. You would like to see them perhaps?'

I explained that I had been one of his pupils and wanted to make contact with him.

The manager frowned. 'A few months ago it would have been simple; for he was staying here. We have a studio apartment on the top floor and we were pleased to let him have it when he escaped from Florence during the—er—renewal of hostilities. But now, he has returned to Florence.'

It was hardly surprising. I had been in hospital for nearly six months and Florence had long since resumed its status of Allied occupation. Naturally Umberto would have gone back to his beloved city.

Strangely I felt little rancour at thus being cheated once again of a possible clue to my Fiamma's whereabouts. (A frail hope anyway, for Umberto was unlikely to know any more than he had before.) But another flame had been kindled in my heart just by the indirect contact with him: the overwhelming desire to *paint*.

*   *   *

It was unexpectedly easy to arrange. Sangallo's offered to lend me the studio apartment. It was

581

within easy distance of the hospital so that I could attend daily for my therapy; and it was there, in the big studio with its north light, that I began to paint 'The Last Battle'.

*   *   *

Looking back, I can see that a form of obsessional frenzy possessed me during the painting of 'The Last Battle'. Some force was released within me, like the proverbial genie from the bottle. These things are inexplicable, of course. To be able to explain them would be to be able to explain the mysteries of creativity; which may sound as though I am claiming creative genius for 'The Last Battle'. Far from it. I know my worth as an artist. My work has always been uneven in quality, uncertain in technique, because complete mastery of the palette knife, my favourite medium, could have been achieved only in the years that were snatched away by the war.

'Do not worry,' Umberto used to say merrily, 'the technique will come. Let the *espressione* have its way for the—' snapping his fingers.

'Time being?' I prompted.

'So: the time being.' And with hand to chest, 'Let the heart have its way. The fingers will follow.'

The heart had had its way with 'The Blue Nude', with 'The Yellow Nude', and several other pictures Duveen had seen and found promising enough to want to 'launch' me.

What I wanted to express in 'The Last Battle' was not just the horrors of war but also the deprivations and indignity that came in its wake—an Armageddon of the spirit concentrated into the death throes of a single unknown warrior. It was a conception too vast, too stark, for any but the greatest artists. And, as I say, I have never been in that company. But the frenzy of inspiration and occasion forced me on into activity. It was easy to arrange my therapy in daily doses at the hospital. The doctors were delighted that at last I had 'taken up a hobby' and added that, if I kept it up, there would be no danger of a nervous breakdown. 'It's all in the mind, old man.'

So I did the basic work—the chalky foundation wash and the primer—in the early morning, not even bothering to dress after I had carefully eased myself out of bed in the curiously awkward manner that avoided some of the pain. The light was poor, but that was less important during the early stages when I was concerned more with treating the canvas, and doing studies in composition on big sketch pads, than with the main work. There were colour studies to be made too, for contrasts symbolising the cosmic battle of the forces of good and evil were at the heart of my vision—which sounds as if I had every detail outlined in my mind; but nothing could be further from the truth. I had only thought that at the time of the picture's conception, when the stark agony of sudden death had leered at me across the fountains of dust and rubble in Cassino field hospital. But between conception and execution there is a great divide, as I soon learnt.

Every day I zealously did my exercises at the hospital and suffered the lessening tortures of the osteopath as my injury took its course towards healing. My cumbersome steel-and-whalebone support was still needed, and I still felt happier using a stick when walking out-of-doors; but my journeys back to Sangallo's ('Avoid transport, old man, give the old pins their freedom') were like release after a penance. I might have only three or four hours of the midday light to work by, but I crowded into them all the pent-up energy of my inspiration, feeling at the end as exhausted as if I had run in a marathon.

Gradually the picture took form. Its composition emerged from beneath my knife and brushes like a structure controlled by an external force. I cannot recall now how long I worked on it. Time in those days of feverish creation seemed to have no value. But I have a feeling it was not much more than a week. And when I had completed it I slept dreamlessly for a day and night, sapped of all energy.

The picture's impact was terrific—I knew that. Even I gasped at its startling juxtaposition of angles and gouts of vivid colour. From beneath a translucent vaporous cloud the death's-head mask of the victim of 'The Last Battle' barely concealed the anguished look of a man suddenly facing, and accepting, doom. Though but a small part of the whole composition, he dominated it—triumphing even in death over the symbols and accoutrements of war, the shellbursts, marching feet, aircraft wings, smoking ruins, that were woven into the design.

I felt it to be good. I *knew* it to be good. I did not even need an outside opinion to reassure me; but I invited one all the same—from Sangallo's manager. He could barely express its impact on him.

'Remarkable, Signor! The power ... the ... *expressione* ... The Professore would be delighted.'

584

'We'll see,' I said.

*   *   *

I intended to take the picture to Florence, feeling sure that Umberto would be back in his flat. Travel was relatively easy now, though the trains could never be relied on to keep to any timetable; and I felt reasonably fit. But Access claimed me back as soon as he knew I was what he called 'walking wounded', and I had to do a stint of routine duties at HQ. I also saw Steve and Lella at infrequent intervals and joined them for an occasional meal.

But I did not offer to show them 'The Last Battle'. I am not quite sure why, except that I felt I wanted Umberto to be the first to have what I rather conceitedly thought of as the 'privilege' of a private view. But I did mention to them that I had committed to canvas what I thought was rather a good picture.

'Gee, Ham,' Steve said. 'Give! Let's have a look-see.' He turned to Lella. 'Betcha it's marvellous, eh, Lell?'

'Of course it is. But if Ham wants to sharpen our appetites by being mysterious—'

Steve shrugged. 'Okay, okay.'

And after that we talked sadly of Kurt and Roz and of the continued mystery of Fiamma's whereabouts.

CHAPTER THIRTY-FIVE

I went to Florence a few days later, taking 'The Last Battle' with me. It was not a big picture—concentrated power rather than size had been in my mind—and it fitted comfortably into one of the thin leather portfolios Sangallo's supplied for artists to 'tote their pix in', as Lella put it. (She absorbed American idioms like a sponge.)

I suppose it was the aftermath of the frenzied energy that had gone into its creation, but I felt strangely tranquil. Perhaps I am wrong—memory sometimes cheats—but Florence seemed tranquil too, almost somnolent in an early spring haze that veiled the mirrored sunlight on the Arno. It was hard to believe that political and industrial unrest were rife in the city. General Clark's unwise re-arming of the Mafia had given them a new strength which they were masking with 'official' sanction to aid police, military, the Prefettura, and the Guardia Segreta. Their probes were everywhere, surreptitiously re-establishing their 'families' and amassing wealth by extortion, blackmail, racketeering, and by undermining the tottering rationing schemes with black market food, clothing, and petrol. Nor was it easy to believe that, in the north, fierce fighting was still going on right across the peninsula, with the American Fifth Army planning offensives on the highways to Bologna, and the British Eighth Army aiming at Ferrara.

My impulse was to go straight to Umberto's studio in the Borgo San Jacopo and show him my picture—a reflex, I suppose, of the white-hot concentration with which I had painted it. My impulse demanded his critical evaluation—*now*. But I subdued it. Could there have been a tiny seed of fear in my suppression—a fear that he might shake his head sadly to intimate that I had failed? After all, I had only the opinion of Sangallo's manager, who would certainly not have wanted to offend a client; and perhaps the same little seed of fear had prompted my refusal to let Steve and Lella see it. I am not sure. At all events, I booked into the Lungarno and loitered away an hour or two before I climbed the stairs to the studio and pressed the bell, half hoping that Umberto had not returned. But he had, and my fears increased despite my pleasure at seeing him, for I knew he would be incapable of softening his opinion for the sake of friendship.

After an emotional greeting and much adjusting of the beret back and forth on his forehead my old master pointed excitedly at my portfolio.

'I knew! This is work you bring to show me! Something special for the old Professore!'

All else was forgotten in his enthusiasm—catching up with everything since our last meeting, the real worlds of war and want, were all reduced to trivial importance beside this event that was so much nearer to his heart.

He delightedly took a canvas he had been working on off the big easel and sat himself on the model's dais while I unfastened the portfolio and set the picture on the easel. My heart was pounding, but at the edge of my apprehension I noted that Umberto was beaming with pleasure at the thought of seeing a new work by his pupil.

'There!'

He rose, rubbing the charcoal from his hands on

his stained trousers, and shuffled to a position a few feet from the easel.

For a moment or two he was silent. I could see his eyes taking in, evaluating, every detail. He stepped forward, then back, then sideways for different views while I waited, fidgeting like a schoolboy waiting while his father reads a headmaster's report.

At last he spoke, his fingers combing his beard and leaving a deposit of charcoal dust. His eyes seemed to be glistening—I think with tears.

'Ham! A masterpiece! Capolavoro!' He took my right hand in both of his and pumped it up and down. 'Such strength—power! Here is everything in your heart—experience, pain, love—'

He chattered on about technical details, colour values, form and so on; but he had said all I wanted to hear. My heart—my artist's heart, that is—was singing.

*   *   *

It is a strange thing that an elevation of the spirit can leave not only the tranquillity I had felt on my arrival in Florence, but also its opposite, a valley as low as the height of joy. It was this that now possessed me. I put it down to a recurrence of my hospital depression; but I know now I was hiding from myself the truth that it was the return of the emptiness of my life without Fiamma and the boy, and the hopelessness of my search. I knew that success as an artist was within my grasp. Umberto had said as much after all the hand pumping and emotional display:

'Yes, yes, Ham! This picture will make you

588

famous. It has the touch of genius. It shows you have the skill at your command, and when you are inspired with a subject—'

But to me it seemed an unimportant achievement. Umberto could not understand at first. He was enthusiastically talking of getting in touch with the London gallery Duveen had arranged to handle my work and no reminder that the world was still at war would sway him. But when he saw that I had deeper troubles on my mind than speculation about my success or failure as an artist, he became astonishingly practical. As we sat together on the dais drinking grappa from cracked cups—a bottle he had secreted in his bedroom at the top of the spiral staircase 'for an occasion like this when we celebrate a fine artist'—he summarised the points on his stubby fingers:

'One: go to Magari. It sometimes helps to—to'—he chuckled as he thought of a ludicrous comparison. 'It sometimes helps to re-visit the scene of the crime, as they say in detective stories, does it not?'

I smiled weakly, still feeling indifferent. In those golden days there had been nothing but the crime of happiness.

'And the trolleybus runs again now, though sometimes they do not come when you want, and sometimes they stop because electric too comes to a stop. But if no bus comes you walk—it is good to make strong your back, I think. No, no—' (for I had begun to protest) '—do not make me to stop. Perhaps at Magari some clue awaits the detective seeking the lost loved one.' He smiled archly and folded forward another stubby finger.

'Two: you visit also I Tatti and Poggibonsi. I

589

think Prince Caeseri invited Signor Berenson to go to Brindisi to help our king to study Roman antiquities. But now perhaps he is returned. Who knows? And there perhaps is more clue.'

'Who knows?' I echoed with little hope in my voice.

'These two things you do,' Umberto said sternly. 'No rock you leave unturned.'

'Stone,' I corrected morosely.

*　　　*　　　*

I had no trouble finding the cheery American, Bill Vine, who was having an easy time in his liaison job.

'Sure, sure,' he said when I begged the loan of a jeep, 'no problem. We're rounding up vehicles here for the big push north to the Brenner Pass and a link-up with the southbound Seventh Army there. But that ain't gonna be for a spell yet. There's supposed to be some negotiations going on between our man in Switzerland, Allen Dulles, and the big-boot of the SS in Rome, Wolff; and that may delay things more. So help yourself, buddy.'

I decided to go to Poggibonsi first—fruitlessly as it turned out. Evidently Umberto's rumour had been right. The place was deserted except for a couple of platoons of British infantry guarding it. The two sergeants in charge to whom I presented my credentials spoke of their job being a waste of time 'but the cushiest billet ever—guarding a lot of comic pictures, women with four tits and square eyes, and houses with flowers growing out of the chimney'.

'Never seen such a load of crap,' the other

sergeant put in.

Nothing had gone since my previous visit except the packing-case addressed to Goering. 'The Blue Nude' was still among the canvases stacked against the wall. I stood gazing at it for a long time. I could see the sergeant was puzzled but I did not bother to enlighten him.

'Like it, do yer?'

'I do rather.'

'Well, horses for courses. Nice looking tart she could be, I s'pose. But what's she naked amongst all that junk for? Can't understand these bloody artists, can yer?'

'They are difficult sometimes,' I agreed solemnly.

'Give me a nice picture of sunset over the sea or summink like that. I've got one at home in Ealing.'

I smiled and thanked him for his co-operation and was on my way.

I Tatti was no different except that the guard was bigger and the young Air Force officer in charge slightly more informative.

'Sort of stately home we have here, full of valuables belonging to a professor chappie who's in Brindisi with the king—of Italy, I mean. My sprogs and I were all told off by the medics for light-duties, so we got this little number. The pictures and books are nice but of course the rooms have to be kept locked, so we don't see them.'

'What a waste,' I said.

There was no clue there for me, so I said cheerio and told him I was going up to Magari.

'Watch the road for bomb craters,' he warned me. 'A couple of sticks fell around here—demolished a house near that Magari villa. They've got a bulldozer there now, clearing it.'

591

My heart missed a beat. There was only one house it could have been.

*   *   *

This was the occasion (which I have already described) when I revisited the Villa Magari, where everything had changed, where the only person to greet me had been old, sad Enrico. He, as resident caretaker, took me round the forsaken garden, showed me the family's canine cemetery, and proudly indicated the first few tiny wild strawberries; but he was inconsolable at the family's departure.

After bidding him a slightly abrupt 'Arrivederci', I drove back down the hillside to Florence. As I passed the Sappers and their bulldozers, I felt tears well in my eyes, for, by some bitterly ironic chance, the piano on which Kurt used to practise had survived. It was standing, somewhat lop-sidedly, beside the rubble of our old house and a young Sapper in fatigue dress was thumping out 'In the Mood'.

*   *   *

'I remember you well, Capitano,' said the little clerk in the Housing Authority office in Rome, trotting his fingers across his desk. 'You were enquiring about a house in the Via Lisbona when all was in chaos. I remember you; but you do not remember to come back, and of course I cannot get in touch. But the house now is taken by the food rationing people—their office, you understand?'

I understood all right, but saw little point in

going there—except that I had Umberto's admonition on my mind—'No rock you leave unturned'. It was that admonition which had led me once again to countless offices when I got back to Rome. I spent hours poring over lists of names of displaced persons, hotel residents, registrations for petrol, hospital patients and staff—all of them, it was true, unreliable as everything is in the aftermath of Occupation and the machinations of black marketeers and corrupt officials; and all of them bafflingly unrevealing of any clue to Fiamma's whereabouts. The hospitals of course had been my priority: they surely must need every nurse they could get. I had even sought the help of Dr Galdi, but he had shaken his head discouragingly.

'Nurses come and go. Normally of course they're on a register, to be posted as required, some of them in permanent places in different hospitals, others mobile to act as reliefs or to reinforce those who have emergencies to deal with—railway accidents and the like. But in wartime—' He shrugged. 'All is different, unstable.'

So I went to the Via Lisbona more out of a sense of desperation than of hope. Or perhaps it was partly because my Intelligence training had so strongly emphasised the importance of winkling out the hidden detail.

The woman who saw me—middle-aged, charming and sympathetic—reminded me of C's Miss Pilbeam. She peered over half-moon spectacles and listened attentively while I explained my problem as briefly as I could and added, 'There's absolutely no reason I can think of that she should be anything to do with food rationing, but—'

'Ah,' she said, 'but every corner of every carpet

must be turned back. Her ration card will be registered, of course, but with the address she gave at the time; and that would be this house if she was living here then; and as a nurse she would not have to re-register.'

She took off her glasses and thought for a while. 'But I wonder ... you see we have many centres for feeding displaced persons, those without homes, those who have lost their cards. These are manned by casual workers, many of whom took on the job originally for the sake of the extra food that comes their way as a ... a bonus, shall we say?'

'You mean the soup kitchens?'

She nodded and smiled delightfully. 'I do mean the soup kitchens—though I have always fought for a more dignified name for them. It sounds so ... so *grovelling*, don't you think?'

She put on her glasses again and went to a filing cabinet from which she extracted a looseleaf file. It was labelled Food Centres (Casual) and had attached to it a folding street map of the city.

'Here are listed all the—er—soup kitchens in Rome and the names of the staff who work in them. You have a tedious task, Captain Johns, for though the names of the centres are in alphabetical order, there is no index of the names of staff. But with such a quest as yours—' Again the charming smile.

It was a good hour before I had perused the book as far as letter T. And there the name Triangolo leapt out at me; and beneath it in print that seemed to burn itself into my consciousness, I read:

Direttrice: Fiamma Caeseri.

594

CHAPTER THIRTY-SIX

Fiamma Caeseri.

Direttrice.

Triangolo!

For a moment it seemed as if a series of electric currents was passing through every nerve in my body. The shock blinded me to the truth in front of me. It could *not* be! Fiamma at the Triangolo! Of course the old 'drop' had been turned into an emergency soup kitchen long ago; and I had passed it time and again with no more than a thought of pity for the queues of displaced persons and others caught in the bureaucratic nonsense of the rationing system. But why, for God's sake, had I not turned my head? Why had Fiamma not turned *her* head at one of the many moments when I was passing? Futile questions. One might as well ask why fate shapes our destinies with such malefic twists.

My shock gave way to the pounding of joy. *Fiamma! Fiamma my beloved!* My legs were trembling, my hands were damp.

'Are you all right, Captain Johns?' The kindly face of 'Miss Pilbeam' looked at me anxiously across the room. 'You cried out.'

'I am sorry,' I replied. 'I hadn't realised ...' I bent down to pick up my stick, then pointed to her looseleaf file. 'She's here! I have found her. *I have found my wife!*—Do you realise? I—' I choked on the words.

'Indeed I do, Captain Johns.' A smile, halfway between reproach and amusement. 'And may I say how glad I am—for both of you?'

595

I hooked my stick over my arm and took her hands in mine. Had she been younger, and less gracious, I am sure I would have embraced her there and then and whirled her round. As it was I kissed her on both cheeks and she coloured charmingly.

'There aren't the words to tell you how grateful I am. But now—'

'Of course. I understand. Away with you, Captain Johns. And all happiness to you both.'

*   *   *

For a moment at the Triangolo my joy was punctured.

There were steaming dixies of soup on long trestle tables, Bologna sausages suspended from the ceiling, the pungent smell of garlic and unwashed bodies. The unfortunates who crowded the steamy place wore the blank faces of bewilderment and despair. The staff dispensing the food were slightly less depressing—perhaps, I thought cynically, because they were better fed. And perhaps the cynicism was part of the momentary lowering of my spirits.

There was no sign of Fiamma.

The feeling that once again fate was cruelly laughing at me throbbed through my veins. Almost hesitantly I approached one of the servers, a thin foxy man with soup splashes down the front of his grubby white overall.

'Direttrice?'

He said nothing, merely pointed down the long crowded room to a door at the end.

I pushed through the people milling about, my

heart beating wildly. I could feel beads of sweat gathering on my forehead and upper lip. I heard mutterings from the people I shouldered aside, felt their eyes following me, their resentment almost tangible. Who was this uniformed English captain? Was he going to cut their lifeline?

The door was the one I remembered as leading to a cubbyhole where a hat-check girl used to sit and scowl at customers who did not tip enough. Now, it opened on to a short passage leading to another door on which was a lopsided card lettered.

DIRETTRICE

I entered without knocking . . .

She looked up from the shaky wooden table at which she was working. Files and pads of official-looking forms surrounded her. On the walls there were curling admonitory posters giving warnings about air raids and locations of shelters and stirrup-pumps for putting out incendiary bombs. Beyond her was a grimy window that overlooked a courtyard. Her head was silhouetted against it, her blonde hair gathered into a tidy plait and pinned close, as when in uniform she wore her nurse's cap. Now, though, a nimbus of light filtered through the window lit it up as if it were spun gold.

I took in all of this in the fraction of a second, the pulse in my temples throbbing, tears of joy pricking my eyelids. The radiance surrounding her seemed, indeed, for that fraction of a second to turn her into a flame.

'Fiamma! My love!'

She wore a blue overall, nondescript as that of any factory worker; but she invested it with the erotic femininity that had so fascinated me in those first days in Umberto's studio when she had shed the old towelling robe and posed, awkwardly innocent, in the chair on the dais.

Now her lips parted and the colour drained from her cheeks as she looked up and saw me. The pencil fell from her fingers, rolled to the edge of the table and dropped to the floor with a tiny click. My stick dropped too, a loud clatter. She rose and ran towards me, nearly upsetting the table in her rush.

Then we were in each other's arms. Words were choking me, tears were mingling on our cheeks.

'My darling, oh my darling ...' she whispered the words again and again, her hands cupping my face fingers tracing my forehead, eyes, chin, as if convincing herself that I was real, not some insubstantial vision of her imagination. 'My own beloved Ham ...' A pause as she saw my stick, and a look of anxiety. 'Oh—'

I assured her, rather more blithely than I felt, 'I'm well on the mend now. But I have to be careful with my back.'

Words are not really needed to celebrate the reunion of lovers; but they bubble up inconsequentially, joy seeking expression in the richness of language—though I can claim no richness for the triviality I uttered as at last we tenderly released each other from our embrace and I smiled down at her slender blue-clad body and her upturned face:

'Blue but not nude.'

★   ★   ★

So much to tell each other ...

But even in the perfect bliss of reunion practical details have to be taken care of. I phoned Lella at the Excelsior.

'Ham, honey,' she said, 'I can tell by your voice you're bubbling over with excitement; you're tripping over your words. Cool it, Ham, and speak slow and solemn.'

I told her briefly. 'And I'm not going to let her out of my sight. She's standing here beside me and I'm clinging on to her hand.'

'Gee! That's great, Ham! Say no more. I guess I know what you want—somewhere to double-park, huh? We'll have a grand get-together later. But tonight—the world's for you two. Right?'

'Right,' I said.

I could hear her tapping her teeth with a pencil. 'Ah! I've got just the thing. Some four-star general has just moved out and his suite's free. It's not bridal, but it's comfortable enough. There'll be champagne in it and a Do-not-disturb sign to hang on the door. One-two-three—easy number to remember, huh? Just ask for the key in reception. I'll keep outa the way. This is no time for threesomes.'

'Bless you,' I said.

'Think nothing of it. Just part of the Sister Lella service.'

★   ★   ★

Yes, so much to tell each other . . . Yet strangely we spoke only a little during that first evening. Even the champagne did not add much to the wonder of the easing of the anxiety that had possessed us both for so long, so many months. I sensed that to press for the story of those intervening months would bring the pain of reminiscence, perhaps of horror ... and it did not matter anyway, now. She was with me, we were alone, we were in each other's arms, reluctant to yield our passionate embrace to the urgency of getting our clothes off—but succeeding at last in a flurry of torn underwear and brutally ripped off buttons.

We took each other hungrily—even pain absorbed in that first impassioned union—until, exhausted, we wordlessly—almost puritanically— shed the rest of our crumpled clothes and lay side by side on the wide bed, perfectly still—'like Daphnis and Chloë in the long grass', I murmured, recalling from somewhere the pastoral poem.

'Who?' Her eyes were half closed, her mane of golden hair streamed across the pillows.

'Never mind,' I whispered. 'They were young lovers. Greek, I think.'

'Oh.' I could feel, rather than see, her smile. My cheek was touching hers and I felt it dimple. Her breathing was quiet now, her breast beneath my hand firm and smooth, almost boyish in its tautness as her arms lay extended—one over the side of the bed, the other above her head. The silence was blissful and I think we slept for a while, perhaps half an hour; I had no means of knowing, for I did not want to open my eyes and look at my watch, the peace and joy were so great.

Then her fingers began to explore my body again. This time there was no urgency—not to begin with anyway. It was the prolonged arousal of desire by gentle fingers touching delicate surfaces, sensitively lingering. I could feel her rib cage beneath the silky flesh and I wondered vaguely if she had been

600

getting enough to eat, but it would have been ludicrous to ask at that moment. My hand travelled down to the thick triangle of hair and she gave a little moan.

I could feel her fingernails indenting the flesh on my back. 'Now!' she said. 'Now ... oh Ham ...' and because my longing was as great as hers I willed the pain in my back to be less violent until her desire could no longer be contained and she cried out with longing and crushed her lips against mine...

After—long after, for I remember the tinge of dawn that stained the sky framed by the window—she murmured something in her sleep as she clung to me with all the ardour of a child seeking protection. I could not catch the words, and it scarcely mattered anyway. I enfolded her more tightly in my arms and kissed her forehead, as if she were indeed a child to be comforted. Later still—as once again I had grown beneath her hands and we were enjoying the sweet aftermath of exhaustion—she said matter-of-factly:

'Ham, beloved—let's get married.'

'Married?' I could not believe my ears. '*Married*? But darling Fiamma, we *are* married.' For a second I thought that perhaps her mind ...

'No, of course I haven't forgotten!' She raised her hand and pointed to the oversize ring that was still padded with a bit of Elastoplast to stop it falling off. 'But how can we *prove* it? We've got no certificate, nothing but the memory of that dear padre. And as he said, it couldn't be *legal*—'

'—and that it was in the sight of God,' I completed for her. 'Surely that's enough for anyone?'

'For us, of course. But there are all sorts of times in life when you have to prove marriage.' Her ring finger rested in the crook of my elbow. I could feel the gold cool to my skin. 'Our children, for instance—'

The touch of primness amused me; but I did not let my amusement show. Of course, I thought, a woman keeps her marriage lines with pride—perhaps there's something primeval about it, a need to prove that she's won someone's heart, an instinctive safeguard. Whatever it was, I understood it perfectly.

'All right,' I said. 'St Peter's, nothing less.'

Fiamma giggled. 'You are ridiculous, Ham! You know how impossible it was for Steve and Lella to get married in Santa Maria in Florence; St Peter's would be even more impossible although Papa knows the Pope. In any case I don't want a grand ceremony. Our bedside wedding ... well, it *was* by a man of God and in the sight of God. It's just—'

'Say no more,' I said, swinging my legs to the ground carefully. 'Just the civil ceremony.' I turned and kissed her. 'I know what to do.'

★   ★   ★

It was true: I knew exactly what to do. Sir D'Arcy Osborne was a viceroy; there could hardly be anyone more highly qualified to perform the simple legal ceremony of marriage. And so it proved. A few strings had to be pulled and it was Access, in an almost jovial mood, who made the arrangements; and he and Lella were witnesses. The ceremony could hardly be called a ceremony at all as time was of the essence for the Minister was between engagements; but even he lingered a while afterwards in the ante-room for champagne and smoked salmon sandwiches. The Prince telephoned from Brindisi with his congratulations, and BB's too, and Fiamma kept looking at the heavy deckle-edged paper which certified that Captain Hamilton Johns and Signorina Fiamma Caeseri had agreed a contract of marriage in the presence of His Britannic Majesty's Minister to the Vatican City 'to which contract they have put their signatures in the presence of the witnesses hereto subscribed below'. As I kissed Fiamma I said, 'It's all very simple and rather beautiful.'

'Simple and beautiful,' she whispered back, 'like our love.'

*   *   *

That evening Fiamma and I walked hand-in-hand in the Vatican garden. Dusk was falling and there was a heavy scent of wallflowers. In the distant shadows we could see a tall white-clad figure approaching and I felt Fiamma go tense.

'It's the Holy Father,' she murmured. 'He often walks here. Should we—?'

'Go back? No. We are doing no harm. He's taking his evening stroll. We're taking our evening stroll too.'

As we drew nearer we saw the gleam of the magnificent jewelled cross on his white soutane. Perhaps we were overawed. I do not know; but it seemed right, as he drew close to us, that we should kneel down. A thin austere man, he nevertheless had a kindly smile in his eyes screened though they were by steel-rimmed spectacles.

603

He paused. 'I think I have heard something of this from Sir D'Arcy. You are the daughter and the son-in-law of my good friend Giorgio Caeseri?'

Fiamma made a whispered acknowledgement. 'Yes, Your Holiness, we are.'

Eugenio Pacelli, Pope Pius XII, extended his hands and touched us lightly as we knelt.

'Bless you, my children, each and together,' he said softly; and passed on silently into the deepening shadows.

Fiamma was later to say that the blessing of the Pope signified more to her even than the religious and civic ceremonies of marriage. Nothing now, and no one, could part us. For myself I can feel the cool touch of his hand on my forehead to this day.

EPILOGUE

SETTIGNANO, TODAY

EPILOGUE

... To this day.

'Happy?'

Fiamma's voice edged into the thoughts I was enjoying as one enjoys the reverie that divides sleep from half-awake contemplation of the day—the sort of day when there are no anxieties to face.

This day.

'Absolutely not,' I said with mock dejection. 'How can anyone be happy with all that noise going on?'

The noise came from the Indian pool. It was the happiest noise imaginable, that of children playing, high-pitched chatter and sudden shrieks of laughter as one of them was pushed into the pool. Just like ...

Fiamma's hand was cool in mine as we sat in rattan chairs on the terrace; but the summer sun bathed Magari in warmth that was balm to my back. I had long discarded the stick but lengthy spells at my easel still brought on a certain amount of discomfort, even with the support of my 'chastity belt'; and during the morning I had been working on a canvas that would not let me out of its grip. It was an idea that had been with me for many years: to express in a painting the name 'Magari', for the 'if only', the 'ah! would that it were so!' that, as the Prince had once explained, it means. An elusive idea when it came to expressing it in form and colour. But it was working out. I was achieving something near the effect I wanted by superimposing one image on another—the forsaken

607

Magari I had returned to in 1945 with the ghostly figure of Enrico picking wild strawberries gripped by tentacles of bindweed, and, behind it and seen through a translucent veil of colour, the Magari of past and present—*present* because I had restored it to its pristine state.

'And thereby hangs a tale,' as Vanni was fond of remarking, thus clearing the conversation for me to enlighten the friends of our sons and daughters and grandchildren as they came and went in the transitory way of young people nowadays.

'The Last Battle' had become what amounted to a best-seller success. Duveen's London gallery had catalogued it at an unbelievably high price.

'For some, price equals prestige,' Duveen's man had said with a wink, but he added hastily, 'Not that that for a moment detracts from the merit of a very fine picture.'

It had been snapped up by an American collector who, I guessed, had been 'wised up' by Steve, though he denied it with suspicious vehemence. But that sale was only the beginning. The gallery, acting as my agent, had shrewdly incorporated a 'reproduction' clause in the bill of sale and authentication certificate, and by one of those strange flukes of fortune reproduction prints had been sold all over the world. On every postcard or other reproduction I received a royalty. So fame and a modest fortune came my way.

I used some of it to buy back Magari from the Milanese businessman who bought it as a speculation from Giorgio Caeseri when the Prince decided to stay on in Brindisi as the king's ADC.

'I know I'm "burning my boats", as the saying goes,' he acknowledged ruefully; 'but there doesn't

608

seem any possibility of renewing a life that war has destroyed.'

I knew what he meant. Though there was no open rift between him and the Principessa, she did not want to return to Magari. It held too many painful memories—'some of them too closely related to my conscience', she admitted sadly—and she had decided to remain in Interlaken. After the war ended in May 1945 and the king had been persuaded to abdicate (he went to live in Egypt and died there two years later) the Prince joined Donna Margarita in Interlaken and there were exchange visits between them and us; but the Prince too found Magari too heady with memories—'It is for the young: your children and theirs, Ham, and we are best at a distance.' They were both beginning to show their age.

When Giorgio died in 1957 the London *Times* gave him a dignified obituary mentioning almost with reverence 'his undercover work for the Allies during the long, difficult, and controversial campaign in Italy'. The Principessa died peacefully in her sleep a couple of years later, leaving her sizeable fortune in trust for her grandchildren—'present *and* future' she had added with a touch of Yorkshire practicality. But by that time our families were complete; and it delighted Fiamma that, when we went to London in 1965 to deal with my father's estate, that chatterbox journal the *Tatler* displayed a picture of 'Sir Hamilton Johns, MC, RA and Lady Johns, with their four children Hamilton II, Giorgio, Lucia and Maria'.

'It's like a warm welcome into the English aristocracy,' she smiled. And when Steve and Lella paid us the first of several visits from their home in

Atlanta, Steve could only murmur 'Gee! That's *real* class!'

'You don't have to get an inferiority complex about it,' I joked. 'After all, you too married the daughter of a prince. Baronets come much lower in the pecking order.'

Roz also visited us from time to time. Kurt's death had left a scar on her life that only dedication to the Church could partly conceal, and she had become what she called 'a lay nun' with the Sisters of St Vincent de Paul in the Vatican, helping with the administration of the commissariat that was responsible for feeding the residents of the city, 'including the Holy Father himself, so I don't feel it's an unworthy task'.

I nodded gravely. 'Indeed not.' And sometimes I wonder whether, in a way, Rosanna is not the happiest of the daughters of the Prince.

Fiamma interrupted my thoughts again. 'Ham! You don't have to tell me—you're dreaming again.'

'Only the pleasantest of dreams. Recollections. Addings-up and subtractions.'

'And what's the total?'

'Happiness—utter and complete.'

'You don't have to tell me: I haven't been married to you for nearly fifty years without knowing there's a shadow there somewhere.'

'There are always shadows,' I said with mock profundity. 'Otherwise you wouldn't recognise the light as light. And that is the professional observation of a painter.'

'It isn't,' she said with a grin that was almost puckish, 'it's what Padre Scofield said.'

'So it is,' I said with genuine astonishment. 'I had

610

quite forgotten.' I had too; but my mind slipped back easily enough . . .

*   *   *

There had been a small party right at the end of the war—instigated by, of all people, Access. 'It's all over bar the bloody shouting,' he called out. 'Hitler's shot himself and his wife and his dog and left Doenitz to carry the can. Let's have a binge.'

'What's it in aid of?' I asked, using the current idiom. 'The end of Hitler or the advent of Führer Doenitz?'

'Neither, you clot. It's in aid of you and your missus. The most married couple in Rome. Set on the road to ruin by an army padre, licensed by the king's representative, and blessed by the Pope. I'd say that was worth a binge—huh?'

It was at the Marsina and it was very lively. Everyone was tense, waiting for the end of the war to be announced, and it was that anticipatory liveliness rather than anything specially laid on for us that gave the whole occasion its swing. But an *ad hoc* band managed a very *ad hoc* version of Mendelssohn's 'Wedding March', which confused those who did not know us and thought we had been married that morning; but as Access said, 'Who cares, eh? It's just one big jolly party. And there are two chaps coming along who *do* know.' He winked. 'Even I can dig up surprises sometimes.'

The two were Dr Turnbull and the chaplain who had officiated at our bedside wedding.

'Captain Scofield, chaplain to the forces,' Access said with affected formality. 'You know each other, I believe?'

The padre smiled. I remembered the smile that

611

seemed to emerge from behind a veil of sadness. 'Indeed yes; Doctor Turnbull and I conspired—'

It was Fiamma who remembered the ring first. She slipped it from her finger and took the padre's hand in hers. Tears glistened in her eyes. 'This is yours, I think.'

He looked down at the ring gleaming on his third finger. 'Thank you, my dear. It belongs to a sad corner of my life. But without the shadows we cannot know about the light.'

★   ★   ★

Fiamma is elegant still—trim of figure and still retaining much of the nimbleness of youth. When BB, Mary Berenson, and Miss Mariano returned to I Tatti and invited us over to discuss the progress of the Arts Commission he told her she would never grow grey—'Pale, perhaps, but never grey. The pigmentation of your hair is like that of gold leaf: in time it loses its sheen but never its colour.' And it never has.

BB died in 1959. He was ninety-four then and his passing was mourned by the art world. After I Tatti became a shrine dedicated to the Renaissance art that had been his life there was a certain amount of debunking that centred round his so-called devious methods; but no one denied his contribution to culture—not even Umberto. My old mentor and dear friend died a year later—almost as if, with BB's passing, the zest of disagreement had vanished with him. I have his portable easel still, and sometimes I take it into the streets of Florence as he used to, and trundle it about as he did, and set it up as he did when a promising street corner or a particularly brilliant shaft of sunlight seems for a moment to offer a subject. And I can hear him saying, as he said a hundred times, 'The end is what you are after, not the beginning.'

And there is Fiamma now, moving gracefully across the terrace, past the terracotta dogs and into the drawing-room; and there she will stand for a few moments looking at 'The Blue Nude', spanning the years.